Break the Glass

By S.A. Levy

MiToo Publishing

MiToo Publishing
Copyright © 2015 by S.A. Levy
ISBN: 978-0-9962066-1-7

For Katy

You make everything possible

Table of Contents

Acknowledgments

SPRING

Microfiber tablecloths, Rebekah thought. A miracle of modern dinner parties.

Someone had accidentally tipped over her entire bowl of matzo ball soup. Broth and chunks of carrots had been wiped away, but bits of the spongy matzo ball managed to cling to the tablecloth. Empty plates had been stacked in front of their previous proprietors, and empty glasses of wine stood sociably in close proximity. Dishes once loaded with roasted asparagus, baked Brussels sprouts, and brisket had been abandoned in the kitchen.

"Well," Daniel Cohayn said. He leaned back in his chair. "I'm glad we only do this once a year."

Judith Cohayn turned to her husband and raised an eyebrow. "And you didn't even cook anything."

Daniel patted his stomach. "Eating is enough, thanks."

"Do you like gefilte fish?" Megan whispered to Rebekah. She poked her finger at the gelatinous gray mass on her plate. It shivered, and then reverted back to a lifeless lump.

Rebekah shrugged. "It's salty. Like a pickle."

Megan raised her eyebrows. "Like a pickle, huh? A fish pickle?"

Megan Nimble had short brown hair cropped closely around her head, a pixie cut invaded by half a dozen uncivilized cowlicks. When she and Rebekah first met nine years ago, her hair had been longer, nearly shoulder-length. She'd cut it shorter and shorter over those years, each time out of increasing frustration with the demands of self-grooming.

Otherwise, Megan looked very much the same as she had in college, although a few strands of white cropped up out of her scalp now, and the lines in her forehead were vaguely more noticeable. She was tall, so tall that she awkwardly towered over her friends. But Megan was not particularly imposing; she sat with her shoulders slumped, as if she had spent much of her life trying to accommodate her shorter peers by slouching.

Megan made a face. She slipped the spoon underneath the gefilte fish, picked it up, and dropped it onto Rebekah's plate.

Rebekah smiled at her girlfriend. She flexed out one foot and surreptitiously slid it over Megan's.

Nine years, Rebekah thought. She let her gaze linger on Megan's face, taking in the sight of her nose, her lips, her smile. So familiar now.

Megan's eyes widened. "What?" She reached up and touched her lips. "Do I have something in my teeth?" She bared her teeth at Rebekah, two rows of straight prongs that had received a course correction in junior high.

"Oh, you're fine," Rebekah said.

Megan pursed her lips. "I'll floss."

Rebekah looked to the head of the table, where her parents were picking at the plate of macaroons in front of them. Judith liked to keep her Passover Seders small, and she weighed them down with enough food to feed the entire city of Portland. Judith and Daniel invited only Judith's mother, Simchah, and their children, Rebekah and David.

David hadn't come in nine years.

There was an empty chair in the corner of the dining room that Judith had set out every Seder since David stopped flying home for Passover. When Daniel tried to convince her that a live human could make better use of the chair, Judith rebuffed him. "He may not be here," she said, glaring at her husband, "but we can still have a place for him."

Judith was a small woman with delicate shoulders. Her brown hair hung down and curled just past the nape of her neck, and she had a sharp chin that jutted out an inch beyond her lips. She chewed on her words as she spoke, as if she had been harboring them in her cheeks for months before pushing them out, rapid-fire. When Judith got determined like that—when her eyes widened and her lips set, narrow as matchsticks—Daniel raised his hands and backed away, understanding that fighting was an exercise in futility.

So the chair sat in the corner of the room, regal in its isolation, a placeholder for Rebekah's older brother, who would most likely never come to his parent's Passover Seder again. But Judith hoped. She hoped that one day, David would wake up and decide to re-engage with his family. She hoped that David would tell his mother he was flying up from Los Angeles so that the family could be stitched together for the first time since his wedding. Judith hoped, and she arranged the chair just so, and she tried to wish her family into completion. Tonight, the empty chair was just a missed stitch. Grandma Simchah sat next to Daniel, a familiar scowl carved into her face. Simchah was bent over, white-haired, and frail, a bitter archaeological excavation. Grandma Simchah had been coming to her daughter Judith's Seder every year since her husband, Mendel, died. She came without fail; and she complained, unceasingly.

"Five hours," Simchah said. "I've been sitting in this chair for five hours. Who needs a five-hour Seder?"

Judith cleared her throat. "Daniel, should we wrap things up?"

Daniel touched his fingers to the graying widow's peak in the middle of his forehead. He was small, like his wife, with an elvish quality that he liked to draw attention to by dressing up as a hobbit on Halloween.

"I suppose we should," Daniel said. "Before it gets too late."

"It's already too late," Simchah said. She crossed her arms and tucked her chin into her chest.

"One more thing," Daniel said. He held up one finger.

"Daniel…" Judith started.

"No, no, we've been ending the Seder this way every year since we starting hosting, and we're not going to stop now," Daniel said. "Here's how we're going to end: we're going to go around the table and each of us are going to say where we hope to be, or what we hope to see in the world, at this time next year. 'Next year in peace.' 'Next year in togetherness.' You know, whatever." He raised his glass, still half-full of wine. "Next year in good health. L'chaim."

"Next year, when our family is together," Judith said. She glanced at the empty chair in the corner of the dining room.

Rebekah rolled her eyes. Would her mother never learn that David wasn't coming? She looked at Megan to commiserate.

Megan was sitting stiffly, a furtive smile on her face. Her eyes were shining. Suddenly, Rebekah realized what her girlfriend was about to do. She grabbed Megan's arm.

"Megan, no!" She whispered. "Stop!" She pressed down on Megan's foot under the table.

Megan shook her off, kicking her foot so that Rebekah's toe hit the table leg.

Rebekah closed her eyes. Megan, unlike Rebekah, wasn't interested in keeping secrets. Megan didn't like living in a hologram world, didn't like hiding her affection, didn't like pretending that they could float above the muck. Megan relished the muck, and was dragging Rebekah into it with her.

"Next year, if there is a next year," Simchah said. She took a delicate sip of wine of wine.

Megan stood up and raised her glass. Rebekah stared at the table. "Next year, at our wedding!" Megan declared. The room fell silent. Judith furrowed her brow. "What?" She looked at Daniel. "What?" Daniel glanced from Judith to Megan. His eyes dilated in shock. Megan placed her hand on Rebekah's shoulder, and her girlfriend was too mortified to shake it off. A tense silence hung in the room, like the charged pause before a wave. Rebekah hung her head. Mr. and Mrs. Cohayn leaned forward.

"Next year at our wedding!" Megan repeated. "Rebekah and I are getting married!"

Birth
1982

During the late afternoon of September 27, 1982, Judith Abrams Cohayn found herself lying prostrate on her hospital bed. Her blue and green-checkered hospital gown had come undone at the shoulder, and she had bruises on the tops of her knees from hours of leaning over a birthing ball. Judith had been pushing for the last hour and a half, after twelve hours of straining through regular, unceasing waves of lower back pain. Her eyelids were wet sandbags and her legs quivered with exhaustion and dehydration.

At this moment, Judith thoroughly regretted the unfortunate set of events that had brought her here: her choice to have a second child, her refusal of pain medication, and even her marriage to Daniel. The on-call nurse had tried to coach her through deep breathing and visualization. The breathing worked at home when Judith did it with Daniel, and it worked for the first few hours at the hospital. It worked—until all of a sudden, it didn't, and there was just pain, and more pain, and a baby pushing its way out of her cervix.

"I think there's a contraction coming," the nurse said.

Judith gritted her teeth, her cheeks popping out in pain, as she breathed deeply and heavily through her nose and mouth.

"Arrrhhhhhh," Judith yelled. She squeezed her eyes shut and bore down on the bed.

Daniel Cohayn sat outside the obstetrics wing in the hospital waiting room. He hadn't been much help during labor, trying to rub Judith's shoulders when she didn't want to be touched, telling her he loved her and getting a taut dismissal to the waiting room in return.

Today was Yom Kippur, the Jewish day of repentance. He wasn't supposed to eat, drink, or think about anything but the evolution of his soul. His four-year-old son, David, was asleep next to him on another waiting room couch, sweetly oblivious to the bedlam of baby production. His sixty-year-old mother-in-law, Simchah, clucked at him from the armchair in the corner.

"Daniel," she said. "Should it be so terrible to help your wife deliver your second child?"

"Yes," Daniel said. "Apparently it is."

"My daughter, giving birth on Yom Kippur," Simchah said. She shook her head and slowly undid a missed stitch. "Bad luck. God should not create life on the Day of Repentance."

Daniel turned his face away. His mother-in-law had always been a terrible, pessimistic malcontent. He often wondered how such a woman could have produced his wife, a disciplined perfectionist.

"Really, Simchah?" Daniel said. "I've never heard of anything in Judaism that says that being born on Yom Kippur is bad luck."

"Well, I've been around longer than you, haven't I?" Simchah said. "Trust me. God is judging us today. And God sees my daughter, my Judith, giving birth, and her husband doing *bubkes* on the couch. My granddaughter—if she is born healthy—will know for the rest of her life that she was born on the day when the *beit din,* the heavenly court, is determining life and death. You think the court needs the distraction of a birth?"

"I think the heavenly court will do just fine."

"Ach, you don't know," Simchah said.

"Simchah, stop it," Daniel said. "It's not like she had a choice." Daniel rubbed his forehead. Daniel had less of a widow's peak then. The hairline on either side of his face had just begun its creep back toward his ears.

"At least your firstborn wasn't born on Yom Kippur. He has a summer birthday like a normal person." Simchah looked over at David. "See how smart he is? Napping now so that he can be awake to meet his little sister later."

Daniel didn't answer.

"You must be hungry," Simchah said. "Is that why you're not helping? I'm hungry, you're hungry, she's hungry." We're all hungry and trying to produce a baby. That child will be born into a world of hungry people. Maybe you should eat, Daniel. You don't look so good."

"I'm fine."

"God will forgive you," Simchah said.

Daniel sat up. He had a headache. "Maybe I should go back in there."

"Ach, don't trouble yourself. You'll just be in the way. Stay here. Be quiet and count your blessings."

Forty-five minutes later, the nurse came to tell Daniel that his daughter had arrived.

By the time David entered the room, Judith had been cleaned up, settled into clean sheets, and was holding little Rebekah Rachel Abrams Cohayn in a receiving blanket.

"My sister?" David asked. He rubbed his eyes with his left hand and held his yellow blanket with his right.

"Yes," Judith said. "You want to kiss her?"

David stood on the tips of his toes and blew a wet kiss in Rebekah's direction.

"Wow," Daniel said. He took a swaddled Rebekah in his arms. She had small tufts of dark hair and the mottled, wrinkled face of a newborn. "Rebekah Cohayn. Welcome to the universe."

"May you be happy, and may your life be full of richness, little Rebekah," Judith said.

"May you find love and be well loved, little girl," Daniel said, kissing his daughter's forehead.

"May you avoid too much suffering," Simchah said. She pursed her lips.

"Mom," Judith whispered from the bed. "Stop."

"It's important to be realistic," Simchah said. "This world is a difficult place. And this one, born on Yom Kippur. What does that mean? She's born with a fist to her heart."

Judith shook her head. She touched the baby gently. "May you be smart, talented, and beautiful, little Rebekah," Judith said, looking at her mother pointedly.

"Ach, beautiful?" Simchah said. She shook her head and clucked again. "No, no. Don't wish that on a little girl. It's more trouble than it's worth."

Simchah bent her head down close to Rebekah. "May you be reasonably attractive and nothing more, little one. A reasonably attractive girl gets just the right kind of man."

As a toddler, Rebekah had dark curly hair that cascaded down the sides of her head, a round face, and a delicate nose with a perfectly rounded tip. Her eyes conveyed a gentle sweetness, a sense of passive observance that one might see in a doll sitting on a bookshelf. She would look around a room, keenly inhaling movement and noise, without seeming to comprehend any of it. "Rebekah!" adults would say, waving their hands to get her attention.

Rebekah would turn her head slowly, her mouth slightly open and her eyes wide.

When Rebekah began walking, she often walked into things, sometimes big things, like the couch in the living room, or the glass screen door leading to the backyard. Sometimes Rebekah would be distracted by something mid-stride and simply sit down, as if she had forgotten where she was going in the first place. When Rebekah turned four, and still had not mastered the art of avoiding large, immovable objects, Judith took her to an eye doctor.

Dr. Cho of Big Bear Optometry worked in a strip mall in southwest Portland on Barbur Boulevard. A five- foot-tall carved wooden black bear stood guard by the door. Sometimes the bear carried mints and business cards in its outstretched palm. On Halloween, the bear passed out circular tubes of floss.

When Rebekah and Judith walked into Big Bear Optometry for the first time, Rebekah shook her dense mop of unkempt black curls, clung to the back of her mom's pants, and buried her head in her mother's thigh.

"Mommy," she whispered. "I don't wanna go."

"Shhh," Judith said. She stroked Rebekah's head.

"Mommy," Rebekah wailed.

The secretary sitting behind the welcome desk looked up at the Cohayn family. She wore a salmon-colored suit over a white blouse, and white-framed glasses sat on her nose, standing out against her salt-and-pepper hair. A brown nameplate on the front desk read, "Alma."

Alma smiled. "How may I help you today?"

"Yes, hi," Judith said. "We have an eye appointment for my daughter, Rebekah."

"No!" Rebekah yelled. She cried and pulled on her mother's hand.

"Oh, Rebekah, honey, please. It's going to be fine," Judith said. She looked at her daughter. "Please?"

"What's wrong…Rebekah, is it?" Alma asked.

Rebekah sniffled. She hugged her mother's leg. She shook her head.

"Are you afraid of the doctor?"

Rebekah shook her head.

"Good, because he's really nice." Alma opened a drawer under a desk. "How about some crayons? Do you like to draw?"

Rebekah shook her head.

"Bekah!" Judith tried to corral her daughter into the office. "What's going on?"

Rebekah pointed to the front door.

"The door?" Judith looked around, bewildered.

Alma stood up, and looked to where Rebekah was pointing. Then she laughed.

"Are you afraid of the bear, sweetie?" The wooden brown bear, standing nearly six feet tall, drooped awkwardly near the door. Rebekah clung to her mother and nodded.

"Yeah, I understand. That bear is a little scary. But you know what? There are no real bears here. That bear isn't real. He can't hurt you. The office is just named after him, that's all. Do you want a tour? We can look inside every room to check for bears. Mom, you want to come with us?"

During Alma's tour of the examination rooms, bathrooms, and even the closets, Rebekah dubiously accepted the absence of non-human mammals in Big Bear Optometry. Alma coaxed Rebekah into an examination room with a little white chair, a box of toys, and a ceiling painted with cartoon animal scenes. An hour later, Dr. Cho diagnosed Rebekah with 200/175 vision.

"Rebekah will need to wear glasses for the rest of her life," the slight Dr. Cho said, when Judith met him in his office after the examination. He had a thick accent and spoke slowly to make sure his patients understood him. Rebekah sat in the corner of the office, playing with a set of blocks and Lincoln Logs he kept in a clear plastic container for his younger patients. "She is very, very, near-sighted. I would be surprised if she could see more than one foot in front of her face." The doctor held up his hands to show the distance. "Has she been bumping into things?"

"Yes," Judith said.

"Yes," Dr. Cho said. "This is from poor eyesight. The good news is that we can fix. Easily fixable problem. We like those, yes? Yes. I've got some plastic frames, good for Rebekah—we will get her started."

Rebekah knew a few important things from an early age. She knew she needed to wear her glasses or she couldn't see. She knew that she lived in Portland, Oregon, and that it rained a lot, so much that she needed to wear her red raincoat almost every day, from February through May. The other, and perhaps most important thing that Rebekah knew, was that she was David Cohayn's younger sister. Cain, Esau, and David Cohayn: Firstborn sons with a birthright. Perhaps it wasn't appropriate for David to hold such a place in his family. Perhaps his family never consciously articulated how David held so much sway over their affairs. But there it was, hovering just below the surface of their family dynamic, like an oxygen-starved fish: David was his mother's favorite, his father's son, his sister's king.

David was an unusually charismatic child, with a deeply dimpled smile, bright blue eyes, and an infectious laugh. He was calm and remarkably sure of himself. He started walking and talking earlier than his peers, possessed superior eye-hand coordination, and exuded the sort of natural grace that translated as a gravitational pull. Judith and Daniel had been struck by the self-assurance of their tiny son. He was a natural born leader, they told themselves. Astoundingly gifted. Even Grandma Simchah affectionately referred to her grandson as "King David."

"Ach, King David wants some fruit loops," she would say. "Judith, can you pull them down off the top shelf? I can't reach that high."

By the time Rebekah was born, David had carved out a powerful role in the family. He quietly demanded the attention of his parents, and gently led his sister with the touch of a royal. Rebekah meekly entered the world in his shadow, and never thought to challenge his authority.

Because of their age difference, they spent exactly one year together in school: the year Rebekah was in first grade, and David was in sixth, at Theodore Roosevelt Elementary School. Even in first grade, Rebekah knew that she was terrible at sports. She was the last picked and first out. The one who would accidentally shoot the ball in the wrong basket, or kick the ball in her own net.

As a result, Rebekah viewed her recess time at Teddy Roosevelt as an obstacle, a challenging time slot in an otherwise pleasant school day. Rebekah did her best to conform to what was expected of her during the forty-five minutes of the school day she spent on the playground. She hung on the periphery of foursquare games, sometimes getting in line to play a round or two, before acknowledging that she was severely outmatched by the other kids who had mastered things like "lowies" and "corners." Rebekah could hit neither lowies nor corners, so she usually spent much of her time in line waiting to get out again, craning her neck to see where David was on the playground.

David had always blended in much more easily with his classmates than Rebekah. When she saw him high-five his friends, Rebekah would turn around and try to high-five others in the four square game. When Rebekah saw David throw back his head and laugh, Rebekah would find something to laugh about, too.

Once every couple of weeks, David would wander over to see Rebekah. He never said much to her, just stood quietly next to the foursquare game. Rebekah tried hard to impress him then, and usually failed, even more spectacularly. When Rebekah whiffed on a hit, she would steal a glance at David.

"Come on, Bekah," David would say quietly, nodding his head in encouragement. He would cross his arms, smile, and watch her with a studied seriousness.

A minute, maybe two minutes, and David would be gone again, back to the older kids' playground. But his visit was enough. He had taken the time to walk over to her, and formulate his thoughts into concrete deliverables.

When David wasn't around, Rebekah would sometimes follow Ruth Kinder around the playground. Though they were the same age, Ruth was much taller than Rebekah—four inches, at least—and thin, with the pale musculature of a girl who disdains sports and sunny days equally. Her two largest sets of joints—her knees and elbows—dominated her physical appearance. When she was forced to run in P.E., she ran pigeon-toed, her elbows sticking out like chicken wings.

But what Ruth lacked in physical skill she made up for in gregariousness and wit. Where Rebekah was shy, with a serious, deadpan delivery, Ruth was all buoyancy, a flashing neon sign compared to Rebekah's carved wooden shingle. Even as a child, Ruth could entertain a room full of adults with a joke or a short story. At her older sister's bat mitzvah, it was eight-year-old Ruth who, with every inch of her lanky frame, danced with such vigor and gawky grace that the video camera was trained on her for most of the night.

Rebekah had watched her then. There was something so astonishing in the way Ruth danced, as if her bones were about to fly out of her sockets, her mass unbound by Newtonian gravity. She was so free, so unrestrained, a pure soul compared to the other kids on the dance floor.

Have I ever danced like that? Rebekah had wondered. She looked down at her feet. They were slightly pigeon-toed, even when she was sitting. Rebekah's calves were white and soft, unacquainted with regular exercise; her thighs were slender but limp. When she tried to dance, she moved awkwardly, as if her joints had been fused together with brittle rubber instead of cartilage.

Rebekah rarely tried to dance.

Rebekah was also friends with Jacob Green. When Rebekah first met Jacob, she expected that he would be one of the boys everyone picked on. He was Jewish, like Rebekah, one of the five children in their grade who didn't go to school on Rosh Hashanah and Yom Kippur. He was weak, gawky, and pale, with oversized ears and feet that looked as if they had grown at twice the rate as the rest of his body. He had sandy brown hair and glasses, like Rebekah, with lenses almost as thick as hers. He was also smart. He was the first in their class to figure out why triangles are more stable for building than squares, and he came up with the best design during the class's toothpick bridge project. Everyone wanted Jacob Green's help in building their gingerbread houses during Christmas celebrations, and the teachers marveled at Jacob Green's exquisite cursive handwriting.

But it wasn't Jacob's intelligence that saved him from bullies: it was his propensity for luck.

Jacob Green was lucky. He always won something in the school's quarterly fundraising raffle. When speakers came to the school and sought audience participation, they inevitably picked Jacob Green. He won a trip to Universal Studios in Hollywood when he sent in ten cereal box tops during a General Mills contest.

Jacob was a hero to the class geeks and an aloof untouchable to the popular kids. He floated between these groups like an ousted double agent. He seemed completely unaware of his special status, only sometimes acknowledging accusations of his special serendipity with a shrug, a shy smile, and upturned hands. It was a gift he had never asked for.

The Finish Line
1992

"Rebekah! Come on!" David leaned on his bike, hands on his handlebars, body turned three quarters of the way forward so that he was looking over his shoulder. David's friends Tyler and Chris stood nearby with their own bikes.

Rebekah was little more than a spot on the edge of Hilltop Road—the main drag through their neighborhood—peddling furiously to catch up to her older brother at the construction site. She pedaled standing up off her seat, her back tire fishtailing as she churned her legs. Her chest hung low over her handlebars, her back parallel to the ground, and the top of her helmet the farthest thing out in front of her bike. Her glasses hung precariously from the corners of her ears. About one minute later, Rebekah pulled her bike up over the sidewalk and into the soft dirt.

She looked up into David's face. He stared intensely, his expression inscrutable. Rebekah, now seven years old, could barely see his eyes because his helmet was pulled so far forwards.

Judith Cohayn liked to tell her friends that David had a "seasoned" face, just as Daniel did when he was David's age. David's face was unusually long and lean, with hollow cheeks for a boy of eleven. These cheeks were beautifully thin, quick-to-blush, red swatches that extended from his temples to his chin. He had a mop of curly hair on his head—black and thick, like Rebekah and his mother. But David's most striking facial feature was his chin, a well-defined, square chin jutting out beyond his neck like a balcony for his lips. When he clenched his jaw, his face was all angles. When he was relaxed, or contemplative, it looked as if he was pouting over the slow shrinkage of the universe.

David stuck his chin out at Rebekah as she rode up. "Geez, Bekah, took you long enough."

"Sorry." Rebekah could barely get the word out because she was breathing so hard.

"If you come with us, you've gotta keep up with us. That's part of the deal."

Rebekah nodded.

David studied her. His eyes swept over her face.

"You ok?"

Rebekah nodded. She straddled her bike, her chest heaving.

"You sure you're up for this?"

Rebekah nodded again. She held her breath, hoping David wouldn't notice how winded she was. David examined her, chin out, eyes narrowed.

"Fine," David said. "You know what to do, right?"

Rebekah blew out the air in her cheeks. "Yeah."

"Cool." David looked at Tyler and Chris. "My sister's got it, guys. Let's go."

The three boys jumped back up on their bikes and took off toward the other side of the construction site.

The site sat on the edge of a residential neighborhood at the intersection between Hilltop and Jackson streets, a narrow intersection that dead-ended in two long cul-de-sacs. A furniture store occupied the corner of the opposite street. The store was an old structure built at the turn of the century. The new owners had painted it white, and a large, brightly lit neon arrow was nailed to the top of the roof.

A tall, steeply sloping mound of dirt sat at the end of the construction site. The mound was thirty feet tall and one hundred feet wide and nearly completely flat on top. Because construction had been idle for a few months, a couple of the neighborhood boys—present company included—had turned it into a racecourse. David, Tyler, and Chris skidded to a halt at the front of the mound, shouldered their nearly identical small trick bikes, and attempted to run up the hill. David stayed on his toes, using his calf muscles to propel himself to the top. He got there first.

While the boys biked away, Rebekah dropped her bike, removed her helmet, and ran over toward the sidewalk closest to Jackson Street. When she reached the sidewalk, she dropped her heel into the dirt and walked backward, slowly, creating a clear, distinct line.

My sister's got it, guys. David's words were a gift, a nibble of his birthright.

Rebekah had only walked a couple of feet when she found the line she had made last weekend. She veered slightly to the right and retraced the track that was already there, making it deeper. David had complained the last time they raced that he couldn't see the finish line. This time, Rebekah dragged her heel in the dirt with force—the finish line was deeper and wider than it had ever been before.

The boys had one objective: to cross the finish line first. David—and it was always David—would yell, "onyermarkgetsetgo!" The boys would take off, peddling furiously down the hill, until they got across the line marked off by Rebekah's heel. David trusted her to determine the winner. It was the only way David would allow her to tag along with them.

Rebekah stood on the sidewalk, squinting into the sun and trying to ignore the dirt smudged onto her glasses. David waved to show that the boys had made it to the top. They appeared six inches tall to Rebekah, specks in the distance, crouching over their bikes like jockeys at the Kentucky Derby. They had raced down this mound a dozen times now. Success in daring feats breeds an illegitimate invincibility, and Tyler, Chris, and David were three of the most invincible boys in the neighborhood.

Rebekah saw the boys brace themselves at the top of the dirt mound. They were pointing to each other's bikes, making sure that no one had even an inch of advantage in the race. Fairness counted when it came to bike racing. She saw David look over to her. Rebekah waved.

She heard David yell. "Onyermarkgetsetgo!" David, Chris, and Tyler took off down the hill, pushing themselves off their seats, pulling their handlebars back and forth to create maximum speed. They started close to each other, so close, in fact, that Chris swerved away from David's bike to avoid a collision.

"Hey!" Chris yelled. He fell back into third place and immediately slowed down. As the boys reached the bottom of the mound—a delicate transition from soft soil to a much more compacted earth—Rebekah saw that the race would be neck-and-neck between Tyler and David.

Rebekah bent her knees slightly, one foot in front of the other. David had coached her not to watch the oncoming bikes, but to keep her eyes focused on the finish line. She heard yelling and chains rattling against metal. David and Tyler strained against their bicycles, their heads way out in front, bikes wobbling.

The boys approached quickly. Rebekah stared at the finish line, listening for bike tires in the dirt, the sound of sneakers against metal pedals. They were over in a flash, two bikes and two boys all at once, before Rebekah could discern who was in front. She stood up quickly, just in time to see David raise his right arm over his head and jerk his bike slightly to the left, directly into Tyler's front tire. "Watch out!" Rebekah screamed.

They were going too fast. David's bike spun around. He flew off backward, landing on the right side of his body. Tyler catapulted straight over the handlebars, and his palms and helmet hit the sidewalk simultaneously with a grisly crack.

Rebekah froze. Chris rode up next to her, threw down his bike, and ran over to Tyler, who lay partially in the middle of Hilltop Road. Rebekah looked back at David. He was writhing on the ground, clutching the right side of his body.

"Bekah," David said. Rebekah ran to him. He sat up, holding his right arm. "Bekah," he said again.

Rebekah looked down. His arm looked bent between his elbow and wrist, giving her the impression that he had an extra joint. Rebekah looked up into his face in horror. David started to cry.

"Is it broken?" Rebekah asked.

David didn't answer. He looked up at her, his lower lip quivering. Then he closed his eyes, hunched his shoulders, and wailed.

"Oh," Rebekah said. "Oh, crap. I'm going to ride home, ok? Don't move."

Rebekah ran over to Chris and Tyler. Chris, a small, blond-haired boy with a round face, had pulled Tyler out of the street. Tyler stared at them with a vacant expression. He tried to sit up.

"Just stay down, man. Just stay here, ok?" Chris turned to Rebekah. "You going home?"

"Yeah. I'll get my parents. I'll be right back."

"Yeah," Chris said. He shook his head.

Rebekah picked up her helmet, ran back to her bike, and pedaled as fast as she could back to her house.

David watched his sister pedal away. She was a blur of arms, legs, and metal, a speck, then gone. He looked down at his arm, bent crookedly on his lap. Broken.

David sniffled. Chris looked over.

"Is he ok?" David asked, nodding towards Tyler.

Chris looked down at Tyler. "You ok?"

Tyler moaned. "What?"

"I think he hit his head," Chris said.

David lay back down on the dirt and turned his face away from Chris so his friend couldn't see him cry. He tried to muffle his erratic breathing. David knew he probably wouldn't be able to play soccer this year—not with what was likely a broken arm. He knew that one of his friends lay on the sidewalk with unknown injuries. What if Tyler had a serious head injury? What if he never recovered?

David also knew that he would be in trouble for playing at the construction site. This likelihood loomed larger to eleven year-old David, more ethereal and terrifying than any other potential consequence.

David rarely got into trouble. Trouble happened to other boys. He was careful and meticulous. Confident and idealistic.

He also possessed an extraordinary set of moral principles, rigid and dogmatic, to which he adhered with nearly obsessive devotion. Things were black and white, right and wrong, in or out. David hated uneven numbers; they seemed out of place and unjust. He gravitated towards stark primary colors, and shied away from pastels. Something was blue or it wasn't. Aqua was not a color.

Sometimes David would walk up to the line of permissibility, dip a toe over the other side, and pull his foot back without leaving a ripple. He could peer into the abyss and step away.

David prided himself on being able to step away.

For months, David had worked on mentally molding his habit of racing at the construction site to fit his rules. There hadn't been any people or equipment there for months. He and his friends never littered or left any permanent damage. It was safer than playing in the street, and there wasn't anywhere else for them to play on their bikes in southwest Portland. Until today, no one had ever gotten hurt.

Today was different. An aberration. An anomaly in what had been an unusually charmed pre-pubescent life. He inventoried possible explanations that might satisfy his parents: the dirt was softer than usual, possibly from the light rain that had fallen the week before; a van from the furniture store had driven by right as they crossed the finish line, distracting them; they had been wearing their helmets (as all of their parents had asked!) preventing much worse injuries.

David certainly wouldn't tattle on his friends or his sister. Tattling was for rats, for little girls, for the mob guys who always got killed by the end of the movie. This was just one of those unfortunate, unpredictable accidents. It was no one's fault.

Half an hour after the accident, Judith and Daniel pulled up in their red hatchback, a tearful Rebekah in the back seat. Judith jumped out and ran to David. Daniel walked over to Chris and Tyler.

"Tyler," Daniel said, kneeling down. "Tyler, you ok?"

Tyler closed his eyes. He had dirty blond hair, a little dirtier than normal from his crash. He was the tallest and thinnest of the three boys. His legs lay in front of him, splayed out, so that his toes were pointed in opposite directions, perpendicular to his body. His Seattle Seahawks t-shirt was smeared with red dirt.

"Umm, I think so," he said. He swallowed. "My head hurts."

Daniel nodded. "Ok, you're going to be ok, we're going to get you to a doctor. I think you probably banged your head pretty good. Can you move your hands and feet?"

Tyler wiggled his feet and lifted his arms. His palms and forearms were scratched all the way to the elbows.

"Great," Daniel said. "Can you sit up for me?"

Tyler slowly sat up while Chris and Daniel reached their hands around to his back to steady him. He swayed, his head tipping forward.

"Ok," Daniel said. "Let's just sit here for a minute, and then we'll get you into the car and go to the hospital."

While Daniel and Chris crouched next to Tyler, Judith bent over David, Rebekah hovering at her heels. The boy had stopped crying, but was sniffling indignantly.

"My arm hurts," David said.

"I bet it does," Judith said. She stood over David, hands on her hips. David—her first child. David, the bony pile of flesh and blood with whom she'd fallen hopelessly in love from his first tiny breath. David, her kin, her suckling life, her boy who bridled with naivety and precociousness in equally generous helpings. She couldn't imagine being deprived, the mother of an ephemeral first son, a ghost with an outline. She always seemed to be walking a step behind David, as if she was destined to look only at the back of his head.

David had fallen, Rebekah had said, as she rushed in to the house (Judith's heart stopped). His arm was broken (Judith's heart skipped, stopped, restarted). Tyler hit his head (Judith walked across the kitchen to grab her car keys). They were playing at the construction site (Judith yelled for Daniel, grabbed Rebekah's arm, and pushed her out the door). Her face was set in a mask: emotionless, focused, cold. This was what Judith was best at. Action.

"Come on, get in the car," Judith said to David now. "Let's go to the hospital." Judith helped David stand and led him stiffly to the van.

"Mom, it wasn't my fault!" David said. Judith had a hand on his left shoulder, steering him in front of her. David started to cry again. "We didn't mean to. It was an accident!"

Judith didn't respond.

Although David had tried to prepare for this moment during his long minutes alone with his broken arm, now that he was actually with his quiet, angry mother, he didn't know what to say. Tattling on friends was cowardly. The accident wasn't his fault, and his mother certainly didn't seem to be in the mood to accept any other explanation for the incident.

"Mom, it was Rebekah!" David said. "She made the finish line, and she made it too deep, and it caused us to crash!"

Judith's head snapped towards her daughter. Rebekah stared at David, her mouth open.

"Rebekah, get in the car, the back seat," Judith said. "Now."

Rebekah sat in a large, blue waiting room chair at the hospital next to her mother, her legs dangling over the front. Daniel had gone into an x-ray room with David. Tyler was in an examination room with his parents, who had rushed to the hospital after a phone call from Judith. Chris's mother, Ann Belfrey, had rushed into the waiting room half an hour ago, grabbed Chris by the arm, mouthed a "thank you" in Judith's direction, and pulled her son through the automatic double doors. Judith sat slumped next to Rebekah, her eyes closed. Rebekah swung her legs back and forth. She had been so deeply hurt by her brother's accusation that she hadn't said anything during the 20 minute ride from the construction site to the hospital, and she had not even been able to look at David when he'd gone into the x-ray room with her father. David had kept his head down, eyes closed, seemingly focused on the pain in his arm.

Rebekah's glasses were still smudged. Her black spandex shorts with the yellow stripe down the side were ripped in the front, where she had caught them on her bike pedal. Her favorite yellow "Sunshine Sally" shirt, the one with the big yellow sunflower, was wrinkled and dirty.

There were others in the waiting room: old men in wheelchairs, hunched over and coughing, as though they were breathing through the tattered remnants of one fouled-up lung; young men on stretchers, blood oozing from various orifices, while they held hands with female companions standing near them; a few families with children, some of whom looked sick, some of whom looked to be in pain, and others who were stretched out on benches, sleeping. Rebekah had never been inside an emergency room before. It seemed like a sad, bilious place, a limbo between a world of wellness and the hospital's inner sanctum.

But Rebekah couldn't think about anything but David's betrayal. The others in the waiting room seemed so small, so unimportant. Whatever their problems were, the doctors would fix them. But the white coats and deliberate touch of the healers here, with their cool, medical aloofness, had no magic for Rebekah. She felt small and alone, physically inept, perversely ill among the sick.

"Mom?" Rebekah whispered.

"What?"

Rebekah looked at her legs. "Mom…was it my fault?"

Judith didn't answer.

"Mom?" Rebekah asked again. "Was it my fault?"

Judith sighed. "Oh, Bekah," she said.

Rebekah looked at her mother. Her face was a coat of latex paint. Rebekah started to cry.

"Oh, Bekah," Judith said again. Her skin cracked; weak rays of light shone through her pores. She reached down and took her daughter's hand. "None of you should have been there in the first place."

Rebekah nodded. "I know, but David said…"

"I know what David said," Judith said. "None of you should have been there. Playing on a construction site is dangerous. And I know you followed your older brother, but next time, you need to think about what you're doing and where you're going, ok?"

Rebekah nodded again. She wiped her eyes.

There was a noise at the end of the hallway, and Rebekah saw the double doors that led inside the hospital open. David and Daniel walked out. David looked so small standing next to his father, his arm in a blue sling, a white cast sticking out. He stared at his shoes as they walked towards Rebekah and Judith.

Judith stood up. "Broken arm?"

"Clean break," Daniel said. "He'll have to wear the cast for at least six weeks, maybe longer."

"Any news on Tyler?"

"Haven't seen them," Daniel said. "We can call and leave a message when we get home."

Judith closed her eyes and took a deep breath. She knelt down next to David and put her arms around him. "You ok?"

David sniffled and nodded.

"We're going to talk about this more later," Judith said. After squeezing her son, she stood up again. "Are we all done here?"

"Yeah, let me check with the front desk." Daniel walked away.

David looked up. His eyes were red rimmed, his square chin tucked into his neck like a sheathed sword.

"I'm sorry, mom," David said. His voice sounded small and tinny, as if he were communicating through a tin can on a string.

"I know," Judith said.

David looked at Rebekah, then up at his mom. His lower lip quivered. "Mom…it was my fault."

Judith looked from her son to her daughter. David was looking at the ground again, fighting back tears. Rebekah was staring at her older brother with a mixture of surprise and awe. Judith felt touched by David's words, by the way they came out like Jell-O and the way he looked at Rebekah before he spoke. He had clearly been considering them since blaming Rebekah at the construction site. This little man, her little man, was trying. With his arm in a sling and his head hanging down, David reminded her of a petty thief paying penance in front of a judge.

Daniel walked up. "We're done. Let's get out of here."

Daniel walked towards the emergency room doors. Judith walked behind him, steering David in front of her. Rebekah fell in behind her mother, following in their footsteps.

SUMMER

"I can't believe you did that."
Rebekah looked out the window. A light drizzle painted the roads with dark splotches, Rorschach tests for night drivers. It always rained in the spring in Portland, a steady drip-drip-drip of precipitation that started in February and didn't let up until July Fourth. Portland had been Rebekah's home for twenty-eight years, save for the four years she spent at college at the University of Southern California in Los Angeles. Eighteen of those years had been spent in the undulating hills west of downtown, the side of Portland where streets looped and circled like strands of spaghetti. Two-lane roads wound their way around cul-de-sacs and tucked-in neighborhoods, climbing steeply into the fog before descending back into the steaminess of the Willamette Valley. When Rebekah heard her mother give directions to their house, it sounded like she was directing cowboys to the mercantile.

"Make a right at the white house," Judith would say. "Go forward for about an eighth of a mile, then make a sharp left up the hill at the green house with the big front yard. When you get to the top of that hill, go left back down the hill, until you pass the park. Our house is the second on the left."

Portland's Eastside, where Megan and Rebekah lived, was the flatter side of town. There were sidewalks, bike lanes, and close-knit neighborhoods. The Eastside was where the twenty-somethings went on midnight zombie bike rides, neighborhood associations held weekly parades during the summer, and where trendy brunch spots with hour-long waits served patrons bacon-infused Bloody Marys and pig cooked a dozen different ways. It was the sunnier side of town, because the sun couldn't disappear here, the way it did into the folds of the southwest. It was where musicians played outside of coffee shops, and entertainers on unicycles rode down main streets in tuxedos, clown costumes, and Darth Vader masks.

"Why?" Megan asked. "We've been talking about telling your parents about the wedding for weeks."

"We've been talking about it. We hadn't decided anything. And didn't we talk about how I was going to tell my own parents?" Megan shrugged. "Well, you hadn't. And it seemed like a good opportunity."

"I was going to. I had a plan."

"You had a plan, huh?"

"Yeah."

"Were you planning on sharing your plan with your future wife?" Megan asked.

"It wasn't that kind of plan."

"So, it was a secret plan?"

Rebekah turned to look out the passenger's side window again. "It wasn't secret," Rebekah said. "It just wasn't ready for the big reveal."

"Ah," Megan said. "So it still needed some polishing."

"It was a rough draft."

"A 'beta' wedding announcement plan."

Rebekah shook her head. Megan took one hand off the steering wheel and slipped it over Rebekah's. Rebekah relaxed her hand and allowed Megan to slip her fingers through her own.

"Beks, I know this stuff is difficult for you," Megan said.

"You don't know."

"I do know," Megan said. "How long have we been together?"

"Ten years."

"Can you believe that?" Megan asked. "Ten years? I guess that's right. We met in 2001. It's been a long time, Bekah. I think I know you."

"I don't think you know how difficult it is. Because if you knew, you wouldn't give me shit about it."

Megan turned onto the Morrison Bridge to cross over the Willamette River. It was the same river that Rebekah and Megan crossed every morning to go to work: Rebekah for her job at Stella, a non-profit organization that supported art in schools, and Megan for her job at Ingénue, a software engineering company. The glittering lights of downtown Portland were behind them now. An incandescent sign, in the shape of the state of Oregon framing a white stag, lit up their side mirrors. "Portland, Oregon," the sign read in cursive script, a welcome for travelers entering downtown from the Eastside. The sign had been there since 1940, transitioning through various ownerships and advertising schemes, while remaining in its prime spot on Northwest Couch Street. The stag—added by White Stag Sportswear in the late 1950's—remained on the sign as an amusing non sequitur. The species of animal had been gently transitioned from a stag to a reindeer, its red nose lighting up as homage to Rudolph.

Rebekah considered the reindeer. The red-nosed buck was as much a symbol of Portland as anything else. We have Mount Hood, Portlanders might say. We have noble firs, perfect for your Christmas Trees! We have the Willamette River, and the Columbia River, and roses that grow with prolific abandon. And we have the leaping neon stag. Welcome to Portland.

She felt like a neon non sequitur sometimes, a deer in the headlights, a gay Jew in a white, Christian town. There were lesbians here, no doubt. Many of them had children, golden retrievers, dirt-streaked Subarus, and honest-to-God flannel shirts. She and Megan talked about that life. A settled life.

"Bekah, I guess…" Megan paused. She loosened her hand from Rebekah's and put it back on the steering wheel. "I guess you're right that I don't understand. Your parents have known about us for…how long?"

Rebekah didn't answer.

"Nine years. Since college. I've been part of their lives for the last decade. And if we want to get married next year, then you can't take a year to tell them about our wedding."

"Just because they've known for nine years doesn't mean that they've been cool with it for nine years."

"They're cool with it now, aren't they?"

"It doesn't matter!" Rebekah said. She pounded her knee with her fist. "You know what I went through to get there?"

"So it took some time," Megan admitted. "But they were happy for us! It turned out fine!"

Rebekah rolled her eyes. After Megan made the announcement at the Seder, her parents had looked at each other in shock. Judith had slowly stood up. Daniel put his hand to his temple. Rebekah stared at the little drops of wine that had pooled on the microfiber tablecloth. They were too small, too dark for her to see her reflection in them. Daniel finally broke the silence. "Well, mazel tov!" Daniel said. "That's wonderful news."

Judith had looked at Daniel, then back to her daughter. "Honey—that's great," she said. She clapped her hands together. "That's great news! Mazel tov. I'm…I'm a little surprised, but…" Judith composed herself. "You two are a delightful couple."

Daniel had stood up to join his wife. His face, like Rebekah's, was bright red. "That's great. Very nice."

Rebekah had slumped in her chair. She felt as though she had been hauled to the town square naked, then lit on fire so everyone could see her intestines pour off her body. Her skin felt hot to the touch. She wanted to run outside screaming, rip her face off, and steal someone else's.

"We're going to get married next year," Megan said. She looked down at her fiancée. "That's the plan right now, anyway."

"Does David know yet?" Judith asked.

Rebekah shook her head.

"Oh," Judith said. She took a deep breath and pressed her lips together in a thin smile.

Daniel gestured with his wine glass. "A toast, then! To my daughters! Next year, at Megan and Rebekah's wedding!"

"Maybe it turned out fine," Rebekah said to Megan in the car, "but I wish we could have done it at a better time."

"That was the perfect time. There was no better time. Were you planning on driving back over there to tell them? Tell them over the phone? They know now. They're happy for us. I took care of it. I think you just need to stop stressing and get over it."

Rebekah shrugged.

Megan shook her head. "Beks, next year, we're going to be getting married. You're going to be getting up in front of your family—your entire extended family—and our friends, and sharing with them how much you love me and how we're planning on spending the rest of our lives together. And you know what's going to happen at the end of the ceremony? You're going to kiss me. We're going to be standing up in front of everyone, and you're going to kiss me. It's going to be two women, kissing."

Megan pulled up in front of their apartment. They lived in the basement of a house located on the north side of northeast Broadway, about thirty blocks east of downtown and just a short walk to an array of bars and restaurants. The house was an old Portland craftsman-style structure, built at the turn of the twentieth century and still upright, despite century-old pipes and a sagging, dilapidated front porch. The light blue paint on the exterior of the house was peeling, and two of the awnings above the upstairs windows had fallen off due to disrepair. In the front yard, well-tended magnolia trees, rhododendrons, and Japanese maples had been planted at even intervals when the house was built, and now towered over the street like natural sentries.

"I'm on board," Rebekah said. She stepped out of the car. "You know that. It just happened really fast."

Megan locked the car door, and they started up the sidewalk for the house. "I'm glad you're on board. Because I don't want to go through with planning a wedding, only to have you back out of the last minute because you're scared."

"I won't."

"I've been dealing with this with you since we met," Megan said. "You're the only person I know who hasn't evolved with the rest of the country. Why do you fucking hate yourself so much?"

Rebekah kept walking. She stared at the sidewalk.

Megan caught up to Rebekah and put an arm around her shoulders. "Sorry. I didn't mean it like that. You're a wonderful person, and I love you so much. There's just no reason for you to hold onto all this crap you bought into years ago."

"Not that long ago, babe."

"Long enough."

The two were interrupted when the front door of the house opened. It was the Judge.

"Hello, you two!" the Judge said. "I've been looking for you all evening!"

"Hey, Mark," Megan said. "What's up?"

The Judge, Mark Mellon on his Social Security card, had advertised the basement apartment on Craigslist six years ago. Rebekah messaged him about the place; Mark wrote back immediately, asking if she was *the* Rebekah Cohayn, daughter of Judith and Daniel Cohayn, who attended Beth Chaver? Rebekah had responded in the affirmative. "Amazing!" Mark had written. "What a small world. I've known your parents for years, and even though you might not know me, I had the pleasure of watching you grow up. Why don't you come over and see the house, and we'll talk about price?"

Mark had given them a good deal, cutting two hundred dollars off the advertised rent.

A lifelong Portlander, Mark had retired from being a county judge twenty years ago. He had been a judge in Family Court, where divorcing couples fought openly and bitterly about their houses, children, and 401ks.

"Our court is considered a social service agency," the Judge told Rebekah. "Social service, my ass. You want social service? Teach these people how to communicate. They end up with me because they can't talk to each other."

After the Judge retired, he switched to performing civil marriage ceremonies in his front yard. He wanted to be on the eating end, instead of the shitting end, of marriages, the Judge liked to say. Rebekah would often come home and find a couple and a small crowd huddled near their door. She would walk around the back of the house, through the kitchen, and down into the basement, so as not to interrupt.

The Judge almost always wore robes. When he married couples in his yard, he wore a long black robe, buttoned up near the collar, over a pair of gray dress slacks and shiny black shoes. Off duty, he walked around his house in a long, faded blue bathrobe. It came down to his mid-calf, leaving exposed the Judge's withered lower legs and ankles, as well as his feet, shoved into a pair of gray Haflinger slippers. Once or twice, Rebekah and Megan had seen him leave the house in jeans. It was like seeing a bull-wrangler step out in tennis whites.

The Judge had a head of white hair, and a white, waxed mustache. He had a distinctive low, gravelly voice, one Rebekah thought she might hear announcing a baseball game.

"Where have you two been?" Mark asked.

"We were over at my parent's for a Seder," Rebekah said.

"I figured as much. It was just Claire and me tonight. We've still got a whole bunch of wine left. You two want to join us?"

Rebekah hesitated.

"Oh, come on," said the Judge. "You guys haven't met Claire yet. She's real nice." He lowered his voice. "Cute too."

Megan cleared her throat.

"It's good wine, I promise. You don't have to stay long."

Rebekah looked at Megan. Megan shrugged.

"One glass," the Judge said. "That's all I'll let you girls drink, anyway."

"Well…ok," Rebekah said. "We'll go up for a little bit. We just need to drop some stuff off in the apartment."

"Great," the Judge said. "See you in a minute." He closed the door. Rebekah turned to Megan. "I can't believe I just agreed to do that," Rebekah said.

"So he's got a lady now, huh?" Megan asked.

"Apparently."

Rebekah followed Megan to the side entrance into their apartment. The basement was surprisingly spacious, with two bedrooms and a thousand square feet. Ten-foot-high ceilings and large wooden beams broke up the monotony of the living room. The Judge had completely renovated the apartment prior to advertising it; he said that he couldn't, in good conscience, let someone live in what he had called the "catacombs" of his house. Now the walls were furred out and insulated. The kitchen was small, but functional, and the apartment remained bone-dry, even through the thickest Portland storms. The only knock on the space was that there wasn't much natural light, despite large windows. After their first winter in the house, Megan, a native of Los Angeles, had purchased a sun lamp. The apartment's rent was less than they could have afforded. Megan made nearly eighty thousand dollars a year at her engineering job, and Rebekah pulled in about half that from Stella. But Rebekah had insisted that she wanted to split the rent fifty-fifty. It meant that they didn't have a place as nice as they could have, but weren't they saving more? Maybe for a house? Or to pay off their student loans faster? Weren't they comfortable? It felt weird, she had told Megan, not to be an equal contributor.

Megan tossed her bag into the basement and pulled Rebekah in after her.

"Kiss me," Megan whispered.

Rebekah put her lips on Megan's and kissed her gently. She smiled through the kiss, thinking of the Judge and his new girlfriend and the way her mom's jaw had dropped when Megan announced their wedding.

Rebekah pulled away. "Shit, did you see the look on my mom's face?"

Megan kissed her neck. "Uh-huh," Megan said.

"Classic."

"Did you happen to look at your grandma?"

"No," Rebekah said. "Why?"

"That lady. She's pretty fucking twisted."

"What?"

"Your grandma," Megan said, "had the biggest shit-eating grin on her face."

Rebekah and Megan walked upstairs.

"Mark!" Rebekah heard a woman yell when they walked in. "Go put on some clothes!"

"Darling, I'm comfortable," the Judge called back. "Maybe you're overdressed."

Rebekah walked into the Judge's living room. There were two fat candles sitting in metal holders on the wooden coffee table; long drips of wax had fossilized on the sides. The candles were gratuitous bits of mood lighting, since the room was well lit, with lamps in every corner and an overhead light in the center of the room.

Though the exterior of the house looked a century old, the Judge had completely redone the interior. He had torn down the walls between the living room, dining room, and kitchen. Glossy gray and white countertops capped new oak cabinets. Stainless steel appliances, including a double oven and built-in microwave, had been embedded in the walls. A large, industrial-sized vent hung over a massive island that divided the kitchen from the other two living spaces.

The living and dining room had been re-painted cozy beige and blue, respectively. Crown molding adorned the corners of the rooms, giving them an old-school formality that matched the era of the home. Floor-to-ceiling bookshelves lined the walls of the living room, filled with leather-bound books with fraying edges. An old encyclopedia collection took up the bottom two rows of one of the shelves. The rest of the books looked to be reference or research works: plant types in the Pacific Northwest, essay collections by political theorists, summaries of religions around the world. The Judge, Rebekah noted, didn't do fiction.

A blond woman who looked to be in her late 40s was sitting on a brown leather couch in the corner of the room. She was wearing blue jeans tucked into black boots and a loose-fitting black sweater. Waves of blond hair hung down past her collar. She had a pleasant face with a wide nose, blue eyes, and lips that seemed to take up half her chin. Not quite conventionally beautiful, Rebekah thought, but all of her facial elements together seemed to work. The Judge was puttering around in the kitchen in his tattered blue bathrobe.

"Oh, Mark, you're embarrassing me." The woman turned to Megan and Rebekah.

"I'm so sorry about him," she said.

"We've seen it before," Megan replied.

"Oh, I bet you have." The woman stood up and offered her hand. "I'm Claire."

Megan and Rebekah introduced themselves.

"Is he like this all the time?" Claire asked.

"I think he puts on clothes to go food shopping," Megan offered.

"She's right," the Judge called from the kitchen. "I sure do."

"Right," Claire said. "At least there's that." Rebekah and Megan sat down on a pink loveseat across the room.

The Judge walked in from the kitchen. His bathrobe was cinched tightly at the waist. He was carrying a plate of cookies.

"Cookies, cookies, who wants cookies?" The Judge asked in a singsong voice. "They're kosher for Passover." He bent over to place the tray on the coffee table next to the candles. His robe rode up, just enough for Rebekah to catch an eyeful of upper thigh before she turned her head away.

"Mark!" Claire said. Rebekah turned back to see the Judge smiling broadly and Claire shaking her head at him.

"Come sit next to me," she said, tapping the couch.

"First, dance with me," the Judge said. He offered Claire a hand. Claire raised her eyebrows. "I don't dance with men in bathrobes."

"In front of guests?" the Judge asked. The Judge crooked one arm around an imaginary partner and held his second arm out for balance. He spun and twirled, humming a waltz.

"I had no idea you were so graceful," Megan said.

Indeed, the Judge did move with surprising grace. His thick hairy legs bounced effortlessly over the carpet, and his back stayed ramrod straight. He danced with his eyes closed and a mischievous smile on his face.

Claire shook her head. "Cute, isn't he? Mark is actually a really good dancer. Do either of you dance?"

Rebekah shook her head. "Never."

"Aw, come on, Megan said. "You're not bad."

Rebekah looked at Claire. "I only dance if I'm pretty sure I won't remember it the next day."

"Oh, whatever," Megan said.

"I look like a three-legged horse learning to walk."

Claire laughed. "It just takes practice. You girls should join us sometime!"

The Judge waltzed around the coffee table, sat down, and crossed one leg over the other. Claire immediately reached out to make sure that his robe was providing adequate coverage.

"Mmmmm," the Judge said. He reached out and took a cookie. "I've gotta tell you girls, I make fabulous kosher-for Passover cookies. It's all in the matzo meal and the kind of flour you use. I used to do it from a mix, but I think it's more fun from scratch. Wine! You ladies need wine!" The Judge started to stand up, but Claire pressed on his thigh.

"I'll get it for them. You stay here." Claire walked over to the kitchen, grabbed the bottle of wine and two tumblers, and poured them each half a glass.

"What kind of wine is this?" Megan asked.

"It's from one of my favorite wineries, Louie Farms," the Judge said. "I love their Pinots. They're really good, dark, with a nice bite at the end."

The Judge swirled his glass and took another sip. "So, how are you girls? What's going on?"

"We're good," Megan said. "We're just doing our thing…working, living. You know how it goes."

"Oh, I know," the Judge said. "Yeah, I know." He uncrossed his legs, and crossed them again in the other direction. Claire put her hand out over his crotch.

"How are your parents?" the Judge asked Rebekah.

"They're fine," Rebekah said. "Same old, same old."

"Are they still working?" the Judge asked.

"They are," Rebekah said. "They talk about retirement but don't have anything concrete planned."

"Well, of course not!" The Judge said. "They're still so young! In their early 60's, right?"

Rebekah nodded.

"Just pups," the Judge said. "I remember them being about 15 years behind me—getting married, having babies, buying a house. They were just adorable when they were younger. Still are! And how's your brother, David?"

Rebekah shrugged. "He's ok."

"Now…he moved to Los Angeles, right?" the Judge asked.

"He did."

"And he's living down there?"

"He is."

"Ah," the Judge nodded. He nodded slowly and squinted his eyes at Rebekah. "And he's happy?"

Rebekah shrugged again. "He seems to be." The truth was that Rebekah didn't know if David was happy, because she hadn't spoken to him for six months, since his last birthday. When they did speak, their conversations were short and superficial: Rebekah asked about his family and his job, and David asked her what was new in her life. But he asked quickly, urgency in his voice, as if he didn't really want to know what was new in her life; he was just performing the expected, perfunctory task of asking the question. Rebekah complied by glossing over her answer, sharing nothing with her older brother except the fact that she was happy and still employed. David knew Megan only as the tall, open-faced, slump-shouldered woman who had been Rebekah's roommate since college.

The Judge nodded. "He was always so driven, that boy. I remember when you were kids, he had this way of walking." The Judge moved his shoulders from side to side, forward to back, as if each of them were his primary means of locomotion. "Like this. Like he always knew where he was going. David always had a destination. There were no wasted movements."

"Yeah," Rebekah said. "He's a pretty intense guy."

"I bet," the Judge said. "Always so striking. Memorable. I always wondered what would become of him." He took another sip of wine and looked from Rebekah to Megan. "And how about you two? What's new?"

"Nothing new," Rebekah answered quickly. She glanced at Megan, who was looking up at the ceiling.

"Nothing, huh?" He continued looking from one to the other. Megan looked quickly at Rebekah and then back at the Judge. Rebekah immediately put her tumbler of wine to her lips.

"We've been talking about getting married, but we can't get married yet," Megan said. "It's not legal." Megan looked at Rebekah. *You can thank me later.*

"Well, gay marriage will be legal! It's right around the corner! And you don't need it to be legal for someone like me to marry you," the Judge said. He winked at them.

"Mark, stop it," Claire said. She put her hand on his knee.

"They've been together for a long time, and when you get to be an old man like me, you like to see people you care about settled," the Judge said to Claire. He looked from Megan to Rebekah and smiled again. "And you can also ask questions like that. Eh? Right?"

"Anytime you ladies want, we can do a ceremony," the Judge said. "We'll have it right here at the house. I'm a registered notary, so I can even sign the domestic partnership paperwork, if that's what you gals want."

"Thanks Mark," Megan said. "We really do appreciate that."

Rebekah held her breath. This was an opportunity. A chance to prove to Megan that she wasn't chicken-shit. That next April, this wedding really would happen. This moment, sitting in front of the Judge and his girlfriend, blew up in front of Rebekah like the yawning maw of a sinkhole. Her pulse quickened, her face was red with anticipation. Rebekah adjusted her glasses and shook out her curls. "Well actually," Rebekah said. She looked at the Judge, who sat placidly in his chair with his legs crossed. He was gently toe tapping the air with the leg that was on top, studying the wine in his tumbler.

Rebekah leaned forward. "Actually—"

"Sorry to interrupt, Rebekah," the Judge said. He held out his wine glass. "I'm truly sorry, but I just can't contain myself. This wine really is quite good. Don't you think, Claire? I think it's one of the best wines of the year from Louie Farms. They really do such a good job. And they've improved so much over the years. I've been with them since they started, you know—I've known those boys since they were just kids—and they've really done it. This by itself is a cause for celebration." He raised his glass. "To good wine!"

Megan, Rebekah, and Claire obediently followed suit. "Good wine," they said.

"L'chaim!" the Judge said.

"L'chaim," the three women repeated. A moment of silence followed as they all sipped from their wine glasses.

"So what were you going to say?" the Judge asked.

"Oh…" Rebekah said. She sipped her wine and looked at Megan over the top of her glasses. Megan shrugged and smiled back.

"I was just going to say that…um…even though marriage isn't legal yet, we shared with our parents tonight that we might have a ceremony next year."

"Might?" Megan asked. She raised her eyebrows.

The Judge looked from one to the other.

"I mean, I guess what I mean is that we announced that we're having a ceremony next year," Rebekah said. "A wedding, I mean. So, um, what I'm trying to say is that we're engaged."

"Mazel tov!" the Judge yelled. "That's wonderful news!"

"But we haven't picked a date or a venue or anything," Rebekah added quickly. "It's totally preliminary."

The Judge spread his arms. "Who the hell cares? That's still wonderful!" He raised his glass. "To preliminary wedding planning!"

The four clinked their glasses together. Rebekah took a long swig, followed by a deep breath. The upcoming year would be full of these moments: moments of free-fall, where fear would swirl and eddy in her stomach and settle into mild froth.

Rebekah reflected that things were so different now than they were a decade ago. When Rebekah had come out to her mom in high school, Judith had gone pale, clammed up, and requested stiffly that Rebekah keep the news to herself. On November 18, 2003, when the Massachusetts Supreme Court ruled 4-3 in favor of the plaintiffs in a case titled *Goodridge et al v. Department of Public Health*, the world could hardly believe that gay people could have normal relationships, let alone get married. When eleven states passed constitutional amendments banning gay marriage in 2004, Rebekah accepted the development as inevitable whiplash.

Now it was 2011, and there were expectations. Expectations of equality. Expectations of coming out. Expectations of self-acceptance. As Rebekah closed down, the world opened up, like one tight gear curled up in the bosom of another. Now she was expected to celebrate herself, feel free to be you and me, shout to the world that she was just born this way, baby.

Could there be a crueler fate for such a creature of habit? For someone who was born so near-sighted that she could barely see out past the tips of her shoes without glasses?

Rebekah had grown so used to entrenched, institutionalized homophobia that she could scarcely believe a world that was trying to change. She needed to unfurl, unclench, and reset, but there simply had not been enough time. Her parents were trying. Her girlfriend wanted to marry her. And Rebekah felt like she had been left behind.

The affirmation from the Judge was helpful, but it was a bittersweet tonic. The Judge wouldn't be up in front of his family and friends getting married. The Judge married others. The Judge remained neutral.

Mark, Claire, Rebekah and Megan continued to chat. The Judge shared stories from some of the weddings at which he had most recently officiated: the two seventeen-year-olds who arrived with signed waivers from their parents, their only witness a friend from high school; the octogenarians, one in a wheelchair and the other with an oxygen tank, who got married in the Judge's front yard, then threw a raucous party at the groom's house down the street; the couple who got married last Halloween, the man dressed up as a pirate, the woman dressed as a princess, and their zombie priest witness. The Judge told these stories with unabashed delight, clearly relishing his role as a marriage-maker.

Finally, Rebekah checked her cell phone. "Oh, shit," Rebekah said. "It's already eleven. We should probably go."

"But we were just getting started!" the Judge said.

"Mark," Claire said. She stood up. "I'm so sorry."

"No, really, it's ok," Rebekah said. "We talk like this all the time."

"We do," the Judge said. "And I love your company. You should come up here more often! When Claire's not around, I'm just a lonely old man."

Rebekah laughed. Megan grabbed her hand.

"Time to go," Megan said. She turned and started walking toward the door. "Thanks so much, Mark."

"Oh, my pleasure! Please come again! And mazel tov on the wedding!"

"Bye!" Claire said from the couch. "Nice meeting you!"

Megan and Rebekah walked downstairs and closed the door behind them. When they had safely entered their own apartment, Megan grabbed Rebekah by the hand. "That man…." Megan said.

"I think he's a riot," Rebekah answered.

"He is. He's wild."

"And that bathrobe?"

"Disgusting. Hilarious."

"Totally."

Megan stopped walking and pulled Rebekah towards her. "We ok?"

Rebekah put her arms around Megan. "Yeah, I think so."

Megan studied her face. "One day at a time?"

"One day at a time."

"Marry me?" Megan asked.

"I told him."

"You sort of told him," Megan said.

"Well, I tried my best."

"I know," Megan said. "It almost counts."

Megan leaned down and kissed the soft spot between Rebekah's neck and clavicle.

Rebekah moaned in response. "Stop," Rebekah said. "I need to work tomorrow."

"So?" Megan kissed her again, moving her lips counter-clockwise around the base of Rebekah's neck.

Rebekah tilted Megan's face up and kissed her lips. They kissed gently, feeling the contours of each other's mouths.

"That's something for you to think about," Rebekah whispered.

"Uh huh." Megan kissed her again. "I'm thinking about it."

They kissed again, pulled apart, and returned to discussing their landlord, speculating about his health, wealth, and the age of his latest flame.

Rebekah's alarm buzzed at six the next morning. She hit the snooze button only once, rolled over, and curled her body against Megan's. When the alarm rang again five minutes later, she threw off her sheets and stumbled out of the bedroom. By six fifteen, Rebekah was out of the shower. She ate bites of peach yogurt in between drying her hair and rubbing in face moisturizer. At six thirty-eight, she ran back into the bedroom, kissed Megan—who refused to extricate herself until well after seven —grabbed a light jacket, and ran out the door.

Most mornings, Rebekah left the apartment no later than six forty. Rebekah relished her commute: Fifty minutes on Portland's MAX light rail to people-watch and think about her work as newsmagazine editor at Stella, a fundraising non-profit for the arts. *Daft* was the name of her newsmagazine. It was an organ for sharing the organization's accomplishments, its quarterly reports, and the work of kids in its arts programs. *Daft* was also a tool for fundraising, an instrument that had become increasingly important in a climate in which donors were finding it more and more difficult to give to non-profit organizations.

Rebekah ran *Daft* from start to finish. She solicited material from colleagues and children in the program, designed and edited the newsmagazine, and oversaw its digital and hard copy dissemination. Rebekah lavished particular care on the newsmagazine's center spread, which allowed for a bi-fold page design. The center spread provided Rebekah with opportunities to stretch creatively, push the envelope on design, and move past the rather structured outline of the rest of the magazine.

Rebekah was one of Stella's only employees who did not work as an artist. She had never taken an arts class in school unless it was a mandatory part of the curriculum. She didn't know much about art history; in art museums, Rebekah needed a tour guide to explain the different eras, mediums, and styles of each exhibit. As an English major, Rebekah was one of the only employees without an arts degree or an M.F.A.

"So, why do you want to work for an arts advocacy organization, if you're not an artist?" Tony Hernandez, the executive director of Stella, had asked at her interview.

Rebekah thought that she muddled her way through an answer—something about how she believed art was a universal language. She might not understand the mechanics of creating visual art, she told Tony, but she was a reader, and she understood that people liked to tell stories about the human condition. Weren't Dickens and Warhol really in the same profession?

After the interview, Tony told Rebekah that her answer to that question was why she got the job.

"You're the only one I interviewed who compared Victorian literature to pop art," Tony had said on her first day of work. "That's just the kind of weirdness I want in my newsmagazine."

Rebekah usually arrived at Stella's office by seven thirty. Located on Southwest Fifth Street and Washington Avenue, Stella was housed in an old brick office building previously used as an overflow space for the Portland Police Department. It had exquisitely refurbished wooden floors, and the faded brick that lined the walls gave the place an old-world charm. There was a non-operational wood-burning stove in one corner; Tony occasionally threw reports into the stove, only to fish them out a few days later and toss them in the trash. Large canvases, framed in recycled wood, had been nailed into the brick. Tony made a point to frame and hang pieces of student art, which he changed out regularly. Instead of cubicles, Tony had set up computer stations around the space, surrounding an old pine table in the center.

Rebekah entered a quiet office. She flicked on the lights and walked into the small break room kitchen, which was outfitted with a tiny camping stove, a microwave, and a refrigerator. She washed out the coffee pot in the sink and poured in grounds for a new one.

At eight ten, Roberto Lima walked in. He nodded to her.

"Mornin' Bekah," he said. Roberto sat down at his computer.

"Mornin' Roberto."

Roberto turned on his computer. He leaned back in his chair and groaned audibly.

"Long weekend?"

He gave her a look. "Girl…you don't even know."

"You think?"

"I think."

"Try me."

Roberto rolled his chair over to Rebekah's desk. He pulled himself forward with his feet slowly, as if every movement was dipping into an exhausted credit line. He kept his hands on his knees as he moved, holding his kneecaps together.

Roberto was the oldest employee in the office. No one knew exactly how old he was; if you asked, he would say in a low drawl, "Old enough to be appalled." He had a smooth face with a surprising absence wrinkles. His only facial blemishes were two deep dimples in his cheeks, long indentations that extended from his cheekbones to his chin. He had a shock of bright silver hair, as if, Rebekah thought, when the first uneven bits of white appeared in his hairline, he had gone straight to a colorist and asked to trade in his youth for symmetry. Two diamond earrings, one in each ear lobe, set off a pair of icy blue eyes that sparkled, even when he was upset.

Rebekah guessed that Roberto was in his mid 40's, which would make him nearly fifteen years her senior. But he never acted older than anyone else in the office. He went out with Stella's crew to their once-a-month Thursday happy hours, making droll comments about the food or the bartenders. He teased Tony about being an old man, even though the director was most likely his junior. He favored well-tailored, cool-hued dress shirts and dark pants or blue jeans. Today, he was wearing a navy blue polo, black slacks, and black dress shoes with argyle socks.

"You always get in so early," Roberto said. He crossed one leg over the other, stretched his arms out, and yawned.

"It's just so I have time to talk to you."

"I bet." Roberto stared at her.

"So?"

"So…it's just drama. You know. Different weekend, same shit. I don't even know how I get myself into these messes."

"Yes, you do."

Roberto cocked his head and pursed his lips. "You're right," he said. "I do. And I do it anyway. Don't let anyone tell you that you can learn from your mistakes. It's a myth, you know? No one ever learns from their mistakes. You just keep repeating them over, and over, and over again, until you die."

"And your mistakes are?" Rebekah asked.

Roberto held up one finger. "The first is going out on Saturday nights."

"Sounds like it must have been a really bad weekend."

"My epitaph should read, 'Son, brother, and hopelessly optimistic old fag.'"

"So…you gonna tell me about it?" Rebekah asked. She took a sip of her coffee.

Roberto took a deep breath. "We got to Peeple's Bar Saturday. It was like eleven. Me, Teddy, and Mike. The same crew I always go out with, you know? So we waited in line, for like, an hour. It's totally ridiculous. I don't know why we still go when we waste half of the night in line. Peeple's is way too young. Way too 'scene.' Why are we going to bars where all the boys are going to be half my age?"

"Teddy and Mike don't care?"

Roberto shrugged. "They don't care. Peeple's has the best drinks."

"So, you're waiting in line…"

"Yeah, we're waiting in line, and I was getting really impatient. It's not like it's that warm out in Portland in April, you know? And of course, I didn't bring a jacket because I hate coat checks. Anyway, so we finally get in, and before I can even get to the bar, this guy walks over and starts hitting on me."

"Sounds promising."

"He was cute. Not really my type—white guy, skinny. Looked to be in his 30s. Young, but not like crazy young. Not like I-need-to-keep-my-hands-off young. He was wearing this really silly leather jacket. Like he was trying too hard, you know?"

"Right," Rebekah said.

"But the kid offered to buy me a drink, so I took him up on it," Roberto said. "We were standing near the bar, just talking. He was, like, really close to me. He was already drunk, and he kind of had his hand on my shirt. And I was like, 'whoa, we got plenty of time.' But whatever, I didn't mind.

"And we were just talking, whatever. Flirting. Totally flirting. When this other guy walks up to me, and gets all up in my space, and just starts kind of yelling. 'Are you hitting on my boyfriend? You douche bag, step off,' that kind of thing. He was crazy. And so I just started pointing at this guy, like, you know, 'He started it.' So then this guy and his boyfriend—I guess he was his boyfriend—get into this major fight right in front of me. They start pushing each other, and the boyfriend starts trying to hit this guy. So I tried to pull him off—not because I gave a shit about the other guy, but really 'cause I just didn't want them to fight right in front of me—and he elbows me right in the ribs."

Roberto reached down and rubbed his right side. "It still hurts."

"Wow. That sucks."

"Yeah. So the security people came over and pulled them apart, and they both got thrown out. I almost got thrown out too, but a couple of people spoke up and said that I wasn't really involved. But we decided to leave the bar anyway."

Roberto shook his head. "So that was my weekend. Because you asked."

"Damn," Rebekah said. "I haven't had a weekend like that in a long, long time."

"Come out with me next weekend. Next Saturday night, specifically."

"I'll put it to a vote with Megan."

Roberto raised his eyebrows. "I suppose that's as much as I can hope for." He looked at the clock on the wall. "I've gotta start working. If I'm going to die alone, I want to die having accomplished something in my life. We'll catch up more later, yeah?"

"Sure."

The office filled up during the next hour. Jane Salish, the organization's top fundraiser, usually strolled in close to eight thirty, talking on her phone, a Starbucks cup in her hand.

Jane wore pants suits in the winter, well-fitted skirts and blouses in the summer, and a never-ending stock of new, expensive, seasonally appropriate shoes. Jane was tall, but not gawky, and toned, while avoiding the broad-shouldered look of athletic women. Her fingernails were always immaculately manicured.

Jane's real magic was in knowing what to say and how to say it, and always at exactly the right time. She was an emotionally intelligent *savant*, a queen bee, a driven, successful woman who used a soft voice and an infectious laugh to extract money from would-be donors. At least, Rebekah thought, Jane was consistent; she viewed friendship as the currency of social capital, and she chose her investments carefully.

Jane had never struck Rebekah as an artist. Could an artist be as ambitious, as grounded, as financially motivated as Jane? Could she really find the psychological space to create? Did Jane understand chaos?

Jane had made offhand comments about her art in meetings—a painting she was trying to sell, a drawing in a coffee shop. Rebekah had never actually seen one of these paintings. In her darker moments, she wondered if Jane was making everything up. But who was she to judge?

Rebekah heard Jane laughing on the phone.

"Hey, now," Jane was saying. "I just walked into my office. We'll have to finish this conversation later." She paused, laughed again, set her purse down on her desk, and ran her fingers through her hair. "Ok, ok. Is that thing happening tonight? Yeah? Ok. Well, maybe I'll see you there, then. Ok, buddy, talk to you later."

Jane pressed her phone's screen, and then took the earpiece off. She picked up her coffee and walked over to Roberto's office and sat down on the edge of his desk. "Robby!" Jane said to Roberto. "Fun weekend?"

Rebekah saw him shake his head.

"What did you do?" Jane asked.

"Jane, why have I been cursed with a life of drama?"

Jane laughed. She sat down in the extra chair in his cubicle. She whispered something to him.

"Oh, no shit!" Roberto said.

Rebekah saw Jane nod, lean in, and continue speaking to Roberto in a low voice.

A few minutes later, Gregory Rimes, the North Portland Education District manager, walked in with his blue and white Cannondale street bike over his shoulder, helmet in hand, clip pedals clicking on the wood floors. He set his bike down by the door and clicked off his helmet. Instead of walking to his office, he walked directly to Roberto's cube.

"You two look like trouble," Greg said.

Jane looked up and smiled at him. She motioned for him to pull up a chair.

Jane, Gregory, and Roberto ran the office. Not so much in name; all of them were paid roughly the same amount, except for Jane, who earned status bonuses for her fundraising prowess. But Jane had no equal in social power at Stella. She spent most of her time with Roberto and Greg, a gay man and a straight one, respectively, who enjoyed fawning over her.

Rebekah watched the three of them between sips of coffee. They had their heads together, whispering, starting off their Monday by catching up on weekend gossip. As they spoke, their office mates wandered in. The three acknowledged them with waves and head nods, but never broke their conversation to say hello.

At about nine thirty, Tony Hernandez walked through the door. "Good morning," he called. He smiled at Rebekah. "Hi, Rebekah, how was your weekend?"

"It was fine Tony, thanks." Rebekah smiled back. "And you?"

"It was great…but you know me. I'm glad it's Monday! Two days away from Stella is two too many!" He laughed. He turned towards the rest of the office. "Good morning Greg, Roberto, and Jane."

When Rebekah first met Tony, she had marveled at his posture. He stood so straight, his shoulders so perfectly sloped and relaxed, the carriage of his hips perfectly level, that she had found herself sucking in her own stomach and pushing out her rib cage in an effort to mimic his body language. But he was always like that: a man with titanium for a spine. Tony walked with admirable fluidity, feet hitting the ground at a steady, even rate. He never tripped. He did not pronate.

She also wondered how old he was. He couldn't have been more than forty, but his resume listed an impressive array of accomplishments for someone so young. She had memorized his academic and professional history: an undergraduate degree in fine arts, a masters of business administration, a few years with an insurance company, a transition to fundraising for an NGO in New York, and within the last five years, a move to Portland, where he started Stella.

When Tony gave fundraising speeches, he liked to share Stella's origination tale. Tony had been a successful young man living in New York City, who found jobs—any jobs, really—to feed his passion to be an artist. He grew increasingly restless and depressed by his seemingly Sisyphean existence. He followed a girl, a fellow artist, to Portland. When the relationship didn't work out, he considered moving back to New York, where most of his friends and professional connections lived.

But instead of moving back to New York to find a job, he liked to say, he found a boy named Tom.

Walking by the waterfront one day, Tony saw a boy with long dreadlocks pushing a shopping cart filled with a sleeping bag and empty cans for deposit. He had a dirty blanket wrapped around his shoulders and he looked skinny and miserable. Strangest of all, he was alone. Most homeless kids in Portland run around in groups, but this kid was sitting all by himself. It was early October, just cold enough to make being outside without a jacket uncomfortable.

"Who are you?" Tony asked the boy.

"Who are YOU?" the boy asked back.

Tony offered to buy him a hot drink. Much to Tony's surprise, the boy accepted. They walked to a nearby coffee shop, where the boy told him a story.

"His name was Tom," Tony would say to donors. "No last name—just Tom. Tom was only seventeen years old when I found him on the waterfront. He told me that he grew up just north of Seattle. Two-parent household, one older sibling. 'Did your parents hurt you?' I asked Tom. 'No,' Tom said. 'Did they kick you out of the house?' I asked him. 'They didn't,' Tom said.

"'So why,' I asked Tom, 'are you here?'

"Tom couldn't give me a definitive reason why. He said that he'd been to a lot of doctors for depression, been on a lot of drugs, ran away from home a couple of times. His parents didn't understand him, he told me. He didn't like being around other people. He didn't like school. He had never been able to hold down a job. Just seventeen, and already he'd given up on so much.

"'Well,' I asked Tom, 'is there anything you do like to do?'

"And Tom's face just lit up. 'I love to paint,' he said."

Tony would pause for long moment to allow Tom's words to sink in.

"Tom was homeless," he would say. "He had nothing. He had run away from home, given up everything. But art—art still did something for him. Art was the answer. In that moment, I saw that art could save him. It could make this boy whole. It could bring him back to his family.

"'Look,' I told Tom at the coffee shop. 'I can help you. I can try to find you some people who can help you. It's hard to make a living as an artist, but there are lots of jobs that you can do in the art field, or that you can do so you can make art.'

"I told Tom I needed some time to make a couple of phone calls. We agreed to meet back at the coffee shop the next day, at the same time. So I went home, called a couple of my friends in New York, called a couple of the people I had met in Portland, and told them about this kid. They were all open to the idea of giving him a chance. They wanted to know if he was talented and hardworking. I couldn't give them any of that information—I hadn't seen his work—but I did say I would vouch for him. If it didn't work out, I told them, they could blame me.

"The next day I went to the coffee shop. I waited for two hours. No Tom."

Tony would pause again. Look around the room. Take a deep breath, and work his way into his main pitch.

"I never found out what happened to Tom. I never saw him again. Maybe, after our talk, he made his way back up to Seattle and his family. Maybe he went south. Maybe he died. I don't know. What I can tell you is that meeting Tom changed *me*—it made me realize what I wanted to do with my life. And that was to start an organization that helped kids find success through art. Art saved my life. It could have saved Tom's life. And I deeply believe, with all my soul, that it saves the lives of kids who get involved with Stella on a daily basis. When I found Tom, I found my calling. I found myself. And I need your help."

Rebekah knew that donors opened their wallets for Tony. They opened their wallets, believing that art might be the answer to homelessness, poverty, poor performance in school, rape, murder, domestic abuse, and unwanted children. What Tony lacked in experience, he made up for in magnetism. He produced charisma more quickly than carbon dioxide.

Jane stood up. She grinned at Greg and Roberto, then headed for Tony's office. When she got there, she leaned against the doorframe, one foot propped behind the heel of the other, twirling her hair with the hand that wasn't holding her cup of coffee. Tony must have said something funny, because Jane laughed.

April 20, 2011

Megan Nimble had the kind of stature that was accentuated by small spaces. When Megan stood in the back corner of the basement, where the ceiling sloped down to make room for a set of water pipes, her head grazed the ceiling just enough to leave a dusty white streak down the middle of her hairline. When Megan lay down on her bed, her feet often poked out of the bottom of the bed sheets.

Megan was tall, but not oafish. She wore her height well, all five feet ten of her tucked into long calves and modest hips. Her lankiness had never translated well to impressive eye-hand coordination, but friends might have said that she was an exceedingly useful companion, always willing to get things down from the highest shelves or assist her smaller friends to see over crowds.

Being born a Nimble, she was predisposed to cheerful functionality. Her father, John Nimble, was an airline pilot. He was stiff, hard working, and demanding of his only daughter, bequeathing her a blue-collar work ethic and a military-grade stubborn streak. Megan's mother, Amy Abel-Nimble, was a nurse. She tempered her husband's gruffness with warmth and empathy, and she matched his exhortations with an insistence that her daughter cultivate compassion. John insisted that Megan be honest; Amy countered that Megan ought to meet challenges with measured thoughtfulness. John badgered Megan to stand up straight; Amy taught her that she could show real confidence by looking someone in the eye.

John and Amy both possessed a self-righteous streak that grounded them in an even pragmatism. When they passed judgment on others, they did so with an air of fatalism.

"There but for the grace of God go I," Amy would say wistfully.

"Coulda been me, coulda been me," John would agree.

John had been raised as a Minnesotan Catholic, and Amy was California Jewish. The result was that Megan considered herself half-Jewish: committed to celebrating both Christmas and Hanukkah each winter, an equal-opportunity eater of lutefisk and gefilte fish. When Rebekah reacted so poorly to Megan's impromptu wedding announcement, Megan did the only thing she could think of that might make their situation equal: she picked up the phone to tell her own parents.

"Oh, Megan, that's wonderful!" Amy Nimble said. "Hold on, let me go grab your dad." Megan heard her mother put down the phone and call her father.

"Hello? Megs? Ok, your dad's on the phone. You want to tell him what you just told me?"

"Hi, Dad," Megan said.

"Hey, Megan," John Nimble said. "What's up?"

"So…Rebekah and I are getting married," Megan said.

"Oh. Well…congratulations," John said. He sounded as excited as John Nimble could sound, which was only slightly more excited than when he was preparing his flight attendants for landing.

"It is wonderful, sweetie," Amy said. Megan imagined the two of them huddled over the mouthpiece, standing in the kitchen of their little home in Pasadena. "Do you know when the wedding is yet?"

"Next spring. We don't have a date."

"Next spring, well, that's perfect," Amy said. "It gives you an entire year to plan."

"Isn't that the rainy season in Portland?" John asked.

"It can always rain in Portland, dad," Megan said.

"So, did you propose to Rebekah?" Amy asked.

"Oh—not really," Megan said. "We sort of just decided together to get married, and then we—I—told Rebekah's parents last night."

"Oh, well that's nice," Amy said.

"So, I have another question," John said. "Is it ok if I ask?"

"Yeah."

"So…are you actually getting married?"

"What do you mean?"

"It was really just—I was wondering if you two were planning on flying to Massachusetts, or something."

"No," Megan said.

"It doesn't matter," Amy said. Megan imagined her mother glaring at John on the other end of the phone. "Paperwork or not, it will be a lovely wedding."

After a few more minutes, Megan hung up, having secured agreement from her parents that they would be responsible for sharing the news with their extended families. She turned to Rebekah. "Told my parents," Megan said.

"So I heard." Rebekah was sitting on their couch sorting through email.

"You going to announce it on Facebook now?"

Rebekah made a face at her fiancée.

"I'll take that as a 'no,'" Megan said.

"My parents already know. Remember?"

"And your crazy-ass grandma knows."

"She does," Rebekah said.

Megan giggled. "Can you do your impression again? It's fucking hilarious."

Rebekah sat up and cleared her throat.

"Who makes a wedding announcement at a Seder?" Rebekah said in a nasally voice. She waved her hands. "And at the end, like that? With everyone half drunk and falling asleep? If you're going to make a wedding announcement, you do it at the beginning. Or you pick up the phone and call your grandmother first."

Megan laughed. Rebekah kept going.

"I always did suspect something," Rebekah said, shaking her head. "Those two, so close. I have a nose for these things."

Megan sat down next to Rebekah on the couch, and puffed her cheeks out. "But mom," Megan said in a quick, clipped voice, a pitch-perfect impression of Judith. "Are you going to go to the wedding?"

"Ach." Rebekah muttered, blowing air out through her nose. "Why not? Your eldest is a *frum*. Your youngest is a lesbian. What could I have to worry about? I'm just an old woman. Think about how much better my life would have been if I could have married a woman instead of your father."

Megan doubled over laughing.

Rebekah grinned widely and shook her head.

Megan sat up and wiped her eyes. "Uh huh."

"I'll take that as a compliment."

"Who else are we going to tell?" Megan asked. "It's going to be more than just your parents and my parents at the wedding, right?"

Rebekah tilted her head. "I suppose we need to make a list."

"I suppose we do."

Rebekah considered her options. It wasn't the marriage she was scared to talk about, she reflected. She had tried to convince Megan to elope. Costa Rica. Paris. Who cared where it was legal? It would be just the two of them, in an intimate ceremony, formally sealing their relationship. It was the act of talking about getting married to her partner, of drawing attention to herself, of coming out *again*, that sent her spinning.

No matter who she was coming out to, she always felt like a scared teenager again. She saw her mom's shocked face. Felt dad's confusion. Imagined David's disgust—the disgust she'd never seen, because nearly fifteen years after her first kiss she still hadn't come out to him.

Rebekah took a deep breath and pushed up her glasses. "I could call Carrie."

Megan smiled. She flopped on the couch next to Rebekah. "Oh…please do."

Rebekah checked the clock on the computer. "It's eleven o'clock out there. You think she's still going to be awake?"

"This is Carrie…Cline, right?" Megan asked.

"The legend," Rebekah said.

Carrie had been Rebekah's roommate at the University of Southern California in 2000, her first year as an undergraduate. Rebekah remembered the moment she met Carrie. Rebekah was standing in her dorm room, alone, surrounded by brown boxes tight with packing tape, containing supposedly essential dorm-room living supplies.

Rebekah heard voices outside her dorm room door, and a key turned in the lock. Startled, she jumped off the bed, fell forward into her desk, and banged her head on the desk lamp.

"Mom, it'll be *fine*." A tall African-American woman walked into the room. She had arresting light blue eyes and dark brown freckles. She wore a dark blue, ribbed cotton tank top over a white tank top, along with a pair of faintly creased jeans. She had finished the outfit with a pair of Rainbow flip-flops, the kind of beachwear sold at Nordstrom.

The woman stopped and stared at Rebekah, who immediately felt embarrassed by her own homely outfit: well-worn sweats and an old red t-shirt. When she was getting dressed earlier that morning, Rebekah hadn't considered that she would meet her roommate later in the day. Rebekah stared back, unsmiling.

After a few moments, her roommate broke out into a huge grin. "Hey, roomie!" she said in a gentle southern lilt. She approached Rebekah with her hand out. "I'm Carrie Cline."

Rebekah felt her face getting hot. "Hi, I'm Rebekah."

"Well, this is cozy, isn't it?" Carrie looked around the room, at the two desks, back to back, near the window overlooking the campus, the twin beds pushed up against opposite walls, and the two small closets, practical parallel indentations, near the door.

Rebekah peeked around her. A man and a woman stood in the doorway.

"May we come in?" the woman asked.

She approached Rebekah with an incandescent smile. She was as equally stunning as her daughter, if not more so: She was slightly taller and thinner, and she moved with a poise and confidence suggesting that she had—in some realm of her life—reached levels of bureaucratic ascendancy and social influence. She was darker skinned than her daughter and didn't have the same spread of freckles across her nose, or the blond streaks in her hair. But she had clearly passed on the trait of self-assurance.

"Hi, I'm Angela." She shook Rebekah's hand. Her hands were warm and soft, the handshake firm.

"Marcus," a deep voice said behind Angela. "Marcus Cline."

A freckled, oval face with sapphire eyes popped out over Angela's shoulder. Marcus was dressed in a sports jacket over a pink polo shirt, paired with light brown khaki shorts and white tennis shoes. Together, the whole family looked as if it had stepped out of a commercial for a summertime getaway on Cape Cod.

"So, you're our daughter's roommate, huh? Where are you from?" Angela asked.

"I'm from Portland, in Oregon," Rebekah said.

"Ooh, Oregon, very nice!" Angela said, pronouncing the state O-re-GONE. "I've always wanted to spend some time in that part of the country. I hear it's just beautiful."

"And you? Where are you from?"

"Northern Virginia," Carrie said. She was already lying down on her mattress. "Hey, these aren't bad. Did you bring an egg crate, Rebekah?"

"Yeah," Rebekah said. She lifted up her bed sheets to reveal her new yellow egg crate mattress—another tip she'd picked up from David.

She felt relieved that the Clines had decided that an egg crate was a worthy choice for a dorm room.

"My older brother had one in his dorm room, and said it was awesome," Rebekah said.

"Oh, I just read about it on a website," Carrie said. "Something like the top fifteen things you need for your dorm room."

"What Carrie really means is that her mother found it on a website and forwarded it to her," Angela said.

Carrie rolled her eyes at Rebekah.

"I'm going to start getting your stuff moved in here," Marcus said, heading for the door.

Carrie and Angela turned to follow them. And Rebekah, hoping to ingratiate herself with this new, impressive family, followed them out the door, as well.

"Oh, Rebekah…no, it's ok," Angela said.

"No, no, really. What can I take?" Rebekah asked. She picked up the handle of a large rolling suitcase and wheeled it into the room. "I'm going to put this by your desk, that ok?" Rebekah asked.

"Sure, anywhere," Carrie said. She had just dropped a large box labeled "clothes" by the closet.

Rebekah followed the Clines out the door a few more times to pull in the remaining boxes. Carrie Cline from Northern Virginia seemed to be a creature from a much more sophisticated universe, the perfect roommate to start afresh with in a new city and new school. Even though they had only been together for a few minutes, she knew she had much to learn from Carrie, who could help her transform herself into the person she wanted to become. She had already decided that she needed a pair of Rainbow flip-flops.

Rebekah smiled at the memory. *So much history*, Rebekah thought. She reclined on the couch and dialed Carrie's number.

Carrie picked up on the first ring. "Bekah!" Carrie yelled into the phone. "Bekah, Bekah, Bekah! What's up, my friend?"

"Oh…you know," Rebekah said. She exchanged a glance with Megan. "How are you?"

"I'm fine, I'm fine. A little tired—totally ready to take some time off work."

"Yeah, I hear you."

"But good, otherwise," Carrie said. "Everything is good. But how are *you*? What's going on?"

"Nothing much."

"Nothing much, huh?"

"Well, maybe something," Rebekah said.

"Something?"

Rebekah waffled. She considered lying, making something up, telling Carrie that her mom was sick, or that Stella had fired her, or that she was going to rehab. Rebekah slid her eyes sideways at Megan, who was smiling at her with a big, open smile.

"Spill it!"

"Um, well…"

"Oh, God, Bekah, you always do this."

"Megan and I are engaged."

"Oh, my God, Bekah!"

Rebekah pulled her cell phone away from her ear.

"You did it, you did it, you did it! Oh, my God! I can't believe it! Oh, my God Bekah, I'm so happy!"

Rebekah tilted her cell phone so that the microphone was close to her chin but the speaker was still a fair distance from her ear.

"Thanks, Carrie."

"A wedding? Is there going to be a wedding?"

"Yes, there will, at some point," Rebekah said. She cleared her throat.

"Aw, I love weddings! I'm invited, right?"

"You are."

"How's your family? Did your parents not even know before this?"

"No, I told my parents."

"How'd they take it?"

"Pretty well, considering."

"Really?"

"Yeah. They were cool."

"Good," Carrie said. "And David? Have you told your brother?"

"Ohh…" Rebekah shifted uncomfortably. "I haven't told him yet."

"Ah." Carrie said. She was silent for a few seconds.

"Well, whatever," Carrie said. "So what are you guys going to wear?"

Rebekah looked at Megan. She paused for a long moment. "Shit, Carrie. We haven't even talked about it."

"You haven't talked about it," Carrie repeated.

"No."

"Who *are* you? Is it possible I taught you nothing in college?" Rebekah laughed. "Do we really need to talk about what you taught me?"

"Oh, shut up. Do you even know, like…are you guys going to wear dresses?"

Rebekah ran her fingers through her hair. "Honestly, I have no idea. I guess I've just assumed we would. I have no idea what Megan has been assuming."

"Oh, my God, Bekah. Matching wedding dresses would be so beautiful."

"Or lesbian-campy."

Carrie laughed.

"No, really. Everyone would think we were overdressed bridesmaids."

"Not everyone. I'd love it."

"Of course."

"Ok, I'm going to start researching this tonight," Carrie said. "I'm going to Google 'lesbian wedding dresses' and see what I get. I'll send you pictures and links. I bet I can even find something on sale!"

"When I hear 'lesbian wedding dress,' I think khaki."

Carrie laughed again. "Well, khaki wouldn't be so bad. You guys could do, like, a light tan cloth. That would be beautiful!"

"Uh-huh."

"Don't worry about this part, Bekah. I got it covered."

"How are your parents?" Rebekah changed the subject.

"Oh, they're fine. Same old, same old."

Carrie shared a winding update about Mr. and Mrs. Cline: their well-connectedness at D.C. dinner parties, their joint knack for political shape-shifting, and their continued pressure on Carrie to follow in their footsteps.

Carrie had, in fact, charted a path that would make many parents—those not named Angela and Marcus Cline—fairly proud of their offspring. After graduating from USC summa cum laude, as the vice president of the Betas, and with an undergraduate degree in business, she'd returned to Virginia to accept an unpaid internship with the campaign of a rising democratic politician named Joe McCann. Rebekah knew that Carrie's parents could have set her up with a paid job, almost any job, working for McCann. But Carrie insisted on competing for the internship and earning it on her own.

McCann won his competitive district and earned a seat on the state senate. Carrie, as one of the most active members of his fundraising campaign, had been given a staff position as a policy advisor. McCann was actively fundraising for a possible governor's run in 2012, and Carrie had become an integral cog in his campaign machinery. It was not unthinkable that, if McCann won the governor's seat, it could serve as a springboard to the U.S. Senate, or perhaps, nearly unimaginably, the presidency.

Mr. and Mrs. Cline had been badgering Carrie to return to school for an advanced degree. A degree in business administration would only get her so far, they gently admonished; with a masters or a Ph.D. she could become a policy advisor to national campaigns. Despite her success, her parents told her, Carrie would get out-competed.

McCann was a politician at heart; when the right time came, he would hire and promote the people who gave him the best chance to win. It was simply a matter of time, they said, before McCann stiffed Carrie.

"So, no time for dating, huh?" Rebekah asked during a break in Carrie's story.

"No." Carrie spoke definitively. "There's not. And there's no one I've met in the past two years who even comes close to someone I'd want to date, anyway. Don't worry. I'm fairly confident that I'll be attending your wedding alone."

"Well, you have plenty of time to decide. And you're of course welcome to bring someone."

"Honestly, I don't miss it. I'm working long hours and really enjoying it. I really don't miss the drama."

You just need to decide to date someone who's not an asshole, Rebekah wanted to say. But she swallowed the thought. "Well, like I said. You're welcome to bring someone to the wedding, even if it's just a friend."

"Oh, well, maybe I'll bring a girlfriend, then!"

"That would be fitting."

The two spoke for a few minutes longer, then begged off. It was close to midnight on the east coast, and Carrie, who woke up at five every day to check her email, said that she needed to go to sleep to be ready for the upcoming week.

May, 2011

"Megan," Rebekah said. They were sitting at their table in the living room in the Judge's basement, finishing dinner. The sounds of Beethoven's Fifth drifted in from upstairs.

"Yeah, babe."

"Have you thought about what you're going to wear to the wedding?"

Megan shrugged. "I just thought we'd figure something out this summer. Buy dresses or something."

"You want to wear a wedding dress?"

"Maybe," Megan said.

"Megs, have you ever worn a dress? In your life?"

"There's a first time for everything."

Rebekah raised her eyebrows. "You want to wear a dress for the first time at your wedding?"

"Now that I think about it, it wouldn't be the first time. I think I wore a few dresses when I was a kid."

"I'd like to see pictures."

Megan stood up and started clearing the table. "What else would I wear?"

"Do you want to try a suit on?"

"No. That would feel even weirder, I think."

"Why?"

"Wearing a dress would feel a little bit like I was dressed in drag," Megan said. "But wearing a suit would feel like…I don't know. Drag inversion."

"How about a pants suit? Ellen DeGeneres-style?"

Megan laughed. She walked into the kitchen with a stack of plates. "Yeah, I guess that's a possibility. But I bet she has her clothes custom-made. You can't just pick that stuff up off the rack."

"We could get it tailored."

"I know I'd end up just looking like I was going to a business meeting."

"Right."

"What about you?" Megan asked.

"Oh…" Rebekah flicked a crumb from the table onto the floor. "I don't really know, either. Carrie asked about it."

"Did she? What did Carrie want to know?"

"She was just curious about what we were planning on wearing. I didn't really know what to tell her."

Ever since her conversation with Carrie, Rebekah had spent hours thinking about what to wear. *Lesbian wedding chic*, she thought. *A fashion niche as unexplored as the subterranean surfaces of Mars.* Rebekah and Megan had both survived social functions with formal wear that could be classified as business-casual: well-fitted slacks and blouses, paired with thick-heeled clogs and sensible, water-resistant jackets. These worked for business meetings, dinner parties, friends' weddings, and date nights. But business-casual didn't feel right for their wedding. It was too stiff. Too habitual.

"Want to go to William's Bridal?" Megan asked.

"The dress place?"

"Yeah."

"Can we afford stuff there?"

"Well…" Megan paused. "We probably can't afford their most expensive dresses. I don't know. Do they have anything for a couple hundred dollars? We really didn't budget much for clothes."

"Ummm…" Rebekah navigated to the store's webpage on her laptop. She scrolled down the homepage. "You really want to go here?"

William's Bridal was the number-one wedding dress seller in America. It was part of the corporate behemoth that set trends, fashions, and styles; it established the rights and wrongs of wedding days for brides in America. William's promoted the idea that a wedding is a very specific kind of celebration: beautiful and stiff, the bride regal in layers of taffeta, the entire affair held together by twin girdles of money and expectations. Its homepage was a celebration of sales, sparkles and lace, flowers and long hair, summers and glittery accessories.

To Rebekah, William's was tar pit, a sinkhole, a palace of unfair expectations and heterosexual fantasy. She didn't think she belonged there. What could an awkward, semi-butch lesbian find in a quarry of tulle?

Megan shrugged. "Why not? It's a place to start."

"Or to end," Rebekah said under her breath.

Megan grinned. She ran in from the kitchen and gently pushed Rebekah down onto the couch. Rebekah screamed.

"Say you'll go with me!" Megan yelled. She began tickling Rebekah and planting light kisses on her face and neck.

Rebekah laughed and tried to push Megan off her. Megan slid her hands up Rebekah's shirt, and started to unhook her bra. Rebekah swatted her hands away.

"Say you'll go!" Megan commanded.

"Fine, I'll go, I'll go!" Rebekah said.

Megan lifted one of her hands triumphantly and lightly kissed Rebekah's lips. "Nothing like a promise under duress."

"Or a promise under dress," Rebekah punned.

Megan rolled her eyes. She stood up. "You're going with me. You're going to make the appointment tomorrow."

The next evening, Rebekah phoned William's Bridal.

"Whatever I wear, I want it to have pockets," Megan said, as Rebekah phoned the store.

"I'm not sure there are that many dresses with pockets."

"I've totally seen them," Megan said. "I want pockets."

"Hello, William's Bridal, this is Crystal. How may I make your dreams come true today?"

Rebekah blanched. "Um…well, I—I was really just calling to set up an appointment. I think it said on your website we needed to do that?"

"Of course! That's so exciting! Congratulations on your engagement!"

"Thanks."

"What day would you like to come in?"

"I was thinking this Sunday."

"Sunday, Sunday—oh perfect. We've got one slot available at eleven a.m. on Sunday."

"Oh, ok, well—this appointment needs to be for two women."

"Oh, well, don't worry about that. Anyone you want can join you. We have a whole seating area for friends and family."

"No, no, I mean, we need two appointments. At the same time."

There was a long pause on the other end of the phone. "Two appointments?" Crystal asked.

"Yes."

"At the same time?"

"Yes."

There was another long pause. Then Crystal laughed.

"Oh…I get it! You and a girlfriend are trying dresses on at the same time, right? Because you're both getting married this summer?"

Rebekah raised her eyebrows. She glanced over at Megan.

"Uh…yeah. My girlfriend and I are trying dresses on at the same time."

"Oh, perfect. That's so much fun. Ok, well I have two slots on Sunday at four. Will that work for you?"

"Yeah."

"Great!" Crystal said. "I'll be working that Sunday, so I can help you two. Again, congratulations on your engagement."

"Thanks so much." Rebekah hung up.

Rebekah and Megan arrived a few minutes before four o'clock on Sunday. William's Bridal was divided into three distinct spaces. On the right side of the store were rows upon rows of what appeared to be dress-filled clear plastic bags. These racks, which looked like rows of cocooned silkworms, were divided by size (0 to 16), silhouette (cocktail, mermaid, A-line), and designer (Calvin Klein). The sale rack was where one might find a deal: last year's dresses, dresses too big or small for the average woman, dresses in pink or jade.

The center of the store housed the dressing room area. There were six of them, lined up back to back, with large, body-length mirrors flanking each room and elevated stages for the future bride to stand on. Each stage was surrounded by couches and easy chairs.

The left side of the store was oriented toward the bridal party: bridesmaids, flower girls, mothers, and grandmothers of the bride. If a bride wanted her entire party to wear tea-length, jade, strapless dresses, William's Bridal could make it so.

Three parts, interconnected, made up William's: the diva, her audience, and the supporting cast. It was the holy trinity of bridal mythmaking.

Crystal greeted Megan and Rebekah at the front door.

"Welcome to William's Bridal!" Crystal said. "Which one of you is getting married?"

Megan and Rebekah looked at each other, then back at Crystal. They pointed to each other.

"Oh, that's great," Crystal said, pressing her palms together in front of her. "It's always so much more fun to try on dresses with your girlfriends." She pressed up on her toes and clicked her heels together. "Well, follow me, I need each of you to fill out some paperwork—it won't take long, I promise—and then we'll get you into some dresses, mmkay?" She nodded, flashed a smile, and turned to walk towards her desk.

Megan began walking towards the dresses.

"Where are you going?" Rebekah whispered loudly.

"To look at the dresses."

"She said we needed to fill some stuff out."

Megan took another step towards the dresses. "Bekah, she just wants to get her claws into you so that they can spam you for the rest of your life."

"Well…"

"I know you'll do a great job." Megan walked away.

Rebekah followed Crystal to her desk.

Crystal was waiting, arm outstretched, holding a piece of paper. She had straight blond hair, adroitly curled to hang just past her shoulders, a slim face, and thin lips. She couldn't be more than one year out of high school, Rebekah thought.

"Ok. Where's…?"

"Megan. She'll be right back."

"Ok, no problem. This will just take you one minute."

Rebekah studied the form. There were some standard information blocks near the top—name, age, address, telephone number, and email—which, Crystal explained, was not for telemarketers, but rather in case a serious issue arose with their William's Bridal experience. It was standard practice, she assured Rebekah, at nearly every bridal store.

Rebekah filled out her form. She left the email address blank. If a serious issue arose with her William's Bridal experience, surely they could resolve it by telephone.

She glanced down at the second half of the form. All of the questions were about her groom. What was his name? How tall was he? Where was he planning on buying his tux? And most importantly: what was his phone number?

Rebekah swallowed and pushed down the knot in her stomach.

"Do I need to fill out this part about the groom?" Rebekah asked.

"Yes, please do," Crystal replied. "It just helps everything go much more smoothly."

Rebekah sighed. She picked up her pen, and wrote "Megan Nimble" in the space provided for the groom's name.

Rebekah looked up at Crystal. She was standing across the table, eyes wide, eyebrows up, her mouth forming a small "O" in a slowly growing sense of understanding.

"Oh!" Crystal said. She giggled. "I thought—I thought you were girlfriends…?"

"We are," Rebekah said.

"Right, right, girlfriends! Of course. I'm so sorry. So, um…" Crystal reached out across the table and put her hand over the form. "Why don't you never mind about this. It's fine." She pulled the form towards her and placed it, unfinished, in the top drawer of her desk. She looked up and smiled at Rebekah. "I'm really sorry," Crystal giggled. "I didn't, like, get it when you were making your appointment."

"That's ok," Rebekah said. "'Girlfriends' just has so many meanings."

"Oh, I know." Crystal leaned in to whisper to her. "I talk about my friends as 'girlfriends' all the time, and sometimes I wonder if people think I'm a lesbian."

Rebekah leaned in and nodded. "Me too."

Crystal smiled, turned away, and walked towards the showroom floor.

"So, let me tell you two how this works." Crystal pressed her palms together. "Dresses are organized by size and style. If you don't find the dress you're looking for, we can order it. We have our own seamstresses here, and they can just make magic happen with dresses that don't quite fit right. You can try on as many as you want—that's part of the fun, right?"

Crystal walked over to the nearest dress and unzipped its plastic sheath. "One more thing. All of our dresses are flammable, so please, no lighters or flames, ok?"

Crystal's head swung around as she noticed five women walk into the store. They were pointing toward the dresses. "I'll be right back, you two. Why don't you pick out a couple of dresses you'd like to get started with?" Crystal turned and jogged towards the front of the store on her tiptoes.

"Hey, you got a lighter?" Megan asked, as she held up a dress.

Rebekah surveyed the row of dresses. "Are you seeing anything you like?"

"No. Not even close."

"Not even…this?" Rebekah held up a sample dress, one of the few not zipped up in a bag. It had copious amounts of lace and ruffles, as well as what looked like a fifteen-foot train pinned to the back.

"Ummmm…." Megan made a face. "I could wear that. But I would look like a drag queen. And not just a drag queen, an ugly drag queen."

Rebekah dropped the dress and held up her hands. "That's it," she whispered. She put her hands on Megan's shoulders. "We should have a drag wedding."

Megan shrugged her off and walked past her. "I'd much prefer a drag bachelorette party. Karaoke at our wedding would just be so gauche."

"Are we even having a bachelorette party?"

"Might be awkward for both of us to be at the same strip club." Megan put her hands on her hips. "So, are we done here? I'm really not seeing anything worth trying on. And I really don't want to put on a dress and go stand up on that stage like a hog at the county fair."

"You're not a hog."

"Thanks. Let's go."

Megan walked up behind Rebekah and gently pushed her towards the door.

When Rebekah broke the news to Carrie Cline that she and her fiancée hadn't even tried on dresses, Carrie expressed her disappointment with a series of shrieks.

"What?" Carrie asked. "You went all the way to William's Bridal and didn't even put anything on? Aw, honey, I can't—that's pathetic. How did I raise you? Were you really my roommate for four years?" Carrie clucked. "You really need me to move out there, don't you?"

"I suppose I do."

"How do you even get dressed in the morning without me?"

"It's a struggle."

"What happened?"

Rebekah shared the whole story— walking into the store, the paperwork, Megan talking about feeling like she was wearing drag. "That's when I think it really sunk in," Rebekah said at the end. "Nothing in there looked like it was for us."

"There are lots of dresses out there, Beks. And not just dresses, but wedding outfits."

"Yeah, but Carrie," Rebekah said. "It's just not me. I walked in there, and felt like an alien. Wedding-wear just wasn't created for girls like me."

"Sure it was! You just haven't find the right thing."

"There is no right thing," Rebekah said. "You don't understand. It doesn't exist."

Carrie sighed into the phone. "Ok, this is serious. You all need an intervention. I can't get out there right now, but I'm going to help you figure this out."

During the next week, Carrie sent Rebekah links—sometimes dozens a day—to dresses she had found online. She sent her purple dresses and see-through dresses, "lightly worn" wedding dresses, and dresses made entirely from felt or polyester. Rebekah looked at all of them, and wrote back to Carrie that none of the dresses were quite the right thing.

One week after the debacle at William's Bridal, Carrie sent a link to a store called Brenda's Dresses. Located just east of Portland, in Gresham, the store advertised itself as an "independent, counter-culture dress shop for brides seeking non-traditional wedding wear."

"This looks perfect for you guys!" Carrie wrote. "Give it a try. For me. Love you xoxoxoxo!"

Buoyed by Carrie's confidence, Megan and Rebekah drove to Brenda's Dress shop on a Saturday afternoon. It was located on a quiet side street, between a liquor store and a tailor, in what looked like a former garage or auto repair shop. An abandoned lot sat across the way. The storefront itself was nondescript; they saw the small, beat-up "Brenda's" sign only after driving past three times.

The interior of Brenda's dresses was totally unlike William's Bridal. The store was long and narrow, like a castle hallway guarded by mannequins. The floors and walls were gray cement. There was a high ceiling, well ventilated, as if to suggest that the store's previous life had required fresh air to be pumped in at regular intervals. The large water or heating pipes on the ceiling had been painted a bright white.

The back third of the room was covered in mirrors: six-foot tall mirrors, all adjacent to one another, creating the appearance of one continuous, repetitive reflection for shoppers. When Rebekah stood in the middle of the room, she could see herself reflected back again and again, smaller and smaller images of herself in the same sweatshirt and jeans that she always wore on Saturdays. She imagined herself looking like one of these mannequins, glimpsing a new image of herself hundreds of times in Brenda's mirrors.

The mannequins were draped in dresses in a wild variety of colors: blue, black, jade, pink, and red. Some dresses were long and beaded. Others were short and strapless. The mannequins were spaced about three feet apart from each other, all the way down the back of the store. Brenda's was a cement palace, attended by frozen, well-dressed mademoiselles.

Rebekah looked around the store. It felt desolate, separate, and disconnected in a different way than William's Bridal. If William's was a golden retriever—overeager, slobbery, common—then Brenda's was a slinky black cat. Hiding. Haughty.

There were so many dresses—but was there really one here for her? As Rebekah and Megan stood at the front of the store, they heard a loud clicking from the right. A woman stepped out of a hidden door in the cement wall and walked towards them.

"Hi," she said. She stuck out a hand. "I'm Jamie. Welcome to Brenda's."

Jamie wore curiously large glasses, stretching from midway up her forehead, down to her lip, past the hairline on each side of her head, and nearly meeting over the bridge of her nose. The frames were a thick black, like two dark handcuffs shackling her eyes into place. She had long black hair, which was pulled in front of her shoulders on each side, wide brown eyes, a small nose, and thick lips.

Jamie possessed the well-kept look of the delicately ironic, the intentionally unmoneyed creative class, poor in equity but rich in self-awareness. Her black knee-high boots sported mesh webbing on the sides, worn leather on the fronts, and pointed toe boxes that were surely painful. She was wearing a short, burgundy corduroy skirt over gray leggings and a three-quarter-length mesh sweater and black tank top.

"I'm Megan," Megan said, shaking her hand.

Jamie nodded at her.

"Rebekah," Rebekah said.

"Great." Jamie crossed her arms over her chest. "How can I help you?"

"We're looking for a couple of wedding dresses," Megan said.

"Uh-huh. Are both of you getting married?"

Megan and Rebekah nodded.

"To each other, right?"

They looked at each other.

"Yep," Megan said.

"Awesome. We get a lot of lesbians in here. You guys came to the right place." Jamie tapped her toe on the floor, and examined Megan. "Suit for you?"

Megan laughed. "Oh, no, I think I want to wear a dress. I'm just not sure what kind yet. We went to William's Bridal and didn't…"

Jamie cut her off mid-sentence. "Never mind. Come with me." She lightly touched Megan's arm and steered her toward a mannequin near the center of one of the walls.

The mannequin stood out from her counterparts for the bold, dramatic lines and colors of her outfit. At first glance, it looked like a tuxedo fitted for a woman. The suit top was cut in at the waist and the lapels were wide, designed to show off a woman's bust. A white, ruffled lace top peeked out underneath. The pants hung just short of the ankles, flaring out around the mannequin's stiletto heels.

"I think you would look so great in this," Jamie said. "It's one of our most masculine pieces."

Megan smirked. "Oh…I don't know. Really?"

Jamie turned towards her and folded her arms across her chest. "It won't fit you perfectly—we can have it tailored for that—but I think you should try one on. Just to see."

"How much is it?"

Jamie pulled up the price tag. "$499. Not including tailoring. That's a bargain, you guys. This piece is one-of-a-kind. Have you looked at the prices of other wedding dresses?"

Megan looked at Rebekah. Rebekah shrugged. "It would make Carrie happy."

"Oh, fine," Megan said. "I guess if it would make *Carrie* happy." Jamie nodded curtly. "Great. Follow me."

She led Megan and Rebekah to the back of the store, past the wall of mirrors, and into a small, cramped dressing room. Once Megan was situated, Jamie disappeared for a few minutes, then came back with a suit that—like the dresses at William's Bridal—was sheathed in white plastic.

"Come out when you need a hand," Jamie called through the door. "We can help you with buttons or whatever." She turned to Rebekah. "And what about you?"

Rebekah shrugged. She felt intimidated by the store. For all of its triteness and classy affectation, William's Bridal had seemed more welcoming to Rebekah. She understood corporate artifice much better than she understood hipster cool.

"Well…I guess I'll just wait for Megan to come out. See how she looks, and go from there."

"Ah, I see," Jamie said. "Because you want to match her?"

"Maybe."

"Is one of you going butch and the other going femme?" Jamie smiled. "That's my favorite. I *love* that. It's such a clever play on heteronormativity, you know? What a statement about gender roles. It's like, by *choosing* that, you're really un-choosing. Get it?" Rebekah nodded.

"I really do love gay weddings," Jamie continued. "There's just so much more freedom in what you can do. It makes my job a lot more fun. Every once in a while we'll get a couple of guys in here who don't want to look drag-queeny, but sort of feel like they don't want to wear a suit. Or at least a super-masculine suit, you know? So they're looking for something with ruffles or pastels, or suits that can show off their waists."

"Do you carry those here?"

"No, we do dresses. But it's fun when they come in anyway, because they tend to love our stuff."

"I bet."

"So anyway, the challenge with lesbians is getting two women who get to wear what they want, but still look right together. A suit tends to look good with anything. But dresses, you've really got to work to make two fit together. It can't be matchy-match; that would be horrid. But they've got to complement one another."

The dressing room knob turned, and Megan poked her head out. "You ready?" Jamie asked.

Megan stepped out. Jamie dropped her jaw, and clapped her hands together in studied excitement.

"Perfect," Jamie said. "Simply perfect. What a statement."

Megan spun around. The pants were too short and the suit jacket too tight, but Megan *did* look handsome. The pants suit hung perfectly on her tall body and broad shoulders, while still very clearly showcasing her feminine body. She looked slender and curvy, strong and soft. Rebekah raised her eyebrows.

"It's cute," Megan admitted. "Really cute." She pulled at the lapels, examined her butt in the mirror, and then turned to Jamie. "But I'm not sure."

"What? Why not?"

"I like it. It's just not what I imagined I would wear on my wedding day."

"Fair enough. So what did you imagine you would wear on your wedding day?"

Megan looked from Rebekah to Jamie. She shrugged. "Well...I don't know if I imagined anything," she said.

"Fine, fine," Jamie said, waving her hand. "You can take it off. We'll try something else. This would be a *statement* outfit. But we've got plenty of other things that I think would look nice on you."

"I just don't know if we're into statement outfits," Rebekah said.

"Well..." Jamie stuck her chin out. "Sorry Charlies, but you're going to be making a statement, no matter what you wear. It's 2011, and lots of gay people are getting married, but we're not at the level where it's passé, know what I'm saying? Why not *own* it?"

Jamie shook her head. "Look, you guys should be comfortable and feel good. That's what's most important. But I feel like part of my job at Brenda's is to help you feel comfortable in wedding wear that shows off your best selves, what you're about. That's what fashion is. It's about self-expression. And there's no better time to do that than at your own wedding. But we'll keep working on it. We've got all afternoon, right?"

Jamie shooed Megan back into the dressing room and disappeared back out onto the mannequin floor, ostensibly to hunt down some more dresses. Rebekah watched her walk away, her black boots clicking dully on the cement floor. After she was gone, Megan poked her head out of the dressing room.

"Hey," she whispered to Rebekah.

"What?"

"So what did you really think?"

"I thought you looked really good. You looked totally hot."

"Really?" Megan grinned. "I like it when you tell me I'm hot."

"You're totally hot. And that suit thing was totally hot on you."

"Like wedding-hot?"

"Why not?"

Megan shrugged. "I dunno. I think I just need to think about it. I can always come back."

"Wait, I need to at least take one picture for Carrie."

Megan walked out of the dressing room, placed her hands on her waist, and stuck one of her hips out. Rebekah snapped a picture on her phone.

"Great," Megan said. "I'm going to change, and then we can leave. Unless you want to try something on?"

Rebekah shook her head. "Nah."

Megan closed the door of the dressing room. After a few minutes she stepped out, wearing her jeans and the green t-shirt she had walked in with. There was something deliciously comforting to Rebekah in seeing Megan dressed like that. It wasn't as elegantly sexy as the suit, but it was a homey sexy, like seeing Megan in pajamas, eating breakfast on a Saturday morning.

Rebekah stuck one of her arms through Megan's. "Maybe you should just wear jeans to our wedding."

"Don't tempt me."

They walked into the center of the store. Jamie was standing next to a tall blond woman, pointing to a mannequin in a bright, strapless purple dress. The woman was nodding, and Jamie was speaking animatedly, waving her hands.

"I guess she forgot about us already," Megan said. "Whatever. Let's get out of here. We'll tell Carrie that unless she flies out here, we're likely to just show up to the wedding naked."

Rebekah's eyes flickered over her computer screen. Stella had released the June issue of *Daft* the previous week, and readers had flooded the message boards with comments about the lead story, "Art Bus." The Art Bus was a unique-to-Portland phenomenon, one of those city-defining enterprises that drew people from around the country to settle, live, and try to build their own niche in a town saturated with niches.

The legend, as Rebekah reported in *Daft*, started with a health insurance customer representative. Sam Jackson was his name. He was in his late forties, a former software engineer. Laid off in late 2008, he had searched fruitlessly for a job for two years, before finally accepting a position answering questions about Medicare for a health insurance company.

Sam Jackson hated donuts holes. Donut holes, the kind that costs taxpayers thousands of dollars. Donut holes, of the sort that came in the mail, in the form of bills printed on crisp white paper, folded in thirds to fit in standard-sized envelopes. Donut holes that showed up when a customers called in with innocent questions about drug coverage—and hung up understanding that their government-funded medical coverage would take a chunk out of their savings.

"You pay your deductible," Sam Jackson found himself saying over and over again. "Then your coverage kicks in until you reach twenty-eight hundred dollars. And then—I'm so sorry to have to tell you this, ma'am—but you're responsible for all payments up to forty-five hundred and fifty. It's a donut hole in coverage. Once you hit that, you're good. You'll only have to pay a minimal amount towards drug coverage, after that."

After three days of work, Sam Jackson decided he was done with donut holes. He quit, walked off the job, and impulsively purchased a yellow school bus.

Sam Jackson drove around town for a week, eating at food carts, walking through the Portland parks. Single and childless, Sam discovered that no one cared about what he did. He'd been jobless for two years, and no one except the government seemed to give a fuck.

He built his first art installation at the top of Mount Tabor in southeast Portland, two weeks after walking off the health insurance job. The installation was created from cans stolen from people's recycle bins, bottles, and trash that he considered clean enough to reuse. It was shaped like a giant donut, complete with a perfectly circular hole, topped with sprinkles made from shards of glass.

Then donuts started popping up all over town. Small donuts appeared at busy intersections, like the corner of Thirty-Ninth and Southeast Powell. Donuts showed up in the middle of the quiet residential neighborhoods, blocking the middle of streets. Donuts appeared in parks, outside restaurants, on sidewalks, in food cart pods.

Sam Jackson's donuts had simultaneously drawn a cult following and the ire of annoyed residents and city officials. Most *Daft* readers seemed to sympathize with the angry, laid-off salesman. A few thought the man ought to find a real job.

"Please," Benny657 wrote to the magazine. "You really think city officials need to put up with this guy? I go to my job every day so that I can put food on the table and pay my taxes to the city of Portland. There are more important things for the city to spend money on other than cleaning up this shit. If this guy really wanted to make a statement, he'd start leaving real donuts—the kind you can eat—on the working man's doorstep."

Rebekah shook her head and switched back to her email. She scrolled through her inbox. There were dozens of unread messages from *Daft* readers. She would eventually reply to all of them, copying-and-pasting one of a few pre-written responses she kept on her desktop.

"Thank you for taking the time to write in," her emails began. "We sincerely appreciate your continued support of Stella and the arts education in Portland."

Rebekah's phone rang. She picked up the receiver. "Hello?"

"Hey, Bekah, this is Tony."

"Oh. Hi, Tony."

"You busy?"

Rebekah closed her email. "Nah, not really," Rebekah lied. "You need something?"

"Yeah, can you come to my office?"

"Be right there."

Rebekah hung up the phone and walked towards Tony's office. She looked over at Roberto, who was staring intently at his computer screen, talking to himself. Roberto was so striking, with his thatch of silver hair and graceful comportment that he managed to look composed even in personal moments. He was wearing a black vest over a white dress shirt today, showing off a pair of gold cufflinks that Rebekah assumed were more expensive that the shirt itself. Rebekah had always admired his beautifully long fingers, now resting on his chin. When Roberto folded his hands together in front of his waist, the length of his fingers added a sort of credibility to his pose, as if a man with such long fingers would never lie.

Roberto's eyes flicked up as Rebekah walked by. "Hey, girl," Roberto said. He nodded his head in deference.

"Hey."

"Lunch today?"

"Sure," Rebekah said. "After I meet with the boss?"

"You got it." Roberto turned back to his computer.

Rebekah glanced over at Jane Salish, sitting on the opposite side of the office. She was on the phone, animated, speaking with her hands and eyebrows and neck and shoulders. Jane didn't notice Rebekah. When Jane was speaking with a client, she gave her utmost attention to their conversation, as if that person were physically present. It was what made Jane so good, so formidable, so valuable and influential at Stella.

Rebekah pushed open the door to Tony's office. A black polished table sat in the middle of the room, flanked by short, black leather chairs. A few black bookshelves lined the interior walls. They held tomes on management and non-profit leadership, as well as wider, coffee-table-style art books. But most shelves showcased various awards and sculptures, along with expensive knick-knacks made solely by local artists. Tony had a small wooden desk, just big enough for a laptop, pushed into a corner of the room, next to a large window that overlooked the southeastern end of downtown Portland. Tony liked to say that you needed to show money to raise money.

Tony was standing by the window when Rebekah walked in. Micah McDonald, Stella's assistant director, was leaning back in her chair at the table, fingertips resting on the tabletop.

"How are you?" Tony asked.

"I'm fine. You?"

"I'm good, I'm good," Tony said. "Beautiful day, huh?"

"Oh…yeah, it's ok," Rebekah said. It was cloudy and overcast. "It looks like it might rain."

"Well…I'm an optimist," Tony said. "It's June, and the weather looks pretty good right now, so that's what I'm going with. Why don't you have a seat?"

Rebekah pulled out one of the chairs next to Micah.

"Hey, Bekah," Micah said. She stretched her neck and adjusted the stack of paper in front of her.

"Hi, Micah."

While Tony exuded charm and exuberance, Micah possessed an equal amount of icy linearity. Tony dazzled with magnetism; Micah did her job with a bluntness that seemed mundane in comparison. She possessed not a whit of glamour, but knew the organization's mission, finances, and directives better than anyone else at Stella. When Tony wanted reports, numbers, or the history of their contracts and agreements, he asked Micah. When Tony needed a heavy—to lean on educators, donors, or partners—he relied on his second-in-command. If Tony brought witchcraft to his job, Micah brought analytics.

Micah had straight, shoulder-length brown hair, not quite long enough to tie with a band, but long enough to constantly brush away from her face with the back of her hand. She favored V-neck sweaters over dress shirts that were tucked into fitted trousers, tailored to hang just at the ankle. Micah owned an impressive array of clogs, enough pairs to go with most of her outfits.

Micah was also one of only three employees at Stella with children. She had two, both in elementary school. Every year she placed new school pictures on her desk. Both kids had straight brown hair and blue eyes, like their mother, and both seemed to have inherited the family frostiness. Neither smiled in their school photos.

"So, what's new?" Tony asked.

Rebekah stared back at him. It had been almost two months, and she still hadn't told anyone at work about the engagement.

"Oh…you know. Same old, same old."

"Yeah?" Tony said. "How's Megan?"

"Oh, she's fine. Great, actually. She's really great."

"Great," Tony said. He glanced at Micah, and then looked back at Rebekah. "Rebekah, how long have you been working here?"

Rebekah swallowed. She resisted the urge to count on her fingers. "About five and a half years."

"Right, five and a half years. Almost six. You've really been with us since I started Stella."

Rebekah nodded.

"How do you like your job?"

"I like it."

"Are you still happy?"

Rebekah considered the question. She did like her job, and she *was* still happy. But what did it mean when your boss asked you questions about your job satisfaction?

"I'm happy," she said. "Really. Before I came in here, I was reading comments about the Art Bus article. Did either of you read it?"

"I did," Micah said.

"Was that the one about Sam Jackson?" Tony asked.

"Yeah. We got a whole bunch of comments, mostly positive that we were covering the story. When that happens, I just feel like, wow. You know? People are reading our stuff. We're touching a nerve. It's cool."

Tony nodded. "You know, Rebekah, last night I went to an opening. An exhibit opening. It was for an artist named Dom Turken. Ever heard of him?"

"He sounds familiar."

"He's nineteen years old. Grew up just outside of Portland, in Gresham. Got involved with Stella when he was fifteen. He was one of our first kids. He was like…the hope, you know? We looked at Dom, and we were so excited. He was it, exactly what we were looking for. A talented, aimless kid. I built Stella for kids like him.

"He was fifteen, but he was mature, as if he was going on forty. Dom has the oldest eyes of anyone I've ever met. You look into them, and I swear, it's like you can see all the way back to the time of the dinosaurs. Some days, he'd say and do stuff that made me wonder: how old was this kid, really? There was one day when we were taking a walk together outside of his school. We walked past a homeless fellow asleep in a sleeping bag under a bus stop. I kept walking, but Dom stopped. He stared at the guy for a while, then dug into his pocket and slipped a five-dollar bill under his head. It's not like five dollars was that much, but it was all Dom had. He was going to buy lunch with that money.

"And then there would be days when he'd just fall apart. He'd become a five-year-old throwing a temper tantrum. He'd explode, need to be escorted out of the art room. He was really a challenge for us in that way. We'd talk to him like an adult, and then the next minute we'd be scraping this fifteen- year-old kid off the floor."

Rebekah nodded. She had grown up with kids like that, kids who were so talented that it oozed out of them, angry, like lava.

"Dom was also…well, let me back up. His mom died when he was little. Not sure what happened to his dad. He had an aunt, who I think formally adopted him at some point. But she had, like, four other kids, so Dom sort of got the butt end of the baguette, you know what I mean? She struggled. I'm sure she did her best. Dom struggled. It was just the situation.

"He never got into trouble, but by the time we got to him, it didn't look like there was much chance that he'd graduate from high school. It just wasn't his thing.

"Dom came to Stella the first time with his guidance counselor. She walked him into the classroom where we were staging, and I remember shaking his hand. He barely shook my hand, I remember that, but when I started talking about what we did, he got interested. I remember his eyes. Those old eyes. His hands were in his pockets, and he didn't look at me much, but when he did, I knew we had him.

"So Dom started coming to our after-school program. It was immediately clear that he was immensely talented. Like, once-in-a-generation talent. All he needed was paint. We didn't even give him canvas for the first few months. It was all on paper. Paint and paper. And he just had this amazing ability to mediate. You know what I mean by mediate? Connect. Channel. My facilitator at the time, Jackie, brought one of his first paintings here into the office, and—oh my God."

Tony put his hand over his heart. "I got chills just looking at it."

Rebekah shivered. She got chills thinking about Tony getting chills.

"Dom had a gift," Tony continued. "And we nurtured it at Stella, all the way through high school. And now he's *producing*. And people are offering him thousands for his paintings. This kid has the chance to be the next big thing. And we *raised* him. It's a turning point for us. People will ask Dom where he learned to paint, and he'll say,

'Stella.' Maybe he would have gotten there without us. But he didn't.

"He had a showing this past weekend," Tony said. He cocked his head. "I was thinking about you."

Rebekah raised her eyebrows. "Oh, yeah?"

"Yeah. I was thinking about you because you joined Stella shortly after we started working with Dom. In fact, I think I saw his first painting the day I interviewed you. And I felt so good about it, that it was like, man, I should take a chance on this person. It's a sign. And I hired you. And you've helped us develop *Daft* into a really good product. A great product, really.

"But," he said. "But."

Rebekah wiped her hands on her pants. Tony furrowed his brow. "You know what you didn't have, compared with some of the other candidates?"

Rebekah shook her head.

"A portfolio. An art portfolio. Rebekah, have you ever noticed that you're one of the only people in this organization who's not an artist?"

"Really?" Rebekah asked. She looked at Micah. "What about you?"

Micah shook her head. "That's not what I was hired for," Micah said.

"That's correct," Tony said. "I hired Micah precisely because she wasn't an artist—because I thought she would be able do things that no one else in this agency might be able, or want to do. Rebekah, do you know what kind of person you should hire to manage your money if you ever start an organization?"

"What kind of person?" Rebekah asked.

"Someone who's smarter than you and meaner than you."

Rebekah raised her eyebrows.

"Meaner?" Micah said. "Really, Tony?"

"I say that with the utmost love and respect, Micah," Tony said. "You're a very warm person off the job. But when it comes to Stella's money, you're as hard-hearted as they come. And that's just how I like it."

Micah smiled. It was a cold smile. "Thanks. I think."

"It's a compliment," Tony said. "Take it. You have the financial and analytical skills to keep an organization full of bleeding-hearts on track. You're the reason we are as successful as we are. We couldn't do it without you."

Tony turned back to Rebekah. "I needed someone who was the opposite of me. Who had completely different skills. I needed a compliment, not a clone. And I think Micah does a great job of that. But you, Rebekah—you're an English major, right?"

Rebekah nodded.

"So you *know* art in the sense that you know Hemingway and Plath and Stegner and Woolf. But you don't produce art, as far as I know, right?"

Rebekah searched her mind for something she could share.

"Not besides *Daft*, no."

"Right. And Rebekah…frankly, *Daft* doesn't really rise to the level of art in my mind. At least not yet."

Rebekah nodded again.

"So here's what I want from you, Rebekah. I want two things. First: I want you to turn *Daft* into art. I want you to do with *Daft* what Dom Turken does with a blank canvas. Raise it to that level. When people look at *Daft*, I want them to be blown away by the layout and font and style and writing. I want them to want to keep it and show it to their friends. I want it to be something that we are proud of showing to our donors, not just a throw-away thing. This is not just an arts organization. This is an organization of artists. Do you think you can do that? Do you think you have the skills to pull that off?"

"Well," Rebekah said. "I would be more than happy to do that. I'm really excited by what you're proposing. But I think I'd need a bigger budget."

"I can't give that to you."

Rebekah pursed her lips. "So, that means that I can't do more color spreads, I can't work with contractors for original art or photography. It's the little stuff, Tony, that would take it to the next level."

Tony shrugged. "Be entrepreneurial. Be an artist. Figure it out. Maybe you can find a grant. And if you can't, then just make it happen. Work with other people on the staff if you need to. Jane, Greg. Those folks might be able to help."

"Right," Rebekah said. She ground her nails into her thigh. Do more with less: the mantra of non-profit organizations.

"Second," Tony said. He glanced at Micah. "Micah, you want to take the lead on this?"

"Sure," Micah said. She folded her hands on the table. She stared at Rebekah. "So, here's the deal, Rebekah. It's been a really tough fundraising climate in recent years. I'm sure you've deduced that."

"Yeah."

"The economic collapse, political infighting—everything, just everything. It's become more and more difficult to find people who want to give to arts or education, and particularly, arts education. It seems like a luxury. How can they give to Stella when people are starving, out of jobs, moving back in with their elderly parents? I get it. But my job is to keep Stella afloat. And to keep Stella afloat, we need to step up our fundraising efforts.

"Rebekah, *Daft* needs to do a better job of bringing in money. We want you to think about how you can do that. It's always been a fundraising tool for us, but not really an explicit fundraising tool. We've never included donation envelopes when we send out the newsmagazine. We've never included letters in our mailings asking people to donate. We've never done profiles of our donors. Now, I think we need to start considering things like that. You understand?"

"So," Rebekah said, "if I'm hearing you both correctly, you want *Daft* to become more artistic and raise more money? At the same time?"

Micah nodded. "Art and money."

"You know, it's funny, Rebekah," Tony said. "When I first started Stella, it was all about the mission. Bringing art to kids. Bringing art to the world. But you can't do any of that without money. Money is like the molecular underpinnings of change. It's the hydrogen and oxygen. We can't all be idealistic. We need to be pragmatic, too.

"I want you to remember something, Rebekah, something very important," Tony said. He leaned forward and stared directly at Rebekah. "The objective of any organism is to grow."

Rebekah swallowed. She could hear the clock tick on the wall of Tony's office.

"I'll say it again: the objective of any organism is to grow. The objective of a person is to grow. The objective of a business is to grow. Governments. Departments, agencies, and staffs within governments. Organizations. They all want to grow. If you understand that, and look at it with a cold eye, you'll have a much better grasp of how the world works. Stella wants to grow. And we need money to do it."

Micah nodded at Tony. Tony stood up. He was tall, and seemed taller when Rebekah looked up at him from a sitting position. He pushed his shoulders back and shoved his hands in his pockets.

"Good. I'll assume you know what you're doing, then, Rebekah. Work with Micah so that it's on point. If you need help with fundraising messages, work with Jane. If you need help with art, find the resources you need. Got it?"

"Got it."

Tony smiled at her, that fund-raising, entrepreneurial, celebrity-by-40 smile. Rebekah's face flushed.

"I know you can do it," Tony said.

Rebekah wanted to believe him.

"Now, get out of here. Thanks for all you do. You're doing a great job."

Rebekah stood up, nodded to Tony and Micah, and left the office. She walked back to her chair, passing the loudly chirping Jane Salish on the way and motioning to Roberto for five more minutes before they left for lunch. Rebekah sat down. She opened up her inbox and hit "reply" on the email to Benny657.

July 4, 2011

The spring rains in Portland stopped gradually, as if someone was slowly tightening a faucet with a leaky O-ring. Starting in March, the clouds dripped with steady regularity. They misted and drizzled, then suddenly erupted into volcanic downpours that tested gutters and drainage systems citywide. In April and May, the trees budded and bloomed, grasses flourished, and flowers popped out of the earth and shook off the sleep from a long winter. The rain still came, but it was interspersed with days of brilliant sunshine. Gardeners loaded up planting boxes with lettuce, herbs, and snap peas. Soil dried out. The asphalt streets steamed from wetness and heat. Commuters carried sunscreen and umbrellas to work.

In June, the sun unleashed an assault on spring. It was impossible not to notice the steady upward creep of the daily temperature, the weather forecast predicting multiple days of sunshine, or the wood chips, lighter fluid, and cases of beer that lined the front aisles of supermarkets. Sunshine lowered itself from between thin, wispy clouds and smote the remaining vestiges of winter.

Every year on July Fourth, Rebekah and Megan left their newly arid city to fly down to always-parched Pasadena for the long holiday weekend. They left yellowing grasses for stiff palms, left the current threat of Oregon wildfire for the ubiquitous possibility of California's severe drought and earthquakes, or the chance that the whole state might burn up in one giant conflagration. They flew from sun to sun, never leaving their time zone or left-leaning voting cohort. But when Rebekah and Megan left Portland for Pasadena, they knew they would have the mandatory, patriotic, Fourth of July celebration with the Nimble family, and there would be visiting time for Rebekah and her brother, David.

Rebekah and David saw each other once a year during the holiday weekend. When David had made the decision to convert to Orthodox Judaism, he'd given up celebrating classic American holidays: Halloween, Thanksgiving, and the Fourth of July.

"We have an independence day," David had once told Rebekah. "It's Yom Ha'atzmaut, the day Israel declared its independence."

"But you live here, David," Rebekah said.

"I live here, true," David said.

"I believe your passport has an American flag on it," Rebekah said. "I believe you celebrate the freedoms and opportunities that come with living here. And you pay taxes. Might as well have a barbecue to celebrate being done with taxes."

David shrugged. "We take the day off on the Fourth of July, just like everyone else. And I'll have a barbecue on Yom Ha'atzmaut."

Rebekah struggled to understand David's stubbornness. What would it take away from him to have a barbecue on the Fourth of July? What would it take to bend a little, to fit in, to try to be a part of the majority—instead of always apart?

Yet there was a little burn of envy inside of her, a festering, slowly steaming blister. David had rules. David had moral clarity. David had what he had always had: righteousness. He could choose not to celebrate the Fourth of July, because he had something that he actually believed in.

I just go with the fucking flow, Rebekah would think. *What do I believe in?*

Righteousness. The word defined David. When he was a child, he walked with his head high and chin out, seeming to evade the raindrops. When he was an adult, he was a man of faith and religious rigor. David had the Torah. David had Yom Ha'atzmaut. David would always be a rung above, simply because people around him believed him to be.

For the first time since meeting Megan, Rebekah was dreading her visit to Los Angeles. She was terrified at the thought of telling her brother about the wedding. Rebekah's fear was founded in the assumption that her brother would wholly reject her, simply based on the articles of his faith. Rebekah had no evidence for this assumption that she could clearly articulate to Megan. David had never made a homophobic comment, had never mentioned voting against politicians who supported gay marriage, had never, in fact, said or done anything to give Rebekah any indication that he placed religious emphasis on the biblical passages that prohibited homosexuality.

And yet, even the possibility of rejection was enough to make Rebekah lie to her brother, obfuscate the nature of her relationship with Megan, and pretend for the previous decade that she was David

Cohayn's straight, uncomplicated younger sister. The possibility of rejection—the hypothetical, non-existent, potential that David would throw her out—was paralyzing. Worse, Rebekah considered, than its reality.

David still occupied a mythical role in Rebekah's mind. Her older brother had been her spiritual and moral compass when they were kids. The way he doled out little drippings of love to his younger sister used to make her feel like a drug addict. She dreaded telling him that she was gay and getting married as much as she would dread confessing a murder to a police officer, or telling a priest about an affair.

The Nimble house was located on the northern edge of Pasadena, in Los Angeles County. It sat on a block that ran up and down, north and south, each house occupying its very own twist in the road. It was the only house on a small, flat stretch of land in the middle of a hill, like a decorative knob on a fulcrum. On the left side of the house, an asphalt driveway led up to a one-car garage. A well-maintained lawn fortified the front of the house and was split down the middle by a white concrete walkway. On either side of a short staircase leading up the door were two small flowerbeds. Amy Nimble lovingly tended to her small garden, occasionally picking a flower to place in a single-stem vase in the center of her dinner table. The house itself was a single-level, ranch-style home with three bedrooms and two bathrooms. Amy and John Nimble had always thought they would move out and find a bigger place as their family grew. But after having Megan, John and Amy decided that one phase of sleepless nights, toilet trainings, first days of school, and college tuition was enough; they would lavish their attention on their only child. So Amy kept tending their small garden, and John finished the mudroom and replaced the fixtures. After thirty-two years in the same house, very little of the hardware was the same as when they'd moved in, but the essence of the house remained.

The interior felt clean and light to Rebekah. The re-finished wood floors, scuffed from years of running feet and furniture-moving, gave the place an air of bucolic charm. The furniture was simple: a small oak table, wooden, hard-backed chairs, a brown leather three-person couch, and a faded light blue reclining arm chair. The kitchen counters, paved in white tile, were old but functional. The gas range was sturdy and reliable. The cabinets were beefy.

Rebekah remembered feeling struck by how different the Nimble house was from her own parents' place. It wasn't anything she could pinpoint in particular, just a sense of order that the house she grew up in had lacked.

Her own family home was located on the top of a hill in southwest Portland, a prime location in a city full of shadows. It was a house Judith and Daniel wouldn't have been able to afford, save for its unexceptional condition. The real estate advertisement had called it "charming." A generous, optimistic buyer might have termed it a fixer-upper. When they had first seen the place, dilapidated white gutters hung from the sides, taped together with white painters tape, so that water ran from the roof to the gutter, then down the sides of the house and into the basement. White paint peeled in streaks down the front of the house, and the blue border near the roof—a trim color, the real estate agent clarified—had the weathered, beaten look of a ship's hull.

Inside, the house was a split-level; the family room occupied the lowest part of the house, the living room and kitchen were in the middle, and a small staircase led up to three bedrooms at the top of the house. Nothing had been updated since 1953, the year the house was built. Pink flowered wallpaper lined the kitchen walls, and the old claw-foot bathtub had worn grooves into the water-damaged bathroom floor.

Rebekah's parents had eclectic tastes in furniture and art, seeming to collect rather than design. Her own mother's garden was inevitably a mess of weeds before it produced anything edible, and her father's garage was in constant need of organization. But there was something familiar about that chaos, something that felt like home to her. Her house had ridges and twists, nooks and crannies. Where in this spotless little house had Megan played hide and seek?

On her first visit to the Nimble house, Rebekah had nearly tip-toed across the floors. But that evening, in a fit of laughter, Megan leaned back too hard in the arm chair, spun unwittingly, and knocked a lamp into the television set, shattering both. Amy had clucked, and John shook his head. Megan apologized profusely and offered to buy them a new television.

"Just come visit more often," John growled.

When Amy pulled up to the Nimble house on the morning of July Fourth, Rebekah noticed that a large American flag had been mounted onto a bracket beside the front door.

Rebekah stepped out of the backseat of the car, and walked up behind Megan. "Your dad's not going to make me recite the Pledge of Allegiance, right?" Rebekah asked.

"What?"

Rebekah nodded towards the flag. "Does he always put that up? I've never noticed it before."

Megan turned to the front of the house. "Oh. That. He used to put it up every year when I was a kid. I guess he must have stopped for a while. I bet my mom was going through the garage and told him that if he wasn't using it, he would need to give it away. So now he puts it up again."

Megan twisted back to the car and pulled her luggage out of the trunk.

John Nimble came striding out of the house. He was barefoot, wearing a red polo shirt and blue jeans.

"Megs!" he said. He wrapped his long arms around his daughter and planted a kiss on her forehead. Megan was almost as tall as her father, so John had to stand on the tips of his toes so his lips would reach above her eyebrows.

"Did you have a good flight?"

"We did," Megan said.

"The pilot did ok?"

"Yeah." Megan rolled her eyes. "There was a little kid sitting behind me who kept kicking the back of my seat the whole flight, but other than that, it was fine."

John squeezed his daughter's shoulder. "When you were two years old, we flew to the East Coast to visit your cousins. You didn't stop screaming from the time the plane took off to when the wheels touched down. I felt like I had to apologize to all the stewardesses myself. Consider this karmic retribution."

"Thanks, Dad," Megan said. She rolled her eyes.

John walked up to Rebekah. "Beks," he said. He gave her a hug and a kiss on the forehead, this time bending down to her. "So nice to see you, too. It's great you girls could make it."

"We wouldn't miss it," Rebekah said.

John jingled his keys in his pocket. "Well, I'm off to the store to get stuff to grill. Ribs ok with everyone?"

Megan glanced over at Rebekah. "Pork or beef ribs?"

"Well, I was thinking pork," John said. He looked at Rebekah. "Oh, good point. You can't eat pork, right? I should probably get beef ribs, too."

"Yeah, get some beef, dad," Megan said.

"Really, Rebekah?" John asked. "You keep kosher?"

"Oh, well, I guess," Rebekah said. "I don't eat pork, but it's more out of habit. My parents never cooked pork, and I never ordered it at restaurants growing up. So it's not really something I think about eating. I'm not super strict about it. I don't have two sets of dishes or anything."

Not like David, Rebekah thought. *David has two sets of dishes.*

"Oh," John said. "Well."

"If it's too much trouble to cook beef and pork ribs, I can just eat the pork ribs," Rebekah said. Her ears burned.

"It's no trouble at all, sweetie," Amy said. She stepped between Rebekah and her husband. "I prefer beef, too. I just didn't feel like I could say anything early, because today…"

"Today is my independence day!" John interrupted.

Amy looked at Rebekah and shook her head. "I don't typically eat pork, either, but I've determined that God values the intactness of my marriage over the occasional foray into pork and shellfish."

"And your more-than-occasional foray into bacon," John said.

Amy pursed her lips. "Yes. I admit it. Bacon is a vice."

"What my parents are trying to say is that they're half-kosher," Megan said.

"I suppose that's fitting, since we're half-Jewish?" John asked.

"Um…dad, I don't think it works like that," Megan said.

"Why not?"

"You can't be proportionally kosher to your percentage of Jewishness. According to, you know, the people who know these things."

"Rabbis?" Rebekah asked.

"Yeah, rabbis," Megan said. "According to rabbis, you're either Jewish or you're not. Like, either your mother is Jewish, or you converted, or you're not Jewish. You can't really be half-Jewish. And you can't really be half-kosher."

"So, if your mother is Jewish, your father is Christian, you celebrate Christmas and Hanukkah, you eat pork ribs on July Fourth and bacon occasionally for breakfast…what does that make you?" John asked.

"Um…" Megan said.

"Rich in culinary experiences," Amy said.

John nodded. "We are what we are. And on that note, I'm off to the store for pork and beef ribs. Anyone opposed to corn on the cob and watermelon, on religious grounds, or otherwise?"

Encountering no opposition to the rest of the dinner menu, John climbed into the car and drove away.

The rest of the day crawled by slowly. John sat in a lawn chair in the backyard, drinking a beer and stoking the coals on his Weber. Amy had changed into a red and white polka-dot sundress, and she cleaned the house before joining her husband in the backyard. Megan and Rebekah loafed around indoors, watching movies and drinking homemade lemonade.

At six thirty, John called Megan and Rebekah into the backyard, where the Nimble's large pine picnic table had been overlaid with a red and white polka-dot tablecloth and set with blue plastic plates and utensils. Plates of steaming beef ribs sat next to a tray of pork ribs, slathered in barbecue sauce. Bowls of potato salad, yellow corn, freshly baked rolls and tomato and cucumber salad rounded out the remainder of the meal. A cooler of beer sat at the foot of the table. John banned wine from his Fourth of July celebrations; beer or lemonade only, he told his family.

Rebekah and the Nimbles ate until the sun disappeared behind the trees in their backyard, and the sky changed from a fierce blue to a mellow gray. The automatic lights in the backyard came on.

"It's hot out there, isn't it?" Amy said. "We haven't had any rain since February. I bet the wildfires are going to start early this year."

"We should do some structure protection," John said.

"Structure protection?" Amy asked. "What on earth are you talking about?"

"You know. Clearing out brush from around the house. If a fire does start, making sure we've taken care of all of our flammable greenery."

"Oh John," Amy said. She opened another beer. "We live in the middle of the city. I think we'll be fine."

"That's what those good folks in San Diego said—when was it? 2007? They evacuated two million people, or something."

"Oh," Amy said. "Really?"

"Sure did."

Amy looked at Megan. "I'm sure everything will be ok."

"I'm not worried, Mom."

John looked from his wife to his daughter. "Well, now, you're making me really think. Megan, if we did have to evacuate, what would you want me to take?"

"What?" Megan asked.

John looked at his wife. "I suppose we should probably pack up her varsity letter. From when she played basketball in high school."

Megan put her hand to her forehead. "Dad. Wow."

Amy stood up. "Well, are we ready for dessert? Watermelon, anyone?"

Amy reached under the table, pulled up a giant watermelon, and handed it to John. John picked up a large butcher's knife and began carving.

A few moments of silence passed. John Nimble artfully sliced the watermelon, spraying bits of juice onto the tablecloth. Rebekah closed her eyes and took a deep breath. The air was so dry, she noticed, compared to Portland. It was almost stifling.

Amy cleared her throat. "So. I just wanted to tell you how excited we are for your wedding."

"We are, we are," John said. He took a hack at the melon. "Committed relationships are a wonderful thing."

"Have you started planning at all?" Amy asked.

"We looked for wedding outfits," Megan said.

"Oh?" Amy said. "Did you find anything?"

"Not yet. We're still thinking about it." Megan smiled. She put her arm around Rebekah.

"Oh, that's great, honey." Amy glanced at John. She set down the teapot and sat down. "So, just so you know, John and I have set aside some money for you two. If you need help, you let us know."

Megan glanced at Rebekah. "Wow, Mom, that's really generous. How much?"

"Just a couple thousand dollars, sweetie. Maybe enough to pay for one thing? Photography? Your wedding dinner?"

Megan nodded and shifted in her chair. "Mom, that's incredibly generous of you. Thank you. I'm sure at some point we will need help. Rebekah and I need to sort through our expenses and figure out what everything is going to cost. We're really trying to keep expenses down, but everything just seems to cost a lot of money for weddings."

"I know, honey," Amy said. "It would be our pleasure to help you with your costs."

"Thanks, Mom," Megan replied.

John Nimble cleared his throat and put the knife down on the table. He folded his hands in front of him. His mustache twitched. "I've got something to say," John said. He stared at the table. After a few seconds, he looked up at Megan.

"Megs," John started. He paused again. "I love you so much. So much. You're my daughter, my only child, and you just mean everything to me." His voice cracked.

"Thanks, Dad." Megan's voice quavered.

"I am so happy that you've found happiness. It means the world to me." He looked at Rebekah. "I love you, too, Bekah. You are so wonderful, and so good for my daughter."

Rebekah nodded at him and stared at the table. She couldn't speak. John cleared his throat again. "I've thought about this moment. The time when you would come to me and talk to me about your wedding. Before I knew you were, you know, gay, I thought—well, of course I thought you would marry a man. And I would walk you down the aisle, and hand you off to a guy that I had threatened to kill and dump in the ocean if he ever mistreated you."

"John," Amy whispered. She wiped her eyes.

"Well, you know, I'm allowed my fantasies, aren't I? That was mine. That my beautiful daughter, my only child, would meet a great guy, a great guy. But there would be no guy good enough for my daughter, and so I would like him, but, you know, I would have to work to like him. Because he would be taking you away from me…" John's voice cracked again. "And I really don't like to think about that.

"And then you told me you were gay, and, you know. I didn't really think about weddings anymore. Because how long ago was that? You were in high school, Meggy. And I didn't know if what you were telling us was true. Maybe you weren't gay. I thought maybe you'd grow out of it. I mean, I don't know what girls in high school really do, and I thought maybe this is something that girls did, but we just didn't used to talk about it like we do today."

Megan exchanged a glance with Rebekah. She'd told Rebekah the story of her coming out many times, hoping that it would inspire Rebekah to come out to David. Megan had been terrified of telling her pilot-father and nurse-mother about being gay. She was worried about her father in particular. He was so traditional, so no-nonsense, that Megan wondered how he would handle this crooked little piece of information.

Megan was surprised when her parents reacted with the equivalent of a giant shrug.

Megan had sat them down in their living room one night. She was a senior in high school. It was cold out, one of the coldest days in southern California on record. Frost had crept up on the corners of their windows. A cold wind was blowing against the house. The Nimble's furnace had been acting finicky for a few days, and so John had kept the thermostat at a cool sixty degrees.

She sat down in their fabric armchair. She pushed her shoulders back and sat tall, her spine straight. Her parents sat across from her on their brown leather couch. Megan took a deep breath. "There's something I need to tell you," she said.

Neither of her parents responded. John stared back, inscrutable; Amy fidgeted and played with her hands.

"I'm gay," Megan said.

John furrowed his brow. "Gay?" he asked.

"Yes," Megan said.

"As in, you want to be with women?"

"Yes," Megan said.

John looked from his wife to his daughter. "Really?" John asked. "You sure?"

"Pretty sure."

"How do you know?"

Megan shrugged. She had watched *Silence of the Lambs* over and over, just to see Jodie Foster. She felt squishy and hot around Janey

McGee, her school's yearbook president and the captain of the soccer team. These weren't the details that she wanted to share with her parents.

"I just know," Megan said.

John nodded and slapped his palms on the tops of his knees.

"Well, that wasn't what I was expecting, but ok," John said. "So that means I don't have to worry about you getting pregnant, right?"

"Um…no," Megan said. "For me to get pregnant right now would take a virgin birth kind of deal."

"Works for me," John said. "Those are the best kinds of births. So, is that it?"

"Yes, that's it," Megan said.

John checked his watch. "Ok, well, I need to go downstairs to check on the furnace again. I really don't want it to give out tonight, with the weather the way it is." John disappeared from the living room. Megan heard his heavy footsteps in the garage.

Amy stood up. "Sweetie, come give me a hug." Megan walked towards her mother and wrapped the smaller woman in her arms. When she pulled back, Amy had tears in her eyes.

"It's ok, honey," Amy said. "Don't worry about your dad. He just needs some time to process. He thought you were going to tell us that you were pregnant."

Megan raised her eyebrows. "Me? Pregnant?"

Amy giggled. "He was ready to drive over to the guy's house, you know."

"That's really not necessary," Megan said. "For anyone I date. Ever."

Now, Rebekah looked back at John Nimble.

"And then you met Rebekah," John said. "And I thought, ok. My daughter is really gay. And I couldn't think about doing to Rebekah what I had imagined doing to a guy for so long. Or saying what I thought I would say. Or feeling like I thought I would feel. And it just…" John paused, put his hands up in the air, and looked bewildered. "It was what it was. You were happy, and so, you know, I was happy. How could I not be happy?"

Megan was staring at her father, her shoulders slumped and her lips apart. She would tell Rebekah later that she'd never heard her father string so many words together at the same time. Amy would say later that in forty years of marriage, the only other times she'd seen John cry were at his mother's funeral and Megan's birth.

"But…" John gestured again, this time towards the door. "Things have changed. And I…I can't say I understand it all. But here you are, telling me you're going to get married, and you're going to spend your life with someone you really love, and…" John eyes filled with tears. "Megan, I'm just so happy."

Megan started crying.

John stood up from his chair and walked over to Megan. He knelt in front of her and wrapped his arms around her. "My little girl," he whispered. "My little girl."

Amy, who had started crying from the moment John started speaking, walked over and wrapped her arms around her husband and daughter.

Rebekah stared at them. She couldn't decide whether she ought to leave the table, or simply sit silently and wait. Rebekah thought about the moment when she came out to her own mother, about the tension, the tears, her mother's instinct to pretend and diffuse. Rebekah watched the Nimble family hold each other, framed by their tight, snug little house. She pushed down the sense that her own family life was a mess, that the Cohayns were falling apart, that their dynamic had been built a few decades ago and nothing had been done in the way of renovations. She blinked back tears and swallowed the lump in her throat.

After a few seconds, Amy looked up and motioned Rebekah into the hug. Rebekah stood up and obediently wrapped her arms around the Nimble family. The four held each other, weeping.

After a few minutes, Amy looked at Rebekah. "Welcome to our weird little family, dear," she said. John and Megan laughed.

John sat back down in his chair. He wiped his eyes. "So, have you two given any thought to what kind of ceremony you're going to have?"

Rebekah and Megan looked at each other. Megan shrugged. "Not really," she said.

"Well, what about a Jewish ceremony?" Amy asked. She looked at Rebekah. "Would you want a Jewish ceremony?"

"Oh, well…" Rebekah paused. "I suppose. But…" She looked at Megan again. "We'll really just need to talk about it. We'd need to find a rabbi."

"Of course," Amy said. "I didn't mean to pry. I was just curious."
Amy was interrupted by a low rumble, followed by three short pops. "It's the fireworks!" John said. He jumped up from his chair. "The best damn part of this holiday, besides the fact that I get to cook whatever I want. I bet we can see them from the corner of our yard." He motioned for Megan and Rebekah to follow him.

Rebekah stood behind John, peering over the fence to the city beyond to watch the fireworks displays light up Los Angeles. As the sky ignited in a rainbow of color, she thought back to the crucible of her own childhood: the night she came out to her mother.

The Fog
November, 2000

HAMLET: The air bites shrewdly; it is very cold.
HORATIO: It is a nipping and an eager air.
HAMLET: What hour now?
HORATIO: I think it lacks of twelve.
HAMLET: No, it is struck.

Rebekah shifted to rest her head on the back of her hand. She was lying underneath the three-foot-high stage on her stomach.

HORATIO: Look, my lord it comes!

Rebekah reached out and turned on the fog machine. White smoke poured out and snaked its way underneath the stage to where Horatio, Hamlet, and Marcellus stood in the cardboard graveyard.

HAMLET: Angels and ministers of grace defend us!
Be thou a spirit of health or goblin damned,
Bring with thee airs from heaven or blasts from hell,
Be thy intents wicked or charitable,
Thou comest in such a questionable shape
That I will speak to thee. I'll call thee "Hamlet,"
"King," "Father," "royal Dane." O, answer me!

Rebekah turned the fog machine off again. She could only leave it on for ten seconds before the coils of smoke obscured the actors.

HAMLET: Where wilt thou lead me? Speak; I'll go no further.
GHOST: Mark me.
HAMLET: I will.
GHOST: My hour is almost come,
When I to sulphurous and tormenting flames,
Must render up myself.

Rebekah turned the fog machine on. This was her favorite scene in *Hamlet*, the scene in which Hamlet's dead father bids him to seek revenge for his death. Greg Askey was playing Hamlet's father, the ghost. Greg was a senior with a deep, steady baritone. He sat in a small, dark storage closet in the bowels of the theater with a microphone, articulating the vengeful wishes of Hamlet's father. Jacob Green, Rebekah's friend from elementary school, had won the role of Hamlet. He had grown into a well-proportioned, good-looking teenager, with dark, curly hair and dark eyebrows. Jacob had also cultivated a charismatic, intense stage presence, and he had starred in multiple school plays. According to those who'd witnessed the tryouts, no one had come close to equaling Jacob's portrayal of Hamlet. His Hamlet was full of depth, pain, and a curious darkness that Jacob articulated through curled lips, a tight jaw, and a constant, wide-eyed distress.

Rebekah had grown to be a little intimidated by Jacob. He walked around campus with ease, cruising through unseen barriers between social groups to eat lunch with the popular kids, spend breaks with the theater kids, and stay after school to talk about books with his English teacher. He wielded his social prowess with a joie de vivre. Even after all these years, Jacob Green was still "Lucky" Jacob Green to Rebekah.

GHOST: I am thy father's spirit
Doom'd for a certain term to walk the night
And for the day confined to fast in fires
Till the foul crimes done in my days of nature
Are burnt and purged away. But that I am forbid
To tell the secrets of my prison-house,
I could a tale unfold whose lightest word
Would harrow up thy soul, freeze thy young blood,
May thy two eyes, like stars, start from their spheres,
Thy knotted and combined locks to part
And each particular hair to stand on end,
Like quills upon the fretful perpentine:
But this eternal blazon must not be
To ears of flesh and blood. List, list, O, list!
If thou didst ever thy dear father love—
HAMLET: O God!

GHOST: Revenge his foul and most unnatural murder.
HAMLET: Murder!
GHOST: Murder most foul, as in the best it is;
But this most foul, strange and unnatural.

Ten seconds. Rebekah turned the fog machine off. The vapor lay heavily on the stage now. Rebekah shifted, laying her cheek on the cold floor of the theater.

By the time Rebekah reached ninth grade, she had grown into a sweetly awkward teenager, gangly and quiet, prone to playing with the thick curly hair that hung down just past her shoulders. She wore a pair of thick black horn-rimmed glasses, nearly the same style that she had worn as a toddler. She still bumped into things, despite her much-improved vision; it was more that she was constantly distracted and didn't pay much attention to where her feet were taking her. Judith and Daniel liked to joke that Rebekah had not changed much since she was a baby. The only difference was her evolved vocabulary.

"If you didn't talk back so much, I would swear you were still my sweet little five year-old," Judith would say. Rebekah would roll her eyes in response.

Rebekah had sworn to herself, with a bit of wobbly resolve, that she would get involved in something, anything, in high school. During the first week of school, Rebekah saw signs recruiting students to help design the set for *A Midsummer Night's Dream*. Though Rebekah had been vehemently opposed to actually appearing on stage, she liked the idea of being a part of a production. Set design seemed innocuous, helpful and safely out of the spotlight.

Four years later, in November of 2000, Rebekah was now a senior at Calvin Coolidge High School in southwest Portland, and a veteran stage designer. She had guided underclassmen through designs for the graveyard and palace scene and had insisted that she work the fog machine herself.

High school was nearly behind her, college in front of her, as if she were straddling a massive fault line that separated universes governed by two different sets of physical laws. Rebekah's parents, not yet empty-nesters, still each worked fifty hours a week in an attempt to pay off their mortgage. David was in his third year of school at the University of Southern California, majoring in political science.

USC was one of the universities Rebekah was planning on applying to, along with the University of Oregon and the University of Washington. Rebekah hoped to follow her brother to USC and major in political science, just like him. She imagined going to coffee shops with David, discussing politics, impressing her older brother with her command of current affairs. He would smile, compliment her, invite her to join student organizations he'd participated in, and tell his friends what an asset she could be. She imagined the dip in his chin, the warmth in his eyes.

GHOST: Swear.
HAMLET: Ah, ha, boy! Say'st thou so? Art thou there, truepenny? Come on—you hear this fellow in the cellarage—consent to swear.

Rebekah leaned forward to try to get a better view of the stage. If the fog dissipated too quickly, she sometimes piped in a little more at the end of the scene. Rebekah craned her neck—and dropped her jaw in horror.

The fog hadn't dispersed at all. It hovered on the stage, nearly obscuring the audience's view of the actors. Everyone was breathing it in, straining to see through a pea soup of machine-generated murkiness.

Rebekah twisted her head to peek over her shoulder. She saw Mr. Donald's face, backlit by the light from the art room, poking through the small opening underneath the stage.

"No. More. Fog," he mouthed, each word punctuated by a slashing motion at his throat.

Rebekah gave him a quick nod and faced forward again. She unplugged the fog machine.

Just then, a loud beeping noise, like the ringing of a telephone, blasted over the loudspeakers. The actors stopped moving. A few people in the audience began whispering.

The ringing stopped. After a few seconds, Hamlet began to speak.
HAMLET: Well said, old mole! Canst work—
The ringing started again. The actors fell silent.

Rebekah finally recognized the noise she was hearing: the fire alarm.

Rebekah saw Jacob take two quick strides towards the center of the stage. He shouted through the ringing.

"Father?" Jacob ad-libbed.

The audience laughed.

Jacob cocked his head to one side while the alarm rang again. He was almost invisible in the thick cloud of smoke. He looked up towards the speaker on the side of the theater.

"Father, is that you?" Jacob said.

Jacob paused for dramatic effect, knowing that the alarm would ring again. It did. Greg Askey, who was still sitting in his storage closet with his microphone, took advantage of the moment.

"It is I!" Greg said, in his deepest, most solemn baritone. The audience roared.

"Rest, rest perturbed spirit!" Jacob said, with a wave of his hand. He ran off stage. Mr. Donald stepped through a side door toward the center of the stage.

"Please exit the theater to the right," Mr. Donald yelled over the clapping. "I believe we've inadvertently set off the fire alarm. Hopefully, this will only take a few minutes to fix, and we can continue the play."

Rebekah pivoted on her stomach, crawled out the back of the stage, and walked directly into the back of the theater.

She saw Ruth Kinder, Aldon Coombs, and Ricky Martinez standing together. They were laughing.

"Hey, Fog," Ricky called out.

Rebekah put her hands up and looked at them skeptically. "Um...was that me?"

"Yes," Ricky and Ruth said at the same time. They looked at each other and laughed.

Rebekah rolled her eyes. "Oh, come on, it couldn't have been. I've been doing the fog every night for the last two weeks, and I haven't done this before."

"That's because the last two weeks, the air conditioner was working," said a voice behind her. Rebekah turned around. It was Jacob. He was grinning at her. His eyelashes stood out stiffly under his stage mascara.

Rebekah turned back to look at Ricky, Ruth, and Aldon. "Really?" she asked.

The four of them started laughing again.

"Oh, shit," Rebekah said.

Ricky reached down and ruffled her hair. "Hey, don't worry about it," Ricky said. "You couldn't have known. And it was like, a totally perfect special effect."

"IT IS I!" Greg Askey's voice boomed through the doorway.

Ricky and Ruth began laughing uproariously again. Rebekah shook her head.

"Hey guys, Mr. Donald wants us out of the art room because of the fire alarm." Greg jerked his thumb behind him. "He says that we can stand behind the building."

Rebekah turned around and began to walk out of the theater. She felt a hand on her shoulder.

"Hey, really, don't worry about it, ok? Could have happened to any of us."

Rebekah saw Ruth Kinder, under full makeup, smiling back at her. Ruth had grown into the sort of gregarious, affable creature that lived for performance. Rebekah had seen sparks of it when they were kids; Ruth was always one of the first in school to sign up for the talent show, and she was always putting on little plays for her parents. But Rebekah had never seen anyone flourish so capably under the bright lights of the CCHS theater. Ruth auditioned for every play, stole every scene, used her natural wiriness for physical humor.

Rebekah had joined the theater program partly because of Ruth. She could freely admit that going to the set design meeting for a *Midsummer Night's Dream* was infinitely easier because Ruth was auditioning. If David cast a long, principled shadow over Rebekah's life, then Ruth seemed to pave a way forward with ease and light. Rebekah thought David lived the way life ought to be lived; Ruth simply lived.

Ricky Martinez and Ruth Kinder played Rosencrantz and Guildenstern, the treacherous courtiers who spy on Hamlet for King Claudius. Though Ricky and Ruth had been friends before *Hamlet*, the play had forced them to spend nearly every minute of every rehearsal together. Ricky was the cynic to Ruth's Pollyanna, the dark wit to her infectious laughter. After a few weeks, the Shakespearean snoop duo started walking around school together, holding hands, giggling, and whispering in each other's ears. The senior class at Calvin Coolidge assumed that they were dating.

Rebekah shrugged. "It just sucks," she said. "I screwed up."

"Yeah, but who cares?" Ruth said. "It happens. Hey, are you going to come to P.J.'s with the crew tonight?"

"Nah, I don't think so," Rebekah said. Eating at P.J.'s, a diner about a five-minute walk from school, was a CCHS theater tradition. But after tonight's debacle, it didn't sound appetizing.

"Oh, come on! Come tonight. Me, Ricky, Greg, Aldon, and Jacob are going."

Rebekah sighed. It was a Friday night. This was a nearly-required social outing, an unspoken rule of being in the theater community. If she said so, she might not be invited again.

"Fine," Rebekah said.

Ruth pumped her fist. "Hah! Awesome. Meet us in the parking lot after the show."

P.J.'s was a bedrock of greasy late-night fare in Portland in the 1990s, a local Pacific Northwest chain that out-cooked IHOP and out-sleazed Denny's. A fellow named P.J. had conceived of the joint in the 80s as an old-meets-nouveau diner, a 50's throwback concept with a futuristic twist. Booths with bright red laminate facings lined the walls; bright red bar stools sat adjacent to the counter that faced the kitchen; and the floors were black-and-white checkerboard linoleum. Pictures of old Hollywood stars and political celebrities hung on the walls in glass frames: Marilyn Monroe, Elvis Presley, Dwight D. Eisenhower. Each picture was signed in black marker. The signatures were widely thought to be forged by none other than P.J. himself, since all were written in the same, left-leaning scrawl, the T's uncrossed, and the I's dotted with slender hearts.

P.J. had made an early decision to pair his diner motif with gaudy futuristic touches. Large tubes of fluorescent lighting hung on the ceiling. Some of these flickered every few seconds, as P.J. was slow to replace old bulbs.

P.J. had also installed a jukebox near the kitchen, which carried popular tunes from the 50's and 60's, as well as some more modern rock and grunge hits. A patron could drop in a quarter to play "Mr. Sandman," then drop in another quarter a few minutes later to play "Smells Like Teen Spirit."

But perhaps the most notable—and popular—aspect of P.J.'s was its most regular inhabitants, the dedicated souls who turned P.J.s from a dive into a late-night cult hit: its waiters.

P.J. had given the folks working in the front of the house the option of dressing in 50's style or "future style" (a choice termed "skates or blades" in the waiters' manual). Both roller skates and rollerblades had been banned at P.J.'s since the late 1980's, when a waitress at the end of a long shift had accidentally skated over a boy's outstretched foot, fallen forward, and spilled hot coffee over a solo diner sitting nearby. The boy had walked away, none the worse for wear; the roller skating waitress, having landed squarely on her right side on the linoleum, was picked up by an ambulance, taken to a hospital, and promptly diagnosed with a broken hip. The man sitting nearby, with a ruined suit and a bruised sense of pride, had sued P.J.'s for his wasted time and emotional distress.

Since that day, the wait staff had been given strict instructions to wear sturdy, thematically appropriate, and non-mobile shoes to work. One waiter, named Tom—or Mr. Tom, as he insisted on being called— wore a white button-down shirt, a green bow tie, black pants, and black Chuck Taylors to work every day. He had long, white hair that hung halfway down his back, kept together (reluctantly) in a ponytail. He also had a long, white mustache that he curled upwards. Mr. Tom had been working at P.J.'s for fifteen years. He liked to tell patrons that if he died on the job, he wanted to be buried in the outfit he was wearing.

But the students' favorite member of P.J.'s wait staff was Esmerelda. She had bright, curly red hair that she liked to dye partially green around Christmastime. Esmerelda wore her own take on the future: leather jackets, knee-high leather boots, black jeans, t-shirts with band names or political messages, and chains: chains hanging down from her pants pockets, baubles on her wrists, and piles of necklaces around her neck. She had a thick New York accent that she could thicken on command, dropping her r's and slurring her consonants. Whenever she saw a batch of Mr. Donald's theater students walk in, she would yell across the restaurant, from wherever she was, that their table was hers.

"I got these kids," she said, when she saw Rebekah, Ruth, Ricky, Aldon, Greg, and Jacob walk through the door.

"Esmerelda!" Ricky said.

Esmerelda squinted at him. Her hair was pulled back into a messy bun that sat on top of her head. Tonight, she was dressed in her usual outfit, wearing a shirt that said "Morose Galactica" on it, written in letters that looked like light sabers.

"Somethin' wrong with your mouth?" she rasped.

"It's just lipstick." Ricky had wiped all of his makeup off, except for his lipstick. He blew her a kiss. "We had a show tonight."

"Uh-huh," Esmerelda said. "Still Hamlet or whateva, the one you guys were in here tellin' me about last week?" She grabbed six menus. "I gotta sit you kids at the booth in the back tonight. I don't got space in the front." She walked quickly toward the back and laid the menus on the table. Ruth, Ricky, Aldon, and James slid into the booth. Greg Askey and Rebekah took the chairs on the other side.

"You guys take as much time as you need, ok? I'll bring drinks. We close in an hour and a half." Esmerelda turned and walked away.

"God, she is so great," Aldon said.

Greg put his arm around her. "Good old Esmerelda." He kissed Aldon's cheek. The two had been dating since junior year.

"What are you guys getting?" Rebekah asked. She was studying the menu. P.J. had taken a few of the greasiest breakfasts, the most gut-busting desserts, and a smattering of appetizers, and put them on a half-price "Late Night" menu.

"Nothing that will set off the fire alarm," Greg said.

The table burst out laughing. Rebekah rolled her eyes at him over the menu.

"No, dude, seriously, I know we're teasing you, but that was so fucking epic," Greg said. "Did you hear me over the loudspeakers?"

"I didn't," Ruth said.

Greg put down his menu, put his right hand over his heart, and held out his left hand, as if he was addressing a crowd.

"IT IS I," Greg boomed. "HAMLET, I AM YOUR FATHER."

"Shut up," Jacob hissed at him over Aldon's giggling. "You're going to get us kicked out."

"We're not going to get kicked out," Greg gave him a ferocious grin. "Esmerelda loves me."

"Loves you?" Ricky asked. "Like, she wants to have your babies?"

"Probably," Greg said. "Who wouldn't?"

Ruth raised her hand.

Greg reached over and threw a sugar packet at her.

"What's goin' on ova here?" Esmerelda had walked over after taking orders at another table. "What, I leave you for two minutes, and already we're havin' a food fight?" She looked at Greg. "And for the record, I want nothin' to do with your babies." She pulled her notepad from her back pocket. "But in the meantime, Mr. Hamlet, what can I get for you?"

Jacob, who had turned bright red while Esmerelda was talking, peeked at the menu. "Um—can I just get a plate of fries please? And a diet coke?"

"Yep." Esmerelda scribbled on her pad and turned to Rebekah. "And you?"

"Root beer float please, vanilla ice cream." She handed Esmerelda the menu and grinned at Greg. There were few who could dish a plate of comeuppance like Esmerelda.

"And over here, this side of the table?"

Greg, who still had his arm around Aldon, said, "We're going to share a plate of fries too, please. And two coffees."

"Mmhmm. And over here?" Esmerelda said, nodding at Ricky.

"And...*we* are going to share the brownie with ice cream, please."

Ricky smiled at Ruth and handed the menu to Esmerelda.

"Got it," Esmerelda said. "A couple of cute couples we got here." Esmerelda looked at Aldon. "Looks like you got the short end of the stick," she said, with a jab of her head toward Greg. Esmerelda turned and walked away.

"Ohh," Jacob said, cupping his hands over his mouth. Aldon rubbed Greg's back. Greg put his forehead down on the table.

"She hates me," Greg said.

"She doesn't hate you," Ruth said. "She just thinks you're a cad."

"A cad?" Ricky asked, looking at her in surprise.

"What did you call me?" Greg asked, looking up.

"Ruth's in honors English, you guys," Jacob said.

Ruth cracked her knuckles and grinned at Greg. "You know. A cad. A bum. A douche-bag."

Greg waved her off. "Words, words, words," he said.

Ricky leaned in close to Ruth. "I think there's something rotten in the state of Askey," he said.

Greg glared at him. "Get thee to a nunnery," he hissed.

"Ok, you guys, like...seriously?" Aldon said.

"I have an idea," Greg said. He looked at Aldon. "Let's play Ten Fingers."

Ruth groaned. Jacob shook his head.

"We don't have to play, if you guys aren't into it," Aldon said. She looked at Greg. Greg was staring at Ricky.

"You in, man?"

Ricky sighed heavily. "I guess. I just think this is a dumb game." His demeanor had changed considerably in the last few seconds. His shoulders were slumped forward instead of up and back. His lips were set in a grim smile.

Rebekah adjusted the collar on her jacket. She had played Ten Fingers only once before, at the cast party for *A Midsummer Night's Dream*. The game was simple: Everyone held up ten fingers. One at a time, each player revealed something that they had never done. It was an unstated rule of Ten Fingers that all identified behaviors would be sexual, although some games permitted other vices to be mentioned, such as drug or alcohol use. Any party who was guilty of committing the named transgression lowered a finger. The first person to lower all ten of their fingers won the game—and secured the dubious status of being considered a leader in debauchery and depraved ventures.

Rebekah hadn't done much that would cause her to win the game. She'd never had sex, never given a blow job; she hadn't even kissed a boy, unless games of spin the bottle counted. Her problem wasn't that she would put too many fingers down. It was that she might not put any down at all.

Rebekah considered the moment. Her face felt hot, her throat dry; she was nervous, excited, and inexplicably charged with a crackling energy. The mistake at the theater had been embarrassing, but it had put her into an inadvertent position of distinction. She was the court jester, the accidental star, the tech hand who stole the show. She felt a secret permission to be different tonight, to step out of her clumsy skin and play a different character.

Rebekah was not afraid, because she couldn't be afraid of something she didn't know. She had a vague sense of discomfort, as if in a land far, far away, she could feel the soft outlines of a black hood coming down slowly over her head. But that all seemed so distant. Now things were just open, thrilling, waiting to be explored.

"Anyone else object?" Greg asked, looking around. Rebekah shook her head. Jacob gave a thumbs up. Ruth had put her arm around Ricky.

Greg nodded at Rebekah. "Ok, Fog, why don't you get this party started?"

Rebekah, surprised at having been called out, nodded. How to start? She was interested in retaining whatever low levels of cool quotient she might have with these friends. Coolness, in these circumstances, was measured in experience.

"Ok, you guys, here's an easy one: Never have I ever…fucked a man." *Too awkward,* Rebekah immediately thought. She forced herself to grin. She felt her cheeks getting hot.

"Ooh," her friends said, all at once, then softened into laughter. Ruth and Aldon put their fingers down. Rebekah saw Ruth and Ricky exchange glances. Ricky's blush had deepened to a dark purple.

"Did you really just say, 'fuck a man?'" Greg asked.

"Or a boy," Rebekah added.

"Ewww," Aldon said.

"Such language," Greg said.

Rebekah shrugged. She cleared her throat. "I haven't yet been presented with a fuckable fellow."

"Fuckable?" Greg repeated. He looked Aldon. "Am I fuckable?"

"Barely," Aldon said.

"I beg to differ, Aldon," Jacob said.

"The night's still young, Jakey-poo," Greg said.

"Gross," Aldon said. She elbowed her boyfriend in the ribs. "Don't be gay."

Esmerelda walked up behind Greg with a tray of drinks. She looked at their table skeptically.

"What's goin' on now? Whaddaya all doin' with your fingas up? Is this somethin' I gotta tell Mr. Donald about?"

"Ten fingers," Greg said. "Want to play?"

Esmerelda laughed and started setting drinks down on the table. "Honey, trust me, that's game's as old as the universe. And you don't wanna to play with me. Ten questions, and game over."

She picked up her empty tray. "Your food will be out in a few minutes. Stay outta trouble until then, ok?" Esmerelda turned and walked away.

"So, Rebekah," Greg said. He leaned into the table. "Would you like to fuck a man?"

Aldon hit him in the shoulder. "Stop."

"Not an offer. Just a question."

"Um…" Rebekah tried to laugh. "I suppose if the right guy presented himself, sure, I'd, you'd know."

Ruth raised her eyebrows. "Would you?"

"Wouldn't you?" Greg asked, looking at Ruth.

Ruth turned to Ricky and smiled. "This boy is all I need." She kissed Ricky on the cheek.

Greg rolled his eyes. "Whatever." He pointed to Jacob. "Now that we've established that Rebekah is a slut, Jake, it's your turn."

"Hmm," Jacob said. He drummed his fingers on the table. "Never have I ever…" his voice trailed off. He stared thoughtfully out the window. Then he snapped his fingers. "Never have I ever…" he turned to face Greg. "Never have I ever had sex with Aldon!"

Aldon turned red and then started giggling. Greg shook his head at Jacob and put one of his fingers down.

"Hey, man, you're the one who wanted to play the game," Jacob said.

Greg shrugged. "Whatever. It's true. I'm not ashamed of it." He looked around the table. "No one else has their fingers down, right?"

"Well…what about Aldon?" Ruth asked. "You know, does that count? Can she have sex with herself?"

Aldon threw back her head and laughed. When she faced the table, there was delight in her eyes. She slowly put a finger down. Greg stared at her incredulously.

"What, babe?" Aldon asked. "A woman can't pleasure herself?"

Rebekah, a neophyte in these discussions, felt giddy watching the back and forth between Aldon, Jacob, and Greg. She knew about sex and masturbation from the copy of *Our Bodies, Ourselves* that her mother had given to her after she'd gotten her period. But she had never heard it discussed so openly, or with so much pleasure. She certainly would never have expected to hear Aldon admit to masturbating.

"Um, ok then," Greg said. He looked both amused and completely discombobulated. "My turn? Ok. Never have I ever…kissed Ruth." He craned his neck to look past Aldon at Ricky.

Ruth let her jaw drop. Ricky stared back at Greg. He waved nine fingers at him.

"Oh, come on!" Greg said. He looked at both of them. "Seriously? Aren't you guys dating?"

"Who says we're not?" Ricky asked.

"So, you're dating but haven't kissed?"

"That wasn't your question," Ricky said. "You didn't say, 'Never have I ever dated Ruth.'"

Greg rolled his eyes. "Sorry. I thought we were at a point where we did more than hold hands at the mall."

Ruth glanced at Aldon and smiled. "If Aldon can put a finger down in response to Greg's question—about having sex with Aldon, then I'm going to put my finger down to this question.'"

"You go, girl!" Aldon yelled, and put her hand up for a high five. Ruth reached over to slap her hand.

"Damn," Greg said, shaking his head. "I really, really want to hear more about this stuff from both of you ladies."

"What do you want to know?" Ruth asked.

"Well, you know." Greg lowered his voice. "How do you do it?"

Ruth raised her eyebrows. "Really?" She looked at Aldon. "You've never showed him?"

"She's showed me," Greg said hotly. "I think I'm pretty damn good at it."

"You're ok, sweetie," Aldon said.

"But, when you're masturbating, do you go inside yourselves?" Greg asked. "You know, like a dick, but with a finger?"

Ruth laughed. Aldon patted her boyfriend on the shoulder.

"What?" Greg asked.

"You can, I guess," Aldon said. "But…" Aldon shook her head and started giggling.

"Oh, c'mon!" Greg said.

Ruth slipped her arm around Ricky. "I guess you could do that if you had a vibrator or something. But the money spot is on the outside."

"The clit?" Greg asked.

Ruth winked at him. "You got it."

Greg turned to Rebekah. "And what about you? You in on this?"

Rebekah shook her head. "I have not had sex with Aldon, and I've never kissed Ruth. And if you want to know any more, you'll need to ask in the form of a 'never' statement."

Greg grimaced.

"Ok, let's move on," Jacob said. He tapped his fingers on the table. "Next."

"What?" Greg asked. "Dude."

"Stop it," Jacob said. "You're bothering these ladies."

"Oh, whatever," Greg said. "They love talking this stuff."

"Not with you," Jacob said. "Aldon, it's your turn."

"Ok," Aldon said. She kissed Greg on the cheek. "I'll show you later, baby."

"Uh huh."

"Never have I ever…" Aldon paused. "Never have I ever kissed a girl."

Rebekah looked around the table. Greg, Jacob, and Ricky had each put down a finger. And then Rebekah noticed that Ruth had two fingers down.

"You've…kissed a girl, Ruth?" Aldon asked.

Ruth nodded. "I have."

"Who?" Greg wanted to know.

"The 'who' shall remain unnamed, for now," Ruth responded. She shrugged. "We were at a party, and we got drunk and just did it. It happens. Stop looking so shocked, you guys! I had no idea you all were a bunch of Puritans."

"Was it better than kissing boys?" Greg asked.

"In many, many ways, Greg," Ruth said.

Rebekah felt a slow tingling make its way from her toes, up through her hips, to her fingertips. She was a foreigner without a passport. She felt so green, so vanilla, so goddamn chaste—she had experienced nothing, not even a kiss. What if they knew? Would they judge her? Expel her? Send her back to third grade with a sippy cup and an overgrown diaper? The possibility of such acute loneliness made Rebekah feel sick. She was a senior in high school. It was time. What was a little lie? Rebekah slowly lowered a finger.

"Whoa!" Jacob said.

"Really?" Ruth asked. The word came out high-pitched and abrupt, like the sudden braking of a car. She was staring at Rebekah curiously.

Rebekah nodded solemnly.

"I have to ask," Greg said. "Who?"

"I plead the Fifth, like my good friends Ruth and Ricky."

"Pussies, all of you," Greg said.

"Ok, you guys, clear a space here, I've got your food." Esmerelda had arrived with two trays with plates of food on them. She set them down one by one. "You know, I was your-all ages once. Enjoy it, you guys. You have it good. Enjoy." She bowed deeply, with an arm sweep, then turned and walked away.

"Bye guys!" Ruth yelled across P.J.'s parking lot. "See you tomorrow? Four o'clock?"

"Bye!" Greg shouted back. He was leading Aldon, Jacob, and Ricky toward the white minivan on loan from his parents. It was nearly one, and Esmerelda had summarily kicked them out of the diner.

"Bye, Ruthie! I'll miss you tonight!" Ricky blew a kiss toward Ruth and Rebekah.

"I'll miss you, too, baby!" Ruth called back.

"Wish I was going home with you, instead of this cad," Ricky said, with a playful look toward Greg.

Greg stopped mid-stride, turned around, and ran back toward Ricky. He picked him up in a bear hug. Ricky screamed.

"I love you man," Greg yelled into Ricky's chest. Greg dropped Ricky and threw back his arms. "IT IS I!" Greg bellowed.

Ricky grabbed the keys from him, opened the driver's side door of the van, and stuffed Greg Askey into his seat. He gave one last wave to Ruth and Rebekah, and then disappeared into the passenger side.

Rebekah looked at Ruth and laughed. Ruth was shaking her head and rolling her eyes.

Ruth had inherited a car from her dad, an old, black four-door BMW sedan. It was a good car, still running well for carrying 200,000 miles. Ruth had offered to give Rebekah a ride home, since they lived in the same neighborhood. Rebekah strapped herself into the passenger seat while Ruth adjusted the rearview mirror.

"Ah," Rebekah said, rubbing the dashboard. "How long has it been since I've been in this car?"

"Oh, man," Ruth responded. She turned the key in the ignition. The engine guffawed a few times, but eventually turned over.

"A while, I think, Ruth said. "You weren't around for the cast parties last year, right?"

Rebekah shook her head.

"Yeah. Well…I don't know then. Eighth grade? Has it really been that long?"

"Yeah, I guess," Rebekah said. "How's your family?"

Ruth sighed. "My older sister Emily went to college this last year, which means that my dad isn't paying as much child support. Which means that my mom is talking like she's going to try to take him to court again."

"Oh, shit. Well…I mean, what does that—?"

"I don't think we're going to need to move," Ruth said, matter-of-factly. "My mom can afford it. She just needs to, like, get over it, you know?"

"Yeah," Rebekah said, nodding.

"It's not a big deal. My dad's a good guy, and my mom's a good person. They just don't get along, and over petty shit, too. They fight over where I'm going to be on Christmas break." Ruth came to a stop at a red light and turned to face Rebekah.

"Isn't that ridiculous? And my dad is saying that's he's going to Mexico for a few days, and I should come, and then mom says that if he can afford to go to Mexico, he can afford to help her out with the house a little more, and how selfish he is, and blah blah blah." Ruth faced forward again and shook her head. "It's just dumb."

"Yeah, that sucks," Rebekah said.

"Like I said," Ruth said, moving the card forward again, "it's not that big of a deal. But you'd think that now that they're divorced, they'd stop fighting."

"How long has it been, again?"

"Two years. After twenty-one years together. I still can't believe it." Ruth stared out the windshield. Rebekah wasn't sure what to say. Rebekah used to see Mr. and Mrs. Kinder quite a bit. Ruth talked about how they fought a lot, but Rebekah had brushed it off. Didn't everyone's parents fight?

"Anyway, moving on…so how are you, Bekah? How's your family?"

"Oh, you know, same old, same old. David is still at USC, my parents are still doing the same thing. Not much has changed."

There was an awkward silence. They were about two minutes away from Rebekah's house. Rebekah watched the familiar scenery pass out the window: the gnarled oak tree on the corner; the place where the sidewalk dipped, then disappeared into the asphalt; the house with the tarp over the front, whose owner hadn't replaced the siding in two years.

Rebekah turned back to look at Ruth. "So, what's going on between you and Ricky?" Rebekah asked carefully.

Ruth started to laugh and glanced at her. "You too?"

Rebekah shrugged. "Well, you guys act like you're together."

Ruth rolled her eyes. "Oh, man." She was silent for a few seconds, staring out the windshield. Finally she spoke. "I'm going to tell you this because we've been friends for a long time, ok? But you can't talk about it."

Rebekah felt her heart flutter with excitement. "Ok," she said.

"Ricky and I are definitely not together. We've spent a lot of time together lately, because of, you know, the play and everything. And I enjoy his company, and I think he enjoys mine. And when we're together, we just hang out, or rehearse, or do whatever, and it's not a big deal."

"But you guys hold hands around campus and stuff."

"Yeah, but that doesn't mean anything. We just hold hands."

Rebekah considered this for a moment.

Ruth pulled up in front of the Cohayn house and turned off the car. She faced Rebekah. "Bekah...Ricky isn't into girls."

Rebekah raised her eyebrows. "What do you mean?"

Ruth stared at her. "I don't think he's into girls," she repeated.

Rebekah stared back. "So...you mean...he's...like...gay, or something?"

Ruth shrugged. "Does it matter?"

"Wow," Rebekah said. "Well, I guess not."

"Good." Ruth faced forward again. She was leaning forward, her arms draped over the steering wheel.

Rebekah, still sitting in her seat with her seatbelt on, searched Ruth's face. She saw confusion and sadness, a wistfulness that had been absent for the previous few hours. It was a look she had never seen before. Rebekah thought back to the Ten Fingers game—to Ricky's reluctant reaction, Ruth's empathy. Suddenly, Rebekah started forward.

"Oh!" Rebekah said. "So...does that mean you're gay?"

Ruth sighed deeply. She put her head on the steering wheel.

"I don't know, Bekah," she said into her lap.

"Oh. Well don't worry about it. It doesn't matter to me." Rebekah leaned back into her seat and swallowed hard. Her face was flushed, her stomach in knots. She sat no more than a foot from Ruth, and could feel the heat from their bodies filling up the small car. She didn't know why she suddenly felt so nervous. She shifted her feet, pressing the sole of one shoe into the toes of her other shoe. The crackling energy she had felt earlier in the night was different now, fuzzier, harder to explain.

Ruth looked at Rebekah. She had tears in her eyes. "You're the only person who could know, besides Ricky. But, like, I don't know what I am, you know? It just…it just, like, makes my head hurt to think about. So I try not to." She wiped at her eyes. She smiled. "But thanks, Bekah. You're a good friend."

"Hey, no problem." Rebekah looked over at Ruth. Ruth was looking at her wide-eyed, desperate, trying to read Rebekah's face. Rebekah smiled back at her, hoping Ruth couldn't detect her anxiety. She could feel the blood pulsing in her temples. Her lips felt thick and dry.

"Hey, well…I should probably get going," Ruth said.

Rebekah swallowed and looked away. "Me too. I bet my mom is sleeping on the couch in the living room, waiting for me to come in."

Ruth laughed. "Just like your mom, man. Go tell her she can go to sleep."

"Ok. But seriously, Ruthie—any time you want to talk, ok?"

Ruth nodded. "Ok."

Rebekah pushed open the car door, and stepped out into the cool night. "See you tomorrow, Ruth."

"See ya, kid," Ruth replied.

Rebekah closed the car door and slowly walked into her house.

The Awakening
December, 2000

Rebekah did not have any distinctive physical characteristics that would have marked her as an undesirable commodity. Her face was nice enough, symmetrical. Her glasses showed off her high cheekbones and the softness of her eyes. She was awkward, but not clumsy enough to be picked on; graceless, but self-aware enough of her flaws to avoid attention. Rebekah was healthy, active, and pleasant. Distinctly unmemorable.

Rebekah had never been crushed on, and in return, had never crushed on anyone else. The world of love and lust, of passion and desire, seemed so outside the realm of possibility to her that she simply never expended any energy on it. Her feelings toward peers whom she found attractive had been more along the lines of curiosity and admiration.

But Ruth.

Ruth and Rebekah had been friends for a long time. So how was it possible that one night, one conversation could awaken Rebekah to the possibility that Ruth could be something more? Were friendships so changeable? Were feelings so flammable? Were the lines between friendship and love, admiration and lust, so permeable that they could be crossed innocently and unwittingly?

During the next few weeks, Rebekah walked her school's hallways with a pounding heart, her head down, thumbs looped into her backpack's arm straps. When she walked past the school theater—where Ruth, Ricky, Greg Askey, and some of the other theater kids hung out—she glanced towards it hungrily, hoping to spot Ruth. She usually did, spying her friend sitting cross-legged on the cement with Ricky, engaged in a conversation as impenetrable to Rebekah as if it had been in a foreign language.

Sometimes when Rebekah walked by, she would catch Ruth looking out towards the school quad. If they caught each other's eyes, they smiled and waved. Rebekah would feel her face flush. Her thighs quivered. Her groin flushed with heat and pleasure. Sometimes

Rebekah paused, wondering if she should walk over to say hi. She never did.

One frosty December morning, Rebekah walked by the theater and saw Ruth watching her. Rebekah waved. Ruth waved back, but this time waved her over. Rebekah froze, midstride. She glanced at her watch—seven minutes before she needed to be at her next class. She hurried over to the theater, where Ruth and Ricky were sitting under the overhang above the doorway.

"Hey, girl," Ricky said, squinting at her. He was wearing black cargo pants and a long-sleeve white shirt. "Damn, I shoulda brought my sunglasses to school today."

Ruth looked at him. "It's pretty gray out. Portland, remember?" She looked up at Rebekah. "Hey, sit down for a minute."

Rebekah obeyed, dropping her backpack and sitting cross-legged between Ruth and Ricky.

"What are you doing this Saturday?"

Rebekah answered quickly. "Nothing."

"Ricky was going to come over, and we were just going to hang out and watch a movie. Wanna come?"

Rebekah's heart pounded. It had been years since she'd been inside the Kinder's house.

"Yeah, that would be great," Rebekah said. "It will be nice to see your mom, too."

Ruth nodded and smiled. "Awesome."

Ricky looked at Rebekah skeptically. "And...aren't you going to ask what movie we're going to watch?"

"Sure. What movie?"

"Have you seen *The Big Lebowski*?" Ruth asked.

"*The Big Lebowski*," Rebekah repeated. "Maybe. Is that the one about bowling?"

"I guess it's sort of about bowling," Ricky said. "It's about bowling the way *Pulp Fiction* is about boxing."

"I haven't seen the whole thing."

That was partially true. Rebekah hadn't seen the whole thing because she hadn't actually seen any of it.

"Well, Ruth told me that she hadn't seen it, and it's just like, one of my favorite movies, ever, so I told her we had to watch it," Ricky said. "I don't know what's wrong with you guys. It came out two years ago."

Ruth smiled at Rebekah. "It's supposed to have a really good cast."

"From the little I saw, it does," Rebekah lied.

"Great," Ricky said. Ok. See you Saturday, then?"

"Yeah." Rebekah stood up. The first bell rang, indicating that they had only two minutes to get to class. "Well, see you guys."

"Bye!" Ricky said.

Rebekah walked away feeling stupefied. She felt the same way that she had at PJ's: hot, agitated, like she was stepping into a sauna. Her feet shuffled forward unconsciously, carrying her to her next class. She opened her mouth, sucked in air until her chest was full, and then breathed out through a smile in shaky, anxious spurts.

"Bekah! Hi!"

Paula Kinder wrapped her arms around Rebekah in a tight hug. After a few seconds, she stood back and examined her daughter's friend. "Gosh, time flies, doesn't it? You've grown so much. How are your parents?"

"They're good," Rebekah replied with a smile. "How are you doing?" As she spoke, Rebekah tried to peek past Paula into the family room, where she could hear Ruth and Ricky laughing.

"Oh, I'm doing ok, I'm doing ok," Paula said. She gave Rebekah a kind, tired smile. "And how's David?"

Rebekah nodded. "David's good, I think. He lives in L.A. now, so I don't see as much of him anymore. But he seems happy."

"Great." Paula paused and studied her intently. Paula had always been an intense, thoughtful woman. Her ex-husband, Dale, was a civil engineer with the Department of Transportation. Dale was quiet, awkward, and painfully nerdy. Paula, who worked as a psychologist at an elementary school, was warm, attentive, and easy to talk to. Ruth had never explained their reasons for divorcing, but Rebekah wondered how two people so different could have gotten married in the first place.

"You look so nice tonight," Paula offered.

Rebekah laughed nervously. "Thanks." She was wearing a new pair of jeans that she had just purchased at the Gap. It had small, manufactured rips in the thighs. Rebekah also had opted to wear a V-neck, black long-sleeve shirt.

"Well, why don't you go join Ruth and Ricky? I think they're about to start the movie."

"Thanks, Paula." Rebekah took a step forward and nearly tripped over herself.

"You ok?" Paula asked.

Rebekah tried to laugh. "I'm fine, thanks." She turned again—bright red and embarrassed by the exchange—and hurried into the family room.

Ruth and Ricky were sitting next to each other on the Kinder's worn brown fabric couch. They had their heads together, laughing and whispering about something. When Rebekah walked in, they looked up.

"Hey, hey," Ricky said. "You look nice. What's the occasion?"

Rebekah shrugged. "Just, you know, whatever."

Ruth stared at her but said nothing.

"Can we start the movie?" Ricky asked.

"Did you bond with my mom?" Ruth asked.

"Ha ha, yeah. She asked about my family," Rebekah said.

"Of course she did," Ruth said, rolling her eyes.

Ricky picked up the remote control. "Ok, Bekah, the popcorn is made—in the bowl in the kitchen. There's also some soda in the refrigerator." He looked at Ruth and they both grinned.

Rebekah searched their faces. "Soda, huh?"

Ruth peered around the corner. When she was satisfied that her mom was not about to walk into the living room, she held up a beat-up water bottle that was filled with a clear liquid.

"You could mix some of this with your soda," she whispered, shaking the bottle.

"Is that vodka?" Rebekah asked.

"Shhh!" Ruth and Ricky said in unison.

"Shit, Bekah, my mom doesn't know," Ruth whispered. "Keep it down."

"Where did you get it?" Rebekah whispered back.

"I have connections," Ricky said in a low voice.

"Hah!" Ruth said, then covered her mouth with her hand.

"What?" Ricky asked. "I do."

"If by connections, you mean that you swiped some of your parents', then I suppose we can call that connections."

"Well, I got it, didn't I?" Ricky asked.

Rebekah sat down on the couch next to Ruth. This would be her first time drinking hard liquor. *Rebekah Rachel Abrams Cohayn*, she scolded herself. *You WILL be cool tonight.*

Ricky stood up. "I'm going to get this movie started for you girls. And—since Paula seems to have disappeared for the moment— maybe I'll just take this," he said, swiping the water bottle from Ruth, "and fix us some sodas."

Ricky pointed the remote control towards the TV. The screen lit up with a movie copyright warning. Ricky disappeared into the kitchen. Over the sound of the narration coming from the screen, Rebekah could hear the refrigerator door opening.

These would be the sounds filling Rebekah's life during the months ahead: the refrigerator, ice cubes clinking into glasses, and dialogue and gunshots manufactured in a Hollywood studio. This evening quickly became part of a period in Rebekah's life that felt simultaneously stark and fuzzy, as though she was stumbling through a heavy fog in which each water molecule stood out in bleak relief. She didn't know where she was headed, but she saw—and felt—every emotion, and every setting, with raw sensitivity.

Rebekah felt Ruth sitting next to her, so close that if she moved her hand a mere inch to her right, it would cover Ruth's.

Ricky walked back into the family room and handed Ruth and Rebekah each a glass of Coke and vodka.

"Cheers," he whispered. They clinked their glasses and drank.

Rebekah took a long drink. She held the vodka and Coke in her mouth, grimacing, forcing herself to taste it. She relaxed into the couch, surprised by how much she relished the easy warmth of the alcohol.

Rebekah drank a sip every few minutes. The Dude was attacked, his rug destroyed; the Dude sought recompense from the Big Lebowski, only to get tied up in a twisted kidnapping scheme. Rebekah drank slowly, losing awareness of the movie's convoluted plot line, the house, and Ricky. She became focused solely and completely on Ruth: Ruth's breathing, Ruth's hand, Ruth crossing and uncrossing her legs, Ruth laughing, Ruth slowly, imperceptibly slipping a hand on top of Rebekah's.

Three-quarters of the way through the movie, Rebekah was drunk, clinging to a fading grasp of reality. Ruth was no longer human to her, but a mystical creature that had climbed inside her ribcage, grasped her lungs, and was playing piano with her intestines. She was not coherent enough to consider how astonishing this moment was: for the first time in Rebekah's short life, she desperately wanted to be with someone else. And that someone else happened to be Ruth.

At some point the movie ended, and Ruth moved her hand. Rebekah sat on the couch, stunned and drunk, unsure of what to do or say. Ruth stood up. "Hey, you drunkey monkeys, you better stay the night," she said, stretching.

"Oh, yay," Ricky replied. "I thought you'd never offer. And where shall we take to bed?"

"Hm." Ruth looked around. "Do you want the spare room?"

"I suppose that would be adequate," Ricky said. He glanced at Rebekah. "And what about this one?"

Rebekah closed her eyes. With the lights on, the movie done, and Ruth standing in front of her instead of holding her hand, her sense of disembodied integration with the universe began to wear off. Now she just had a headache.

Sitting on the couch with her eyes closed, she missed a silent exchange between Ruth and Ricky. It was the kind of exchange that happens without words, between close friends who are capable of reading emotions in each other's eyes. Ruth stared at him with a pleading gaze; Ricky stared back, puzzled for a moment. Then he snapped his head up, opened his eyes wide, formed an "O" with his mouth, and nodded his understanding. He gave her a hug, rubbed Rebekah's head, and left.

Rebekah, lost at sea under the influence of love and alcohol, vaguely felt Ruth's hand gently grab her arm and help her stand. The next morning, she didn't remember falling asleep or saying goodnight to Ricky. But she did remember Ruth's hand on her arm, gently leading her to her bedroom.

A few hours later, Rebekah sat up with a start. She could tell by the white light filtering into the room that it was late in the morning. She looked down. She was wearing the same clothes that she had been wearing the night before. Her new black shirt was wrinkled and bunching around her stomach. Rebekah quickly pulled it down. Rebekah looked around. She recognized aspects of Ruth's room that looked the same as they had when they were children. Ruth's much-loved brown teddy bear, Alphie, was still sitting on top of her bookshelf. The same small desk, now covered with a desktop computer and textbooks, was pushed up against the wall on the opposite side of the bedroom. The walls, once covered with finished puzzles glued together for her by her dad, were now covered with movie posters: *A Clockwork Orange, The Godfather, Requiem for a Dream.*

She was alone in Ruth's twin bed, which seemed odd to her. Where was Ruth? She threw back the covers and swung her legs over the side of the bed. She was just about to step down when she felt a hand grab her ankle.

"Hey, you're up," Ruth said. She yawned.

"Hey," Rebekah said. Ruth was lying on top of an air mattress on the floor of her bedroom. She was wearing green and white striped pajamas. Her hair was tousled.

"You slept on the floor?" Rebekah asked, confused.

"Yeah, sure did," Ruth replied. "I suppose I could have put you on the floor—you wouldn't have known the difference—but I didn't think that was the proper host thing for me to do."

"Oh," Rebekah said.

"Oh man…you got pretty drunk last night," Ruth said. "Have you ever had that much to drink before?"

"No," Rebekah said. She rubbed her forehead. "I don't think I'm drunk now though. I don't have a headache."

"Well, that's good. But drink lots of water today. I bet you're dehydrated."

Ruth stood up and stretched. "Let's get up. I bet Ricky is still asleep. I'm going to run downstairs and jump on him." Ruth stood up and walked out the door. Rebekah sat on the bed for a few moments before getting up to follow her.

The Crucible
April, 2001

Sexual attraction: the endocrinal activity that marks the end of childhood and the beginning of orientations. Straight and gay orientations. Top and bottom orientations. Vanilla and kinky orientations. Reorientations, disorientations, non-orientations. The epoch of orientations begins when one reaches double digits and ends at death.

If considered primarily from a dermatological perspective, sexual attraction can be characterized as the rushing of blood to the topmost surface of skin. Your face flushes. Your hands sweat. Your nose twitches, and your groin aches. You feel as though the sun is composed of a thousand needles, each one pricking you like a cosmic acupuncturist. Your blood vessels congregate and dilate. Your capillaries actuate.

From a neurological point of view, sexual attraction might be described as a waking stroke, characterized by slurred, stuttering speech, impeded thought, mass confusion. Abnormal, often reckless behavior. Personality changes that may prompt loved ones to search the Diagnostic and Statistical Manual of Mental Disorders.

Sexual attraction: Was that what Rebekah felt toward Ruth? Rebekah found herself rather apathetic about most of Ruth's physical features. Ruth's breasts seemed normal, full, breast-like; probably an annoyance to Ruth, merely an aftershock from puberty. Ruth wasn't overweight, but she wasn't the spindly-legged sprite she had been in sixth grade. Her hips had widened, her shoulders had broadened, and her thighs had become thicker. Her long blond hair fell in waves, rarely blow-dried. Ruth didn't wear make-up unless she was on stage.

But Ruth's face—Ruth's face was a different story. Rebekah fell asleep and woke up thinking about Ruth's face. When Ruth's green eyes twinkled, Rebekah felt her face flush. When Ruth laughed, Rebekah's lungs emptied of air, and she felt herself gasping like a beached whale. When Ruth stared into space, Rebekah's nose twitched and her stomach ached.

At the very least, there seemed to be something else, some indescribable charm that Ruth possessed, that lured Rebekah beyond the bounds of rationality and sound judgment. If a woman's face is said to contain all the elements of enchantment, Rebekah may have admitted that she was neurologically and dermatologically smitten. After the evening at the Kinder house, Rebekah found herself wandering over to the theater to sit with Ruth and Ricky at breaks, at lunchtime, and then after school, during play rehearsals. Ricky and Ruth absorbed their extra appendage with little fanfare, as if Rebekah had always been part of their small group. Spending time with Ruth felt deliciously comfortable.

Rebekah loved Ricky. She loved him for the way he loved Ruth, and she loved him because he seemed to know, somehow, why she was there. He never said anything that confirmed this suspicion. He just smiled kindly at her, and blew her kisses, and put his arm around her to whisper secrets in her ear. Ricky also started coming up with excuses for being unable to make it to weekend movie nights anymore—and Rebekah loved him endlessly for that.

Without Ricky to supply the alcohol, Ruth and Rebekah drank virgin sodas in the evenings. Rebekah would start the movie, while Ruth fixed them Diet Coke with ice in the kitchen. She would come back in, hand Rebekah her glass, sit down next to her on the couch, and put her hand on top of Rebekah's. Holding hands during movie night was just something they did now.

Rebekah always spent these nights at Ruth's. She told herself she was avoiding the dangers of walking home alone, by herself, late at night. She checked with her parents, who approved of the decision and praised her for her foresight and responsible decision-making. After each movie ended, Rebekah and Ruth walked upstairs to Ruth's bedroom. Sometimes Ruth was too tired to set up the air mattress, so she and Rebekah shared the twin bed. They snuggled close together—because of the smallness and the bed and the cold winter nights, which persisted, even through March and April—with Ruth usually pressed up against Rebekah's back. Ruth allowed her top arm to wrap around Rebekah's shoulder, and she twisted her ankles around Rebekah's legs. Rebekah lay in bed on her side, her legs curled up and pressed together, marveling at her luck at finding such a good friend and utterly confused by the fluttering of her heart.

The first time Ruth and Rebekah kissed was in April of 2001.

"Well, hello again, Rebekah!" Paula said, as Rebekah walked through the door on a Saturday evening.

"Hi, Mrs. Kinder," Rebekah said. "How are you?"

"Fine, fine. You know, the usual. I'm just running out to meet a friend for a late coffee date. You two going to be ok by yourselves here?"

Paula Kinder was wearing a black top, a gold skirt, and white pumps. She had put on bright red lipstick and teased her hair into a curled coif.

Some coffee date, Rebekah thought. "Sure, Mrs. Kinder. We'll be fine."

Paula leaned down and gave her a kiss on the cheek. "Of course you will. Be good!"

Rebekah walked into the family room. She was wearing a red polo shirt, blue jeans, and black Chuck Taylors. Ruth, she noticed, had dressed down. She wore gray sweatpants and a blue sweatshirt that was fraying around the collar.

Ruth smiled at Rebekah. "I've been in my sweats all day and didn't feel like changing. Do you mind?"

Rebekah shook her head. "No, no, not at all." She sat down on the couch.

"Did you pick up *Trainspotting*?"

"Well…" Ruth walked over to the DVD player and held up a box. " They were out of *Trainspotting*. I rented *Gia* instead…ever heard of it?"

"Yeah, I've heard of it. The one with Angelina Jolie, right?"

"Yep."

"Yeah, never seen it."

"Good! So you're ok with the switch, then?"

Rebekah nodded.

Ruth popped the DVD into the player, and hit "play." The previews rolled as Ruth walked into the kitchen. Ruth shared the week's gossip: Mr. McDonough, the math teacher and volleyball coach, was rumored to be moving to Seattle to coach a team that won the state championships every year, and the principal was panicking about how to placate angry parents; Aldon Coombs had dumped Greg Askey just two months before graduation because she wanted to be single over the summer, and Greg was simultaneously heartbroken and furious that he hadn't dumped her first; and two boys had decided to streak across the quad during lunch hour as a senior prank, and now faced criminal charges.

"Idiots," Ruth snorted, concluding the story about the senior boys. She walked back into the living room with the drinks.

"So now what? Are they going to be listed on sex offender registries?"

"Yeah, something like that. I bet they'll go to court over it. I also don't know if they're going to be allowed to walk in graduation."

"Wow."

"Fucked up, right? Ooh, and I almost forgot to tell you the most important thing of all."

"What?" Rebekah asked.

"Ricky has a boyfriend."

"What?" Rebekah nearly dropped her drink. She grabbed the remote control, paused the movie and turned to face Ruth. "A boyfriend? Who?"

"He's a college student from Lewis and Clark. They met at a party. They've been hooking up, and now I guess they're kinda dating." Rebekah stared at Ruth.

"What?" Ruth asked. "Is this really that surprising to you? Do you think he just stopped coming to movie night because he didn't like movies anymore?"

I thought he stopped coming to give us time alone, Rebekah thought.

"No, I just…" Rebekah grinned at Ruth. "I guess I just expected him to date high school guys, that's all."

"Psh. He says he doesn't like any of the guys in our school, that they're either hot and in the closet, or out and unattractive."

"What's his name?" Rebekah asked.

"Tommy, I think."

"Ricky and Tommy," Rebekah considered the names. "That's pretty gay."

Ruth nodded and picked up the remote control. "I think so. And I think they like it that way."

The movie came back on, and Rebekah leaned back into the couch. She inched her left hand closer to Ruth in anticipation of feeling Ruth's close over her own. But instead, Rebekah felt Ruth's arm wrap around the back of her shoulders. Rebekah stiffened.

"This ok?" Ruth asked. She seemed relaxed, affecting a nonchalance that belied her usual attentive focus on the movie.

"Yeah," Rebekah stammered. Her throat had closed up. She could barely breathe. They were so close that, if Rebekah leaned in slightly to her left, she could put her head on Ruth's shoulder. Rebekah kept her gaze straight ahead, her head perfectly still, as if she was balancing a tray of hot tea.

Gia would have been a curious choice for any two teenagers. The story of the drug-addled, sexually adventurous, and extraordinarily talented model was provocative and edgy, graphic and raw. Angelina Jolie was hot, intense, at her career-best as Gia. For two girls falling in love, the selection was prescient.

Twenty minutes into the movie, Gia had sex with her makeup artist, Linda. Rebekah and Ruth watched the sex scene unfold in graphic detail. They saw everything: bodies, hands on stomachs and legs, lips and eyes and hair and toes and fingers. They saw Gia's lips, impossibly full with sex and hunger, making their way down Gia's torso.

Rebekah shifted uncomfortably. She pressed her palms against the couch and held her breath, trying to ignore the sound of Ruth breathing. Rebekah felt too warm, as though she was stuck in the back seat of a car with the windows rolled up. For the first time all night, she wished that Ruth would lift her arm from around her shoulders.

And much to Rebekah's surprise, Ruth did.

"I'm hot," Ruth said, as she stood up from the couch. Linda and Gia were still in the throes of their one-night stand when Ruth pulled off her sweater, tossed it onto the kitchen table, and sat down again, this time with her arms at her sides and her hands in her lap.

Rebekah and Ruth sat only inches apart for the remainder of the movie, but those inches constituted an impassable gulf. Something had changed. Something involving a sweatered arm and a sex scene and two girls had blown apart. Now it sat, broken and scattered, in the Kinder family room. Rebekah and Ruth both faced forward, not speaking, pretending to watch the movie.

When the movie ended, Ruth and Rebekah stayed seated on the couch watching the credits roll. Finally, Rebekah stood up and stretched. "Good movie," Rebekah offered.

"Yep," Ruth said. She was staring straight ahead, her lips pressed together.

"Well…I guess that's it." Rebekah looked around the living room. "I'm going upstairs." She turned and walked out of the room and up the stairs, without waiting for a reply.

Rebekah walked into Ruth's room, threw herself onto the bed and faced the wall, willing herself not to cry. If she heard Ruth drag in the air mattress, she knew she would lose it completely. She wanted to be so close to her, to wrap her arms around her and feel her body pressed up against her own. There was something so wanton in the way she thought about Ruth, something carnal and base that went way beyond the bounds of friendship.

This is wrong, Rebekah thought. *Wrong wrong wrong wrong wrong.* Rebekah pushed her forehead up against the wall. She was wrong. These sleepovers were wrong. Everything about movie night and Ruth, and her life, and love and friendship, was wrong and incomplete, immoral and ugly, wrong wrong wrong, and what would her parents say if they knew she felt like this? What would Paula say? What would David say?

The nervous excitement that had carried in her stomach since the night at PJ's had turned into soapstone. It was heavy now, an anchor. She felt darkness closing in around her, the black hood descending around her eyes and nose and mouth.

If Rebekah was terrified of the darkness, she also couldn't quite bring herself to shrug it off. Rebekah loved Ruth, desperately, and she wanted to show her—she wanted to show her, and simultaneously to stuff her feelings into her stomach, and put on her adult face, and pretend that nothing, nothing had ever happened between them but the most Protestant of friendships.

Rebekah heard the door crack open, then shut again. The light clicked off. Rebekah, still in her clothes, closed her eyes and pretended to be asleep. Rebekah heard Ruth walk over to the side of the bed. Rebekah didn't move. Her heart pounded so loudly in her ears that she was sure Ruth could hear it.

After a few long seconds, Rebekah felt Ruth climb into bed. Rebekah involuntarily exhaled—and inadvertently moaned softly. Then she felt Ruth press up against her and wrap her arm around her stomach.

"Rebekah," Ruth whispered.

Rebekah didn't move. She felt stiff and incapacitated. She imagined herself tied to a body board, blindfolded, carried to an ambulance by a phalanx of firefighters. There was safety in stillness.

"Rebekah," Ruth whispered again. "Please."

The firefighters dropped the body board on the sidewalk, and it shattered into nothing. Her ropes snapped. Now she was lying on the sidewalk, alone, the fire truck gone, listening to Ruth's voice. She was free-floating. There were sirens and lights and emptiness, and Ruth's voice was calling to her from the loneliest sky she'd ever seen.

"Just turn over and talk to me."

Rebekah swallowed hard, took a deep breath—a breath marked by hiccups and shudders and a shaky, uncertain exhalation—and rolled over to face Ruth.

The girls held their breaths and stared at each other. Their gaze stretched from nose to nose, as if they were sharing one oxygen mask, connected by a rutted plastic tube. The air was hot. Rebekah felt pressure behind her eyeballs.

Rebekah saw the corners of Ruth's eyes dip. It looked as if she was struggling not to cry. Rebekah raised her hand to her face, to touch her, and Ruth leaned in and kissed Rebekah.

Ruth's lips were warm and soft. The kiss lasted a long second, during which Rebekah closed her eyes and moved her hand to Ruth's shoulder. When they pulled away from each other, their lips felt elastic, as if they were pulling apart freshly baked rolls.

Their eyes met. Rebekah could feel Ruth shivering. "Are you cold?" Rebekah whispered.

"No," Ruth whispered back.

A few moments later, Ruth leaned in to kiss her again. Rebekah didn't stop her. They kissed, slowly, with their mouths closed, content to explore each other's lips. The kiss went on for a few minutes, not a particularly long time, and certainly not the longest kiss the two would share. But at the time, it felt like an immeasurable expanse to Rebekah.

After the girls pulled apart for the last time, Rebekah sat up. It was dark in the bedroom, save for some gray light streaming in from the windows. She felt Ruth touch her back.

"You ok?" Ruth asked.

"I don't know," Rebekah said. The pressure behind her eyes had suddenly transitioned into a full-blown headache. Her throat was still tight, her stomach in knots. She felt as though she was going to vomit. *What am I going to tell my mom?* Rebekah thought. *What am I going to tell David?*

"Ruth, I think I need to go home," Rebekah said.

Ruth quickly sat up. "Why?"

"I'm not feeling good."

"What? Why?"

"I don't know."

"Bekah, we need to talk about this. I didn't mean to…"

"Ruth." Rebekah held up her hand. The room was spinning. "Later. I just need to go home."

Rebekah pushed herself to the front of the bed and stood up.

"Bekah, please." Ruth was crying now. "Don't go."

"We'll talk Monday, ok?"

"No, Bekah, please, please stay. If you're not feeling good, please stay."

Rebekah pushed the door of the bedroom open. She turned halfway back into the bedroom. She didn't want to look at Ruth. She felt too ashamed to see her face, too heartbroken to watch her cry.

"Ruth, I'm sorry, I just can't be here right now. We'll talk later."

Rebekah stepped out and softly closed the bedroom door behind her. She tiptoed down the stairs and ran across the foyer and out the front door. Rebekah was halfway down the front lawn when she realized that she had forgotten her jacket. "Shit," Rebekah hissed.

She briefly considered going back inside, but the thought of another conversation with Ruth was horrifying. Rebekah resolutely turned, crossed the yard, and walked into the street. The rain was falling heavily now, pelting her face and her hunched back. It was only a ten-minute walk to the house, seven if she shuffled her feet quickly, as she was doing now.

I'm not gay. I'm not gay. I'm not gay. I'm not gay, Rebekah repeated to herself.

So what was that with Ruth?

I'm not gay. I'm not gay. I'm not gay.

It became a mantra, to match the pounding of her feet on the street.

I'm. Not. Gay. Breath. *I'm. Not. Gay.*

It felt like a dream. A jagged ripping of her identity. The experimentation that she had wanted so badly had led her to a new self—a self she no longer recognized. Who could she tell? What was she playing at? How had she gone from being a normal, near-sighted Jewish girl living a quiet life in Portland, Oregon, to a lesbian?

The door she had cracked open was now fully ajar, and it looked like a burned out moonscape on the other side.

Rebekah got home dripping wet and gently tried to open the front door. It was locked. Her parents had installed a key box on the side of the house, accessible with a code, in case she was ever locked out. Rebekah padded around to the side of the house, opened the box, and punched in the code. It popped open. There were no keys inside.

"Fuck!" Rebekah cursed quietly. She slammed her palm against the house. She had forgotten that she'd used the code box earlier this week. The keys were sitting upstairs in her room.

Rebekah walked back around to the front of the house and sat on the stoop. She imagined passing the rest of the night here, waiting until morning, when her dad came out to pick up the newspaper. She would be cold and wet. She could make up a story about Ruth having an early Sunday morning event to attend, tell her father that she had only waited outside for ten minutes, tops. Everyone would be happy. No one would ask any questions.

A few minutes later, Rebekah's resolve was wavering. She was so cold, she could barely bend her fingers. She thought of her dad, coming outside in the morning to pick up the paper, and instead finding his daughter's frozen body on the stoop, curled up in a ball. She thought about David, and how furious he would be that she had upset her parents. And she thought about Ruth, poor Ruth, who, Rebekah imagined, would only blame herself.

It was this last thought that forced Rebekah to stand up and, with a trembling finger, ring the doorbell. A minute later, the front door cracked open.

"Bekah?" Daniel asked incredulously.

"Hi." Rebekah said. She pushed her way inside. Both of her parents stood in the doorway, in their slippers and robes, squinting at their wet, bedraggled daughter.

"What happened? Judith asked. "Why aren't you at Ruth's house?"

"It's a long story, Mom. I'll tell you tomorrow."

Rebekah walked past them to her bedroom and shut the door. She sat on her chair and closed her eyes. *I'm not gay. I'm not gay. I'm not gay.* The rain beat a chant outside her window.

Rebekah heard a knock on the door. "Go away!" Rebekah yelled. *I'm not gay. I'm not gay.*

Judith opened the door and pushed her head in. "Bekah? Can we talk?"

"No."

Judith paused in the doorway. She puffed out her cheeks, swallowing the questions that wanted to push themselves out of her lips. She could see the pain etched in her Rebekah's hunched shoulders and dripping black hair, the weary lines in her forehead, and the downward slant of her eyes.

What is a mother's job, other than to protect? Protect, heal, solve, soothe—wasn't that the first element of the job description? Judith remembered how little she had known when David was born. She didn't know how to swaddle. She didn't know how to change a diaper. It took her weeks to figure out how to breastfeed. But protecting him was simple. Judith had immediately wrapped a crying David between her forearms and her chest, pressed him against her sternum, laid his head directly over heart, and whispered to him. *Shhhhhhhh. Hush.*

Teenagers were a foreign species. Independent, obnoxious, foolhardy—a riddle impossible to solve. What would warmth, a beating heart, or soft words do for the disheveled creature that had showed up at her door? Judith thought it might be best to give Rebekah space tonight and speak with her tomorrow. But the moment was ripe. If Rebekah was going to talk, she would talk right now, before she had the chance to swallow it and emerge from her bedroom tomorrow morning with a tight smile and an air-clearing lie. Judith knew that she was certainly capable of pressing her daughter into a conversation tomorrow, if necessary. She was a management analyst, a skilled conversationalist, a consummate negotiator.

Judith walked in, gently closed the door behind her, and sat on the bed.

"Mom, please." Rebekah swung around her in her chair. Her eyes were still squeezed shut.

"What's wrong, Becky?" Judith whispered.

"Mom." Rebekah spoke through gritted teeth. "I. Don't. Want. To. Talk."

Judith cleared her throat. "Fine. So we don't have to talk, then."

The girl and her mother sat in silence for a long moment, Rebekah with her head hanging and her eyes closed, Judith studying her daughter intently. The silence hung between them like a flaccid sail. Finally, Rebekah looked up. "If we're not going to talk, then why are you here?"

"Well," Judith shrugged. "My daughter showed up at my door after midnight, dripping wet, when she should be sleeping at her friend's house. I suppose I'm a little concerned. Is everything ok at the Kinder's?"

"Yeah, Mom, everything's fine."

"How's Paula? Was she home?"

"Yeah, Mom, she was home. For a minute, anyway."

"Just for a minute?"

"She went to have coffee with a friend."

"Oh," Judith said. She paused. "And Ruth? Did you and Ruth have a fight?"

Rebekah instinctively closed her eyes again. Her lower lip started to tremble.

"Was it a fight, honey? What did you fight about?"

"No, Mom, we didn't have a fight." Rebekah was choking back tears.

Judith, sensing an opening, slid off the bed and onto her knees. She sat at Rebekah's feet and put her hand on Rebekah's thigh. "It's ok, sweetheart, you can tell me."

The sweet, genuine plea from her mother struck a chord in Rebekah. The voice that had calmed her as a child was the same voice speaking to her now—sincere, unpretentious, wavering between wanting to know and wanting simply to fix.

Suddenly, Rebekah wanted to confess everything. Setting off the fire alarm in *Hamlet*. Holding hands during movie nights. Ricky's boyfriend. Kissing Ruth. But when Rebekah opened her mouth to speak, all that emerged was a heavy sob. She fell off the chair, onto the floor and into her mother's arms. Judith buried her head into her daughter's shoulder and rubbed her back.

"Shhh." Judith whispered. "It's going to be ok. It's going to be ok."

These words, though simple, and lacking any kind of predictive value or solid explanation, seemed to be a panacea for soothing her children. They were the same words she'd whispered to Rebekah when her daughter was little, not yet six years old, and had tried to flip off the monkey bars at school and landed on her wrist. She'd taken Rebekah to the hospital, where the pediatric doctors had taken a few x-rays and diagnosed her with a sprain. They wrapped a splint around her wrist and sent her home.

See? Judith said to her daughter on the drive home. *It's going to be ok.*

They were the same words that Judith said to Rebekah after bad test scores, fights with her older brother, sickness, the death of grandparents, skinned knees, fear of monsters in closets and bears in shopping centers, hunger, petulance, and anxiety. And now she said them again, this time with the unfamiliar presentiment of an irrepressible heaviness.

After ten minutes of crying, Rebekah ran out of tears. Judith stood up, grabbed a box of tissue, and handed a couple of sheets to Rebekah.

"Where's Dad?" Rebekah sniffled.

"Probably in the bedroom. Don't worry about him."

"Ok."

Judith kneeled down again. "What's wrong? Tell me."

Rebekah started to cry again. "I can't tell you."

"Oh, honey." Judith pressed her daughter into her body. "Please. Let me help you."

"I can't. I can't. I can't." Rebekah started wailing. "I can't, I can't…"

"Shhh," Judith said. She pressed her daughter's head against her shoulder and rocked back and forth. "It's going to be ok. It's going to be ok."

Rebekah took a few deep breaths. Judith let her breathe.

"What's wrong?" Judith asked.

Rebekah swallowed. She looked away from her mother.

"I kissed Ruth."

"You kissed Ruth?" Judith repeated, uncertainly. She pulled back, dropped her arms, tried to get a look at Rebekah's face.

"We kissed."

"Oh." Judith looked at her daughter with confusion. "You mean—on purpose?"

Rebekah started to laugh. Her breath caught on her throat.

"What?" Judith asked. "You ok?"

"Yeah."

"So…you kissed Ruth," Judith repeated.

Rebekah nodded.

"Why?" Judith asked.

Rebekah shrugged.

"Ok," Judith nodded. "Ok."

They sat in silence for a few moments, each on her own square of rug. Judith's hands were on her knees; Rebekah's fists were pressed up underneath her chin.

"So—so what does that mean?" Judith asked.

"What?"

"What does that mean? I don't know if I understand what you're telling me. What are you telling me? Are you—are you telling me you're gay?"

Rebekah shrugged again.

"Are you gay?" Judith asked again.

Rebekah started to cry.

Judith stared at her daughter. She blinked and looked out the window, where the spring rain was trying to beat the ground into submission. Judith squinted her eyes. "Rebekah, I don't know what this means."

Rebekah cried harder. She felt something close up inside her—a metal chain wrapped around a steel crate, the clink and lock of an iron door.

"Rebekah, I'm not trying to…I'm just trying to understand, ok? You kissed Ruth. Fine. But does that mean you're gay? How do you know? Have you ever kissed a boy? Do—do you know what that's like?" Judith spit out the words quickly, nervously.

Rebekah put her hands to her face. "Mom, leave."

"No, we're talking about this now, and I…"

"Mom!" Rebekah screamed. "Get out of my room!"

Judith put her hands up. "Bekah, calm down."

"Get out of my room! Get out of my room! Get out of my room!"

Rebekah fell onto her stomach, sobbing and pounding the floor with her fist. She was hysterical, hiccupping and crying.

Judith sighed. Shook her head. *Fix it!*

She slid close to Rebekah. Rebekah jerked away. Judith put her hand back on Rebekah's back.

"Shhh…hush," Judith said. She rubbed her daughter's back almost mechanically, in small circles. "Shhhhh."

Rebekah kept crying.

"Honey, it's going to be ok." Judith said it conclusively, as if she were issuing a decision. "We'll figure this out. Maybe you need to see a therapist?"

Rebekah didn't say anything. She sat up, pulled a tissue out of the box, and loudly blew her nose.

"A therapist would be helpful," Judith said again. "You're confused, you're young—you had a bad experience. You can work this out."

"Are you upset?" Rebekah asked.

"Upset?" Judith repeated. She realized her voice sounded shrill. She took a deep breath and set her jaw. Judith smiled tightly. "No, honey. I'm not upset."

"What, then?"

Fix it! "I just think we can work through this," Judith said. *Better.*

"I'm not sure what this means. What does this mean? How do you know?"

"I'm not sure what it means, either."

"So you don't like boys? At all? Are you sure?"

"I don't know, Mom," Rebekah said.

Judith took another deep breath and pushed back her shoulders. "You know, when I was a teenager, I did some sexual experimenting. I was a part of a group of friends, and we all played kissing games. And sometimes girls would kiss other girls, you know, just for fun. I don't remember if I ever…"

"Mom, it's ok," Rebekah said. "I don't want to know."

"Ok." Judith looked at her daughter. "Do you have to decide right now? Like—if you're gay?"

Rebekah shrugged.

"Well…maybe you're bisexual," Judith said. "Maybe you like boys and girls."

Rebekah started to cry again.

"Shhh," Judith said. "Don't worry. Ok? Whatever this means, we'll figure it out. We'll figure it out."

"I'm so sorry," Rebekah said. "I don't want to be like this."

"Oh, stop it," Judith said. "You're not! You're not."

Rebekah heard heavy footsteps approaching, and then the bedroom door cracked open. Daniel stood in the doorway, looking at his wife and daughter in shock and fatigue.

"Is everything ok? What's going on in here?"

"I'll be to bed in a minute," Judith responded. "Everything is fine."

Daniel looked skeptical. He was not a complicated man; he was logical, deliberate, rational, and he knew enough to know that an emotional conversation between a mother and daughter may not be reason to panic. But still, they both looked so upset. He touched the top of the widow's peak on his forehead.

"You sure?" Daniel asked.

"Yes, it's ok. Go back to the bedroom. I'll be there in a minute."

Daniel stepped back and closed the door.

Judith closed her eyes, took a deep breath, and looked at her daughter. "Rebekah, let's go to sleep and talk more in the morning, ok?"

"What are you going to tell Dad?"

Judith cocked her head. "What do you want me to tell Dad?"

"I don't know."

She nodded. "I'll feel it out."

"What about David?"

"David…" Judith's voice trailed off. *David.* Her eldest was rigid, idealistic, prone to quick judgment and emotional outbursts. Her youngest, sensitive, sweet, and shy, looked up to her older brother in fearful reverence. The first was radical but rigid, the second traditional but steady. Judith was obliged to protect them both, to keep peace in the house, to help them build a relationship that would survive her and Daniel.

David, a ghost with so much power.

Finally, Judith spoke. "Don't tell David," she said. "Don't tell David yet."

Rebekah fumbled through her suitcase, tossing articles of clothing onto Megan's bed.

"Are you sure?" Megan asked. She was leaning against the doorframe of the bedroom, her arms crossed over her chest.

Rebekah continued rummaging.

"I really think I should be there," Megan said.

"I can't find my socks."

Megan walked in. "You're really frustrating me right now." She picked a pair of socks out of the suitcase. "Here."

"Do you really want to come?"

Megan shrugged. "I don't really want to go. I just think maybe I should."

"So maybe you should."

"Should I?"

Rebekah pulled on her socks, one foot at a time, carefully making sure that the seam lined up with the edge of her toes.

"I just think it's easier if I go by myself," Rebekah said finally.

"Fine."

It's not you," Rebekah said.

Megan sat on the bed and didn't respond.

"Ugh, Megan. I really don't want to fight with you about this. You know my brother. I have no idea how he's going to react. Or how Talia's going to react."

"Rebekah. I'm marrying you. At some point, they're going to be my family, too. Your problems are going to be my problems."

"Lucky you."

"You know what I mean. I just think we should present a united front about this. It's not like we're asking for permission. What's the worst David can do? He's your brother."

"Right," Rebekah said.

"Don't you think?"

"No."

Megan rolled her eyes. "Do whatever you want."

"I just think it's better if I go alone. They don't even know that I'm *gay*, Megan. They still think you're just a roommate."

"Really? You really think they still think that?" Megan pushed her shoulder back and did a couple of neck rolls. "They're not idiots. You really think that they think I've just been this super awesome roommate you've had for the last eight years who goes on vacations with you?"

Rebekah shrugged. David never asked. "Yeah. I do."

"Fine." Megan got up and walked out of the room.

Rebekah followed Megan out of their bedroom and grabbed the keys from the kitchen counter.

"Megan."

"What?"

Rebekah stood by the front door. "I love you."

"Yeah."

"Megan."

Megan looked over this time. "What?"

"Please?"

Megan sighed heavily, stood up, and walked over to the door. She coolly put her hands on Rebekah's shoulders, and then leaned down to plant a perfunctory kiss on her lips. "Good luck."

"Thanks."

"Are you sure?"

"About what?"

"That you want to do this alone?"

Rebekah nodded. "Yeah. I mean, I would love for you to be there. But I think I need to do this alone."

Megan clenched her jaw. She hadn't looked forward to folding herself into the passenger's seat of her parents' car to drive over there through Friday traffic. She hadn't looked forward to a stilted and awkward dinner with David and Talia, the sort of peculiar two-hour conversation in which deviating from polite superficialities would have been a major breach of contract.

"Fine," Megan said.

"Are we ok?"

"Sure."

"Megs…"

"The fact that you don't want me there at one of the major moments of your life doesn't feel so good. But you know, I'll deal."

Rebekah blew a black inkiness into the space behind her eyeballs. "I thought I told you I didn't want to fight about this," Rebekah said, her eyes still closed.

"So fine. Let's not fight." Rebekah heard Megan's footfalls march toward the edge of the bedroom, then the door slam behind her as she left.

Rebekah pulled onto the 110 freeway at five, just as the sun had begun working its way toward the ocean, probing its way through Rebekah's windshield, and glinting off the thousands of cars making their descent southwest. Friday afternoon traffic in Los Angeles was a chrome serpent, a gravel worm covered in diesel-spouting chainmail. The highways were strangely quiet, aside from the dull roar of thousands of engines; drivers didn't honk, so much as just move, aggressively shifting lanes, speeding up to prevent the car next to them from pulling in front of them. Most cars had their windows rolled up to prevent the dust and grit and tiny shards of gravel from flying into their air-conditioned cocoons. The stationary road, the moving, metal amoeba, the smoke and coolant and shimmering heat, bumper-to-bumper at dawn and dusk—it was a universe governed by its own seasons and atmosphere.

There was something in this city, Rebekah thought, which made people seem simultaneously garrisoned and exposed. It was the grit in this town. The grit here was somehow grittier than it was in Portland. The beach was more imposing and overwhelming and raw than the forests and lakes of the Pacific Northwest. There was more concrete here, more stiffness, a thickness of skin that hid a thinness in the blood. People here were tough and over-sensitive, like a poorly cooked flank steak.

She clenched and re-clenched the sticky steering wheel of Megan's father's car. She knew why they had fought: Megan didn't believe Rebekah would actually come out to her brother tonight. Megan wanted to be there to make sure it happened. They had been approaching that dangerous place in which questions slide into accusations, in which couples find themselves arguing over the insignificant, as a richly inadequate stand-in for the significant. Over and over they had trudged through the same material. They would circle and circle their partially clogged drain, remaining on the soapy, scummy outer liquid ring, never settling. Their conversations mostly remained at a low boil, Megan frustrated with

Rebekah's insecurity, and Rebekah retreating from the conflict. It was an off-and-on conversation that had lasted nearly eleven years, since the first few moments of their meeting in college. After dipping into the same cauldron for all those years, and drinking from the same vile liquid, the bitterness of the never-ending exchange was slowly metastasizing into their bones.

An hour and a half later, Rebekah pulled into David's driveway. She switched off the engine and sat in her car to survey the neighborhood. The houses here were built from stucco and cement, their front yards neat with grass lawns and potted shrubbery. All the homes were well kept: grass mowed, roofs cleared of moss, sidewalks swept.

Rebekah stepped out of her car and walked towards the house. The front steps were gray and peeling, badly in need of refinishing; the stucco on the side of the house was intact, but dirty; the roof, now overlaid three times with shingles, was old but, not leaking; the front door, painted a new, cheery shade of red, had a doorknob that stuck and froze and spit out keys as if they were arsenic. It was a house badly in need of self-examination.

She peered into the front window. There was a small living room with a wooden coffee table in the center and a slightly tattered white cloth couch backed up against the wall. There were only a few family pictures on the wall farthest from the door. To the right, she could see the entrance to the kitchen.

Rebekah knocked on the door. There was no answer. She knocked again, this time harder. Still no answer. Rebekah walked around the side of the house, popped open the latch on a side door, and stepped into the backyard. She saw Talia in a crouch, wielding a small shovel, digging weeds out of a flowerbed.

"Hey, Talia."

Talia turned her head. She smiled. "Bekah!" She dropped the shovel and dusted off her pants. "You'll have to excuse me, I'm a little dirty." She walked up to Rebekah and gently hugged her. "How are you?"

"I'm good. How are you?"

"I'm great," Talia said. "We've had some great weather this summer. Hasn't been too hot. I've still had to water every day, but it's not like last summer, when I watered every day, and my plants still died."

Talia wore a black scarf wrapped around her head, a long-sleeved shirt, and long skirt. She was slim, with long, dark hair, and she looked about ten years younger than her thirty-three years. She had an exuberant way of talking and an open-mouthed smile. Rebekah found herself drawn to Talia's eyes, dark craters in an otherwise flawless moonscape.

"It always seems to be great weather when I come down here," Rebekah said.

"Yeah?" Talia said. "Does it rain in Portland in the summer?"

"No, not really. But it's great weather here in the summer, fall, winter, spring…"

Talia laughed. "Yeah, I guess I've never lived anywhere else. But it's not bad here, right? I don't really feel like I'm missing much. Are you hungry? Can I get you anything?"

"No, I'm not hungry," Rebekah said.

Talia looked back at her flowerbed. "See that?"

"What?"

"See all the little holes in the leaves and petals? Like something's been taking bites out of them?"

Rebekah leaned over. She noticed little holes in the flower petals.

"I'm just not sure what it is," Talia continued. A little bug, or a bird, maybe?"

Rebekah shrugged. "Maybe."

Talia smiled at her. "I'm asking you like you're a horticulturalist or something. Nevermind. Let's go inside. I need to start dinner, anyway."

Rebekah nodded. She looked back at the flowers. A few were upright. Most were in a cockeyed state, lying twisted or half-eaten in the flowerbed. Rebekah turned away and followed her sister-in-law into the house.

"How does baked chicken sound to you?" Talia asked. "With rice and asparagus?"

"Sounds perfect."

"So what brought you down here?" Talia reached into a cupboard and pulled out two glasses. "You're visiting people? I never got the full story from David."

Rebekah sat down at a small table just off the kitchen. It was covered with a pale yellow tablecloth that matched the color of the kitchen walls. A small vase with a drooping sunflower sat in the center.

"Yeah, visiting some friends," Rebekah said.

"What friends?"

"Oh…you know. Just friends." Rebekah tried to prop up the sunflower. "Where's David?"

"On his way home. He's walking today."

"Oh. And the kids?"

"They're all a few doors down at a friend's house."

"How are they doing?"

Talia handed her a glass of water and dove into a description of each of her three children. Ben, the oldest, had just finished kindergarten and would begin first grade in the fall. Shira and Chaim were both still in preschool. Her three kids were happy and healthy, Talia said. They had grown up so quickly. It was amazing to think that in just ten years they would all be teenagers.

Talia's hands were busy prepping the chicken and rice. Her eyes glanced between Rebekah, the kitchen counter, and the clock on the wall.

David felt lucky that he was able to walk home from work. How many people in Los Angeles could say that? He zipped up his jacket around his throat. It was July Fourth, and he was still wearing fleece. *You can take a Portlander out of the rain,* David thought, *but you can never really take the rain out of a Portlander.*

The walk home took about fifteen minutes. Ari Dobrin, David's father-in-law and boss, had rented out the third floor of an office building on Pico Boulevard for his medical billing business, where David worked as a salesman. The building was old, built in the middle of the twentieth century, with an elevator that jerked and listed and had a penchant for breaking down at four on Friday afternoons.

David wondered what people thought when they saw him walking home. His cotton khakis were just a bit too short and inevitably slipped into the heel of his canvas loafers. His polo shirts were a bit too big, bought on sale from whatever department store happened to be advertising discounts. Department stores never had medium polos on the discount racks, only the large and extra-large. His *tzit-tzit,* the fringes from his prayer shawl, hung out over the top of his pants. He wore a baseball hat year-round, even though he'd never been to a Dodgers game in his life.

Three months into his marriage to Talia Dobrin, David and his wife were walking down the sidewalk on a Friday night. It was a warm, humid night in the middle of August. The streetlights bathed the sidewalk in a harsh yellow; rock music wafted down from the top floor of an apartment building. They were walking back to their house from evening Shabbat services at synagogue. David was wearing what he'd worn to work: polo shirt, khakis, and canvas shoes. A white woven kippah rested lightly on the top of his dark, curly hair. Talia wore a headscarf, long sleeves, a long shirt, and running shoes.

Ten minutes from their house, four men leaned out of a large, gleaming red truck and wolf-whistled. Talia waved at them. David grabbed her arm and pushed it down by her side. "What are you doing?" David asked. "Are you crazy?"

"They're just saying hi," Talia said. She adjusted her scarf and looked up at him with her big blue eyes. There was innocence there, the charming naiveté that had sucked David in like a translucent vortex.

"They're not saying hi, Tal," David said.

"So what are they saying?"

David shook his head. "Never mind what they're saying."

Talia shrugged. "Should it be so terrible that we live in a world where people wave to each other?"

David grinned to himself. *Ironic, isn't it?* David had wanted to believe in that kind of world. During the first week of college at the University of Southern California in Los Angeles, student organizations held an involvement fair. Dozens of tables were set up along Trousdale Parkway, the main campus thoroughfare. Organizations had been grouped by theme, starting with academic and honors societies, then student governance, community, and political organizations. The pre-law, and pre-MBA groups huddled together, followed closely by the Political Science Undergraduate Association, the International Studies for Undergrads group, and the Public Policy Students Club. The organizations associated with the College of Letters, Arts, and Sciences gradually gave way to a section filled mostly with science-oriented groups. There was 'SC Bugs and Crud, the Biology Student Association, and USC Women in Science. David walked by three different tables for aerospace engineering students: The USC Rocketeers, USC Aerospace Coalition, and USC Aero-Grads.

When David saw the USC Student Government table—and the students standing there, confident, smiling, beautiful, running things—he knew he'd found the people who were waiting for him. *This is right*, he thought. *Doing good with power.*

David threw himself into political science classes. He took courses on political theory, law and politics, and political literature. He stayed on campus late every night planning events. David was elected head of the Liberal Students Association, a loose-knit group of organizations with a progressive bent. David railed against Republicans and capitalism. He protested for peace in Darfur, the legalization of marijuana, and the end of the occupation of Palestine.

David Cohayn was the powerful face of firebrand activism on campus, and he relished the political fights. This felt so fitting, the first step in what would be a storied career in noble politics. In his rigid ledger of right and wrong, practicing noble politics approached a platonic ideal of righteousness.

Late in his junior year, David was sitting in a coffee shop in Santa Monica. Rousseau's *The Social Contract* lay in front of him, unopened. A white ceramic mug filled with a half-consumed cappuccino sat to his left. David much preferred to people watch than to read, and he enjoyed observing the parade of Angelenos coming in for their daily fix.

David noticed a woman walk in. She was short and thin, her head covered by a scarf, and she was wearing a long shirt with long sleeves over an ankle-length skirt. She had big blue eyes that ate up half of her face.

"Mind if I take this seat?" the woman asked him. She was pointing to the chair next to him at the coffee bar. "It's the only seat left."

David looked around. She was right. "Sure," David said. He turned the wattage up on his smile.

"What are you reading?" the woman asked. She stared at him.

David held up his book. "Oh, just something for class. Rousseau."

"What subject?"

"Political science."

"Oh," the woman said.

"I'm a political science major," David said.

"So you want to be a politician?"

David shrugged. "I'm not sure yet. I believe in certain things, and I believe they're worth fighting for. If I can do that as a politician, then sure, I'd consider that."

"So what are these very important things you believe in?"

"Well," David said. He crossed one legs over the other. "For example, I believe that all people have a right to basic necessities for life. Food, water, shelter."

The woman smiled. "That makes sense."

"So…yeah. Amazingly, there are many people in the United States who don't have that. It's absurd. Obscene." David heard himself babbling, but he couldn't stop. "The poverty in this country, with the amount of resources we have, that we spend on our military…if we just spent a fraction, a nibble of that on solving poverty, we could be the first nation-state in the history of the world where no one would be poor. We're closer than you'd think. It's just a matter of political will."

"And you're going to try to make that happen?"

David grimaced, as if she had asked him an embarrassing question. He shrugged. "It would be difficult. But it's worth trying for."

The woman nodded. David stuck his chin out. He could see her taking him in: his ropey muscles and hollowed-out cheeks. David took a long, slow deep breath. Frank Sinatra briefly flashed through his brain. *Smile. Be cool.*

"What are you reading?" David asked.

The woman pushed the book towards him. *Moral Grandeur and Spiritual Audacity*, by Abraham Joshua Heschel.

"What's this?" David asked.

"A book."

"Yes, um, yeah, I uh…" David laughed. "I can see that it's a book. What kind of book is it?"

The woman shrugged. "Philosophy, I guess. Jewish philosophy."

"You're Jewish?" David asked.

"I am," the woman said.

David picked up the book. "May I?"

"Certainly."

"I've read a lot of philosophy before. Mostly political philosophers." David flipped the book open to a page that the woman—Talia Dobrin, he later learned—had bookmarked. He read a highlighted passage: *We are the most challenged people under the sun. Our existence is either superfluous or indispensable to the world; it is either tragic or holy to be a Jew.*

David frowned. "Tragic or holy?"

Talia peeked over his shoulder. "Sure," she said. "If that's what it says."

"What do you mean, if that's what it says?" David asked. "Didn't you highlight this?"

"No," Talia said. "It's my dad's book." She took the book back from him.

"So why are you reading it?"

"For the same reason you bring Rousseau to a coffee shop in Santa Monica."

"Right," David said. A few beats of silence passed. They each stared at their books.

"So…what are you doing after this?" David asked.

"Going home."

"Ah." David nodded, and took a sip of his coffee. He rolled his shoulders and moved his head from side to side. "Maybe we can hang out later? Talk about philosophy or something?"

"Maybe, Talia said. She smiled. "You give me your number."

"And you give me yours?"

"No."

"Oh," David said. He frowned and fumbled with his wallet. "Um…here." He handed Talia a business card.

Talia laughed. "David Cohayn, USC Student Government? You need a business card for this?"

David's ears burned. "Well, you know. I made them as kind of a joke."

Talia laughed again. She tucked the business card into her purse and slid away from the bar. "Ok, then. See you later, David Cohayn of USC Student Government."

David watched her walk out the door of the coffee shop. It was like watching the tide recede into a wormhole.

That night, David lay in bed thinking about Talia, about being a politician, about the line he'd read in Talia's book. The bleak juxtaposition had resonated with David. *Tragic or holy.* His life was either tragic or holy. Black or white. In or out. It was either just a pebble of sand among billions of pebbles, or something more, something that was unique and incredible. Was he just a single organism amidst an Earth full of billions of organisms, or destined for something else?

The impromptu date at the coffee shop quickly turned into dinner, followed by outings at the beach and matinees at the movie theater. For Talia's family, the synagogue was the center of social life. The Dobrins went to services every Saturday morning to worship. They spoke a mix of English and Hebrew at home. Their Judaism was more than just an identity layered within the fragmented fusion of other identities; it was a contract, the central mode of communion with the universe, a faith that bound them to the coherent and incoherent.

David found himself slowly spending less time with student government and more time with the Dobrins and their Jewish community. The Dobrin family seemed so authentic, so humble, so single-mindedly driven by something bigger that David had never previously considered. The students at USC were idealistic, inspiring, ambitious; the Dobrins were idealistic and inspiring, but rejected material ambition as a detractor from faith. To be faithful *was* their ambition. To be open to God, to experience holiness, to know things through prayer, study, and meditation, was the most magnificent achievement that existed.

It was foreign to David, seductive. He was drawn to the idea of a set path, where achievement was measured by commitment, participation, and belief. For his whole life, he'd sought out right from wrong; in this community, right and wrong were discussed, deliberated, and ultimately laid out for him.

In Talia—and by extension, her family—David found a combination of passion and righteousness: a wife who could dedicate herself to him completely, while forcing him towards a more virtuous ethical canon than he had ever known. As a devout Jew, her life seemed both more circumscribed and uninhibited. With rules for living, she could simply be.

Student government seemed so small compared to the Torah and the Talmud, compared to five thousand years of miracles.

Three months into the relationship, it struck David that Talia was the most complete woman he'd ever met. Complete, as in certain. Complete, as in whole. Complete, as in the one who could compliment his new ambitions. He sold himself to the Dobrins as a convert, *their* convert—born-again into a religion in which birth determined peoplehood. Talia loved him for his magnetism, for his commitment and intensity. Who wouldn't love a man who completed rearranged his life around his sweetheart's family?

His parents had raised him to think of Judaism as a wide path, like the kind of trail you encounter in a National Park, one paved with gravel and fit for wheelchairs and families. They're easy to walk on, with no more than a six percent grade. You could probably roll a corpse down one of them, if you attached wheels to its feet.

But you can't get to the backcountry on those trails. You can't get to the jagged peaks and the pristine rivers; you can't see the grizzly bears and the marmots, and the trees so big that you can strain your neck, just trying to see the tops. Those wide trails—the ones made for everyone—can't take you to the kind of solitude that makes your bones feel like they're brewed from the granite sticking up out of the earth, and like you could lay down in a high mountain meadow and fall asleep for a hundred years, and the grass would grow up and around you and yet you'd still feel more alive than you had ever felt. David began going to synagogue on Saturday mornings. He started studying Jewish texts and philosophers, paying attention to the Jewish arcana that his parents scoffed at. He bought separate plates for dairy and meat meals, and then an entire set for Passover. He bought a new tallit and a woven kippah. He grew out his facial hair and began saying prayers multiple times a day. He found a home with the Dobrins. He set his ambition on a search for faith. One year after meeting Talia, David graduated from USC with a degree in political science, then immediately went to work for Talia's father, Ari Dobrin.

By design, his marriage to Talia was a small affair. They married in Talia's synagogue, in front of their immediate families and Talia's rabbi. David didn't want too much association between his family and the Dobrins. He didn't want them to know each other. What would his parents and sister know of the new David, the one who found solace in meditation and prayer? What would they think of the David who got into long arguments with other men in his community over esoteric details of their faith? Would they recognize the David who led prayers on Saturday, who danced with his hands to the sky on Simchat Torah, who bent his waist rhythmically in prayer during the Amidah?

David could barely remember the person he used to be, the one who wanted to wear suits and wingtips and hand out business cards. This new David, Talia's David, possessed a calmer confidence than the old David. An assurance that, despite his previous coolness, he'd always lacked. This David was the right David, the one that felt more right than all the other Davids.

He remembered his parents during the marriage ceremony, standing quietly to one side, his sister on the other with Talia's siblings. Rebekah had looked at him with curiosity and longing, that same look she'd given him since she was born. Rebekah, his quiet younger sister, who possessed an insatiable thirst for approval. He had smiled at her, nodded, tried to make her feel comfortable.

The Cohayns and the Dobrins hadn't been in the same room since, even after the births of each of the children. David had managed to stagger the two families' visits. He was always with the Dobrins on Jewish holidays, and the Cohayns at other times of the year. It wasn't difficult. It was simply the way it had to be.

Stepping away from his family had ben either tragic or holy. A fatal, devastating mistake, or a profoundly correct decision. David chose to believe the latter.

Just after six thirty, Rebekah heard the front door open and shut. David walked into the kitchen His cheeks looked more angular and gaunt than they had during Rebekah's last visit. His chin, that sharp facial mantle that had been with him since he was a child, jutted out like a jetty in a harbor. Much to Rebekah's surprise, large glasses with black rims sat on the bridge of his nose. David had always had perfect vision.

"Hi, Rebekah," David said. "Welcome."

Rebekah wanted to stand up and hug her brother, to ask him why his eyes looked so haggard and his face seemed so slim. She wanted to grip him, smell him, hear him tell her he was thrilled to see her. After a few moments, David smiled. It was a genuine, heart-warming smile that sent beacons of warmth into Rebekah's extremities. David opened his arms to her. "So, are you going to give your big brother a hug?"

Rebekah stood up and obediently wrapped her arms around David's waist. He was only a few inches taller, but the way he hugged her, with his arms around her shoulders and his stance wider than hers, made Rebekah feel as though he towered over her. He was like a heroic statue in a city square.

"It's nice to see you, kiddo," David said.

"Nice to see you, too."

David stood back and looked at her. "You look great. A little older, but I guess that's inevitable, eh?"

Rebekah blushed. "I guess."

"You look better than me, anyway. I'm an old man now."

Rebekah smiled. "How was work?"

"It was fine," David said. "The usual." David peeked in the oven. "The chicken almost ready?"

"Just about," Talia said.

"How was your drive here?" David asked Rebekah. He sat down at the kitchen table.

"Fine, if you're into traffic."

"Welcome to Los Angeles. It's how we do it. And your plane flight?"

"Same. Fine. Nothing to report."

"How are Mom and Dad?"

"Same old, same old."

David raised one eyebrow and smirked at his younger sister. "Not much of a storyteller, are you?"

Rebekah laughed. "Sorry, I'll try to be a little more dramatic." She leaned into the table, and looked to her left and right. "So just the other day," Rebekah whispered loudly, "Dad came home from Costco with an extra-large package of toilet paper, and Mom freaked out, because she thought Dad was going to tell her that he was incontinent."

David threw back his head and laughed. Talia looked over her shoulder and grinned at Rebekah.

"Well done." David nodded approvingly. "That's exactly the kind of news I want to hear."

Rebekah glowed. "I do what I can."

By seven, Ben, Shira, and Chaim had returned to the house, and the family assembled in the kitchen. David was dressed in a clean white dress shirt, black pants, and a kippah. He closed his eyes and led his family in the blessing before the meal. The children squirmed and poked each other; Talia stared absent-mindedly at her husband. To Rebekah, the prayer sounded familiar enough, close to what she'd heard repeated in synagogue during Hebrew school, or on the rare occasion when her parents hosted Friday-night dinners.

"Amen," David said.

"Amen," echoed Talia and the children.

"Did everyone wash their hands?" David asked. He grabbed one of Chaim's hands. "Your hands look dirty. Talia, can you check their hands and make sure they've washed?"

As Talia walked to the sink with the children, David sat down and shook his head at Rebekah. "Just wait, you'll see," he said.

"Children are wonderful, but they're a handful. They're a blessing. You'll have them someday, and you'll see. And their hands—always dirty."

"Ha, yeah, I can imagine." Rebekah picked up the metal serving spoon and dished herself a drumstick. She passed the plate to David and picked up a few spears of asparagus.

"So what's new?" Talia asked. "How's Portland?"

"Portland is fine."

"Yeah? How's work?"

Rebekah shrugged and kept chewing. "It's work," she said through a mouthful of food.

"What are you working on?"

"Same stuff. Working for Stella on the newsmagazine. Writing. Designing. Copy-editing." Rebekah swallowed a cheekful of food. "The usual."

"Any chance of a promotion on the horizon?" Talia asked. Her eyes were large and round, her expression childlike.

"Ha!" Rebekah laughed. "Definitely no promotions. Just more challenging work with the same pay."

"But maybe your boss will raise your pay if you do a good job?" David asked. "Tal—Chaim is about to throw his chicken. Chaim, food on your plate, please." Two-year-old Chaim dropped a piece of chicken on the floor, and was about to drop another, when Talia grabbed his plate from him.

"It's possible, but not likely," Rebekah said. "We're hurting for money. I don't think they'd give me a pay raise unless I paid for it myself, if you know what I mean."

"Sure, sure, I hear you," David said. He took a bite of his chicken. "How's Megan?"

"Megan?" Rebekah repeated.

"Yeah. Your roommate, right?" David asked.

"She's fine."

"What does she do, again?"

"She's an engineer."

David raised his eyebrows. "An engineer, huh? Impressive. I should have done that. I could be making more money." David glanced at Talia.

"We have enough money, honey," Talia said. She was completely focused on Chaim now, who had as much food on his face as he'd gotten into his mouth.

"Enough, but we could use more," David said. "Remember that, Rebekah—if you ever have a change of heart about your career, pick one that makes you a little bit of money. It's worth it in the long run, not always feeling like you're trying to play catch-up. Ben, Shira, please stop fighting. If you're done with dinner, you can leave the table."

Ben and Shira stood up and chased each other out of the kitchen.

"It's not like Megan makes that much money," Rebekah said. "She makes a little more than me, but I work at a non-profit. If she got into management, she'd make a lot more. But I don't think she's into that."

"I'm going to give Chaim a bath," Talia said. "David, can you handle clean up tonight?" She looked from her husband to Rebekah. "I'll be back after I put Chaim down." She reached into the high chair and pulled out her youngest child, who let out a high-pitched wail of protest.

David looked at Rebekah. "See how it goes? Let me give you a piece of advice, Rebekah: When you say no for the first time to your children, mean it. Your kids will never respect you, otherwise. These kids, my kids—they respect us. And it's because we've meant what we said." David adjusted his kippah. "It's about respect. That's where it begins and ends. Parents are in the right. And if your kids believe that you're in the right, then you can teach them how to be good people."

Rebekah's phone buzzed in her pocket. Rebekah pulled it out. It was Megan.

"Excuse me, David, I need to take this."

David waved his sister away. "Sure. I need to clean up."

Rebekah walked into the living room. "Hello?"

"Hi," Megan said.

Rebekah sat down on the couch. "Hi."

"Did you tell them?"

Rebekah could hear Megan chewing. "What are you eating?"

"Pistachios," Megan said. "Did you tell them?"

"No."

"Why not?"

"It wasn't the right time."

"Ugh, Bekah." Rebekah heard the crack of a pistachio shell.

"Megan, I'm telling you, it wasn't the right time." She lowered her voice to a whisper. "The kids were there, and we were talking about family stuff. I'm not just going to drop this on my brother in front of his children."

Megan didn't answer.

"You weren't here."

"I know I'm not there." Megan said it like an indictment.

"Megan, I don't know what to tell you," Rebekah whispered. She could hear her brother washing the dishes. "I need to handle my brother the way I know how to handle him. What do you want me to do?"

"You could have told them from the beginning. For example: 'David. Talia. I have something to tell you.'"

"That's so awkward."

"It's going to be awkward, no matter what."

Rebekah dug her fingernails into her thigh. "I'm sorry, ok? I don't really know what to tell you. It wasn't the right time, and it didn't happen."

"So when are you going to tell them?"

"I'll tell them."

"When?"

"I don't know. Tonight."

"You're going to tell them tonight?"

Rebekah pulled the phone away from her ear and squeezed it.

"I'll do my best, Megan."

Megan didn't respond.

"I'll find a time. I'll make it happen. You need to trust me. I will tell them."

"Ok." Megan sounded skeptical. Rebekah heard the crack of another pistachio shell.

"Can I just call you later?"

"Sure."

"I love you."

"You, too."

"You what?"

"I love you, too," Megan said. There was an intentional staleness in her voice, as though she'd activated an automatic message.

"Bye."

"Bye."

Rebekah hung up the phone in disgust. She walked back into the kitchen. David's back was toward her as he washed the dishes, whistling softly. He didn't notice Rebekah walk back in.

Rebekah sat down, and watched David wash dishes. He had always hated his hands: the slender palms, long fingers, and skin so papery white and thin that he needed to put lotion on them year-round. Rebekah had always admired David's hands. Her own hands were warm, red, and a little sweaty.

Rebekah turned to look at the sunflower in the center of the table. She wondered if a lack of water made it droop, or too little sun, or something altogether different. Maybe it had been cut too long ago. Maybe the vase was too small. Maybe sunflowers didn't belong indoors.

David was wiping his hands on a dishtowel when Talia came back in.

"Chaim's down," she said. "He seemed really tired and cranky tonight. I hope he's not getting sick."

"Did he have a fever?" David asked.

"No, I don't think so," Talia said. "He was just a little bit fussy." She turned to Rebekah. "He's not quite at the stage where he can really communicate what's wrong with him yet, so if he's not feeling good it still comes across as crankiness. It's hard to tell what's what with Chaim, because it seems like he's always a little bit under the weather."

"You just baby him," David said.

"I'm raising him just like our other kids, David."

David sighed heavily. "Well."

Talia nodded. "Well."

"So you probably better get going soon, huh?" David said to Rebekah. "It's getting late."

"Wait," Rebekah said. Her voice came out froggy.

David raised his eyebrows. "Yes?"

This was not it. This was not it. This was not the gentle segue. This was not what she was waiting for. This was not the moment.

Talia and David looked at her.

"There's something I wanted to tell you."

Talia raised her eyebrows. David cleared his throat.

"I'm seeing someone." *Seeing someone? After eight years?*
Talia smiled at Rebekah. She clapped her hands in front of her.
"Oh, that's great news!" she said. "I wanted to ask you, but since
you didn't bring it up, I didn't know if you wanted to talk about it.
Oh, that's great news, Bekah."
"Yes, great news," David repeated. He looked surprised.
"What's his name?"
Rebekah looked at her plate. "Oh. Well…"
Talia looked back, wide-eyed. David leaned forward.
"Megan," Rebekah said quietly.
"Morgan?" Talia repeated.
"Megan," Rebekah said, a little louder.
"Megan?"
"Yes, Megan."
"Megan." Talia looked skeptically at David.
"Yes."
"You're dating a boy named Megan?"
"No. I'm dating a woman named Megan. My roommate. Megan
Nimble."
Talia sat back in her chair. "You're dating your roommate?"
David looked at his wife, then at his sister.
"Yes."
"Why?"
Why? "Um…why? Because…."
"Wait, what are you saying, Bekah?" David asked. His eyes were
hard.
Talia looked from her husband to her sister-in-law.
"Um…"Rebekah looked from her brother to her sister-in-law.
"Yeah. I don't know what else there is to say."
"You don't know?" David asked.
Rebekah turned her eyes away from him. "Yeah."
"But what does that mean?" David asked.
"It means that…you know, I think I'm gay."
"But how can you think you're gay? Isn't that the kind of thing you
know?"
"Ok, I misspoke. I know I'm gay."
David thrust his chin out. "I don't understand. I don't understand
what you're telling us. Have you ever even…been with a man? First

you're not sure; you think you're gay, but you're not sure, and now you know? You know for sure? How have you confirmed it?"

"David," Talia said.

"What?" David stared at his wife. "She's telling us she's gay. This is news. I've known her my whole life, and she's never been gay before. I think I have the right to ask her some questions."

He dropped his hands beneath the table; Rebekah imagined that they were balled into fists. His lips looked like two uncooked pieces of linguini tucked into his chin. She thought about seeing him in the emergency room when they were kids, his broken arm in a sling, his eyes staring at the ground. He had apologized to her then for betraying her.

Now, David just looked angry.

"So what you're telling us is that you're gay, and that the person you've led us to believe is your roommate for the last eight years was actually your girlfriend, correct?"

Rebekah nodded. "Right."

"Well," David said, glancing at Talia. He cleared his throat again. "I suppose it's unfortunate that you lied to us for so long."

Rebekah closed her eyes and took a deep breath. *I'm not lying to you now, am I?* Both of them sat silently, staring at her.

"I'm still not really understanding," Talia said. She had unclasped her hands and was leaning forward, elbows on the table. "You've been dating Megan? Like…having a sexual relationship with her?"

Rebekah took a deep breath. "Yes." She opened her eyes. "Clear now?"

Talia nodded. Her forehead was drawn and knitted.

"Megan is Jewish, right?" David asked.

Rebekah started to laugh.

"What?"

Rebekah shook her head. "I don't know. It's just a funny question right now."

"She is though, right?"

"Yeah."

"Both parents?" David asked.

"Just her mom."

"Right. Megan *Nimble*." David stood up and began to pace in the kitchen.

Rebekah squeezed her napkin in her fist. She had to finish this.

"There's something else."

"Great," David said.

"Megan *Nimble*"—Rebekah emphasized the last name, just as her brother had—"and I are getting married."

Talia's jaw dropped. She looked at her husband.

"What?" David asked.

"We're having a commitment ceremony. A wedding. Next year."

David put his hands to his ears. "How? What are you talking about? How?"

"What do you mean 'how'? We're just going to do it. Like other people do it."

And who do you think is going to come?" David's voice had gotten soft, almost to a whisper.

"David…" Talia said.

"Who do you expect to be there? Our parents? You think they're going to support their daughter's *gay* wedding? You expect Aunt Sophie and Uncle Isaac, Stedman and Leanne—you expect them to bring their kids? And what about our grandparents?" David laughed. "You think Grandma Simchah is going to come? Our crazy grandma, who came to this country to make a better life for her children? You think she's really going to support this kind of freedom?"

"David." Talia put her hand on her husband's arm. "Please."

David withdrew his arm. "Don't tell me what to do. My sister lied to me for most of her adult life. And being gay?" David threw up his hands. "You know what's in the Torah, don't you?"

"David." Rebekah struggled to keep her voice under control. "Why do you think I lied to you for so long? Because of this. Because I expected this. Because I knew this was how you guys would take it, and this would all be about you, and Mom and Dad, and how this all affects you. Mom and Dad already know, and they're ok with this."

David laughed. "Right."

"They are. Rebekah swallowed. Her voice sounded strangely calm to her own ears. "David, this is our decision. We're having a wedding next year, and I guess you're both invited. But if you can't handle it, then you don't have to come. We only want people there who want to be there."

"Rebekah." David turned away from her. "It's not about that."

"So what is it about?"

David turned back. His brow was furrowed and face was red. "You lied to us. Continually. For nine years. You told us your girlfriend was your roommate. And beyond that, what the hell am I going to tell my kids? I can't take them to a gay wedding. This isn't something we do."

"Oh," Rebekah said. She took a couple of ragged breaths and tried to laugh. "Not something you do."

"You can do whatever you want," David said. "Frankly, I don't really care. I mean, I care because you're my sister and I want you to make good choices."

"Choices?"

"Yeah. Choices. You're making a choice to be with a woman, are you not?"

"I was born this way, David."

"Who you are and what you do are two different things."

Rebekah closed her eyes.

"Bekah, do you not get it? There's no one gay in our community. My children have never met a gay person."

"They've met me."

"But you've been lying!" David roared.

"I was scared," Rebekah whispered.

David shook his head. "I can't. I can't get my children mixed up in this."

"Mixed up in this?" Rebekah repeated.

"We wish you the best," David said. He tried to smile. Breathe. "Really. We wish you all the love and happiness in the world."

Rebekah stared at her brother. There he was, the same boy that she had worshiped throughout her childhood. He stood in front of her, his terrible power pulsating from his rib cage, that polite, charming smile still locked on his face.

Rebekah stood up and walked to the coat rack to grab her jacket. She looked down the hall. There was no sign of her niece or nephew. In the kitchen, Talia was sitting with her head down, staring at the table. David was looking at his sister.

"I'm taking off," Rebekah said. "Thanks for dinner."

She saw Talia look up and smile weakly. There was no movement from David.

Rebekah walked through the front door, closing it gently behind her. She ran to her car, fumbled for her keys, unlocked the door, and twisted the ignition. She paused in the driveway to see if either of them would walk out and stop her from leaving.

After a few seconds, she threw the car into reverse, backed into the street, and headed back to Pasadena, hot, angry tears flowing down her cheeks.

FALL

From time to time, life forces us to pirouette. These are awkward turns—feet flat, toes splayed, legs wobbly and uncertain, arms straight out to the side to maintain balance. You can fall flat on your face and strain a muscle, break a bone, or suffer degrading, crippling humiliation.

Rebekah was pirouetting. She was spinning and tripping and falling to the earth, landing on her front and back and side and head, all at the same time.

From the outside, nothing seemed out of the ordinary. Rebekah still rode the Portland light rail to work, staring out the window, as if she was trying to read all the billboards. At home, she dusted the coffee table, did the dishes after dinner, switched the laundry to the dryer, and folded clothes with meticulous care. Rebekah called her parents regularly, at least once a week on Sunday, but usually more often. They talked about work, Grandma Simchah, Megan, the slow pace of wedding planning.

When Judith and Daniel asked about her conversation with David, Rebekah simply stretched the truth. "Oh, you know," Rebekah had told her parents after the visit. "David kind of freaked out, like I thought he would."

"What did he say to you?" Judith asked.

"I don't really remember," Rebekah lied. "It was a really quick conversation."

"Did he say if he was going to the wedding?"

"Didn't say, Mom," Rebekah said. "Maybe you should ask him."

So Judith did ask him. She called him one evening a few weeks after Rebekah's visit. The conversation lasted an hour, much of which Judith spent pleading with David. David didn't budge.

"Mom, it's not the gay wedding that bothers me," David had said. "I mean, it bothers me, but I could get over it. Talia and the kids would get over it. I even looked up a *halachic* justification. Suspect, but feasible."

"Homosexuality is ok now?"

"To some. Lots of discussion about anal sex and marriage. You don't want to know."

"So what's your problem then?" Judith asked.

"So…you lied to me!" David yelled. "You and dad and Rebekah all lied to me for years! How could you do that? I feel betrayed by my own family."

"You feel betrayed?" Judith asked. She puffed out her cheeks. "How do you think your sister feels? That you're not going to her wedding?"

"I don't care. I don't even feel like I know any of you anymore! Rebekah told me that Megan is Jewish. Is that even true? She's lied to me about so many other things."

"She's half Jewish. Her mother's Jewish."

"And what rabbi is going to marry them? A rent-a-rabbi?"

"David, please!"

"Is this even legal, like, in a secular way?" David asked. "Can they get married?"

"I…I don't think so. But I don't know."

"So what's the point of having a wedding, if they can't get married?"

"David, if you make this choice, I'm warning you," Judith said. "It's going to cause irreparable harm. This is the kind of thing you can't fix. Not going to your sister's wedding…I don't even know what to say. That's not how I raised my eldest son."

"So don't say anything."

"David, please!"

"Mom, you're in the wrong here. Not me. You're the ones who lied to me." Judith heard the line go dead. She stared at the receiver, imagining David calmly setting his phone down on the kitchen table and walking out of the room. He would be walking with perfect posture, a charming smile plastered to his face, his chin defiantly extending out over his chest. Talia would never know.

"I'm so sorry about him, Bekah," Judith later said to her over the phone.

Rebekah swallowed the lump in her throat. "It's fine, mom. Don't worry about it."

"How can I not worry about it?" Judith asked. "He's your older brother. And he's being a shmuck, pardon my Yiddish."

"Right."

"He's always been like that, Bekah. He's always been stubborn." Judith lowered her voice to a whisper. "You know, he's a little bit self-righteous."

Rebekah laughed despite herself. "You think?"

Judith sighed. "I'm so sorry. There's nothing I can do about him. Are you going to be ok?"

"I'm fine," Rebekah said. "Really."

Grandma Simchah had a more stoic explanation.

"King David is who he is," Grandma Simchah told Rebekah. "You think a king bows to anyone?"

Each passing day became a drop. The drops congregated deep in Rebekah's belly. After a few weeks, Rebekah felt bloated with humiliation. *David can't love me,* Rebekah thought. *How could he?* Rebekah could never say these things out loud. They would sound tinny and harsh, comical even.

July turned into August, and August into September. Rebekah thought about David every day: the shock and disgust on his face, the way his chin stuck out, like an indictment, his utter lack of comprehension about what she was telling him.

Gay? Over and over in her mind, she kept replaying the way he had said that word. He'd said it as if it was catching.

October arrived with a torrential rain shower. Over the course of a few days, front yard lawns all over Portland came back to life, transitioning from matted yellow to luscious green. Gutters filled up with water and dead leaves. Rebekah and Megan checked the corners of their basement every morning and evening to make sure it wasn't leaking.

Fall meant moisture. A heavy inversion of fog settled into the cedar trees in the west hills of Portland. The fog was there when Rebekah arrived at work in the morning, and the fog was still there when Rebekah left at night. Everything was dripping. Everything would drip until next July.

Fall also heralded a flux of holidays: Rosh Hashanah, the Jewish New Year; Yom Kippur, the Day of Repentance; Sukkot, the harvest holiday; Simchah Torah, a celebration of the Torah; Rebekah's birthday, a day of accidental solemnity. This year, Yom Kippur fell after Rebekah's 31st birthday.

Rebekah and Megan made plans to attend Beth Chaver, Rebekah's childhood synagogue, for Yom Kippur services. They would go with Rebekah's parents, as they did every year. For Rebekah and Megan, Yom Kippur services were an annual pilgrimage, a physical tithe to the constructs of their faith.

Beth Chaver's Kol Nidre service started at eight, after the sunset. The synagogue hadn't changed much since Rebekah's childhood. It still sat, tall and imposing, at the top of a hill on Portland's west side. The synagogue's long driveway, that seemed to wind its way from the bottom of the Willamette Valley to the top of Oregon's coastal range, was still paved with black asphalt. Inside, there were still rows of benches and chairs facing the bimah, or raised stage, with its ark enclosing a Torah scroll. The synagogue's constancy was sheathed in its mottled rock walls and velvet chair covers, its plush red carpet and ornate, decorative wall hangings. If Beth Chaver ever changed, it would be in small increments: a rug refinished one year, a ceiling repainting the next. Too many physical changes would seem too jarring, a reminder that its builders were mortal, not spared from death, despite their faith.

Rebekah, Megan, Judith, and Daniel walked into the synagogue at seven forty-five. The front rows had already filled up, so the Cohayn family slid into seats near the back.

Rebekah looked around. When she was a child, she had thought that everyone who attended synagogue was old. Parents of newborn babies were old, the rabbi was old, hunched-over people with canes and walkers seemed ancient. The synagogue's demographic hadn't changed much in the last thirty years. Parents of newborns—children themselves when Rebekah was little—pushed black strollers through the synagogue doors, opting for aisle seats, if they were available. Childless couples who appeared past child-rearing years huddled together in groups of two, sometimes with canes or walkers, scarves wrapped around their necks, hats tucked under their chairs. Children squirmed in their seats, feeling grown-up and important in their synagogue clothes, playing games with their hands and laughing at jokes that no one else could understand. The adults looked stiff and insecure. Their hands were folded in their laps. They watched people walk in, playing with the collars of their shirts and adjusting the hems of their pants. They stole glances at their children, at their neighbors, and at the front of the synagogue, where the rabbi was making last-minute adjustments in preparation for the service.

There were also the synagogue regulars, people wearing cloth shoes and long, flowing white clothes, who were walking around, greeting other people. These were the ones on synagogue social and planning committees, the ones who had official titles and who solicited donations, the ones who seemed so imposing in their kindness and spiritual confidence. The synagogue regulars were at home here, welcomed and welcoming, as if they had been born into their administrative roles.

Ten minutes after eight, Rabbi Joshua Miller approached the microphone. He had short white hair and a full beard. He was wearing a white robe, white fabric shoes, a white tallit, and a white kippah. In a different context, he might have been able to walk unobserved through a snowstorm, a short, bespectacled, and rather well put-together snowman.

"Gut Yontiff," Rabbi Miller said into the microphone.

"Gut Yontiff," the audience murmured back.

"For those of you who don't know me, I'm Rabbi Joshua Miller," he said. "Welcome to Beth Chaver. Thank you for joining us tonight." The rabbi motioned to someone sitting in a chair at the back of the bimah. "Rabbi Jacob Green will be leading our prayer service over the candles."

Rebekah leaned forward. Jacob Green?

Rebekah had last seen Jacob Green when they were graduating from high school. Jacob had looked so confident and smart in his red robe, his curly hair poking out beneath his mortarboard, a careless smile on his face. He was the valedictorian of the class, and he had led the processional down to the football field, where he'd given a clever speech about how his acting roles for the Calvin Coolidge High School Theater had informed his identity.

"Do we ever really stop acting?" Jacob had asked the assembled students and parents. "Or is to call our behavior 'acting' simply a more honest assessment of our constant struggle to figure out who we are?"

Jacob had written "Cal" on the top of his cap, advertising that he was headed to UC Berkeley to study biology. An odd choice, Rebekah had thought at the time, for a Hamlet. Wouldn't he have chosen to major in theater, or English? To write, to create, to study art and artists? Maybe Jacob thought he had a healing touch? Or: talent to heal, that the extraordinary luck he had carried throughout his childhood could be extended to his patients.

Here he was, walking to the microphone, looking far more like a rabbi than a doctor. Jacob's curly hair was short, neatly tapered around his head. His face looked thinner, his cheekbones poking through nearly translucent white skin. Rebekah was too far away to see his eyes, to determine whether or not he was smiling. He walked slowly, deliberately, his face straight ahead. Rebekah made a mental note to send him an email.

"Shana tova," Jacob said.

"Shana tova," the audience responded.

"I would like to invite Arianne Klein, our synagogue president, to help me light the candles," Jacob said.

Arianne, a diminutive woman with short black hair, walked up onto the bimah. Jacob cupped his hands around the wicks, while Arianne struck a match against a matchbox. The first match she struck went out; she tried again, this time with Jacob cupping his hands around the match and the box. The two leaned in towards the candles, the delicate, wavering flame between them. When they pulled back, the two long, white holiday candles had been lit.

Jacob and Arianne brought their hands to their eyes, and recited with the congregation, *"Boruch atah Adonai eloheinu melech haolom asher kideshanu bemitzvotov vetzivanu lehadlik ner shel Yom Hakipurim."*

Arianne smiled at Jacob, shook his hand, and walked off the bimah.

"Please rise for the opening of the ark," Jacob said. He walked to the side of the bimah, to make room for Rabbi Miller and the cantor.

Rebekah stood alongside Megan and her parents. She looked around. A silence had settled over the congregation. Even the children, fidgeting only minutes before, seemed to sense the gravity of the moment. They stood, little people with cherubic cheeks, holding onto their parents hands. Unable to see over the tall adults in front of them, they looked instead to the side, the back, or up into their parent's faces, seeking visual cues about how to act.

The wooden ark had two doors, opening to either side like stiff, ceremonial curtains. Two members of the synagogue congregation reached inside and pulled out the Torah scrolls. The members stood on either side of the cantor, facing the ark, holding the Torah scrolls above their heads. The three people standing up on the bimah represented the convening of a beit din, or heavenly rabbinical court. The cantor began to sing in Hebrew:

In the tribunal of heaven and the tribunal of earth, by the permission of God, and by the permission of this holy congregation, we hold it lawful to pray with the transgressors.

The cantor sang slowly in a deep, rich tenor. His pitch was pure, the timbre strong. His words floated above the congregation, bridging the gap between sky and soil. Congregants raised their voices to match the cantor's.

In the tribunal of heaven and the tribunal of earth, by the permission of God, and by the permission of this holy congregation, we hold it lawful to pray with the transgressors.

Rebekah felt herself slipping into the physicality of the cantor's voice. She sang quietly, just loud enough to hear her own voice, but not so loud that she sang over Megan or her parents.

The cantor paused. The moment hung. He took a breath. "*Kol Nidre*," he began.

All vows we are likely to make, all oaths and pledges we are likely to take between this Yom Kippur and next Yom Kippur, we publicly renounce. Let them all be relinquished and abandoned, null and void, neither firm nor established. Let our vows, pledges, and oaths be considered neither vows nor pledges nor oaths.

The slow, aching melody seeped straight into Rebekah's skin. The hair on her arms stood straight up. A lump rose in her throat. This song was a memory from her childhood. She used to sing this song standing next to David. She remembered how he never actually sang, but stared at the prayer book, thinking thoughts that he never shared. She imagined him now, standing in his own synagogue singing the Kol Nidre. What did David repent for?

Rebekah looked at Jacob standing on the bimah. He was rocking slowly back and forth, eyes closed, singing along with the cantor. *All vows.* Before coming out, life had fit into a much smaller, simpler frame. Home life was confined to the space within the walls of her parent's home. There were her parents, who loved her. David, whom she loved. Grandma Simchah, who—despite near constant complaining—attended nearly every family function. Rebekah's exterior life was mostly made up of people at school and in her small circle of friends. Life was regimented. There was good and evil. Sickness and health.

All vows. The ideals that used to be so simple had become so complicated. The life she had thought lay before her, like a taut string between two tin cans, turned out to be an infinitely stranded affair, in which right and wrong seemed undefined. Beside her was a woman she loved, to whom she owed an explanation. On the other side were her parents, to whom she owed honesty. Surrounding her was a community with whom she'd had little contact, on the premise that they could never provide the answers she sought in the middle of the night.

And then there was David, singing Kol Nidre a thousand miles away with his family. Of what sin was he absolving himself?

"Kol Nidre…" the congregation sang.

Rebekah closed her eyes, submitting to an overwhelming feeling of guilt. She felt so small, so weak, as though she might melt into a puddle in the heels of her shoes. Her lower lip trembled. She burned at the flakiness of her own soul, raged against her autonomous heart, and burned with humiliation at her own perceived ineptitude.

Always born on Yom Kippur. Always repenting.

People ready themselves for such moments. They seek them in books, from exercise, or in daily ritual, like meditation or gardening. Such revelations are sought by our species. They feel like raindrops that are capable of scrubbing blood and bones. They've got magic in their molecules, and can swell hearts and grow vertebrae. We walk away from such moments feeling like over-exposed photographs: bright, splotchy, and confused, hung up to dry in dark rooms, hoping that when we step out again, we'll be able to function in the world.

"Kol Nidre…" the cantor sang. His voice was so strong. Rebekah felt so weak. She was walking into a Yom Kippur in which she would ask for forgiveness, and she felt she would be given none. If she were written into the Book of Life, then she would walk through the next year, and the year after that, and after that, with a blackened face. If she were written into the Book of Death, then at least her freedom would be taken. At least she wouldn't have to choose between love and her family, her brother and her wife, the fury in her brain and the chaos in her soul.

The Kol Nidre ended. The two people holding the Torahs sat down on chairs on the bimah. As the congregation was sitting down, Rebekah gently squeezed Megan's arm and whispered, "Be right back."

Rebekah put her prayer book down on her chair and walked slowly, on wobbly legs, towards the door. She walked into the bathroom, gently closed the door of a stall behind her, and threw up.

November 8, 2011

Late in October, Rebekah saw a new email pop up in her inbox.

Hi there,
My name is Jacob Green. I'm looking for my friend Rebekah
Cohayn. Is this the right person? I googled your name and found this
email address.
I thought I saw you and your family at Kol Nidre services at Beth
Chaver. You guys were sitting near the back, so I couldn't tell for
sure.
If you're in town, I would love to see you and catch up. Coffee?
Best,
Jake

Rebekah sat back in her chair. How could Jacob have possibly seen her? Her family had sat way in the back, in the bowels of the congregation.

She re-read the email. Lucky Jacob Green, the boy to whom serendipity attached itself like thousands of little burs. He'd seen her, somehow, amidst the thousands of other congregants in the synagogue. Rebekah felt the power of being in his orbit again. Jacob Green's auspiciousness seemed to extend to his social circles, as if he distributed good fortune like a food charity.

Rebekah hesitated. She'd have to come out to him, too, the way she was forced to come out to everyone else. There were no meetings or reunions now that didn't contain this little necessary revelation.

Rebekah shrank from the thought. Coming out to David had been so traumatizing that Rebekah didn't know if she could handle a similar reaction from Jacob. But Jacob was a different soul than David: lighter, freer, less intense. Rebekah wanted to believe that she *knew* Jacob, that her old friend was unlike her brother, that his bottomless well of good fortune had made him less judgmental.

Rebekah pushed down the kernel of anxiety pressing into her throat and hit reply.

Jacob,
It's so great to hear from you. I've been meaning to email you for weeks. I would love to get together for coffee with you. When are you free?
Rebekah

Rebekah and Jacob set up a coffee date for the second week of November. Jacob reasoned that it was after the spate of Jewish holidays and before Thanksgiving, a rabbinic sweet spot of extra time. Rebekah proposed that they meet at Grinder's, a coffee shop downtown. The central location would work both for Jacob, who worked on the Westside, and Rebekah, whose office was just a few blocks away.

Rebekah arrived at Grinder's five minutes early. The coffee shop was set up like a bar, with low light, a long, gleaming counter that stretched from the door to the back wall, and tall tables for standing or sitting. A row of glossy latte machines anchored the back wall of the coffee bar. Drawings and paintings by local artists decorated the walls, and soft, alt-rock music floated down from large speakers on the ceiling rafters.

She saw Jacob sitting at a table near the back, holding a white ceramic mug between his hands.

Jacob looked up. "Rebekah," he waved. "Back here."

Rebekah waved back. She ordered a latte at the bar and walked to the back of the coffee shop. Jacob looked remarkably similar to the eighteen-year-old version that Rebekah remembered from high school. Crow's feet had gathered near the corners of his eyes. He was wearing glasses again, instead of contacts, and he had put just a few pounds onto his gangly frame. When he waved to Rebekah, he did so with the same smile, the same unbridled optimism that he'd had since he was a child.

He wrapped Rebekah in a tight hug. "It's so good to see you old friend," Jacob said.

"It's wonderful to see you, Jake. How long has it been?"

"Since high school. More than a decade, I guess."

Rebekah grinned and shook her head. "We're old."

"No kidding."

"Did you order anything?"

Rebekah held up her latte.

"Good. The best part about coming here is the designs that they make with the foam and milk." He pointed into Rebekah's cup, where the milk at the top of the drink had been arranged in the shape of a flower. "Such a Portland thing, but I love it. It's just like a little bit of artistry with the caffeine drip."

The two sat down. To their left, a thin man with a handlebar mustache and tight black jeans typed on his laptop. Directly behind them, a young man and woman held hands across a table, their foreheads nearly pressed together. They spoke softly with their eyes closed. Rebekah leaned in, so she didn't have to yell to be heard above the music.

"So." Rebekah said. She smiled.

Jacob smiled back. "So."

"It's been a long time."

"Yeah."

"How are you?"

Jacob nodded. "Pretty good. Life is good."

"So…I gotta admit. I was surprised to see you at synagogue. You a rabbi?" Rebekah raised her eyebrows.

"Sure does look that way, doesn't it?"

"How did that happen?"

"Well…" Jacob slowly moved his index finger around the edge of his coffee mug. "It's a good story."

"I bet."

"I always thought I was going to be a doctor."

Rebekah laughed. "Right, I remember that."

"What?" Jacob asked.

"I don't know. I wouldn't have pegged you as a doctor, either."

"Why not?"

"I just always thought of you as the artistic type."

Jacob shrugged. "In seventh grade, we watched this video about kids with AIDS in Africa. Many of the women there don't have access to birth control. The prevalence of AIDS is so high, there's a decent chance that any form of unprotected sex might transmit the disease. And you know who suffers the most? The kids who are born with it. They're born with this disease, and of course have no resources to deal with it. What's their life expectancy? A few years? I was watching that as a seventh grader, and I thought, you know, that's really not fair. All those kids with that disease, and it's really not their fault. It just struck me as something I could do. Try to help those kids. Not a bad dream for seventh grade, right?"

Rebekah thought about the future she had imagined when she was in seventh grade. She remembered telling her mom that she thought she'd be a pretty good teacher. Being a doctor, or a politician, like David wanted to be, had seemed outside the realm of possibility.

"Right," Rebekah said.

"So that was the plan through high school," Jacob said. "It was convenient, because it made my parents happy. They could tell all their friends that their son was going to grow up to be a doctor. And since they were happy, I was happy."

"I thought you might have become an actor."

"Yeah, I would have loved that. But I think I brought it up with my parents once, and they weren't really into the idea. They said, 'Jacob, if you want to act, act. But why not have a real job, too?"

Rebekah laughed. "I could totally see your parents saying that."

"So I went to UC Berkeley."

"I remember that."

"When I got to college, it was like…wow. Are you fucking kidding me? I'm in *Berkeley*. There was just so much going on. It was like a professional Portland. You know what I mean by that?"

Rebekah shook her head.

"Here, it's like…life is pretty slow. You've got your coffee shops, and your bicycle lanes, and your zombie bike rides, and your organic food. Life is awesome. But Berkeley…Berkeley had all that, but, you know, more intense. People here sit in coffee shops to read books, or maybe grow their own business. People there sit in coffee shops to read books and pitch their startup to some zillionaire down the street in Silicon Valley. It was like going from college to the big leagues. That's how it felt, anyway.

"So I get there, and I'm going to school with all these ultra-competitive kids who all want to be doctors. And I still liked the idea of being a doctor, but I had to get through all these undergraduate biology classes. And I just kept thinking, Jake…what are you doing, man? There was so much to do. There was campus stuff going on every day. And then there was the city. Or cities, really. Berkeley. San Francisco. The Castro and MOMA and the whole entire city of Oakland. Forget the west side of the bay, man, I just loved walking around Oakland. The people. The vibe. I just thought, why am I staying on campus when I could be out *there*?"

"Uh huh," Rebekah said.

"So I continued with my science classes. With my electives, I dabbled in some other stuff. Philosophy. Eastern religions. I took an astronomy class that was pretty cool. But none of it was really hitting for me. I went to class so that I could go out and do other stuff. Because if I dropped out of school…" Jacob grinned again. "There goes my meal ticket. School for the most part was just like— go to class, try to stay awake, come home, study, go to a lab, do some ridiculous experiment, write it up."

Jacob leaned in. "You know what bugged me the most about those labs? That every single student who had taken the lab before and, I don't know, maybe hundreds, or millions, of students across the country were doing the same thing, the same experiment, and all getting the same result."

"But isn't that the point?"

"Yeah, but if that's the point, who cares? I felt like a damn goat being herded by a giant, multi-billion dollar shepherd, telling me: 'Here you go. If you spend an ungodly amount of time and money doing blah blah blah to get a blah blah blah degree, we'll give you a piece of paper that says you're just one step closer to putting on a white lab coat and telling people why they're constipated.'"

"Or…I suppose, in your case, helping children with AIDs in Africa." Jacob took another sip of his coffee.

"Yeah, you're right. I guess I'm reflecting how negative I felt at the moment. It was hard to keep sight of that goal when I felt so restless. I really just kept doing it because that's why I was there. Because my parents kept telling their friends about their son, the doctor, their only child who was going to save the world."

Rebekah nodded.

Jacob looked straight up at Rebekah. "So, then, my senior year, my dad got sick."

"What? What kind of sick?"

"Stomach cancer."

Rebekah's jaw dropped. "Oh, shit Jake. Stomach cancer? Is he ok?"

Jacob smiled. He flexed his jaw. "You've never known anyone with stomach cancer, have you?"

"No."

"You haven't because they're not around for long. Stomach cancer's a quick one. It might start in your stomach, but it progresses so quickly…" His voice caught. "It doesn't take long for it to get to your kidneys, liver, colon, lungs. And that's maybe even before you figure out you have it. Because when you go to the doctor with stomach pain, they usually tell you to stop drinking milk or coffee, or to eat more fiber. It's not until they feel something that they order a scan, and by then, it's too late."

Rebekah stared at Jacob with her mouth open. She felt guilty for worrying about David and the wedding. It seemed so petty now. "Wow. I'm so sorry."

"Thanks. It really just went by fast. I remember him telling me over the phone that he wasn't feeling well and he was going to the doctor, and the next conversation was like, 'Well Jake, I'm meeting with my estate attorney, because I've got stomach cancer and three months to live.' I don't really remember what else we talked about. It just seemed so unreal. I kept asking him over and over again if he was joking. I kept insisting that he was an asshole and lying to me. I just remember thinking that it couldn't possibly be true."

Rebekah didn't think it could possibly be true, either. Not to Jacob Green.

"Wow, Jake…I don't know what to say. That's just so sad."

Jacob nodded. "At least it was quick. He was in a lot of pain, but they found it so late that it wasn't for long. So—you remember my dad?"

"Very well."

"He was always a real jackass." They both laughed. "Do you remember him?"

"I do," Rebekah said. "I remember that he was always talking—talking about work. Loudly. And he smoked, right?"

"He did. He smoked first thing in the morning, and right before he went to sleep at night, and nearly every hour in between. I hated it. Remember how I insisted he hang that scented thing in his car?"

Rebekah remembered that Gary Green had owned an old white Cadillac with a red polyester interior that smelled like air freshener-propelled pine and cigarettes. Jacob's dad smoked a pack and a half a day, abstaining only when there were children in his car. It was Jacob who insisted that his dad hang the air fresheners from the interior rearview mirror.

Rebekah nodded.

"As soon as I left for college he took that out. I think he really just liked the smell of his own cigarettes, or something. Anyway, my dad—he was still himself all the way until the end. Funny. Loud. Bombastic and ridiculous. He died at home. A hospice nurse would come over and take care of him. And he was so drugged out that he was conscious for only part of the time. But when he was alert, he'd be bossing people around and telling them where to go and what to do, asking for his PalmPilot as if he was going to jump out of bed and start working again. 'Watch out! Joe Green is back from the dead!'

"So the second-to-last morning before he died, my dad woke up. He sat up in bed. He had a short conversation with my mom. He asked about the weather."

"The weather?" Rebekah asked.

"Yeah. Here he was, lucid for the first time in a few days, and he wants to know the weather. My mom was like, 'Well Joe…I think there might be some rain.' And my dad looks out the window. 'Rain,' he says. 'Of course.'

"Then my mom left the room for a minute, and my dad called me over to his bed. 'Jakey,' my dad says." Jacob mimicked his dad's croaking voice. 'Jakey, get me a cigarette.'"

Jacob opened his mouth wide to show his reaction. "What the hell, right?" Jacob whispered loudly, smiling. "Here's my dad, dying, asking for a cigarette. So I said, 'Um, Dad, I don't think you should smoke right now.'

"And Dad chokes out, 'Jake…' again, and then he just points to his briefcase at the foot of his bed. It was his work briefcase that he insisted be in the room. So I searched through his briefcase, and sure enough, there was one cigarette, hidden in an interior pocket."

"What did you do?" Rebekah asked.

"What was I going to do? I opened the window as wide as I could, lit the damn thing, and put it to his lips."

"Could he smoke?"

Jacob snorted. "No. He could barely breathe. He tried to take a drag, but he started coughing. So I put the cigarette out on the windowsill, tossed it, tried to fan the air with a pillow for a bit, and then called the nurse.

"When the nurse got there, she checked his drip, calmed him down a little. And when he was finally calm, and the nurse was gone, he looked at me and gave me this little nod. Like…you know. He got his last smoke in."

"Ha." Rebekah shook her head. "How's your mom?"

"Oh, she's ok. This was hard for her. It was really hard, actually. She was a wreck for about six months after. But she's ok now. It took a little bit, but she's ok."

"That's good."

Jacob nodded again.

"And how are you?"

"Oh, I'm fine now. After my dad died, not so much." He took another sip of his coffee and smiled tightly into his mug. "It happened my senior year. So here I am, going through the motions to get into med school, and Dad gets stomach cancer and dies."

He pushed back on his chair, so that he was balancing on its back two legs. After a few seconds, he let go of the table and allowed the chair to fall with a thud.

"You know, I learned far, far more about medicine in the three months my dad was sick than I learned in my four years at one of the supposedly best universities in the world. I had no idea how messed up our medical system is until I witnessed that. Do you know what chemo is? It's poison. Doctors pour poison into your body in the hopes that it will kill you more slowly than your cancer. My dad was riddled with tumors. They were…you know. Everywhere. The situation was clear? Ok? Crystal fucking clear. I'm no oncologist, but when I saw the scans, I knew what my dad was up against. I knew it wasn't worth the fight. But the doctor suggested we do surgery and chemo. For what reason? Why? Why would we do that?"

Jacob shook his head.

"So after that first semester senior year—it wasn't much of a semester, really. I had taken a bunch of time off to fly up to Portland and be with my dad. I didn't expect anyone to save him, but it was shocking how much the system failed him. The doctors failed him. And I saw it. And I just didn't want to do it anymore. It made me sick."

Jake was spitting his words now. He looked visibly angry. He tipped his coffee mug back to his lips, then drew it back and looked inside.

It must have been empty, because he took a deep breath—a long, slow drag of air—and set his mug back on the table.

"I about bombed my finals," he continued quietly. "But, you know, it seemed so unimportant. I had just lost my dad. I went home over break to be with my mom. And I really didn't want to go back to school after that. About a week before I was supposed to leave, I told my mom I was thinking about taking some time off school."

"And?"

"And…" Jake shrugged and laughed. "And nothing. She just looked at me as if I was speaking in another language. It was…it was totally bizarre. I think she knew I wasn't asking for her permission, but it was pretty clear what she thought about it. She really hated the idea."

"So you went back to school?"

"Yeah. I just didn't want to push it. Her husband had just died, and her Jewish doctor son was threatening to drop out of Berkeley. It probably would have killed her."

"And you had one semester left."

"Exactly. I figured that if I didn't finish now, I never would. I was mentally gone. I don't remember a thing from my classes that semester." Jake lifted his hands in the air. "But somehow I got through it, and graduated, and walked away with a BS in Biology. Barely."

"Uh-huh," Rebekah said.

"Yeah. So then I just decided to get the hell out. I asked my mom if I could borrow a little money to buy a one-way plane ticket. It wasn't until she said yes that I really thought about where I wanted to go, and I decided I wanted to go to Israel and live on a kibbutz for a little while."

Rebekah raised her eyebrows. "A kibbutz?"

"I had gone to Israel as a teenager. My family spent some time on a kibbutz. Do you know what a kibbutz is?"

"Sort of," Rebekah said.

"A kibbutz is a group of people who choose to live communally. It's sort of like a communal farm, where everyone takes part in the work, and everyone takes part in the profits. They've been around since the founding of Israel, an attempt to create these utopian islands of socialism. They've become more capitalistic than they used to be— you know, hiring foreign labor to work in the fields and whatnot—

but a few of them are still the same idealistic little communes that kibbutzniks originally imagined.

"So my family had spent some time on a kibbutz. I had worked in an olive grove back then. And I just remembered feeling so at peace, feeling like this was such a cool idea. I would put in a day of work and get to live in a beautiful place, with enough to eat, and I could turn off my brain about my dad, and medical school, and everything fucked up that had happened."

"And how was it?"

"It was—it changed my life. That year was so tough, and so wonderful, and so emotionally draining, and so healing. I worked. I did a bunch of different things. I worked in the olive grove for a while again. Then I drove a bus. I just did lots of little things, whatever. It wasn't important. I didn't know how to do any of it. I had this degree from a fancy university, but otherwise I was totally useless.

"When I first got to the kibbutz I would go on these long walks. Like, fifteen-mile walks. I wouldn't bring anything, not even water. And I would just think about life, and my dad, and everything that happened in the last year. Have you ever been on a long walk in the desert without water? After just a few miles, your throat begins to hurt. By the sixth mile, your head is hurting, and you begin stumbling. By mile fifteen, things are dangerous. You can barely see. You're stumbling. You're wishing either for water or for death. By the time I got back, I would feel like I was about to pass out. I'd find some water, and drink and drink until I was so full that I could barely walk. Sometimes I would cry. I would wonder if that's how my dad felt before he died. And I did those walks over and over again. And every time, I wondered if I felt like my dad did."

Rebekah looked at her table. She thought about her long walk home from Ruth's house. *I'm not gay. I'm not gay.*

"There's something about being away, like totally away, and being around people who really just don't care about anything, other than whether you can milk a cow or like the same music or video games they do. It gives you some perspective," Jacob continued. "I got perspective. I felt totally certain that I wanted nothing to do with medicine. I thought that I'd rather die than go home and become a doctor, and think about my dad every day, and fail people the way those doctors failed my dad. And it wasn't even like, 'Oh, I can be better than them.' It was the whole system that I wanted nothing do with.

"I went on my last long walk about seven months into my stay on the kibbutz. I got back, drank a whole bunch of water, felt my life come back to me, like I always did. And I—I remember this so clearly—I was sitting on the floor, by my bed, and my head was spinning because I was so dehydrated. And I just…I just had this realization that I didn't need the walks anymore. They had served their purpose. They had drained me, taken my memories, nearly killed me. And suddenly, I just felt done. I had gone on my last one, and I wanted to leave them behind. Then, that Saturday, I woke up in the morning…and I decided to go to synagogue."

"For the first time?"

"Yeah," Jacob said, nodding. "A lot of the kibbutzniks don't care. The synagogue on the kibbutz is sort of—it's like, perfunctory, you know? And lots of people don't even go. They have it because it would be weird not to have one. I had never considered myself religious before. I still don't."

Rebekah raised her eyebrows. She thought about David, the most religious man she knew. David wasn't a rabbi. "Really?" Rebekah said.

"No. But when I woke up that morning and went to synagogue, it just felt right. I got that same kind of meditative time that I did on my long walks, but I didn't need to nearly kill myself to do it. I had this space, this time set aside just to think. I didn't even pay much attention to the service. I just stood up and sat down when I was supposed to, and listened to some of the discussion—the parts I could follow, anyway—but it was like…just three hours. Three hours, just for me. And I could drink water at the same time."

"So that's how it happened?"

"Well, sort of. I went to synagogue every Saturday morning. And then, when I came back to the states after a year, I kept going. Because it was the only thing that kept me connected to my time at the kibbutz. And then, after a few months of living with my mom, I had to find a job, and all I had was this degree in biology." Jacob's voice trailed off. "So why not be a rabbi?"

"Sort of seems like a big commitment?"

Jacob shrugged. "I guess I just figured it was something I could do. I liked being around the Jewish community. I liked the meditative space. And, you know. Maybe I could still go to Africa and work with people, but just in a different capacity."

A beat of silence passed between them. Rebekah stared at the ground. The couple next to them had disappeared, leaving a crumpled napkin and a coffee ring on their table. The man with the handlebar mustache was still beating away on his laptop.

Jacob had been through the muck and back; he'd walked miles in the desert, gone on a journey of self-discovery, beaten himself into a pulp, and then reformed into a believing non-believer.

And me? Rebekah thought. *I'm still lying. A decade of lying, and still doing it.*

But what about you?" Jacob asked. "What's new?"

"Well." Rebekah looked up. She picked up her mug to take a sip, but her tea was cold by now. She put it back down. "Living in Portland."

"Figured that much."

"Yeah. It's nice. I know it well, I'm close to my parents."

"And what do you do?"

"I work for an arts advocacy organization, running a newsmagazine," Rebekah said. "I collect art and articles from people on staff and students and publish it quarterly. It's something I really, really enjoy. The pay isn't great, but I do look forward to going to work everyday."

"That's awesome, the only way to live," Jacob said.

Rebekah nodded.

"Is there anyone special for you?" Jacob asked.

Rebekah cleared her throat. She reminded herself that Jacob was not David, and that it was the year 2011, not 1999. Things had changed; life forms evolved. After waiting a few seconds, Rebekah quietly said, "Yes. I'm engaged to a woman named Megan Nimble."

Jacob smiled. "Well, mazel tov! That's wonderful! Congratulations!"

Rebekah nodded without looking at him. "Thanks."

"When's the wedding?"

"Not until next year. We haven't picked a date yet."

"What kind of ceremony is it going to be?"

Rebekah looked up. "Well…" she said. Her voice trailed off. "Well, we haven't really decided," she said finally. "We're trying to figure it out."

"Ah." Jacob nodded at her. "What kind of ceremony does Megan want?"

"I don't know. Nothing too religious. Her dad is Christian and mom is Jewish, but neither of them have expressed a preference."

"So…what about a Jewish ceremony?"

"We've thought about it," Rebekah said. "The problem is finding a rabbi willing to perform a gay wedding."

"I don't mean to be presumptuous, Rebekah, but I would be absolutely honored to be your rabbi."

Rebekah blinked. Rebekah and Megan had talked a few times about an officiant. It was a difficult conversation, one that they'd continued to postpone, hoping that the right answer would eventually come to them. A Jewish ceremony would be nice, they agreed, but what if they couldn't find a rabbi willing to preside over a gay wedding? Rebekah knew that Jacob had received his religious training through the Conservative religious movement, whose position on homosexuality was rapidly changing. The Reform movement had long ago endorsed the ordination of gay, lesbian, and transgendered rabbis, and Reform rabbis presided over gay marriages regularly. The Orthodox movement adhered to the historical and traditional understanding of homosexuality—that the act of homosexual sex violated biblical edicts. Rebekah had assumed Jacob wouldn't want—or be able to—officiate at their wedding.

"Really?" Rebekah asked. "I thought…I thought you were a Conservative rabbi."

Jacob shrugged. "Sure. I am. But we're not monolithic. I can do what I want. And I want to officiate at a gay wedding."

"Jake, that would be wonderful," Rebekah said. She swallowed a lump in her throat. "Really, really wonderful. Thank you so much for the offer."

"Would Megan be ok with it?"

"She better be!" Rebekah said. Jacob laughed.

"I have to check with her, but I can't imagine that she wouldn't. Really. You're just what we wanted."

"Awesome. I'm thrilled." Jacob looked at his phone. "Well…I'm so sorry to have to do this right in the middle of our conversation, but I've actually gotta run in a few minutes. I'm going to a Hotel Workers Union meeting tonight. Why don't we meet to talk again?"

"About what?"

"Whatever you want. Definitely more about your wedding and the kind of ceremony you're looking for. I want to meet Megan. But really, I think it will be nice just to connect with an old friend." Jacob smiled at her. "Deal?"

Rebekah nodded her assent. The two stood up, hugged again, and pledged to set a dinner date.

When Rebekah shared the news about Jacob officiating at their wedding, Megan pumped her fist in the air.

"Yeah!" Megan said. "Honey! I can't believe you asked him!"

Rebekah didn't tell her that Jacob had offered. Megan's affirmation felt so good, so needed. Megan walked over, kissed her on the face, and beamed.

"I'm so proud of you, Bekah. I know that must have been hard."

Rebekah nodded. She smiled. "Yeah. It was."

The next morning, Rebekah spent her work commute commanding herself to share her engagement news with the staff at Stella. Seven months had passed since her engagement, and each month she had dithered away opportunities. In April, the wedding seemed too unsettled to share the news; in June, she told herself that she was preparing for her conversation with David and couldn't be distracted by drama at work. In July and August, she reasoned that she was recovering from her conversation with David, and September and October passed without much movement in their wedding planning. Rebekah imagined herself walking up to Roberto's desk and sitting down. She would initiate a conversation—breezy, easy, maybe about his upcoming Thanksgiving plans. Their conversation would take on the intimacy of a chat between close friends. It would feel as though they were seated at a restaurant with dimmed lights and discreet waiters, rather than in a work cubicle. At just the right moment, Rebekah would tell him.

"So, I've got some news," Rebekah imagined herself saying. "I'm engaged."

Roberto, shocked, would jump out of his chair. Their intimacy-bubble would be popped, but it wouldn't matter. The deed would be done. Greg would run over to give her a congratulatory hug. Jane might give her a curt smile, a friendly nod. Tony would invite her into his office to talk about wedding details. Rebekah would be gracious enough to extend an invitation to him on the spot.

Rebekah decided to wear one of her two pants suits that morning, a navy blue combination that she paired with a white collared shirt and black clogs. She thought she looked adult, elegant, and decisive. Much like someone who could, theoretically, be married.

When Rebekah reached her office, she flipped on the lights, started the coffee machine, sat down at her desk, and scanned her email. The September issue of *Daft* had come out two weeks earlier. After Rebekah's conversation with Tony and Micah, she had doubled her focus on increasing the artistry of the newsmagazine, while simultaneously intensifying fundraising efforts. Rebekah had tweaked the overall design slightly to accommodate a more artistic look. The new *Daft* featured an enhanced use of white space, smaller, sans-serif fonts, slightly softer edges on the text pullouts and infographic borders, and entire pages devoted to the prints of Stella participants. Advertisements were now given center-space space, cleverly packaged to look like artwork. Artwork bylines had been moved out from underneath art pieces and were now placed at the sides, often accompanied by a short interpretation. The look was cleaner, more streamlined, intended to draw more attention to the art and less to the design elements.

With Micah's blessing, Rebekah had decided to devote this issue's center spread to Dom Turken, one of Stella's first artists, the one whom Tony had anointed "the next big thing." Dom's headshot sat in the upper left-hand corner of the spread, at the beginning of a five hundred-word story on Dom's life and art.

Rebekah had dedicated the majority of the center spread to one of Dom's most acclaimed works, a piece titled "Union I." Union I consisted of two pieces of canvas, landscape-style, set up side by side. One of them Dom had painted a mottled purple. The other was a beaten, brownish-blue. He had cut out a rectangle in one, and a square in the other, and overlaid the holes with stiff black paper. Seen together, the colors seemed to bleed into each other, giving the overarching effect of one piece. Apart, they could stand on their own as distinct, individual works.

Bifurcated but allied, distinct and homogenous, this piece—or pieces—spoke to alienation, estrangement, a cultural split-personality disorder. It showed a deep psychological bruising and a lack of cohesive identity. Who are we? Union I seemed to be asking. Unified or shattered? Traumatized or fragmented? To what depths can we descend—and is there anyone to lift us out again? This piece was just the sort that Tony expected to draw national attention. Dom was speaking to the masses with his dystopian vision.

Daft was always released quarterly, on the first Thursday of March, June, September, and December. The newsmagazine was delivered hard-copy to subscribers, who paid an astounding seven dollars per issue, and it was accessible for free online. Tony justified the print price by saying that it was a fundraising endeavor, and his readers understood that.

During the last five years, *Daft*'s circulation had grown to nearly ten thousand, a number that Stella was proud of. Subscribers consisted of educational organizations, donors, music and art venues, and a few artists and educators who considered the price a worthy investment. It was also sent to would-be donors for free, an outlay that Tony, with the help of Jane Salish and the rest of the fundraising department, tried to recoup.

Rebekah hoped that a rejuvenated focus on one of Stella's most prodigious talents would spur fundraising. The art by itself should be enough to inspire, she had argued to Micah.

A few minutes after Rebekah began working that morning, Jane Salish walked in. She was wearing a short black skirt, black and white argyle socks, and a white blouse. Her blond hair, blow-dried straight down her back, flipped and moved with the soft arc of her shoulders. Jane's skin looked perfect, no doubt enhanced by moisturizer and foundation, the sorts that Rebekah imagined were purchased in expensive department stores by women who offered to paint your face first.

Like a 30 year-old schoolgirl, Rebekah thought.

Jane nodded to her. "Hey, Bekah."

"Hey, Jane."

Jane set her purse down by her computer. "How was your weekend?"

"Oh, pretty good. And you?"

"Great," Jane said. "We went to a piano bar on Saturday night. Have you ever been?"

"No."

"You should go. It's so fun. I'd heard mixed things about it, you know? But we all ended up having a really great time. The piano player was really amazing."

"Yeah. I probably should."

"Is Megan into that kind of stuff?"

Rebekah raised her eyebrows. Jane rarely asked about Megan. "Yeah, I guess."

"Oh, shit," Jane said. She was studying her computer. "Shit, shit, shit. This is not good."

"What's up?"

Jane looked up. "Is Tony in yet?"

"No."

Jane stood up. "I need to call him right now. This is really, really bad. Tony is going to be so upset. You think he'll mind if I use his office? I'd rather make this phone call in private."

"Um…"

Jane walked over to Tony's office and tried the door handle. It turned easily. "See? Unlocked. If he didn't want anyone to go in there, he'd lock the door."

Rebekah turned back to her computer. Jane stepped into Tony's office and closed the door. During the next half hour, Rebekah could hear snippets of her conversation. Every once in a while, Jane raised her voice to ask a question; sometimes she heard Jane laugh, her high-pitched, put-on laugh. Rebekah's sinuses ached when Jane Salish laughed like that.

Tony walked in at eight thirty and immediately shut the door to his office. Half an hour later, Micah rushed into the office, tossed her shoulder bag on her desk, and quickly stepped in behind Tony.

By ten, Stella's office had filled up. Rebekah heard the familiar sound of the ventilation system overhead, and the dull, dependable tapping of fingers on keyboards. She heard Roberto speaking in a low voice on his phone in the cubicle across the walkway from her. From the sound of it—particularly his consistent use of work-inappropriate swear words—Rebekah assumed that he wasn't making a work-related phone call.

Maybe when he's off the phone I'll roll over and tell him I'm engaged, Rebekah thought.

"That guy is such a fucking tool," Roberto whispered. "I can't even believe it."

Rebekah looked at him over her cubicle wall. Roberto raised his eyebrows at her.

"Ok, listen dude, I've gotta go." He paused. "Yeah. Uh-huh. Yeah. I'll call later." Roberto hung up the phone. "What can I do for you, Rebekah my dear?"

"Oh, nothing." Rebekah sidled up to his workspace. "Just wanted to say hi."

"Hi." Roberto leaned back in his chair and interlaced his fingers behind his head. It appeared as though he'd just gotten a haircut; his sideburns and neck had been neatly trimmed and shaved, and his mass of silver hair was neatly combed to one side, gelled so it gently spiked.

"Having a good Monday?" Roberto asked.

"As good as a Monday can ever be, I suppose."

"Oh yeah? Tell me more."

"You first." Rebekah sat down in Roberto's second cubicle chair and crossed one ankle over her thigh.

"Oh no, *you* first," Roberto said. "I always go first. I don't have anything to share, anyway."

"You must have something."

"No, really, nothing, "Roberto said. He sighed. "Rebekah, sweetie, I'm an old bachelor. I have old, bachelor friends. We get together and cook dinner and talk about how ugly we are. We lament the lost days, speculate about karmic retribution, and wonder if anyone is going to try to call up our spirits on an Ouija board after we die. I think about where I'll donate the small fortune I've amassed over my life—the Portland Zoo? Meals on Wheels?" Roberto lowered his voice to a whisper. "Stella?"

Roberto spoke with an air of delighted fatalism. A smile tugged at the corner of his mouth.

"Every day is just one step closer to death, my dear," Roberto said. "Maybe I'll move in with you, and then you'll donate your small fortune to me," Rebekah said.

"Oh no, never. Megan would kill me."

"Not if she knew there was money involved."

Roberto laughed. "I see. A smart girl you've got there. Tell her I'll consider you in my estate. How are you two doing, anyway? You never talk about your woman."

Here it was. Roberto had set her up perfectly. "Well....I have some news."

"News?" Roberto leaned forward and put his feet flat on the floor, his elbows on his knees. He was wearing dark brown dress slacks and a tucked in white dress shirt open at the collar. "I love news."

Rebekah took a deep breath. She looked at the floor.

"Rebekah? Rebekah, where are you?"

Jane Salish had poked her head out of Tony's office. She saw Rebekah standing in Roberto's cube. "Hey, can you come in here?"

Roberto looked from Jane to Rebekah. "Tell me now," he said. "Tell me really quickly."

Rebekah rolled her eyes at him. She sighed in mock annoyance. "I'll be out in a few. We'll go out for coffee when I'm out of the boss's chambers."

"We better," Roberto said. He faced his computer again.

Rebekah adjusted her suit and pushed up her glasses. She turned around and walked into Tony's office.

"Thanks for coming in, Rebekah," Tony said. He was sitting at the head of his long black table. Micah was sitting across the corner from him, her back to the window, Jane's papers on the table next to her. Jane pulled the door closed behind Rebekah. Tony pointed to the chair across from Micah. "Take a seat."

Rebekah took the seat across from Micah. Though Tony was sitting next to her, not across from her, Rebekah felt as though she was on one side of an interrogation table, with Tony, Micah, and Jane on the other. Rebekah looked out of the window behind her colleagues. She imagined it as two-way glass, with the rest of the Stella organization standing behind it, taking notes.

"We need to bring you into what's going on," Tony said. "We got some disturbing news this morning. Mr. Fuentes, who we assumed would be the primary donor for our Arts in the Halls Campaign, is most likely pulling out. He canceled his lunch with me this afternoon and left a vague message about needing to talk. We've been trying to get ahold of him all morning, with no luck."

"Yikes," Rebekah said. "So what happens if he pulls out?"

"We're trying to figure that out. We haven't given up on Mr. Fuentes yet. It's possible that he needed to cancel the lunch for other reasons, and he just needs reassurance about this campaign. So we're trying to figure out what he needs from us. If he really is pulling out, then we're either going to need to find another donor, or we're going to be pulling the plug on the campaign."

Rebekah glanced from Tony to Micah and Jane. The Arts in the Halls campaign was one of their biggest educational events of the year. It was the fundraiser that raised enough money to support them for six months, the premiere showcase for student art, and the set-up party for the rest of the year's fundraising get-togethers. Canceling the event would be a serious blow for the organization. Rebekah shifted uncomfortably and glanced at the thermostat on Tony's wall. It was only 72 degrees in the office, but the air felt stifling.

"Jane's on it," Tony said. "I have confidence in her to figure this out. But it's just a difficult time for a lot of people. The economy hasn't improved, like we thought it would. The climate out there is much more like 2008 and 2009 than we'd like. Things are really tight. Everyone is competing for the same people, the same money. I'd really like to find out what Mr. Fuentes does want to do with his money. I have a hard time believing he's just holding onto it."

"Do we know who else he usually gives to?" Rebekah asked.

"Arts organizations, usually. I'd be surprised if he were making any kind of shift away from that. But I would like to know his reasoning."

Rebekah glanced at Jane, who was sitting with her back erect, her fingers interlaced on the table, looking serenely at Tony. Usually, when a major donor pulled out of a campaign, an organization looked to its top development officer for answers. Such an occurrence should have been seen as a major mistake by Jane, and documented as a catastrophic blow to her job performance. But Jane had somehow convinced Tony that she wasn't liable for such a disaster—and, simultaneously, that she was just the person to fix it.

"Which is where you come in, Rebekah," Tony said.

Rebekah's head whipped around to Tony again. He pulled up the September issue of *Daft*. "Tell me about this."

Rebekah usually met with Micah post-production to evaluate the performance of the newsmagazine. Micah graded Rebekah on a few objective measures: hits per article, length of stay per page, forwarding and repostings for the digital version, changes in circulation numbers and written comments for the hard-copy publication.

Micah McDonald had a thin smile. It was the first feature Rebekah always noticed: lips pressed together, almost white; rounded chin and cheeks pulled back, as though she was hiding food in her gums.

In comparison to Tony's acutely enchanting grin, Micah's smile was a watered-down soup.

She was the calculated tactician to balance Tony's visionary capabilities. She micro-managed Tony's ideas, and turned them into action items. She oversaw the day-to-day operation of the business, while Tony met with donors, artists, and school administrators. The thin smile seemed to be a tired smile, born of a fatigue that came with the required niceties mandatory for anyone who had worked her way up the food chain of the non-profit world.

"Rebekah, sorry I didn't warn you about this in advance, but we thought we'd just have our post-production meeting right now and wrap it into this discussion," Micah said. "We thought Jane might be able to make contributions, too."

Rebekah nodded and gritted her teeth. Jane smirked across the table.

"So, how'd we do this week?" Micah asked.

"Pretty good," Rebekah said. "Nearly ten thousand hits so far on the Turken piece. "A few thousand hits on some of the other pieces—the ones on Cleveland Middle, and 'The Lost Canvas.' Fifteen hundred hits on 'Fall Food Art.'"

"Good. Anything on Facebook?"

"A little bit. I think mostly from Stella students. What's his name— Michael Hurt?"

"Yeah."

"He posted a few comments."

"He always does." Micah put the handout aside. "Did you pull the circulation numbers?"

"Yeah. Got another twenty-three subscribers."

"Ok." Micah drummed her fingers on the table. "So that's it? Nothing else?"

"Not so far."

"How do you think this issue went?"

"I think it went ok."

"Just ok?"

Rebekah considered the follow-up question. "Well, no. I mean, I think it was great. The writing was solid, and the students did a great job. We had some really interesting stories. I suppose if I had to do it again, I might bring the 'Fall Food Art' story out a bit. We had that one buried, and it still got fifteen hundred hits. But with the Turken story, we did a great job profiling one of our premiere talents."

Rebekah turned to Tony. "You told me to focus on two things: ramping up the artistry, and enhancing fundraising. I think we absolutely nailed the first one. The comments so far have been really, really positive about what we did with Turken. All good stuff about Stella and our artists."

"That's fine, Rebekah," Tony said. "But we're not here to talk about that. You're right, you're right…" Tony held up his hand. "And it's important that we give you credit for that. You did a great job with the Turken story.

"But let me spell this out for you, Rebekah." Tony held up one finger. "Remember what I told you last time? The objective of any organism is to grow. Shrinking is dying. Growing is living. If we don't fundraise, if we're not growing, we're dying. It's that simple.

"From what I can tell, that Turken story was not oriented at all toward raising money. I want to know why that is."

Rebekah looked at Micah, her eyes wide. "Well, I cleared everything with Micah, and she read the final proof."

"Micah's got a lot of things going on, Rebekah. Reading your copy isn't her only job. You are the one who's responsible for what happens with *Daft*. Micah is just supposed to make sure you aren't breaking any laws. She's an expert in finance, not newsmagazines. She's not a newsmagazine editor, and she's sure as hell not a copy-editor."

"Rebekah, I think we just had a miscommunication," Micah said. "I thought you were going to include something about making donations to support work like Dom's. When I didn't see it in your copy, I just thought it would somehow be a part of the packaging. That was an assumption I made, my fault. But I need to be able to trust you with this. I'm not a babysitter. Do I need to babysit you?"

Rebekah looked from Micah to Tony. They stared back at her impassively.

"No, you don't," Rebekah said.

"Good," Tony said. "So for this next issue, we're going to do something that's Jane's idea. Jane, do you want to explain?"

"Sure, Tony." Jane smiled at Rebekah again. Rebekah imagined punching Jane in the face, and Jane's head snapping back and smashing through Tony's big window.

"So, Rebekah…for the next issue, you're going to do your center spread on donors," Jane said.

"Donors?"

"That's right. Donor profiles. The whole thing. Depending on what happens with Mr. Fuentes here, maybe you'll make him the star. That might be part of our pitch to him, if he's thinking about backing out. But we want you to profile all of the people who have been supporting Stella, the ones who've made the art possible."

Rebekah blinked. "What about art?"

Tony pressed his hands together. "Of course, art. Art is always going to be most important. That's what we do. That's why we're here. Stella would be nothing without our students, without the production, without our mission to promote arts education in schools. But Bekah."

Tony closed his eyes for a second. He let the silence hang over the room. With his eyes closed, he looked like a wax model, like a man who could have decided to be a Ralph Lauren centerfold, instead of the executive director of a small, non-profit organization. Rebekah suddenly felt frightened of this man, of his intense charisma, of his ability to slice through his own idealism to its impenetrable, pragmatic core. Underneath his glittering veneer, Rebekah imagined that Tony was a modern-day Machiavelli, a man who clearly understood the raw machinations of politics. The goal of every organism is to grow, Tony had told her. When it came to business, Tony viewed the parasite as equal to the host, each engaging in the give-and-take necessary to advance his principles.

"You need to think about money as the handmaiden to art," Tony said. "They can't exist without one another. Who supports artists? Universities, organizations, philanthropies. People with money. We can't exist without money. And if we didn't exist, then arts in schools would suffer. This is about our students, not about us." Tony took another deep breath. "The bottom line is that we need fundraising to take center stage for a little while. When we get our books in order, we can go back to featuring artists. And by the way, I see no reason why you can't amp up the artistry of your donor profiles. Do you understand?" Tony asked.

Rebekah nodded. She stared at the table. "I understand."

"Good." Tony slapped the table with an open palm. "So Jane, when you talk to Mr. Fuentes, I want you to tell him that he's going to be featured in our next newsmagazine. Then you can pick a few other people who Rebekah can focus on for other profiles. I expect to see results from this."

"You will, Tony," Jane said. "I have no doubt." She tossed her mane of golden hair. Rebekah looked away.

"So, Rebekah, how are you otherwise? Tony asked. "How's everything at home?"

Rebekah felt herself sweating through her suit, the suit that was supposed to power her through this meeting, give her the confidence she didn't feel. She felt her pants sticking to her seat, her feet sweating through her socks. The air was so stale that she was breathing with her mouth open, like a beached whale. "Oh, you know, it's good."

"I overheard you tell Roberto that you had some news," Jane said.

Fuck.

"News?" Tony asked.

No, no, no, no. This was all wrong. This felt so wrong. This was exactly the wrong moment.

Jane's hands were folded on her desk in front of her. Tony was leaning forward, his chin on his fist. Micah stopped shuffling her papers.

"What news?" Tony asked again.

Rebekah felt dizzy. She opened her mouth and took a breath. Tony's office was a sauna.

"Oh…." Rebekah said. She tried to force a laugh.

"Is it about Megan?" Jane asked.

How did she fucking know? Rebekah thought.

Rebekah swallowed and forced a smile. "Megan and I are engaged." Everyone froze. The body language of the assembled around the table mirrored Rebekah's: tight and uncomfortable. Rebekah saw Jane widen her eyes, then drop her jaw a little. These were the kinds of moments that pass at a dinner table occupied by strangers.

Finally, Tony spoke. "Well, congratulations!" Tony said. There was genuine warmth in his voice. Rebekah heard murmurs of congratulations from the others. She nodded.

"When's the big day?" Tony asked.

"Next April."

"Good, a spring wedding," Tony said. "Well, congratulations to you and Megan. That really is wonderful."

"Thanks."

"Anything else?"

"Um, you're all invited," Rebekah said. *Fuck.*

"Well, that's very nice, Rebekah," Tony said. "Thank you, I'm flattered." Jane stared at her with a thin smile. Micah looked up at the ceiling.

"That's it," Rebekah said. Her voice sounded too clear and high-pitched.

"Ok, Tony, I need to open the door," Micah interjected. "It's just way too hot in here. I'm dying."

"Fine." Tony picked up his notebook. "I'm leaving at eleven, and will be out of the office for the rest of the day today. I'll be back in tomorrow at eight, then have meetings out of the office starting at two. I hope to swing by Ronald Reagan High School tomorrow around four o'clock."

Micah pushed the door open, and Rebekah stood up. "Is that it?" Rebekah asked.

"That's it," Tony said. "Thanks for joining us."

Micah walked passed Rebekah out of the office. Rebekah felt Jane brush up alongside her.

"Congratulations," Jane said. She gently squeezed Rebekah's forearm. "That's wonderful news."

Rebekah nodded. "Thanks."

Jane smiled at her and walked away, grinning at Greg as she passed his cube. Rebekah walked back to her cube, sat down, and took a long, deep breath of cool air.

WINTER

After Rebekah shared the wedding news with her colleagues at Stella, the event took on a thing-ness. Walking into work, she felt conscious of her status as a fiancée. She was ascribed, attached, soon-to-be wedded.

"So, how's the wedding planning going?" Roberto asked daily.

"Oh, fine," Rebekah would answer. She didn't feel like talking about the three caterers they'd met with, who all seemed to have the same versions of tiny meatball skewer appetizers, scalloped potatoes, and spinach salad with lavender vinaigrette. She didn't want to tell Roberto that she still hadn't picked out a dress, that everything she tried on made her feel like a Ken doll in drag.

So Rebekah lied to Roberto and told him that the wedding planning was going well. She lied to Megan, telling her that she was just tired from stress and fatigue related to work. She lied to her parents, and she told them that she could respect David's decision about whether or not to attend the wedding. It was his life, she told them, his family. He knew himself so well, knew what he believed in. Wasn't that all they could ask?

Rebekah lied to everyone who asked, all those well-intentioned people who acted as though a gay wedding were the most normal thing in the world.

Where were you in 1995? Rebekah wanted to scream at them. *Where were you when I was in high school and coming out? Where were you when it wasn't so easy?*

So much had changed. The world had changed. Gay people were getting married. It had been a weird, crazy thing to think about only twenty years ago, when AIDS and sodomy and perversity dominated the conversation about the LGBT community.

How had it changed so fast? Rebekah wondered. *How did I go from being a pariah—a halfling untouchable—to being in the mainstream?*

It was if she had been transported to a desert island for ten years, and come back to a completely different universe. Everyone around her had changed, and Rebekah was still in a closet, hand-fighting with herself.

With Rebekah claiming exhaustion from work, Megan took on the task of sending out invitations. She designed, assembled, and mailed them herself; a perfect job for an engineer, she told Rebekah.

WITH GREAT PLEASURE
MEGAN COLLEEN NIMBLE
AND
REBEKAH RACHEL ABRAMS COHAYN
KINDLY REQUEST YOUR PRESENCE AT THEIR WEDDING
APRIL ONE, TWO THOUSAND AND TWELVE
FIVE O'CLOCK IN THE EVENING
IN PORTLAND, OREGON

The invitations were simple: white cardstock, black print, and the outline of tree branches with small green leaves and yellow flowers flanking the texting. They were relatively cheap, under two hundred dollars for a hundred sets.

Megan and Rebekah received their first RSVP from Carrie Cline. There was a big checkmark next to "attending," and curly, squiggly handwriting all over the RSVP card. "Just can't wait, ladies!" Rebekah read, hearing Carrie say the words out loud in her Virginia lilt. "I'm so excited! You two are just the best! Love love love, Carrie."

Rebekah's parents sent in their card next. Judith had put an "x" next to attending, along with a heart and a smiley face. Otherwise, the card was blank.

Amy Nimble didn't send back the card at all. She called in her RSVP instead. "Hi girls, I just got your invitation," Amy said. Her voice floated out of Megan's cell phone's speaker. "Can I RSVP for John and I?"

"Sure, Mom," Megan said. "But you're supposed to send back the card. We paid for the postage."

Amy laughed. "I know, but I wanted to tell you. I'll give you fifty cents to make up for the stamp."

"That's ok, Mom."

"You guys getting excited?" Amy asked.

"Yeah, pretty excited," Megan said. "There's a lot to do between now and then."

"Oh, you'll be fine, you'll be fine. Hold on, your father wants to say hi."

Rebekah heard some shuffling as Amy handed the phone to John.

"Hello?" John said.

"Hi, Dad," Megan said.

"Hi, there. How you doing, Megs?"

"I'm good. How're things with you, Dad?"

"Oh, fine, fine. Work is good. You know, the usual."

"Good," Megan said.

So, got your invitation."

"Yeah, thanks, Dad. Mom told us."

"We're very excited, you know," John said. His voice was flat, deep. *We've reached our cruising altitude of thirty thousand feet. You may now use your electronic devices.*

"I know, Dad," Megan said.

"Yeah. So I'm going to have to wear a suit, I guess?"

Megan rolled her eyes. "You can wear whatever you want."

"Yeah, well. Your mom probably is going to make me wear a suit."

"Why don't you just wear one of those tuxedo t-shirts over jeans?" Megan asked.

"Yeah," John said slowly. "Yeah, that's a good idea. We'll just have to slip your mom something so she doesn't notice."

"Uh-huh."

"You guys have your dresses picked out and everything?"

"Um…" Megan glanced at Rebekah. "Not exactly. I'm thinking about wearing this suit-thing that I saw at a store a couple of months ago."

"You're wearing a suit?"

"It's not a suit, exactly," Megan said. It's like a tailored suit. Sort of."

"Oh," John said. He was quiet for a few moments. "Well, I think you've got the shoulders to pull off a suit, Meggy."

"Hah!" Megan laughed. "Thanks, Dad."

"And Rebekah?"

"Oh, well, Rebekah doesn't know yet." Rebekah looked at the floor.

"Ok," John said. "Well that's fine. No rush. You've still got time." John cleared his throat. "Well, ok, Megs. Just wanted to say hi and let you know we're coming to your wedding."

"Thanks, Dad," Megan said. "I'll make sure to include you in the catering numbers."

Rebekah and Megan didn't receive any other RSVPs right away. Daniel told his daughter that his brother Stedman would be there, and he'd be sending in his card. Judith shared that she'd double-checked with Grandma Simchah, and the old woman would be making the trip from New York City. Judith's siblings, the Phillipses, Websters, Aunt Sophie, Uncle Josh, and Aunt Rachel had tentatively said they would come; Judith anticipated that they would all eventually send in their RSVP cards in the affirmative.

No one knew about David's plans. Rebekah still hadn't spoken to her brother since her trip to Los Angeles in July.

One Saturday night in early January, Rebekah couldn't sleep. She tossed and turned, kicked off the covers, and then pulled them back up. She stared through the blue blackness, trying to make out the shapes of the furniture in their living room and kitchen. She imagined the basement flooding: rain water pouring through the windows, doors, and pipes, slowly inhaling their modest living space. The rushing water would be a soothing sound, much like ocean waves. She and Megan might even sleep through it, only to wake up when it was too late, and the water was rushing into their eyes and ears and mouths. The end would be quick.

When Rebekah looked at the clock the next morning, her eyes stung and head pounded. It was only five fifteen. Rebekah tiptoed out of the bedroom and gently shut the door. She started the coffee machine and sank into the middle cushion on the couch. She picked her laptop up, flipped up the lid, and turned it on.

She opened up the guest list spreadsheet that Megan had started. A hundred and twenty   people had been invited. There were only seven RSVPs.

The coffee machine dinged. Rebekah walked into the kitchen, poured herself a mug, and absent-mindedly stirred in a few drops of half-and-half. She walked back to the couch, closed the lid of her computer, and clutched her mug of coffee with both hands. Half an hour passed. Rebekah sat on the couch in silence, staring out the window, watching the sun come up.

She looked up when she saw the bedroom door open. Megan walked out, hair tousled, socks halfway off her feet.

"What are you doing up so early?" Megan asked.

"Hi, honey," Rebekah said. "I love you. You look so cute in the mornings."

Megan made a face and wandered into the kitchen. "Coffee?"

"Made. In the coffee pot."

"You're a goddess." Megan picked up the pot and poured herself a cup. "What time is it?"

Rebekah glanced at the clock. "Six forty."

"Six forty? You woke up at six forty on a Sunday morning?"

"I couldn't sleep.

Megan plopped down on the couch next to Rebekah. She groaned. "I think we need a new couch, babe. This one hurts my back."

Rebekah kissed her on the cheek. "Whatever you need, honey."

Megan smiled at her. "I love you."

"I love you too."

They kissed lightly on the lips.

Megan shook her head. She was about to start speaking when they heard a banging on the door leading up to the main house. Megan grabbed Rebekah's arm. She looked around. "Did you hear that?" Megan whispered.

"Of course I heard it," Rebekah said.

They heard loud knocking again, this time more persistent.

"Who's there?" Megan called out.

"It's me," called a muffled voice through the door. "Mark."

The Judge. Megan gave Rebekah a puzzled look and grabbed a jacket off the hook near the door. She threw it on quickly and zipped it up, then walked up the stairs and opened the door a crack.

"Hi, Mark," Megan said. "Can we help you with something?"

"Oh, yeah. Sorry to bother you so early, but I heard you guys, and I thought you might be awake. Mind if I come in for a minute?"

Megan stepped away from the door, and the Judge walked in. He was wearing his ratty blue bathrobe, which was tied loosely with a big bow. His feet were tucked into a pair of slippers. His hair was uncombed, his eyes watery. He was holding a large red cup.

"Hi, Bekah," the Judge said.

"Hi," Rebekah said.

"Uh, so…" The Judge glanced down at his cup. "All I really wanted to know is if you guys had some flour. I want to surprise my girlfriend this morning with pancakes. I have everything—the milk and blueberries and syrup—and I didn't buy any flour, because I thought I had some, but I don't. Would you guys have any I could borrow?"

"We might," Megan said. "Let me check."

She walked into the kitchen and began flinging open cupboard doors. "How is your weekend going so far, Mark?" she asked.

"Oh, it's just been great. Claire and I spent the day at the beach yesterday. It was chilly, but so nice. You know how lucky we are to live here? I grew up in a place with terrible winters." The Judge shook his head.

"Where?" Rebekah asked.

"Oh…" The Judge's eyes twinkled. "Up north. In a land called Michigan." The Judge held up his right hand, and pointed to a spot just underneath the thumb. "The winters were terrible there. Just terrible. Positively Siberian. I moved to Portland because I thought I could be happy forever living in a place that never had winters like that. And you know? I was right. I don't mind the rain at all."

"I found some flour," Megan said. She held up a small Ziploc. "This is what's left. Looks like it's about two cups. I'm not quite sure how old it is, because we don't do much baking. But you're welcome to it."

"Oh, thank you, thank you so much." The Judge walked towards Megan, the tie on his bathrobe slipping. Rebekah averted her eyes.

"I'll buy some flour and get two cups to you," the Judge said to Megan.

"Oh, really, that's not a problem. Like I said, we don't do much baking. It's probably better for you just to hang onto it."

"Ok, thank you." The Judge adjusted his bathrobe and looked around. "You gals having a good weekend?"

Rebekah nodded. "Yep."

"Yeah? What are you up to?"

"Oh…" Rebekah looked at Megan. Megan was staring hard at Rebekah. The Judge hadn't been on their invitation list.

"Just wedding planning and stuff," Rebekah said, finally.

"Well, that's wonderful!" the Judge said. "When is it, again?"

"April first," Megan said.

"April first, April first." the Judge looked up at the ceiling. "Well, I don't think I have anything going on that day. That's great! Claire and I would love to go."

Megan put her hands on her hips and cleared her throat.

"I know, I'm inviting myself," the Judge said. "I just really want to be there. I think it would be great to see you girls finally tie the knot. I just think the world of you guys."

He looked back and forth, a big grin spread across his face. Rebekah couldn't help thinking that he was tickled by his own invitation. Had he really even come for the flour?

Megan was staring at Rebekah. *Play for more time*, her eyes said.

But what would more time buy them, Rebekah thought? The Judge would just keep pressuring them until they let him go. Why not invite the crazy old coot?

"It would be delightful to have you at our wedding," Rebekah said. "Claire is invited too." She glanced at Megan. Megan crossed her arms in front of her chest.

The Judge clapped his hands. "Oh, great, that's just great. Have you guys sent out invitations yet?"

"Well…" Megan said. "Um, no. I guess we haven't. Not to everyone." Megan took a deep breath. "How about we just hand ours to you and save ourselves a stamp?"

"Oh, yeah, that's perfect," the Judge said. "I mean, the Postal Service needs our support, but I don't think handing me your invitation is going to put them out of business."

Megan went into the bedroom and came out with an invitation. "Do we need to give you an RSVP card?" Megan asked.

"Nope," the Judge said. "Consider me RSVPed for two."

"Will do," Megan said.

The Judge walked over and wrapped Megan in a hug. Megan draped her arms lightly around his shoulders. She was careful to lean forward from her lips, trying not to touch his robe with her body.

"So, what else is new?" the Judge asked. "Mind if I grab some coffee?" He walked past Megan into the kitchen, poured himself a steaming cup, and took a seat in the armchair across from the couch. The purpose of his errand lay forgotten on the kitchen counter.

"Not too much," Rebekah said. "Wedding planning has really taken over our lives."

"That's what happens." The Judge looked back and forth between them. "Do you two have an officiant yet? Or do you need my services?"

"We asked a friend of mine," Rebekah said.

"Just a friend? Does he have credentials?"

"He's a rabbi."

"Oh!" the Judge said. "A Jewish wedding. I wondered if you guys would go that route. Well that's great, just great. Yeah, I wouldn't have been able to do that kind of thing for you. How about your families? Are they excited?"

"The ones who are coming are excited," Megan said.

The Judge raised his eyebrows. He looked at Rebekah. "Your family isn't coming?"

"Um…" Rebekah swallowed. "David might not."

"Huh," the Judge said.

"He's not really on board," Megan said.

"He doesn't like her?" the Judge asked, pointing at Megan.

Megan laughed. "I think they liked me until they found out I knew their daughter in the biblical sense."

"Ah, I see, I see." The Judge nodded. "You know, my family didn't really like my wife. My mom in particular hated her. And you've gotta understand, my wife was a wonderful woman. Just wonderful. She was the sweetest, kindest, gentlest, most wonderful person. And my mom just hated her."

"Why?" Megan asked. She looked interested now, leaning forward on the kitchen counter on her elbows, her shoulders up by her ears. The Judge had never mentioned a wife before.

The Judge adjusted his bathrobe and re-crossed his legs. "Well, I guess you've got to know my family dynamic a little bit. I met my wife in 1958. I was twenty-two years old. In college. I was away from home for the first time, my parent's oldest child, and their only son. It was a different time, you know. These days…gosh, I don't know how you guys do it these days. But I grew up in Detroit, and my dad got a job with Ford after the war, and the expectation was that I would go to school, get a business or engineering degree, and then go to work for Ford, like my dad.

"And then I met Nancy. And Nancy…" The Judge shook his head. He closed his eyes and smiled. "Nancy was just perfect. She was the most perfect girl I'd ever met. A mutual friend introduced us, and I didn't want to be with anyone else after that. We dated for three months, and I proposed. Doesn't seem that long, does it? In those days, it wasn't that crazy.

"So I brought her home to meet my parents. And I couldn't believe it; my mom just didn't like her. Never wanted to like her. To this day, I'm not sure why. But I can only imagine that it was maybe jealousy. Or maybe she didn't think Nancy was good enough for me, for God knows what reason." the Judge laughed again. "My mom, rest her soul, just never treated her right.

"We wanted to get married right away. Really wanted to start a family, and all that. So the summer after my senior year—really, just nine months after we met—we got married in a little church that Nancy belonged to. It was a small wedding, just our closest family and friends." The Judge smiled. "We did consider eloping. Or getting married, and devising a way to keep it from my mother." The Judge sighed, and laughed again. "But…my Nancy said something brilliant. She said, 'Mark, we're going to get married in front of your mother, and your mother's gonna like it.'"

"What does that mean?" Megan asked.

The Judge uncrossed his legs and leaned forward. "She meant that my mom wasn't crazy enough to come to our wedding and screw it up. She knew my mom well enough to know that, if she came, she would be perfectly behaved. My mom just abhorred boorish behavior. And really, would she go to her own son's wedding and make a fool of herself?"

The Judge chuckled. "It was so long ago, but it still makes me laugh. All the pettiness. For what? It's a wedding. And they're both gone now. My mom and Nancy. Probably playing poker in heaven."

The Judge stood up and grabbed his flour. "All right ladies, I've gotta run. There are pancakes that need to be made. Do you two want to come up for breakfast?"

Megan and Rebekah shook their heads.

The Judge shrugged. "Fine. You're missing out. I make some great pancakes." He started walking toward his apartment, his hairy calves swishing beneath his robe.

February, 2012

"Rebekah," Micah said. "Can you join me in Tony's office?" Rebekah stood up. Micah was leaning out of the executive's suite, with one hand on the doorknob. She was wearing a cool gray business suit, her blazer buttoned in the front and cut to hang just below her waist. Micah looked tired and serious. She was staring at Rebekah with studied boredom, as if she was standing outside the elephant exhibit at the Portland Zoo.

"Hey—can it wait a little bit?" Rebekah asked. "I'm in the middle of something."

Micah glanced at her watch, a small gold bracelet that hung loosely on her wrist. "Five minutes?"

Try five hours, Rebekah thought. *Daft* was supposed to be published next week, and this was her crunch time. "Is this our copy-edit meeting?" Rebekah asked. "Because I'm not quite ready for that yet. Aren't we scheduled for tomorrow?"

"No, this is something different. A few minutes, ok, Rebekah? Tony and Jane are already waiting for you." Micah looked at Rebekah over the top of her nose. "Can you fit that into whatever you're doing?"

Rebekah nodded. Micah pivoted and closed the door to Tony's office behind her.

"Ooh," Roberto said. "Got sent to the principal's office again?" He was sitting at his desk, looking at Rebekah around the side of his computer.

Rebekah slumped in her chair. "It just never stops."

"Let it roll, baby." Roberto brushed the top of his shoulder, as if he were dusting off some lint.

"Right," Rebekah said.

"If life was but of slight concern, then death would be a minor turn." Roberto said with a slight bow of his head.

Rebekah raised her eyebrows. "Uh huh. Wish me luck."

"Good luck," Roberto said.

"Close the door, Rebekah," Tony said as Rebekah stepped into the office. Rebekah pulled the door shut behind her and sat down at the table. Jane sat to her left, Tony at the head of the table, and Micah with her back to the large office window. Rebekah shifted uncomfortably.

"Where are you in this next issue of *Daft*?" Tony asked.

"I've received all my submissions, and I'm working with the authors on some final edits," Rebekah said. "Putting the finishing touches on design. Micah should be able to look at a close-to-final proof tomorrow."

"Comes out next week, right?"

"Yeah. First week in March."

Tony nodded. He looked at Micah. Micah shrugged.

Rebekah glanced from one to the other. "What?"

Tony cleared his throat. "We're thinking about making some changes."

"Now?"

"Yes."

Rebekah shook her head. She tried to suppress the bile rising into her throat. "It's too late. We're far, far past the deadline of making any major editorial changes. All of the copy and pictures are set. We're just about ready to proof the thing. If you have a great idea, I'd love to hear it for next issue. That one comes out in June. We'd have plenty of time to incorporate what you want."

"What's the topic of this one?" Tony asked. "I know you've already told me, and I presume you've discussed it with Micah and Jane, like I asked."

"I did," Rebekah said.

"Ok, well…we were all just talking about it before you came in here, and there seemed to be some confusion. Can you explain it again?"

Rebekah cleared her throat. "So you all remember the last issue, right? With the spread on Mr. Fuentes?"

Tony nodded.

Rebekah had set up the center spread with a banner headline across the top of the page in big, black, block letters, reading: "Saving the Arts." The left side of the page featured a large picture of Mr. André Fuentes standing in an art gallery, laughing with the curator, examining student work. Rebekah's text focused solely on Mr.

Fuentes: a child of immigrants who had worked his way up from being a waiter to owning a very successful restaurant chain, Fuentes. Over the years, he'd accumulated a vast amount of wealth, a good portion of which he reserved for philanthropic activity. The thrust of the article was that Mr. Fuentes chose to give to Stella, and as a result of his giving, Mr. Fuentes was a happy, successful, deeply satisfied, and contented man.

After *Daft* came out in December, Mr. Fuentes called Tony to tell him that he was recommitting to the Arts in the Halls campaign. Other top donors increased their donations, as well. Late in January, Jane was still calculating the fundraising windfall; Stella appeared to have nearly doubled its organizational worth since the same time last year. Jane begged Tony to give her the rest of the month of January to keep working the *Daft* issue for other donors. Even though they'd missed the end-of-year cutoff, she said, maybe some of them wanted to make donations early on in a new year. Tony complied.

"Jane is one of our exemplary employees," Tony said at a staff Christmas party. "She's innovative, dedicated, and passionate—a role model for the rest of us." He led the Stella staff in an ovation. Rebekah hung in the back, the tips of her fingers lightly tapping the palm of her right hand. Genteel claps.

After the December issue, Rebekah received a higher-than-usual number of reader responses.

So glad Daft is telling us about all the rich people they rely on to keep their organization running, a reader named Ellersbee wrote. *What's next? A contest for students about who can create the most commercially viable art, with Stella keeping all the profits? Nice to see what your priorities are.*

LindaEagleCap wrote: *What do I need to do to get featured in Daft? Get rich?*

In perhaps the most poignant post, Student1993 wrote, "*Dear Stella, I am the president of the student art organization at my school. We meet at lunch time once a month to talk about art, and sometimes after school. We really like Stella, and would love to do more with you guys. Please feature student art next time in your magazine. We like seeing other kids' stuff.*

It was this last letter that Rebekah highlighted for Tony in early January as part of a report on reader responses. "Tony, I know we've been really successful in fundraising," Rebekah had said then. "But I think we're losing some people. This has been a really, really big change from what our readers are used to. We've zigged pretty hard in one direction by focusing solely on donors. Can we move back a little? Do this next center spread on something more student art-related?"

Tony studied the report. "I want to dispute your characterization that our story on Mr. Fuentes was not art-related," he said. "I think Mr. Fuentes would disagree with that, too."

"Tony, we didn't actually feature any art."

"Yes, but we featured a patron of the arts. What is art without patrons?"

"Ok. Fine. But I want to get back to showing art. This last issue did poorly with our readers."

"I hear you. But I also don't want to take our foot off the gas pedal," Tony said.

"Well, I think we can still use the magazine for fundraising while doing something about student art. They're not mutually exclusive, right?"

"Yeah? What do you propose?"

"See that last letter?" Rebekah asked. "The one written by Student1993?"

Tony studied the report. "Yeah."

"This letter was written by a student at Washington High, where Dom Turken went to school. I bet they're in the same art group. I bet we could do a really cool feature on them. Like, 'We all know about Dom, but what are Dom's friends doing?' If other students see what they're doing, maybe they'll start something similar at their schools. We can tell the story about how Stella can help support their groups, and donors can help Stella do that."

Tony nodded slowly. "You don't think we've done too much on Dom?"

"Well, our readers know him, but they don't know much about his environment."

"Ok," Tony said. "I just don't want to over-expose the kid. Are you going to work a fundraising pitch into the text?"

"Yeah. I will."

"Better than last time?"

"Yes."

"How are you going to do it?" Tony asked.

"Well, first I'm going to describe—and show—the student art work," Rebekah said. "Because student work is what's at the heart of all this, right?"

"Sure," Tony said. He drummed his fingers on the table.

"Then I'll talk about how, with Stella's support, the kids were able to form a student group that meets after school. They have resources because of Stella. They can be successful because of Stella."

Tony nodded. "Ok."

"And then I'll bring it out: Here's how Stella can help other groups. Here's the big picture of what this means for Portland, for art, for these kids in the long run. That's how we can fundraise, Tony. I know the last issue was successful, but how sustainable is that? We've got to get back to our mission. To the heart of what we do. Art and the artists."

Tony put the report down. "Ok. Well, it's ok with me. Make sure Micah is on board, and Jane knows what you're doing. Our goal here is still development, so let's not lose sight of that."

"Right."

Rebekah had checked in with Micah, who grudgingly gave her blessing. Rebekah sent Jane a quick email about her plan, but never heard back. Rebekah took Jane's silence as consent, and she contacted Student1993 to set up interviews and a photography session.

Now, sitting around the table with Tony, Jane, and Micah, Rebekah passed around a copy of her center spread.

"This spread is about the Washington High arts group, the one that Dom Turken grew up in," Rebekah said. Jane sat with her hands folded in her lap, staring at the document, which sat slightly askew on the table in front of her. Tony picked it up and studied it.

"This is good work, Rebekah," he said finally. He set the piece of paper down again. "But I don't think it's what we're looking for."

"What do you mean?" Rebekah said. "I thought you said I could go with it."

Tony looked at Jane. "Jane, do you want to explain?"

Jane gently pushed Rebekah's work to the side and folded her hands in front of her on the table. She looked like a teen pageant gargoyle.

"Rebekah, you did some really great work in the last issue, really, really great work," Jane said. "The spread on the donors was really a huge hit."

"With the donors," Rebekah said.

"Right. With the donors. Rebekah, we were able to nearly double our fundraising in December and January, and it was in part—in part—because of the work you did with *Daft*. I mean, we always bring a little more in at the end of the year, but this year was noticeably more impressive."

"And it was in part because of the work you did, Jane," Tony said. Jane smiled her radiant smile and tossed her hair over her shoulder. "Well, thanks, Tony. It really was a group effort. I think we can all share in the success."

Rebekah suppressed an eye role.

"So we really want to try to build on that success. I know we can't continue this forever, but we can really build on what we achieved last issue. We've got a lot of people's attention. A lot of our heavy hitters are going to be reading *Daft* now, looking to see where they fit in. This is our chance to really put out our fundraising message for the year."

"And I think we can do that," Rebekah said. "I'll add whatever you want into the Washington High copy. It's right there in front of you."

"Well…" Jane said. "I've spoken to Tony and Micah, and we've decided we're not going to feature the Washington High story this time."

"You all decided?" Rebekah repeated. "When did you all decide this?"

"We've been talking about it for a while now," Jane said. "But we just made the decision a few minutes ago."

Rebekah put her hands up. "Ok, so…first of all, as editor of this newsmagazine, I appreciate being involved in major decisions. Like, editorial and copy decisions. Am I not still in charge of this thing?" Rebekah looked at Tony. "Am I?"

Tony nodded. "You are."

"Ok. Then the last decision I was a part of was the one to move forward with the Washington High story as the center spread. *Tony and I* decided," Rebekah said, "that we'd turn the focus back to student art, and that we'd incorporate development messages into the text. I emailed you about this a long time ago, Jane. I can dig up the email, if you want."

"I saw the email," Jane said. "But I never agreed to it."

"You never said anything about it!"

"Well, I was busy, and I was thinking about it, and talking with Tony and Micah about it."

"Why didn't you talk with me about it?"

Jane stared at her. "Frankly, Rebekah, I don't think you understand how this game is played."

Rebekah sat back in her chair.

"We've got a job to do here," Jane said. "We're fighting for our survival. And sometimes we've got to be really explicit about it. This Washington High story?" Jane said, picking up Rebekah's document. "This is nice. It'll make people feel good. It'll show people what awesome work students are doing. But it's not going to help us open wallets."

"Jane's right," Micah said. "If you look at our financials, these last two months were just what the organization needed to feel good about heading into this year. We need more months like that. We've been operating on a bare bones budget for a long time. There's no cushion if a donor pulls out, or if we fall short for a month or two."

Fucking robot, Rebekah thought. *Fucking soulless, gutless robot.*

"Right," Jane said. She folded her hands in front of her again, her manicured fingernails resting on her knuckles. "Our Arts in the Hall campaign is happening at the end of March. I want *Daft* to open the floodgates—to bring people to the event, to get them ready to sign some checks, help them understand what's at stake."

Tony, Micah, and Jane stared at Rebekah.

"Do you understand what we're saying, Rebekah?" Tony asked.

Rebekah cleared her throat. She felt cornered, ensnared, as if she had stepped into the maw of a bear trap. She didn't know what to say, didn't know how to respond to this onslaught, except to give in. She'd been doing that her whole life: going with the flow, avoiding conflict, doing what she could to make people feel comfortable. Jane had entered this fight with a machine gun, knowing Rebekah carried only a paring knife.

"I do," Rebekah said.

Jane pulled up a folder she'd been holding in her lap. "Instead of the Washington High story for the center spread, you're going to publish this letter." She handed the letter to Rebekah.

Dear friends,
Art saves lives.

Art saved the life of Dom Turken, a former Stella student who now showcases his work at the Allen Art Gallery. Art saved the life of Kevin Anderson, a former drug addict and high school dropout who has now earned his GRE and is working towards a degree at Portland Community College.

Art has saved the lives of many, many students who have joined Stella over the years. Because of Stella, they have somewhere safe to go after school. They have a creative, productive means of expressing themselves. They've learned that they can succeed.

To keep doing this incredibly important work, we need your help. Our Arts in the Hall campaign kicks off at the end of this month. Join us and our partners for an evening at The Dapple House, where we'll be showcasing student art and sharing information about how you can get involved.

Help us make art. Help us save lives. Join us in our mission.

Yours truly,

Tony Hernandez

"You want this letter to be the center spread?" Rebekah asked.

"Yes," Jane said.

"And nothing else? Just the letter?"

"Just the letter. I think it will be really bold. People will open the magazine expecting to see what they usually see—a spread of some kind—and it'll just be this letter. It'll really draw attention to the content. I don't think this letter needs anything else."

Rebekah nodded. The letter itself didn't bother her much; in fact, she agreed with much of what it said. Art *does* save lives. Stella *does* need donors. The messages, and even the motives, were sound. What Rebekah felt intrinsically opposed to was the delivery. The bluntness of the letter—the ask so essential to organizational development—felt acidic, capitalistic, grubby. She should have been publishing a story that elevated readers. Art was about feeling, about being. Artistic products could be commoditized, but the artist—and art itself—could take people to a place that turned them inside out, made them feel as though their vital organs were directly connected to the cosmos. That's what saved lives.

"Whatever you want," Rebekah said. She cursed herself for her smallness.

"Great," Jane said. "So at the bottom of the letter, I want you to include a link, somewhere people can go to on our website for information about the Arts in the Halls campaign. Can you do that?"

"I can."

"Thank you, Rebekah," Tony said. "I know this is difficult to do to you at the last minute."

Rebekah shrugged. "Well, you know. Whatever."

Micah glanced at her watch. "Well, I've gotta go. I'm already a minute late for a phone appointment. We done here?"

"We are," Tony said.

Micah stood up. "Rebekah, let's keep our meeting tomorrow. You can show me where you're at with the new layout." She nodded at Tony and Jane and walked out the door.

"I better get to it," Rebekah said.

"Make sure you're working with Jane," Tony said.

"Yeah, Rebekah, I'd like to see the proof. Maybe I can join your meeting with Micah tomorrow?"

"Sure," Rebekah said. "Whatever you want, Jane." Rebekah turned and walked out the door, Jane's letter in her hand. She stood in the middle of the office, looking around. She couldn't go back to her computer right now. She needed to clear her head.

"Coffee?" Roberto walked up to her and slid his arm through hers.

"God, Roberto, I don't think you could have asked at a better time," Rebekah said.

"Well, let's go then."

Rebekah tossed Jane's letter on her computer desk and followed Roberto out the door.

The two walked to a nearby Grinder's. It was their go-to coffee shop from their office: a three-minute walk, with coffee discounts in the early afternoon. If Rebekah wanted to work uninterrupted, she brought her computer and a notebook and occupied a counter space for an afternoon. Today, the coffee shop was about half-empty, and David Bowie's voice floated down from the speakers mounted on the rafters. Bright flyers advertising music shows were pinned to a large corkboard near the door. Rebekah ordered a tall coffee, black; Roberto got a cappuccino. They settled at a small table in the back.

"So, how's the wedding planning going?" Roberto asked.

"It's going alright," Rebekah said. She swallowed. *Lying again.* "We're getting down to the wire, so everything is sort of coming together at the same time. It's actually getting pretty stressful."

"I got an invitation in the mail yesterday!" Robert said. "I'm so excited. Did you invite everyone from work?"

Rebekah looked down at her cup. "I did," Rebekah said.

"Even Micah?"

"Even Micah."

Roberto leaned back in his chair and smiled. He looked sharp in a black vest over a purple dress shirt, his collar folded neatly at his neck. "Gotta do what you gotta do."

Rebekah nodded. "Yep."

"Did you include some anthrax with Jane's invitation?"

Rebekah choked on her coffee. She picked up a napkin and dabbed her lips while Roberto laughed a deep, baritone laugh. Rebekah looked around the coffee shop. "You want to get us arrested?" Rebekah whispered.

"Will that get me out of working this afternoon?"

"Yes. And the afternoon after that, and the afternoon after that."

"You make it sound so appealing," Roberto said. He took a sip of his coffee. "So, tell me, is your family cool with everything?"

"Oh…" Rebekah shrugged. "Some are, some aren't."

"Your parents?"

"Parents are ok. I don't think my brother is going to come." Rebekah looked at the ground. "What can I do? Whoever comes, comes."

"You don't really want anyone there who doesn't want to be there, anyway."

"Right. Exactly. I mean, it still hurts." Rebekah took a sip of her coffee. She didn't want her voice to start wavering. "But you gotta just move forward, you know?" She forced herself to laugh.

"Yeah, totally. So are you guys going to go out of state to get a license? Canada? Massachusetts?"

"Nah." Rebekah swirled her coffee with a cardboard stick. "We're not talking about that right now. Unless we decide to go to Canada for a honeymoon or something. But we filled out the domestic partnership paperwork a few years ago. And I don't think getting a license in another state would help us much, anyway. The wedding is really just…for now, it's just symbolic."

"The exclamation point."

"Um…more like the dot on the bottom of the exclamation point." Roberto laughed.

"Well, really. I mean, at this point, I'm not sure why we're doing it, to be honest," Rebekah said. She swallowed hard. "I think it's important to Megan. But we're not really getting *married*, married."

Roberto put his chin down to his chest and looked at her.

"That's not a flattering look for you," Rebekah said. "You look like you have a double chin."

Roberto lifted his head. "Never."

"So, anyway. It is what it is. We're having a big party."

"You know, I've thought a lot about this. About the domestic partnership thing. A few years ago, I was in a relationship serious enough that we discussed getting a domestic partnership."

"Oh?" Rebekah said.

"Yeah. This guy. Ted. I don't want to talk about it."

"Ok."

"Ted and I ended up breaking up before that conversation went anywhere. But it was like, well, if we got a domestic partnership, how do we celebrate it? Can one throw a 'wedding' after getting a domestic partnership license? Do we need to wait until marriage is legal?"

"Good question."

"Ted and I had decided that if we became domestic partners, we'd go bowling."

"Why bowling?" Rebekah asked.

"Why not?"

Rebekah leaned forward. "I think it's really ironic that all the discussion about this supposedly sacred institution has become focused on parsing out tax and health benefits."

"Right. And do you really need a big party to celebrate putting your partner on your health insurance?"

"In this country? Yes."

Roberto pointed at Rebekah. "Fair enough."

"Unfortunately."

"So, Rebekah, I'm an old guy."

"You're not that old."

"Trust me, I'm old. In the gay community, I'm so old I might as well be mummified."

"What do you mean?"

"Well," Roberto said, "for the longest time, I think only one age existed in the gay community, particularly the gay male community. If you were a young, twenty-something, beautiful, lithe, thing, you embodied the ideal. You were single. You went to clubs and danced. You fell in love and allowed yourself to be loved, and you had glorious nights with men you didn't know. It was so liberating. When I was that age, I felt so alive." Roberto stirred his coffee. "When I hit my thirties, and then my forties, it was like I had passed through this unseen barrier. I was now *old*. If I go to clubs, I'm an old man among the young. I'm like an old mare trying to prance with the colts. Instead of a beautiful young gay, I'm just an old fag."

"Oh, come on," Rebekah said. "You're still totally hot."

"This is true," Roberto said. He smiled. "I am hot. I'm a silver fox. But I'm still an old fag."

"Whatever."

"It's not all bad, though," Roberto said. "Gay marriage—it's changed that equation a bit. Now that men are getting married and having families, raising kids, it's like the old fags have been given permission to be as frumpy as all the old heteros out there. We can be, you know, daddies. We can have spit-up on our shirts. We can be something other than beautiful and twenty-something."

"I suppose that's a fair point," Rebekah said.

"But here's the thing," Roberto said. He cocked his head to one side and continued to stir his drink. "Does our community really want that? Something I've loved about being gay, identifying as gay, is that we've got a culture that's different from straight culture. We have grace. We have beauty. We have drag queens and rainbows and parades. We're forever young, you know what I mean? I don't *want* to be a straight man. I don't want to have spit-up on my shirt. That's not me. That's not who I am. That's not what I identify as."

"Can we have both?" Rebekah asked.

"I don't know," Roberto said. "Honestly, I don't know. Sometimes I worry about what will happen to all the wonderful things about gay culture, if everyone starts getting married. Are you worried about that at all?"

"Worried about what?"

"You know, losing your queer identity and all that. Becoming a *wife.*" Roberto said the word "wife" as if it were smothered in a layer of fat.

Rebekah blinked. "I…um, no. I guess I really haven't thought about that." She looked down at the table. Rebekah realized that she had never worried about losing her queer identity because she had never had one to begin with.

Roberto leaned back in his chair and studied her. "Other things to worry about, huh?"

Rebekah shrugged.

"Well…whatever, you know. Marriage is a great thing. And marriage equality is important. Health insurance, social security, social acceptance; they're all important."

"They are."

"So, to sum up my thoughts," Roberto said with a flourish of his hand, "I really don't think you're giving yourself enough credit. You're getting married," Roberto said, making quotation marks with his fingers around the word "married," "in front of your friends and family, who all believe in you as a couple and as members of your community. In my eyes, that's as legitimate as any other wedding."

"Right."

"So why worry about the other stuff?"

"I don't know," Rebekah said.

"Don't worry about it so much, Rebekah. Just enjoy the day."

"I'll try."

Roberto took a sip of his coffee. "Speaking of not worrying, can we change the subject? I want to talk with you about your wedding, but that's not why I invited you out for coffee."

Rebekah looked at the ceiling. Journey's "Don't Stop Believin'" was playing now. "Sure."

Roberto put his cup down and leaned forward. He looked around the coffee shop. "So, you just got out of a meeting with Tony, Micah, and Jane about *Daft*, right?"

Rebekah nodded.

"And they're leaning on you to make it fundraising-focused, right?"

"Yeah."

"Do you have any idea what Jane Salish is encouraging Tony to do with *Daft*?"

Rebekah shook her head.

Roberto looked around the coffee shop. "You didn't hear this from me, ok? But Jane thinks *Daft* is a complete and total waste of money. She doesn't think it pulls its weight in fundraising, she doesn't think its readership justifies the cost, and she thinks that our money can be better spent elsewhere."

"What the fuck does Jane know about all that? How does she know about our circulation, or our costs? What is she fucking…"

Roberto cut her off. "She knows. She's asked Micah for all of the data. A few months ago, she started meeting with Tony about revamping it."

"What?"

Roberto nodded. "One of two options. Either she wants to get rid of the whole thing and spend the money on hiring more fundraisers, or she wants to turn it into a glossy thing, contract it out, then have fundraisers do all the writing."

Rebekah pushed back in her chair. She felt like throwing up. "How do you know all this?" Rebekah asked.

"Because I heard Jane telling Greg about it."

"Fuck. What does Tony think?"

"I think Tony dismissed her at first. But she's been working him. All the stuff you did in December, that big spread on the donors…it's sort of like Jane is using you as a prototype to develop her product. Did he tell you what he thought of it?"

"Yeah. He loved it. In the meeting I just got out of they want me to scrap my fucking center spread and print a fundraising letter. It's so fucking stupid. They're gutting it." Rebekah felt her lower lip start to tremble. "I thought it was something like this. It's just been so out of character for Tony, how he's been talking to me about all this."

Roberto stirred his coffee.

"So what are they going to do?" Rebekah asked. "Is Jane suggesting that they fire me?"

Roberto shrugged. "I don't know. I don't even know what Tony really wants, just what Jane is telling him to do. I bet, deep down, Tony thinks a fundraising glossy is boring. He's an artist, you know? That's why he started this thing. But it seems Jane has convinced him that it's time for a change."

"Shit," Rebekah said again.

"Do you know where Tony got the name Stella?" Roberto asked.

"No."

"Me neither. I've never asked him. But when I heard of the organization, the first thing I thought of was that scene in *A Streetcar Named Desire* where Stanley—have you ever seen it? The movie or the play?"

Rebekah shook her head.

"Stanley Kowalski is one of the main characters. In the movie, he's played by Marlon Brando."

"I love Marlon Brando."

"Right? He was so good in *The Godfather.* Anyway, in *A Streetcar Named Desire,* he plays this violent, passionate guy. A brute. He drinks. He loves his wife and beats his wife. In the middle of the movie, he comes home one night, dripping wet, really upset. He's desperate to see his wife. And his wife is in the landlady's apartment upstairs, above Stanley's, hiding from him. So Stanley is on the street, trying to figure out where his wife is, and he just starts shouting her name. 'Stella! Stella!'"

Roberto did his best Brando impression, lowering his voice to the appropriate, inside-a-coffee shop growl.

"And Brando is such a genius; you can just see his hopelessness. When he shouts 'Stella,' you can hear everything in his voice. Fear. Loneliness. Hunger. His wife is everything to him. And the thought of her leaving turns him into a little boy and a big, fucking empty man, all at the same time.

"That's how I see Tony. Tony is Stanley Kowalski. He's on the street, dripping wet, and he's this big, fucking empty man, struggling to find his love. I think he imagines that, to some degree, we're all like that. These kids he's trying to help? They're all Stanley Kowalski. They've all got their face pointed upstairs, looking to see a woman in white at the window. We all want to see Stella."

Rebekah raised her eyebrows. "Uh huh."

Roberto shrugged. "I love that movie."

"Maybe he just named the organization after a girl, or something."

Roberto laughed. "Probably. I'm probably totally wrong."

"Well, let's say you're right. What does that mean?"

"It means that you can probably still convince Tony to do something really amazing with *Daft*. I don't think the status quo is going to work anymore. But what can you show him? Tony is searching for something, that magic spark, that inspiration. That reason for being. I bet if you could show him that, he'd drop Jane like a Twinkie into a deep fryer."

"Didn't Twinkies almost go out of business?"

Roberto spread his hands. "All the more reason to go for it."

"Well…I have no idea what to do."

"Just be yourself. You're here for a reason."

Rebekah shook her head. "I have no idea what that reason is. You know, when Tony and I first started talking about this, nine months ago, you know what he said? He said, 'Rebekah, you're one of the only ones at Stella who's not an artist.' What the fuck am I supposed to do with that?"

"Prove him wrong."

Rebekah stared at him.

"Did you know that when I first met you, I thought you were aloof?"

Rebekah laughed. "Shut up."

"No, really. It's because you were quiet and serious. And sort of…aloof-looking."

"What does aloof-looking mean?"

Roberto shrugged. "I guess it's like bitch-face, but a little sweeter."

"Oh, come on. I don't have a bitch-face."

"No. But you know who does?" Roberto leaned forward. "Micah."

"Whatever. She's just smart. She's thinking all the time."

"It's not becoming."

"Whatever."

"Girl, just relax," Roberto said. He leaned back in his chair and crossed one leg over the other. "Just be yourself. Everyone's an artist. You just need to find the courage to express yourself."

"Maybe."

"Trust me. Trust me, ok? I'm old. I've been through the knothole a couple of times." Roberto drained his cappuccino. "Look, we should be getting back. I've got a ton of shit to do for the Art in the Halls campaign."

"And I've got to totally rearrange this issue of *Daft*."

Roberto pushed his chair out and tossed his cup in the trash. "I guess we'll sink or swim together, then."

Rebekah and Rabbi Jacob Green had only exchanged a few emails since their coffee date. Jacob emailed Rebekah immediately afterward to thank her for meeting him; Rebekah emailed back to invite Jacob over for dinner.

Jacob didn't write back immediately. In late February, with Megan hounding her to nail down some details about the ceremony, Rebekah emailed Jacob again, this time suggesting that he come over on a Wednesday evening in the first week in March. Jacob responded in the affirmative and arrived promptly at six thirty. Megan greeted Jacob at the door. "Hello!" Megan said. "You must be Jacob."

"I am."

Megan wrapped him in a hug. She was taller than Jacob by about two inches, and she stooped down so that her hand crooked around his neck and her elbow stuck out beyond his shoulder.

"Come in, come in! Welcome. I just took the chicken out of the oven, and everything else is almost ready. You can sit down, or—you want a tour? Rebekah, why don't you give Jacob a tour?"

Jacob stood at the door, wearing a slightly wrinkled, white collared shirt and brown corduroy slacks. His hair was mussed and damp, puffing out around his kippah and hanging down in loose curls by his ears. Jacob's brown canvas shoes stuck out from his legs like oval duck feet. He shuffled into the basement apartment, looking more like a boy who had raided his dad's closet than an associate rabbi of one of the largest synagogues in Portland.

"Sure," Rebekah said. "I can give you a tour. There's not that much to show. Our place is about seven hundred square feet." Rebekah stepped into the middle of the living room. She swept her arm across her body. "This is our living room."

"Very nice," Jacob said.

Rebekah pointed to a corner of the room, where a small, square wooden table was now carefully set for dinner. "That's our dining room."

"A delightful dining room."

Rebekah walked four steps to her right and pointed down the hall. "Bathroom and bedroom are down that way."

Jacob walked into the hall and poked his head into each room. "Lovely," he said.

Rebekah jerked her thumb in the opposite direction, back to the kitchen, where Megan was standing. "That's the kitchen."

"It's impressive."

"Don't lie. It's small."

"Bigger than mine. You can barely turn around in my kitchen."

"Well, Megan is the cook in our house, and she wanted to find something with enough counter space for at least a cutting board."

"A cutting board and a coffee maker," Megan said from the kitchen. "That's what our counter had to be able to hold."

"And it looks like your counters do wonderfully with both."

Megan walked into the living room, carrying a casserole with crackling chicken and potatoes.

"Oh, my," Jacob said. "That looks so good."

"Megan is the cook in our house," Rebekah said.

"Want to be the cook in my house too?" Jacob asked Megan.

"I'll do anything for the right price," Megan said. Jacob looked at Rebekah and raised his eyebrows.

Rebekah shrugged. "Engineer by day, businesswoman by night."

"Is that what you are?" Jacob asked. "An engineer?"

"Yeah," Megan said. "Electrical engineer."

Jacob turned to Rebekah. "And you work for a non-profit, right?"

"I do. Stella. Have you heard of it?"

Jacob cocked his head to the side. "Vaguely familiar."

"We put on in-school and after-school arts programs for students."

"Oh, right," Jacob said. "I remember you telling me. And you make their newsmagazine, right?"

"For the moment."

"For the moment? Is there a job change on the horizon?"

"I hope not," Rebekah said. She shook her head. "Never mind. Just work drama. Not worth talking about. This all smells really good. Megan, shit, what did you make?"

"I thought you'd never ask," Megan said. She lifted up the casserole dish. "Ok, Jacob, this is just what it looks like: baked chicken with garlic and paprika, and potatoes and carrots on the bottom to catch all of the yummy juices."

She handed the casserole to Jacob, and lifted up a bowl. "This is rice pilaf; I just toasted the rice in a little bit of oil, cooked it in chicken broth, and then added some slivered almonds at the end." She handed the bowl to Rebekah.

"And this," she said, pulling the last dish towards her, "is just kale, sautéed with oil, garlic, and lemon."

"Just?" Jacob asked.

"Is this ok?" Megan asked.

"This is perfect. It looks amazing." Jacob said.

The three dug into dinner and discussed the sorts of superficial topics readily available to new friends. Megan chattered about wedding planning and work; Jacob told them about life at the head of a large synagogue. Their talk gradually moved to the upcoming presidential election, in which President Obama was to go head-to-head with one of the candidates still locked in the Republican primary.

"You know, I kind of like Mitt Romney," Megan said.

Jacob raised his eyebrows. "Why?"

"I don't know," Megan said. "He seems like a genuinely nice, dorky guy. Also…" Megan pointed her knife at Jacob. "Universal health care in Massachusetts."

"Only because it was politically expedient at the time," Jacob said.

"Yeah, but I think it shows he's not bound to ideology. He'll do whatever he thinks is right for the country."

"Whatever he thinks is right," Rebekah said. "Which means he might do whatever."

"Like banning abortion," Jacob said.

"I'm not voting for the guy," Megan said. "I just think he's better than all the other Republicans."

"You're a Democrat, right Jacob?" Rebekah asked.

Jacob nodded.

"Good," Megan said. "I'm not sure I could tolerate you if you were a Republican."

"So I can stay, then?" Jacob asked.

"You can stay."

"I had no idea you were so intolerant," Rebekah said.

Megan gently dropped her knife and fork. Slack-jawed, she stared at Rebekah. "What do you mean, you had no idea? I'm one of the most intolerant people you know."

"Your dad's a Republican."

"Reformed Republican. He was a Republican in the 90's, when it was still cool. He voted for Dole and the second Bush. Actually, he voted for the second Bush the first time, and then he voted for Kerry. By 2008, he was all about Obama. So our family is solidly in Democratic territory."

"How about your parents?" Jacob asked, nodding at Rebekah.

"They're Democrats," Rebekah said.

"Really?" Megan asked.

"Yeah. They're conservative about certain things, but they think Republicans are idiots. Even David is a Democrat, I think."

"Well, you were saying he lives in Los Angeles, right? It would be tough to be a Republican in Los Angeles."

"So they say," Rebekah said.

"Ah." Jacob nodded. "He's pretty religious, right?"

"Yeah. He and his wife. And I guess his kids. They're all Orthodox. Shomer shabbas, strict kashrut, the whole bit."

"Have you come out to them? Or told them about the wedding?" Rebekah looked at Megan. Megan looked at the table.

"Yeah, they know about the wedding," Rebekah said.

"Are they coming?" Jacob asked.

"I don't think so," Rebekah said. David continued to refuse to confirm whether or not he would attend the ceremony. He met their mother's questions with counter questions, like asking whether the food at the wedding would be kosher.

"Does it really matter, David?" Judith would ask. "It's your sister's wedding. I'm sure we could work with the caterer and figure something out."

"It's just one more thing, mom," David would say. "And there are lots of things."

Lots of things. Lots of reasons why David didn't think he belonged at his sister's wedding ceremony. Rebekah swallowed and looked down at the table. Her estrangement from her brother grew daily. It would be so easy for someone like Megan to pick herself up, blame David, and move forward with her life.

But Rebekah had always had trouble letting go. She was afraid David's rejection had lodged itself in her forever, like a rotten vertebra in the middle of her spine.

Jacob considered Rebekah's answer for a few seconds.

"He's an idiot," Megan said.

"He's not an idiot," Rebekah said. "He just believes what he believes."

"Why are you defending him?" Megan asked. "It's inexcusable. You're his sister."

Rebekah shrugged. "I don't know. I guess I'm defending him because I'm his sister."

"Just because they're religious doesn't mean they've got a monopoly on moral authority," Jacob said. He reached into the casserole and pulled out another piece of chicken. "And by the way, I think you're both right. I don't agree with his decision. He can believe whatever he wants to believe and still celebrate your *simchah*. But he's also your brother. Even idiotic brothers are still brothers."

"Ain't that the truth," Megan said.

"My dad smoked," Jacob said. "I hated it. When I was a kid, I'd hide his cigarettes, or throw them out. When I got older, I tried to argue with him. 'Dad, why are you intentionally killing yourself?' And he didn't have a good answer, but he still smoked. He was stupid. Maybe even more stupid than your brother, because he was killing himself. When he got stomach cancer, I was so angry at him. But I loved him—I couldn't help loving him. And I was devastated when he died. I'm still devastated."

"I'm so sorry your dad died," Megan said.

Next to her, Rebekah nodded in agreement.

"It's just so unfortunate to lose someone like that," Megan said.

"Unfortunate," Jacob repeated. "Why unfortunate?"

"Oh—I'm sorry," Megan said. "I didn't mean to offend. I just meant—I just meant that it's hard to lose someone close to you."

"Thanks, but I'm not offended," Jacob said. "I really was just curious why you used the word 'unfortunate.' It suggests that there was an element of luck involved."

"Well, there is, right?" Megan asked. "No one tries to get cancer."

"I don't know. It sure seemed like my dad was trying. After he died, it was difficult not to wonder whether he would have gotten cancer if he didn't smoke. Was he really just one of those unlucky guys to get stomach cancer in his 50s? He certainly increased his risk by smoking, but would it have happened anyway?"

"Why does it matter?" Rebekah asked. "I mean, does it matter why he got cancer?"

"It does to me," Jacob said. He picked up his napkin and dabbed at his mouth. He turned to Megan. "Did Rebekah tell you what kids used to call me?"

Megan shook her head.

"Lucky. Lucky Jacob Green. And to some extent, it was true. I just used to win stuff. Raffles, contests, whatever. My dad used to take me to the gas station so I could pick the lotto numbers. We never won the lotto, but we figured that it was just a matter of time." Jacob shook his head. "I could never explain it, how special it felt. I never thought about cancer, or illness or death. I didn't think it would ever exist for me.

"I had this identity, right? Someone who was lucky. And then my dad gets sick and dies within months. And all of a sudden, I felt the reverse: that I was somehow singled out for unluckiness. Cancer was possible. Death was possible. I felt completely normal and vulnerable.

"But which was it? Was I singled out? Was it all a roll of the dice? Did my dad die from stomach cancer because he smoked? Or did my dad die from stomach cancer because of his genetic makeup, or something, you know, embedded in the fabric of the universe?" Jacob pushed his plate away. "Anyway. Let's talk a little about the ceremony, shall we?" Jacob asked. "How much do you guys know about Jewish ceremonies?"

"I've been to a couple," Rebekah said.

"I've been to just one, my cousin's," Megan said. "But I was really little, and I don't remember much. We flew to Miami, and I remember seeing a lot of palm trees. But that's about it."

"Ok," Jacob said. "So we'll start from the beginning. There's two parts to a Jewish ceremony. The first part is when the marrying couple signs the ketubah, or Jewish marriage contract. Back in the day, ketubahs were used to outline the goods being exchanged by the parents of the bride and groom, like that the parents of the bride would receive one goat in exchange for allowing their daughter to marry the other parents' son."

Megan turned to Rebekah. "So, when are your parents shipping my parents a goat?"

"As soon as your parents send mine a donkey," Rebekah said.

"Right," Jacob said. "Exactly. That's how it worked. Most traditional ketubahs today still contain that kind of exchange-of-goods language."

"Uh huh," Megan said.

"Are ketubahs updatable?" Rebekah asked.

"I suppose it depends on who you ask. For me? Yes. Of course they are. Today we don't really use ketubahs to document dowries. They're more symbolic. The two people getting married are entering into a contract to love each other, share their possessions, commit their lives to one another, and serve their community. Lots of modern Jewish couples even write their own ketubahs. Now, a person like your brother," Jacob said, nodding at Rebekah, "probably has a very traditional ketubah, and would probably never consider changing the language. But for you two, we'd need to do a few important tweaks, anyway. We're going to remove the reference to the groom, for starters."

"What about that selling language?" Rebekah asked. "That seems a little…"

"Crass?" Jacob asked. "Sure. It's actually pretty central to the legality of the document, at least in the Hebrew. But given that your ketubah is going to be non-traditional anyway, we can play with it a little bit."

"So we can read it before you finalize it?"

"Absolutely. I want to make sure it's legal—I am a rabbi—but within certain bounds, we can change it as much as you want."

Megan and Rebekah looked at each other and nodded.

"And then what happens during the ceremony?" Megan asked. "I don't think I've ever seen one."

"You probably haven't, because the ketubah ceremony is usually reserved only for the couple, the rabbi, and a few witnesses. That's actually really important: you'll need to find two Jewish people who are not related to you to serve as witnesses to the ketubah signing."

"Two non-related Jewish witnesses?" Rebekah asked. She looked at Megan.

Megan shook her head. "We're not really involved in a Jewish community."

"Why do they need to be Jewish?" Rebekah asked.

"They're part of the community," Jacob said. "A ketubah is a Jewish document, written according to Jewish law. Back in the day, when Jews used to be segregated from other populations, it was necessary to have only Jewish witnesses. But don't worry. If you guys can't think of anyone, I'll drum up a few folks from my synagogue who I'm sure would be happy to help."

Rebekah's heart started thumping. Strangers? At her ketubah ceremony?

"You may want to invite your closest friends and family for the ceremony." Jacob continued. "But it's not something for the whole wedding party. They're usually much more intimate than that. As far as what happens…" Jacob slowly rolled his head from side to side. "I don't want to reveal too much. I'm going to give the two of you an opportunity to reflect on the significance of the moment. You're leaving your parents to start your own family. You're committing to each other. The document you're signing is one of the most important of your lives."

"How long does it take?" Megan asked.

"Not long. Twenty minutes."

"So we go from there to the chuppah ceremony, right?" Megan asked.

"Right. We finish the ketubah signing, then all head over to wherever you're holding the main ceremony. Do you have a chuppah?"

Megan shook her head.

"No problem," Jacob said. "We've got one stored at our synagogue. The chuppah itself only needs to be pretty simple. It's literally a piece of cloth, strung between two branches or sticks, to cover the marrying couple and rabbi."

"Like a canopy," Megan said.

"Exactly. You need to be able to see through the cloth, so you can't have a chuppah made from metal, for example. At my synagogue, we have a large tallit—a prayer shawl—that we use. There's a lot of different interpretations as to what a chuppah symbolizes, but I like to say that it represents your home. When you get married under the chuppah, you invite all of your guests into an intimate moment in your symbolic home."

"So all of our friends and family can be at the chuppah ceremony?" Megan asked.

"Yes," Jacob said. "The chuppah ceremony is the part of the Jewish wedding that's open to guests. There are a few different components

I'm going to go over: the circling, the Kiddush, the ring exchange, and the seven blessings."

As Jacob spoke, Rebekah could feel the sour taste of acid rising in her throat. Her chest felt tight, as if a life jacket had been cinched around her rib cage. The burning below her breastbone felt like a gnawing hunger in her esophagus.

"Excuse me," Rebekah said, standing up from the table. She tapped on her chest. "Heartburn. I'll be right back. Just need to find some Tums."

Rebekah walked to the bathroom at the end of the hallway, rummaged through the medicine cabinet, and pulled out a jar of Tums. She flipped down the lid of the toilet, sat down, opened the bottle, and popped a tablet into her mouth.

Tropical flavored. That's what the jar said, as if these antacids were going to taste like pineapple and kiwi. What if she got heartburn during her wedding? Would she need to walk down the aisle with her breath smelling like mango?

Rebekah shuddered, thinking about the ketubah ceremony. She imagined her mother there, standing with her feet together, cheeks puffed out, hands clasped in front of her as she shifted nervously from side to side. Her father would be supportive: logical, distracted, encouraging. He'd never had the shrewdness to think beyond his daughter's happiness.

Supportive. That was her parents' word of choice, as if they were holding up a buckling bridge.

And David—God forbid if David actually came. What if he made a scene? What if he stomped out and declared the ceremony a fake or a disgrace? Judith would be distraught. Daniel would be confused. The ketubah ceremony would be ruined.

Rebekah popped another Tum in her mouth. Guava? No, mixed berry. She shook her head. It would be too difficult. The ceremony would simply be too difficult. *We should just get our domestic partnership license and skip this whole thing,* Rebekah thought. *Save ourselves the money and the trouble.*

Rebekah pushed the Tums back into the medicine cabinet and walked back to the table.

"So, if you wanted to involve your families, the seven blessings would be a great time to do it," Jacob was saying. Rebekah slipped back into her chair. Megan was leaning forward, her elbow resting on the table, her chin on her fist.

"Shit, Beks, you just missed Jacob's whole shpiel," Megan said. "Do you want him to start over?"

"No, no, that's ok. I'm kind of familiar with the chuppah ceremony. We can talk more about it later," Rebekah said, nodding at Megan. "To tell you the truth, I'm feeling a little out of it. I've got some bad heartburn. Not sure what it's from."

Megan squinted at Rebekah.

Jacob looked from one to the other. "No problem," he said. "I get heartburn sometimes, too. Maybe it's from the kale and lemon juice? That was a little acidic."

"Maybe," Rebekah said.

Jacob looked at his phone and pushed his glasses up on his face. "Well, I'd better get running, anyway. It's a workday tomorrow, and I've got to give someone a ride to the hospital early tomorrow morning. I'm sure you two need to get up early, too." Jacob stood up. "Well friends, I'm really, really excited about this. Thanks for including me in your wedding. I'm honored."

"No, thank you, Jacob!" Megan said. "Really, this is amazing. You're just perfect. We're very lucky to have a friend like you."

"Yes, very lucky," Rebekah echoed.

Jacob gave them both quick hugs. "We can figure out the rest of this via email," he said. "Or we can meet again, whatever works best for you guys."

Megan showed him to the door, gave him one more hug, and closed the door behind him. "What was that about?" Megan said, turning to Rebekah.

Rebekah shrugged. She picked up the large casserole dish, which had been picked clean. "I got some heartburn, that's all. It happens."

"I think Jacob thought you were kicking him out."

"I wasn't kicking him out," Rebekah said. "I just wasn't feeling very good."

Megan turned on the sink to wash dishes. "So you're ok with all this? The ketubah ceremony? Everything?"

Rebekah clenched her teeth. She finished stacking the plates before she answered. "I think I'm as comfortable as I'll ever be," Rebekah said, finally.

"You know which part I loved?" Megan said. "I loved when he was talking about how, in the ketubah ceremony, we'd have the opportunity to reflect on the momentousness of the occasion. I just imagined looking into your eyes, holding your hands, and telling you how much I love you. How much I want to be with you." Megan turned off the water. She had tears in her eyes. "That part, to me, doing that in front of just our parents…it sounds so meaningful, doesn't it?"

Rebekah set the dishes down on the table. "Megs, is it ok, if I go lie down? I'm just not feeling that great." Rebekah didn't wait for Megan's response. She was already halfway down the hall, focused on getting to her bedroom and closing the door behind her.

She heard Megan's footsteps behind her. Rebekah threw herself onto their bed and pulled a pillow over her head. Megan opened the bedroom door and walked in.

"Do we need to talk?" Megan asked.

"No."

"Really?"

"Megs, I'm just not feeling well. Ok? Am I allowed to not feel well?"

"You're allowed to not feel well. The only problem is that you always seem to not feel well when we start talking about the wedding."

Rebekah pulled the pillow off her head and rolled over. Megan was standing at the foot of the bed, her arms crossed over her chest.

"I'm fine," Rebekah said. "I'm just a little tired."

"From what?"

Rebekah blinked a few times. "I don't know. Maybe from seeing Jacob. Maybe it just brought back a lot of memories."

"You seemed fine the last time you saw him, when you went out for coffee."

"Yeah, well. Maybe this time was different."

"Why?" Megan asked. "Because this time we talked about the wedding?"

"We talked about the wedding when we went out for coffee, too."

"When was that?" Megan started pacing. "October? November? We were just getting started then. There couldn't have been all that much to talk about."

Rebekah raised her arms. "Megan, I don't know what to tell you. Ok? I'm just not feeling well. I'm sure I just need a minute. Just some alone time."

Megan stopped pacing. "Yeah. Yeah, ok. I'll give you some alone time." She stalked out of the bedroom and slammed the door behind her.

Rebekah jumped off the bed and followed her out. "Megan, what's your deal? I just need to close my eyes for a minute."

Megan was in the living room. She picked up her wallet from the coffee table and stuffed it in her back pocket.

"What are you doing?" Rebekah asked.

"I'm leaving."

"What? Why?"

"To give you alone time. Just like you asked."

"Megan, I meant like five minutes of alone time."

"No...no, I don't think you meant that." Megan stood up straight and pushed her shoulders back. Her cheeks were flushed, her lips set into a thin line. "Rebekah, do you have a wedding dress yet?"

"I don't see how—"

"Rebekah, damn it!" Megan yelled. *"Do you have a wedding dress?"*

"No, but I'm going to get one."

"Yeah? When?"

"Soon," Rebekah said.

"From where?"

"I don't know," Rebekah answered. "From somewhere."

"Fine, fine, you'll get a wedding dress," Megan said. "Do you know what we're eating at the wedding?"

"Um..." Rebekah looked around. "I thought you were taking care of the caterer."

"Yes, and I did. I took care of the caterer, and I ordered and sent out all the invitations, and I've been keeping track of the RSVPs. What have you done for the wedding?"

Rebekah thought for a few moments. "I found our officiant."

"Yes, you did. He told me tonight that he offered to perform the ceremony. That you didn't ask him."

"Why does it matter how it happened?"

"And I've been badgering you for weeks now to get him to come over to dinner, correct?"

"Megan, stop."

"No, this is important," Megan said. "I really want to know what part of the wedding planning you've been actively involved in."

"All of it, Megan!"

Megan shook her head. She pushed her shoulders back again. "No, no." She laughed. "I don't know why it took me so long to realize this—maybe I've just been in fucking denial—but you haven't been involved in any of it. You've been involved, in the sense that you've been here. But you've never given a shit. And whenever stuff comes up, you run away."

"I don't know what you're talking about."

"You don't know what I'm talking about?" Megan was shouting now. "How long did it take you to share the wedding news with people at work?"

"They're dumb, Megan, and there was a lot going on."

"And we wouldn't even be here, if I hadn't said something at your parents' Passover Seder last year. Is that not true? Do you deny that?"

Rebekah stared at the floor.

"That was almost a year ago, Rebekah. Passover was last April. Eleven months. Eleven months, and you're still not on board with this wedding. Do you even want to get married? Do you even love me? Or are you so blinded by your own fucking issues that you can't?"

Tears were streaming down Megan's face now. They caught on the edge of her nose and her top lip. Megan kept shouting. "I can't live like this, Rebekah. I can't marry someone who hates herself. It's been like this since we met. Remember when we met? In college? How you ran away the first time you met me?"

Rebekah felt tears well up in her eyes. She couldn't speak.

"A decade. It's been almost a decade. You haven't changed. At all. How is that even possible? Who doesn't evolve, or try to evolve?"

"Megan, my family…"

"Who gives a fuck about your family?" Megan shouted. "Aren't I becoming your family?"

Rebekah tried to speak. "Megan, you are…"

Megan shook her head. "You're a liar. You've been lying this whole time. About everything. You know, I really used to believe that it was your issues. Internalized homophobia. The whole bit. And now? Now I just think it's me."

Rebekah stood up. "Megs, c'mon."

"Rebekah…fuck." Megan grabbed the car keys from the wall hook. "I need to go."

Megan pulled a coat out of the hallway closet, walked toward the front of the house, opened the front door, and slammed it shut behind her. A minute later, Rebekah heard Megan's car start, then peel away from the house.

Rebekah found herself standing in near silence. She heard a dripping sound from the kitchen, where the faucet hadn't been fully turned off. The house creaked and leaned from the force of the rain on the outside walls. Music and laughter floated down from the top level of the house, where, doubtlessly, the Judge and Claire were enjoying themselves.

Rebekah flopped onto the couch. She thought about canceling the wedding, about life without Megan. She remembered the first time they met, ten years ago, at the University of Southern California.

Wandering
Fall, 2000

How do girls fall in love?

Some fall in love at ski chalets. You can find them sitting by the large stone hearth at the northern end of the lobby, skis propped up, the day's snow dripping into the carpet. Their goggles, gloves, and jackets lie in a heap at their feet. They might be holding small foam cups of hot chocolate picked up at the Snowy Snack Shoppe.

Some girls fall in love at bars. They fall in love at gay bars. They fall in love at straight bars. They fall in love at drag bars, bear bars, skeezy bars, and bars that only play hits from the 1980's. They fall in love in big cities and small towns, and at bars in neighborhoods with nicknames.

Weho. Soho. The Castro.

Girls go to bars to find butchies, trannies, lipstick lesbians, soccer players, artists, angry intellectuals, working class girlz and trust fund bois. They dance, play pool, drink double shots of tequila, spin music, and grind on each other's thighs.

And then they fall in love.

To cut through the painful extroversion and alcohol consumption required to meet at bars, some girls try to meet each other online. Online dating cuts through the heavy fog of corporeal interactions, allowing girls to talk about real things: life goals, financial decision-making styles, income. Religious and political beliefs. Vegan, vegetarian, or omnivorian eating habits.

Girls fall in love in public libraries. Sometimes in the science-fiction section.

Girls meet at the beach, at baseball games, truck stops, and day care centers. They meet in all-girls Catholic schools, in non-parochial elementary schools, in girl scout troops, on intramural softball teams, at Greenpeace meetings, at public hearings, in Islamic youth groups, and while volunteering for local soup kitchens.

Some girls meet at the Olympics. And if they do, they deserve each other.

Sometimes, girls meet in places where they'd rather not meet
anyone: addiction recovery meetings. Prison. Hospitals or hospices.
At funeral homes, or during natural disaster recovery efforts, while
picking up the pieces of lives they never expected to go so awry.
Girls often meet at LGBT events on college campuses, sometimes
after trying things out with boys. Like Rebekah and Megan, they
eventually fall in love.

"We walked in, and by that time, it was, like, eleven thirty, and there
were way too many people in there, I could barely get in the door.
And it was me, Jessa, and Colleen—they're in my pledge class. So
we kind of pushed our way in. There was a guy standing at the door,
you know, like, I think he was supposed to be a, like, bouncer or
something—and he helped to make some space for us. And, oh my
God, you wouldn't believe…"
Carrie Cline dropped her voice to a whisper. "I was waiting for the
po-pos to show up and try to clear out the living room. Just on over-
crowding alone." Carrie shook her head and cut another piece of her
waffle. She'd loaded it up with butter, blueberries, and whipped
cream, explaining to Rebekah that carbs were the only thing that
would help get rid of her hangover.
"So we go over to the drinks table, and there's a punch bowl—but,
you know, I never drink that jungle juice crap at parties, 'cause who
knows what's in it? Jessa had brought in a small flask of vodka in
her purse, so we ended up getting some ice and just drinking some of
that. And we had a pretty good buzz going by the time we got to the
party.
"So then—remember that guy I was tellin' you about? Jace? The one
that I'd met at the football tailgater, who I thought was kind of
cute?"
"I believe you told me that he was cute and an obnoxious drunk,"
Rebekah responded. She was sipping coffee, a habit she'd acquired
during her first few weeks of college. They'd been sitting in the
University of Southern California's EVK cafeteria eating breakfast.
Rebekah had already finished her toast and eggs and was watching
Carrie slowly plow through her waffle.

Carrie started to laugh with her mouth full, then put her hand over her lips so she wouldn't spit out any food. Her eyelashes, black and long, even without makeup, fluttered as she laughed. She'd pulled her hair—still stiff from the evening's layers of hair product—back into a tight, curly bun. Carrie's black tank top and gray sweat pants somehow managed to look chic and form fitting, even as they hung loosely over her limbs. Rebekah marveled at her elegant and pulled-together roommate, the picture of easy grace, even as she fought off a hangover.

Carrie swallowed her bite of waffle and took a sip of orange juice.

"Did I say that?" Carrie asked.

"Yep."

"Oh, man, well…so, oh, no." Carrie started laughing again.

Rebekah leaned into the table. "What?"

Carrie shook her head. "I can't tell you now."

"Tell me!"

"You're going to think I'm an idiot."

"Carrie!" Rebekah rolled her eyes. "Come on. I won't think you're an idiot."

Carrie looked around the cafeteria, then leaned in towards Rebekah. "We hooked up last night."

"You and Jace?"

"Yeah."

"Really?"

"Yeah."

Carrie slowly chewed another bite of her waffle. Rebekah raised her eyebrows and took another sip of her coffee.

Rebekah nodded. "So, what did you guys do?"

"Oh, well, you know, I was hanging out at the party, there was some good music going, and Jessa, Colleen and I were on the dance floor, kind of dancing together, and Jace walks up. And he gives me this big hug and says something, and I couldn't really hear him, but he starts dancing with us. And we were just hanging out, and dancing, and well, you know." Carried giggled.

"Uh-huh."

"And it just kind of happened. We kissed, and I think he felt me up, and that's it. And then we went outside and kissed some more. And I think he was trying to convince me to go somewhere with him, but I didn't."

"That's good. You just kissed, then?"

"Yeah. I do have some sense, even when I'm drunk." Carrie flashed Rebekah a smile.

"Right."

"Which isn't to say that he didn't want more," Carrie said. "He kept pushing my head down, like he wanted me to suck him off right there, right on the sidewalk."

"Gross."

"I have my limits."

"And…you actually like this guy?" Rebekah asked.

Carrie chewed thoughtfully. "I don't know. I don't know him that well. I do remember telling you that I thought he was obnoxious after that tailgate. But it was, like, three in the afternoon, and the guy was already wasted, and so I guess I thought that was a little much. But, you know. Guys do dumb shit in college. I figure he's cute, I'm nineteen, and you know—whatever. We'll see how it goes. I won't let myself do anything stupid."

Rebekah pursed her lips and stared at Carrie. Her roommate had been disgusted with this Jace fellow only a few weeks earlier, when, at a tailgate before the football game, he had accidentally spilled an entire beer all over her shoes. Why the change now?

Rebekah hadn't had much of a chance yet to ask about Carrie's life, but she knew some of the basic details. Carrie had attended a private school in Northern Virginia. Her parents, both economists, worked in the DC area. Carrie didn't volunteer much else, deftly changing the subject back to her roommate when Rebekah attempted to inquire about her interests.

Rebekah didn't dwell on Carrie's omissions. They simply became part of her enchantment, the mystery in the myth. Rebekah, too, skirted the truth; when Carrie asked her about past boyfriends, Rebekah quickly said that she'd never had a boyfriend, but that she had scammed with a couple of guys at high school parties.

"So when do I get to meet this guy?" Rebekah asked.

"Hah! Never. You'll hate him."

"Ah, come on. If he's worth seeing again, he's worth introducing to your roomie."

"Oh, I see how you did that!" Carrie laughed. She cut another small piece of her waffle, quickly chewed, and swallowed. "Tell you what—if Jace calls and wants to hang out, I'll say we should go out on a double date. And I'll tell him that I have a friend I've been itching to set up—that's you—and then we'll both get to go out."

"Um, that's ok. I don't think you need to set me up with anyone," Rebekah said.

"Oh, come on, Bekah! It's time you got out there a little bit. It's one date, and I'll pick a super nice guy. There's a couple I know that I've met through initiation stuff. All the nice guys like Betas, because we're the most normal house on the row."

"Whatever. That's not the reputation I've heard," Rebekah said.

Carrie had pledged with the Alpha Beta Betas. They called themselves the "Betas" and had a reputation for recruiting the most beautiful women in a pledge class. It was the house every pledge wanted to get into. "If by normal, you mean the hottest, then yeah, I'd say of course that's the reason all the guys like the Betas."

Carrie shook her head. "Whatever, you know? We're just a bunch of girls. We're cool. Don't worry about it. Anyway, it's settled. If Jace calls, you're coming with me on a double date, and I'm not letting you get out of this one. It'll be fun! Don't worry so much, Bekah. I won't let anything bad happen to you."

Carrie stood up and grabbed her tray. "Let's get out of here. I've gotta get over to the house and do some stuff to get ready for the football game. "

Tommy Trojan was the symbol of tradition at the University of Southern California. He posed in the middle of campus, front leg thrust out and bent at the knee, back leg straight, providing stability. His sword was at the ready in his right arm, his shield held up in his left. The large bronze sculpture watched over Trousdale Parkway, the main walkway through campus. Tommy hearkened back to the ancient Trojan warriors, known best for their determination during a siege. He also called attention to USC's modern warriors: its football team, whose charge was no less than to win a national championship.

For the most part, the powers-that-be in charge of maintaining USC's campus were fond of traditional features, like large reflecting pools, meticulously kept flower gardens, painted benches under decades-old trees, and wide open walkways. Many of the libraries and primary administration buildings were built of beautiful, East Coast-style red brick. A few buildings that snuck in during the 1960's and 70's reflect the unfortunate architectural sensibilities of that time: monolithic concrete structures, maze-like layouts, and small windows. These buildings—the Annenberg School of Journalism, and what was previously the George Lucas Structural Building (mercifully demolished in 2009)—cowered in shame next to their Romanesque brethren.

While there were many important people in USC's mini-economy—administrators, professors, teaching assistants, shuttle drivers, cooks, coaches, tutors, boosters, alumni, and visiting faculty—the students were the lifeblood of the university. USC's student government, clubs, Greek system, and student-run religious and civic institutions were the pulsing, dynamic center of campus life. They operated in ebbs and flows, according to the unique seasons of university life: summer, in which activity slowed to a crawl; the beginning of each semester, during which campus engagement began at a frenzied pace; and the end of each semester, controlled by tests and papers and rigorous finals schedules.

On the thirteenth Friday of the first semester, just two weeks before school let out for winter break, Carrie organized a date night. "The worst that can happen is that Jace will be drunk and obnoxious, as usual, and then I'll write him off forever," Carrie said.
"I can think of much worse things than that," Rebekah said.
"Oh, come on. We'll be together the whole time. I'm not an idiot. I'm not going to let him be alone with me for a second."
"Uh-huh."
"And you haven't even asked me about the guy you're going out with."
Rebekah sighed and lay back on her bed.
"Bekah, you haven't gone out, like, at all, all semester. You need to try a little. It's good for you."
Rebekah rolled her eyes and turned her head towards her roommate. Carrie was sitting on her chair, her stomach pressed up against the chair's back, legs splayed around the front.
"Who is it?"

Carrie smiled. "His name is Andy Rowan. He's a little red-headed Irish guy. Really cute. Very, very nice. I made Jace swear to me up and down that he was worthy of you."

"Sounds promising."

"Oh, Bekah, it'll be great. You'll make a new friend."

"I hope so."

Carrie turned her back to Rebekah so she could face her closet. "Show me what you're wearing tonight."

Rebekah motioned from her feet up to her neck. Rebekah figured she would wear what she had worn all day: jeans, a gray t-shirt, and black Chuck Taylors.

Carrie stopped moving. "Whaa?" Carrie said.

"Carrie, I don't have anything to wear."

"Bekah! You're going out on a date! You've got to wear something sexy! Look at what I'm wearing." Carrie motioned to the outfit on her bed: a gray cashmere sweater over a lime green shirt, a pleated gray skirt, and black heels.

Rebekah shrugged. "I don't have anything. Besides, if Andy Rowan is as nice as you say he is, then maybe he won't care what I wear."

"Oh, my God, Rebekah. He's a guy. I don't care how nice he is. Of course he's going to care what you're wearing." Carrie put her hands on her hips. "If I give you something to wear, will you wear it?"

"Maybe."

Carrie walked over to her closet and began rifling through her clothes. She pulled out one article after another, tossing them all on the floor behind her. When she had accumulated a small mountain of material, she scooped it up with both arms and dumped it on her bed. As Rebekah watched, she went through the pile on her bed, holding up articles of clothing against one another, seeing what matched. After a few minutes, she waved Rebekah over.

"Ok, girl, here we go. You're going to look so hot. And you're not allowed to argue with me on any of this, 'cause you agreed to it, ok?"

Rebekah folded her arms across her chest. One of her contacts was irritating her eyes; she held it closed for a few seconds, opened it again, and wiped at the edge of her eye. Still irritated.

"Hey, where are you going?"

"I just need to put some eye drops in." Rebekah walked over to her cosmetics bag, which was sitting at the foot of her closet. She picked up her small bottle of Visine, tilted back her head, and squeezed a few drops into her eye. When she had finished, she walked back over to Carrie's bed, where Carrie had laid out a small, fitted black shirt, and a black skirt so small that it looked more appropriate for a twelve-year-old girl.

"You want me to wear that?"

"You'll look great."

"I can't wear that. Are you fucking kidding me?"

Carrie picked up the skirt and held it up against Rebekah's legs. "Aw, see? It'll be perfect on you."

"You're smaller than me, Carrie. There's no way I'll be able to squeeze into that."

"Whatever. Try it on. You're not allowed to argue with me, remember?"

Rebekah took the skirt from Carrie and held it out in front of her. She imagined herself walking through campus, her legs long, lean and shapely, just like Carrie's. This short black skirt had been sewn for the Carrie Clines of the world. Might it also be for Rebekah? Rebekah sighed, nodded, and tossed it onto her bed. Carrie handed her the top.

"You can't go wrong in all black. Trust me. You're going to look really, really good."

Rebekah nodded again.

Carrie clapped her hands and tossed her head. "This is going to be so awesome! Ok, you try that stuff on. I'm going to run to the bathroom, and I'll be right back." Carrie laughed and headed for the door. She paused in the doorway and looked back toward Rebekah. "I'm so glad you're doing this with me, Bekah. You're the best." And she closed the door and disappeared.

Rebekah slipped off her jeans, picked up the skirt, and pulled it up to her waist. It was indeed a little tight; Rebekah had to squeeze in her stomach to zip it up and push the top button through the buttonhole. The skirt sat snugly over her hips, a little higher than Carrie would have worn it. As a result, the hem of the skirt was a little higher on her thigh than intended, a good four inches above the top of her knee.

Rebekah tugged it down over her hips as far as it would go, and she turned to the full-length mirror. The skirt *was* a little high. Rebekah ripped off the shirt she was wearing and slipped on Carrie's sequined, tight black shirt. She turned back to the mirror.

Like a white-meat hot dog in a burnt-black bun, Rebekah thought. She felt her eyeballs twitching under her contacts.

Carrie burst through the door. "Ooh!" She studied Rebekah.

"It's too tight," Rebekah said.

"Oh, well…no." Carrie walked around Rebekah, studying her. "No, I don't think it's too tight. I do think it's, like, you know…*right there.* But it still fits." She looked Rebekah up and down again. "I think you look great."

"I look like a sausage."

"Oh, you're just not used to seeing yourself in tight clothing. Really, you look good! You can see your body this way."

Rebekah stared at herself in the mirror. *I wonder what Ruth would say. She probably would laugh at me*, Rebekah mused. *And then she would tell me I look beautiful. Because she always told me that.* Rebekah felt tears welling up in her eyes. All of a sudden she felt really homesick. She turned away from the mirror and headed back to her bed, willing herself not to cry.

"What's wrong?" Carried asked.

"Oh…it's just my fucking contacts. My eyes are really irritated."

"Oh, shit. Well, are you really planning on wearing glasses?"

Rebekah took a deep breath and turned around to face her roommate.

"You can, I guess," Carrie said. "I just think your eyes are so beautiful."

"Yeah, whatever. I'll wear my contacts. I'll just deal."

"Ooh, Bekah! I've got the perfect shoes for you!" Carrie pulled a pair of black wedges out of her closet. "These have a low heel, so they won't hurt your feet. And they'll go really well with your outfit."

She handed them to Rebekah, who wordlessly slipped them on.

"Yay!" Carrie said. "Oh, Bekah." She gave Rebekah a big hug. "You look so good. Andy is just gonna die."

Rebekah smiled at her. Carrie spoke with such certainty, with an air of erudition and confidence that came from years of competently dressing herself for evenings out. Rebekah looked in the mirror again. She saw a young woman—is that what she was?—overdressed, uncertain, a slice of ham trying to fit in among the prosciutto. Rebekah turned away again. Better not to look than to stare and stare at such a phantom.

Jace underwhelmed Rebekah almost immediately. He was short, with slicked-back black hair and an upturned nose that reminded Rebekah of a jump sticking out of a ski hill. He had cold blue eyes and a smile that showcased a row of small, perfect teeth. Jace looked like a throwback, a mid-twentieth century greaser, the kind of boy who wore sleeveless white undershirts and black jeans and hung out near the auto body shop, so his parents wouldn't catch him smoking. He was stocky, like a wrestler, a gym rat who focused solely on body-building.

Jace politely greeted Rebekah with a firm handshake and gentle pleasantries. But his attention was clearly superficial. Jace stared through Rebekah, never quite seeing her, as if he'd immediately thrown her into a bin along with the hundreds of other USC co-eds. After exchanging a few words with Rebekah, he turned back to Carrie and draped her in a tight hug. Carrie gently pushed him away and began searching through her purse, citing a missing hand mirror.

Rebekah was surprisingly pleased to meet Andy Rowan. He had neatly combed red hair that was parted on the right side of his head, bright freckles, blue eyes, and a light dotting of red stubble on his chin. He had a self-conscious, charming air, as if he felt almost apologetic that Rebekah had been put in an awkward situation. He smiled with his eyes, bashfully shoved his hands in his pockets when he spoke, and seemed to be making an effort to balance his friend's deficiencies. Andy shook Carrie's hand, then Rebekah's, and watched Jace give Carrie that unseemly hug. Andy shook his head at Rebekah, gave her a look that hovered between amusement and remorse, and immediately began peppering Rebekah with questions. Where was she from? How did she end up at USC? How did Los Angeles compare to Portland? And was it true that it really rained there every day, even during the summer?

After a few minutes, Jace announced that he was going to lead them all to La Luna, a Mexican restaurant off campus. It was not a far walk, he assured them. Jace guided Carrie's arm through the crook of his own and began leading the way.

Before Jace and Andy knocked on their dorm room door, Carrie had helped Rebekah blow dry and style her hair, then spent half an hour applying makeup to Rebekah's face. When Carrie finished—

stepping back to admire her handiwork by clapping and squealing—Rebekah looked in the mirror and raised her eyebrows in astonishment. She looked like a completely different person.

Now, Rebekah gazed at Andy Rowan with eyes that had been darkened, tinted, painted, and shadowed, and she spoke with lips that had been outlined, lightened, and then darkened again. She willed herself not to tug on her skirt, although she could feel it riding up her thigh, and ignored the sensation that bits of her stomach were spilling out underneath the edges of her top.

Carrie must think this looks good, or she wouldn't have let me go out, Rebekah thought. *And this must be what Andy likes, because Andy seems to like me.*

With every step toward La Luna, Rebekah grew more self-assured. She giggled at Andy's jokes, batted her eyelashes at him, tripped over her own words as she spoke, then giggled again, and apologized for speaking too fast. Andy gently laid his hand on her arm, shushing away her apology, begging her to continue speaking. He was gentle, encouraging, interested, playing the part of a man delighted to be going out on a first date.

After twenty minutes, the four freshmen reached La Luna. It was seven fifteen, the height of La Luna's dinner hour, and a crush of young people were streaming through the front door and into the bar. Hand-painted phases of the moon, artistically rendered in blue and yellow, decorated the walls of the restaurant. Next to the moons, a painted woman with brown skin and long, dark hair, reached her arms to the sky.

A waitress ushered them in and offered them a table for four. Carrie was the first to the table. She reached out, grabbed Rebekah's arm, and steered her to the chair next to her own. For a brief moment, Carrie locked eyes with Rebekah. Her eyes radiated anger.

Rebekah sat down in her chair next to Carrie, tucking her skirt underneath her legs. She tried to sit with her spine as straight as possible, hips facing forward, as she had seen Carrie do almost effortlessly in their dorm room. She wondered if her shoulders sloped gently away from her neck, or if they stuck straight out, like a linebacker's; she wondered whether she was holding her chin at the proper angle, not so high that she looked haughty, not so low that she looked shy. Carrie sat down next to her, cleared her throat, and

picked up her menu. The boys sat down across from Carrie and
Rebekah. Jace was talking about his Spanish professor.

"Dude, you wouldn't even believe how nasty it is," Jace said.

"What?" Andy asked.

"You know, what I was telling you, about how she spits when she
talks. I don't even sit in the front of the room, but she wanders
around when she talks, so you can't avoid it, unless you sit, like,
completely in the middle. She's just totally gross, a real hag."

Jace had a low, raspy voice, one that sounded as it was permanently
afflicted by a mild form of bronchitis. "I'm getting a margarita,"
Jace announced.

Carrie rolled her eyes.

Jace looked at Andy. "How about you, bro?"

Andy studied the menu. "I don't have an ID for that, bro," he said,
over-pronouncing "O," so that "bro" sounded like "brow-wa." He
grinned at Rebekah. Rebekah giggled and felt Carrie kick her
underneath the table.

"I'm going to get a diet Coke," Carrie announced. "And tacos." She
dropped her menu and stood up. "And if you'll excuse me, I need to
use the restroom." She turned away from the table and headed for
the back of the restaurant.

An awkward silence settled over the table. "What?" Jace asked. He
looked at Andy, then Rebekah, and back to Andy, who was slowly
shaking his head. "What, dude? You saying it's me?"

"Come to think of it, I need to use the restroom too," Rebekah said,
pushing away from the table. Rebekah looked at Andy. "Be right
back, ok?"

Andy nodded at her. "Sure thing." He hit Jace's shoulder with the
back of his hand. "Bro."

Rebekah hurried away. She pushed open the bathroom door and
found Carrie leaning against the sink counter. Carrie looked up
toward the ceiling when Rebekah walked in.

"Thank God you're here," Carrie said. She stared into the mirror,
inspecting the makeup on her cheekbones. Rebekah, freshly made-up
and presented with a mirror for the first time since leaving her dorm
room, quickly walked over to the sink and proceeded to do the same.

"Jace is such an idiot. First he makes us walk, like, a mile to this
restaurant. I'm not opposed to walking, but I am opposed to wearing
the wrong shoes—didn't he notice I'm wearing these heels?

Couldn't he have picked something closer, or called a cab?" Carrie scowled. "And he complained the whole time about his Spanish professor, who sounds like a real mess, but probably doesn't deserve all of Jace's abuse. And *then* Jace talks about ordering a margarita. The guy's already been drinking. I can smell it on him."

"Do you want to leave?" Rebekah asked.

"No," Carrie said. "I just can't believe that I got into this situation. I'm just frustrated with myself."

"It's just dinner. We'll go home after that."

Carrie turned to look at Rebekah. "Excuse me? I'll go home after that. The way things are going, you'll go home with Andy."

"What? What are you talking about? Are you upset at me?"

Carrie rolled her eyes again. "No, I'm not upset."

"You seem upset."

Carrie studied her roommate. After a few seconds, she smiled, and the tension seemed to leave her face. She waved her hand. "I guess I just expected things to go differently tonight," she said softly. She looked in the mirror again. "But I'm happy for you. Andy seems like a really nice guy."

Rebekah nodded. "He does."

"He's cute, too," Carrie said, grinning at her.

Rebekah blushed. "Yeah, he's ok."

"Your eyes are hurting, huh?"

"Oh, shit." Rebekah turned back to the mirror. "You can tell?"

"Yeah. Your eyes are bloodshot."

Rebekah inspected herself in the mirror. "Crap."

"Can you just take out your contacts?"

"No. I'll be blind."

Carrie walked to Rebekah and wrapped her in a hug. Then she stood back. "I'm sorry. I should have told you to wear your glasses. Let's continue our dates with Mr. Dumb and Mr. Wonderful so we can go home, ok?"

Rebekah smiled. "Maybe Andy's got some other friends."

"Yeah, maybe!"

The girls walked back into the restaurant, their shoes clicking against the tile floor. When they got back to the table, their waitress had already delivered a round of water glasses, along with Jace's margarita.

"Ladies," Jace said when they returned, raising his oversized glass, as if to toast them.

"Give me a sip of that, Jace," Carrie said, motioning with her hand as she sat down. "I need to drink if I want to get through this evening."

"Of course!" Jace said, handing her the glass.

Carrie took a sip. "Mm, this is good," she said. "You can really taste the tequila."

Carrie handed Jace his glass. Rebekah squinted as Carrie pushed back into her chair, folded one leg over the other, and set her hands in front of her, her long fingers stretched out on the table. In an instant, Carrie had become alluring again, almost desperately so; she leaned toward Jace, laughed at his jokes, flattered him with her eyes and her smile, and lavished him with the kind of attention that a few minutes ago she would have thought unseemly.

Carrie also continued to sip Jace's margaritas. After the first drink ran out, Jace quickly ordered another. She sipped this second one, just as the first, and when the third one came, Jace pushed it toward her.

The evening passed quickly, as the four students fell into easy conversation about their first few weeks on campus. They spoke of their classes and social lives. By the time they left La Luna, Carrie and Jace seemed decidedly sloppy, leaning on each other as they walked back toward campus. They spoke loudly, and Carrie was hardly able to walk in a straight line.

"I think Carrie is totally drunk," Rebekah said in a low voice to Andy. They were walking side by side behind their friends.

"She's not the only one," Andy said with a nod to Jace.

Rebekah nodded. "I usually only see her the morning after she's been drinking like this."

Jace led them to his frat house, a ten minute walk from La Luna, where students were milling about outside, holding red plastic cups. The house itself was a large, square mansion, with lines of boxy windows on the top and bottom floors. It was plain and unadorned, as if a coat of paint on the exterior was all the upkeep its members could manage. The landscaping was equally simple: a few bushes under the eaves of the windows and a faded, trampled lawn that circled the house like a moat. The house seemed to be built for function, rather than aesthetics, to house college-aged men and parties and fundraisers. Three large, red Greek letters hung over the doorway to the house, partially covered by a large banner announcing a jungle-themed party.

Rebekah and Andy walked through the door of the house into the living room, which was illuminated by a red neon light and packed with students. The space was so full that it was impossible to move without rubbing up against someone else in accidental intimacy. Rebekah's mind drifted. Was it her imagination, or had the room fallen silent when she walked in? Were all these men—big, strong men holding little red cups—staring at her? Were these women—skinny, drunk, holding little red cups—laughing at her? Rebekah quickly walked to a corner of the room, sat down on a couch, and draped her coat over her legs. Andy followed behind her.

"Can I get you a drink?" Andy shouted over the music.

Rebekah nodded. Andy turned his back and walked away.

Rebekah searched the living room for Carrie. Through the jumbled mass of people in the living room, she saw Carrie's narrow shoulders and dark skin by the drinks table. Rebekah stood up, pressing the coat against her stomach, and tried to wave, but Carrie was facing the other direction, absorbed in conversation.

Andy returned and handed her a red cup. Rebekah sat back down, tipped the cup back, and gamely took a large gulp.

She looked around the living room. Beer bottles from various craft breweries—Fat Tire, Bell's Brewery, Zero Gravity—lined a shallow shelf that ringed the living room. A sign with the word "open" spelled out in brightly-colored tubes hung over what was serving as the bar: a gray plastic table holding two large punch bowls and stacks of large red plastic cups. From her seat on the couch, she couldn't see into the kitchen or up the large staircase on the other side of the living room. There were too many torsos in front of her, blocking her from seeing more than three feet in front of her.

Rebekah rubbed her eyes. They were tired and irritated.

"You ok?" Andy shouted in her ear. He was leaning over her, his red eyebrows furrowed. His round face looked even more full-figured in the half-light, his facial features partially obscured and his chin tucked into his neck.

Rebekah nodded at him again. She took another big sip from her red cup and began to feel light-headed.

"This is strong," she shouted at Andy over the music. "Do you know what's in it?"

Andy shrugged. "Nothing good," he yelled with a grin. "Want a beer instead?"

Rebekah shook her head. A beer at this point would probably make her feel even worse. She poured the rest of the contents of the cup down her throat.

The remainder of the party glissaded into a mental slush for Rebekah, a disconnected assortment of sounds, colors, and movements. The next day, as she tried to remember what had happened, she recalled feeling warmer and abandoning her coat somewhere, perhaps the chair that she had been sitting in. The living room had smelled like sweat and beer. Rebekah remembered Andy's round face bobbing in front of her, the blazing "open" sign in the background, the pulsing music that seemed to buoy her through the evening. Had she been dancing? If she was, she couldn't remember how, or to what, or with whom, just the sensation of laughing and falling over after getting pushed from behind, and Andy's hand grabbing hers and lifting her up. Rebekah was wet. Something had spilled.

She was definitely laughing—she remembered that. What was so funny? It got cold again, all of a sudden, and there was sidewalk in front of her, and Andy was next to her. Where was Carrie? Her roommate had disappeared long ago, seeping into the walls with Jace and her red cup. But it didn't matter, because now it was cold, and she had Andy Rowan next to her, holding her arm, and then her hand, and then his arm was around her shoulders, keeping her warm. They were walking somewhere, and it smelled like asphalt.

Rebekah didn't remember much else, except that after an interminable amount of coldness, she was finally warm again, getting into an elevator that she didn't recognize. How distant the beginning of the evening seemed then—looking in the mirror at her short black skirt, Carrie dabbing powder onto her nose. It was all one monochromatic memory now, with just a few whitecaps popping up to differentiate one event from another.

She was led off the elevator and down the hall, still laughing. She had so much trust in that arm around her shoulder. Rebekah was warm again, the music was gone, and it was quiet—just her and

Andy, and the sound of a key in the lock, and then the door swinging open.

What was it about the room that clicked things into focus? It could have been the smell: a mixture of cooped-up sweat and old hair gel, a savory, sour mix, not unlike what David's room used to smell like. *David.* Where was David right now? She felt a pair of hands lift her up and gently set her down on the bed. There was a hand on her knee.

"Where are we?" Rebekah asked. "What's going on?"

And then there were lips, cold, dry lips on her lips. Lips, then a tongue that tasted like Altoids and alcohol. Rebekah pulled back.

"Andy, stop, stop for a second. I just…where are we?"

He reached out and touched Rebekah's hair. "In my room."

Rebekah looked around. She was sitting on a rumpled blue comforter that lay untucked on top of navy bed sheets. There was an assortment of socks on the floor, lying haphazardly a few feet from a full laundry hamper. On the wall on the other side of the room were half a dozen posters of bands Rebekah didn't recognize.

She shut her eyes and tried to clear the haze from her head. She felt lips on her lips again.

Rebekah began to think that maybe Carrie had been right; maybe she was going to spend the night at Andy's. Is that what he expected? She certainly didn't feel much like leaving. His lips were the most tangible sensation of the evening since dinner, and they weren't unpleasant. They had moved away from her face, down to her neck, and were slowly making their way up to her left earlobe.

Andy had been so nice to her the whole night, so kind, and understanding, such a wonderful conversationalist. Perhaps all she had to do was talk with him.

"Andy, are you tired?"

"Nope," came the muffled reply.

Rebekah had become quite well skilled in love-making with Ruth. She had come to know how to touch her, how to kiss her, how to make her back arch with pleasure. Andy was kissing her on her neck, and it should have felt the way it always felt with Ruth. But she felt not a whit with Andy Rowan, save an increasing sense of apprehension.

Andy gently lifted up her arms. He reached down to her waist and tugged off her shirt. He gently pushed her down on the bed—her head was resting on his pillow—and he began kissing her collarbone, then her breastbone. After a few moments, he took a break to quickly rip off his own shirt. Then he commenced his kissing again, at the same gentle pace.

Rebekah's impression of the evening had undergone a radical shift in the last few minutes. It had been a pleasant, if not wonderful, evening, until they all got to the party; then it had become terribly exciting. Now, she felt strangely numb. She'd had high hopes of Andy Rowan. He seemed like boyfriend material, like a man who could be a replacement for Ruth. But she was here now, in the very position one would expect a girl with a crush on a boy to be—and she felt anesthetized.

Rebekah squirmed underneath Andy. He took her movement as a sign of pleasure and reached underneath her bra, cupping her breast in his hand and kissing her nipple. She squirmed again, this time more violently.

Andy looked up. "Did I hurt you?" Andy asked.

"Andy, I need to go," Rebekah said.

Andy stared at her, confused. "Go?"

"Yeah, um…I think I need to leave. Go back to my room."

He slowly sat up and leaned against the wall. Rebekah took the opportunity to adjust her bra and grab her shirt.

"Did I do something wrong?" he asked. He was staring at her with a hangdog expression.

"No, no, not at all," Rebekah said. "I just…I'm tired, and I'm not feeling great, and I think I need to go." She pulled on her shirt and tried to get down off the bed. She stumbled when she hit the ground.

"Whoa, hey." Andy jumped off the bed and steadied her. "Are you sure? Can I walk you home?"

"No, no, I'll be fine." Rebekah staggered to the door. She pushed it open, then looked back inside at Andy. He was standing in the middle of the room with his shirt off, his round face hovering six feet above the ground like a small white moon.

"See you soon, ok?" Rebekah said.

Andy nodded. He looked at the floor.

Rebekah walked into the hall, down the elevator, and out of the dorm. She was across campus from her own dorm, and it was cold, colder than she could ever remember it being in Portland. What had happened to her coat?

She wrapped her arms around her stomach, and tried to pull her little sleeves down further over her arms. Her knees felt rubbery, numb from the cold, further weakened from being intoxicated. She gritted her teeth, then quickly squeezed her lips shut when the cold hit her teeth, sending a shiver down her spine.

Rebekah walked through an empty, dark campus. She had the dim sense that perhaps she wouldn't make it back to her dorm room at all, that tomorrow morning, someone would find her curled up in a flower bed, frozen, twin icicles hanging from her eyes. She felt cold and detached, cut off from the warmth of friends and humanity and the carefree living at the frat party. It all seemed like eons ago now, when she had been just one more USC student at a party with a boy on her arm. The elements could overwhelm her. Rebekah could disappear into the sidewalk, turn into gray and stony concrete, and no one would know the difference.

Rebekah was too tired to cry, too stupefied to do much more than shuffle forward on the sidewalk. She thought of how she had felt in Andy's room. There had been no passion, no desire to kiss him back or let him touch her.

There must simply be something wrong with her, she thought, a fatal flaw in her genetic makeup that prevented her from ever falling in love with a kind, empathetic, all-American man. Rebekah walked by Taper Hall, an instructional building where a couple of her classes were held. She peered into the windows to try to see a reflection. She could only see darkness.

A few minutes later, Rebekah made it back to her dorm. She opened the electronic door with her keycard, waited by the elevator, and hurried down the hall to her room. She pushed the door open. When she walked into her room, the light was on. She saw Carrie lying in bed.

"Rebekah?" Carrie sat up. Rebekah saw that she had been crying. Rebekah quietly closed the door and tossed her keys onto her desk. "Wow. What happened? You ok?"

Carrie nodded and sniffled.

Rebekah hesitantly walked to her side of the room and sat on Carrie's bed. "What happened?"

Carrie shrugged. "This was all just a bad idea. You know? Everything."

Rebekah nodded. She rubbed her forehead. She had a headache.

"What happened to you? Where's Andy?"

Rebekah looked at the ground, struggling not to cry.

"Rebekah?" Carrie asked again.

Rebekah opened her mouth to speak. When she did, she started to cry.

Carrie wrapped her arms around her roommate. She whispered to Rebekah, coaxing her to talk, until everything came pouring out. Rebekah told Carrie about David, Hamlet, Ruth, and Andy. She told Carrie about coming out to her parents; Carrie was really only the fifth person on earth, she confessed, beside Ruth, Ricky, and her parents, who knew she was gay. She cried and shook and allowed Carrie to rub her back, and wipe snot from her nose, and brush her hair out of her eyes. After she told Carrie everything, Carrie kissed her on the top of the head and told Rebekah to go to sleep. Carrie climbed back up onto her bed, lay down on her side, and pulled the lamp cord next to her bed. Rebekah lay in bed with her eyes open, staring at the ceiling, the shame in her chest weighing on her like the front tire of a double-decker bus.

Meeting Megan Nimble
Winter, 2001

What is love, misplaced? It is here, somewhere, waiting to be found. Hiding in the freezer? Starved for oxygen under a couch cushion? You, irresponsible and absent-minded, have allowed it to wander off. Loneliness is love, misplaced. It's love that has found another home—there, across the street, where all those happy people in red and green Christmas sweaters are sitting in the living room by the fire, drinking apple cider and wine and laughing at the same, worn, familiar stories they've shared with one another hundreds of times. Loneliness is the kind of love that lives in city parks. It runs away from you as you sit on the park bench, alone. It tells you that you weren't a very good conversationalist. Loneliness is the kind of love that feeds on envy—envy of the moneyed by the poor, of the poor by the moneyed, envy of politicians by the business class, and envy of God by politicians.

After coming out to Carrie, Rebekah's love was precisely this kind of loneliness. It felt raw and gritty, as if she had lost her entire top layer of skin in a freak asphalt bobsledding accident. When Rebekah went home over winter break, she went to sleep early and woke up late. She ate little and hardly left the house. Rebekah blamed her lethargy on the gray skies, the cold weather, the rain. She didn't talk to her parents. She couldn't talk to her parents.

What would her parents know about love, misplaced?

In January, the two roommates returned to school, and they greeted each other as if the ill-fated double date had never happened. Rebekah marveled at how much Carrie had been transformed by her three weeks in Virginia. The heaviness that had seemed to be weighing on her after the evening with Jace was gone, replaced by the ineffable charisma that had so transfixed Rebekah when they first met. Carrie's face was fuller again; she had gotten her hair done, and perhaps even put on a pound or two. Instead of the long, tight curls that she had tamed with an abundance of hair product, she had rows and rows of tight, beautiful braids that cascaded down her back in a rich black weave.

"It looks like your hair got longer," Rebekah marveled.

"Extensions," Carrie giggled. "You like it?" she asked, twirling for her roommate.

The vintage Carrie Cline was back—the high-spirited, graceful, and exceedingly confident woman who was equally intimidating and seductive. Rebekah wondered if Carrie had spoken to anyone in Virginia about their catastrophic double date. She doubted it; Carrie liked to tell the kinds of stories in which life was easy, in which the prince married the princess and the emotional arc of the star character—Carrie Cline—rarely deviated from the path of a marble-cut success. Carrie's new hairstyle was, perhaps, a shallow fix. But it was this very kind of fix, this game of appearances and display of personal power, which the Carrie Clines of the world had so naturally mastered.

"Yeah," Rebekah said. "Hot."

Carrie pulled a folded piece of paper out of her pocket. "I picked you up something at the Involvement Fair."

Rebekah took the piece of paper from Carrie and unfolded it. "USC LGBTQ MIXER," the flyer read. "6:00 p.m. Thursday, Student Union. All are welcome." Rebekah stared at the flyer blankly.

"A mixer!" Carrie said. "Mixers are so fun. Everyone is so awkward. You can totally go, and just be yourself, and talk to people, and have nothing to be afraid of. Everyone is just there to meet everyone else for the first time."

"Uh-huh."

"Well?" Carrie asked. "Are you going to go?"

Rebekah pushed her tongue against her teeth. She didn't speak.

"I'd go with you, but I have class on Thursday night," Carrie said. "You should totally go. Maybe you'll even meet someone."

Rebekah closed her eyes.

"Oh, Bekah, you're so silly," Carrie said. Rebekah heard that easy southern laugh float toward the front door. "You have nothing to be afraid of! You're beautiful and funny and perfect! This is just the thing for you to kick the semester off right." Carrie picked up her towel and shower caddy. "I'm going to take a shower. Be right back, ok?"

Rebekah watched Carrie walk out. She folded the flyer back up, slid it into a drawer in her desk, climbed up onto her bed, and waited for Carrie to come back.

The five days between Rebekah's arrival on campus and the mixer slid by with a slow tension. Every evening, Rebekah would pull out the flyer, re-read the information about the date and time, then fold it up again and set it gently back in the drawer among her pens and scissors.

Rebekah thought of little else until the Thursday evening of the mixer arrived. Rebekah hadn't seen Carrie all day; she knew her roommate's schedule was packed on Thursdays. Rebekah downloaded music, reviewed her homework for the weekend, and trolled the web.

By six fifteen, when Rebekah still hadn't gone down to the cafeteria for dinner, she convinced herself to at least walk over to the event and peek inside. Maybe there would be no one there. Maybe there would just be pizza boxes and plates of brownies, sitting alone in silence.

Rebekah carefully selected a pink polo shirt and her darkest pair of blue jeans. She slid on her black, low-cut Chuck Taylors—tying the laces with a bit more painstaking precision than usual—and picked out a black fleece jacket to wear on top of the outfit.

Rebekah sat down at Carrie's desk and peered into the little oval face mirror that her roommate used so fastidiously. She examined her skin: pale, Portland pale, without any freckles or color or blemishes. Her nose was small, unremarkable. Her hair was coarse, coarser now that she was washing it in the hard water of Los Angeles, as opposed to the much softer, gentler water of the Pacific Northwest. Tonight, as she did almost every night, she had pulled her hair back in a ponytail, and it lay over her shoulders like a bushy head-tail. She had never minded her eyes too much. They were a rich chocolate brown. She couldn't call them particularly arresting, but they weren't muddy or off-putting.

At six thirty, Rebekah left her dorm and headed toward the Student Union. She walked with her head down and her hands in her jacket pockets, shoulders bent against a biting wind, studiously avoiding eye contact with anyone else. She worried as she walked. Was she sure she had the right evening? Yes, she had read the flyer a million times. Had she brought money to get in? Yes, there was ten dollars in her pocket—if she decided to go in. What if no one was there? *If only Ruth was here,* she thought.

But she wasn't, and would never be. It was over between them—a mutual parting borne of drama and petty arguments. They had dated for a few months, figuring out how to love each other slowly, gently, through their fingertips and eyes and tongues and hips. They kept their relationship secret from everyone but a handful of close friends. The constant hiding took a toll on them, and they were fighting over little things. Which movie to watch on movie night. Which friends to tell or not to tell. Who loved who more. Their love was beautiful and intense—and then suddenly it was over, with Ruth telling Rebekah that she wanted to go to college and "discover herself." Rebekah, not wanting to be outdone, told Ruth that she wanted to go to college and "experiment."

They hadn't spoken since. Not even during the holidays when they were both home from school.

Rebekah kicked the sidewalk thinking about it. Since breaking up with Ruth, all she had known was loneliness.

She walked past Tommy Trojan—flexing, silent, strong—and reached the front steps of the Student Union. She opened the door, took a left toward the community rooms, and slowed down as she approached the mixer. When Rebekah was within sight of the door, she stopped. She leaned forward and peered down the hall and into the room.

The room was full. Not half-full, but full-full. The community room wasn't too big, about the size of a one-bedroom apartment, but people were lined up around the walls and clustered into groups in the center. The room was so crowded that students had to turn sideways when they walked past each other, and occasionally even tap strangers on the shoulder, asking them to shift a few inches so that they could pass.

The LGBT Student Association had whimsically decorated the room with multicolored streamers, so that it resembled a snow cone drizzled with a dozen different flavored syrups. A big rainbow flag hung on the back wall, imprinted with the word PEACE in white block letters. A second rainbow flag was affixed to a pole in a flagpole holder just outside the door. A few students sat behind a table just inside the door, all wearing matching shirts with the letters LGBTQ on the front.

She could hear the low beats and high voices of grainy pop music filtering through the open door, most likely from an old boom box. She heard voices, sometimes escalating past one another, culminating in shouting or laughter. People held paper plates with pizza.

Pizza, Rebekah thought. The tangy smell of the pizza made her stomach turn. She took a step back, so that she was hidden from the room by a hallway corner. She stared out through the window. Students were walking by, wearing backpacks and headphones. She could see the side right side of the Tommy Trojan statue; his brandished sword was hidden from view, but the definition in his pectorals and biceps was visible, even from across the parkway and inside a building.

Another quick glance back into the community room confirmed that she didn't know anyone at the event. *This is too much,* Rebekah thought. Rebekah was turning to walk away when someone running in the other direction knocked her to the ground.

"Oh—oh my God! I totally didn't see you! Are you ok?"

Rebekah slowly sat up and rubbed her head. Something sharp had caught her just above the right eye. It was throbbing. She touched a finger to the spot and looked at her fingertips. No blood.

"Oh, fuck. Are you bleeding? Did I elbow you in the head? I'm so sorry. I am so, so sorry. Sam!"   Someone was bending over Rebekah, yelling down the hall. "Sam, I think I seriously injured someone!"

Rebekah kept staring at the ground, afraid to look up. She found herself studying at a pair of low-cut, black and white Chuck Taylors—a pair of shoes so curiously like her own that Rebekah glanced quickly at her own feet to make sure that her shoes hadn't popped off during the collision. Dark-blue jeans hung around the stranger's ankles, the ends of which were frayed from the constant abuse of being dragged against the ground. There were slight indentations in the pant legs near the knees: creases resulting from too much sitting. Slightly higher up, she saw the edge of a black, loose-fitting t-shirt.

Rebekah heard the quick drops of rapid footfalls.

"What did you do, Megan?" Rebekah heard another woman ask. Rebekah looked up. A different woman leaned over Rebekah, her hands on her knees. Her hair was spiked into a faux-hawk; she was wearing a black tank and tight black jeans. She had well-defined arms and two matching star tattoos on her shoulders.

Rebekah had recovered from the collision but felt dizzy and claustrophobic. She blinked hard a few times and weakly held her hand out. The woman with the faux-hawk grabbed it and pulled her up. Rebekah looked around. A bunch of students had gathered to watch the exchange. To her left stood the woman she thought might have run into her, the one with the Chuck Taylors and frayed blue jeans. The woman stared at her with wide eyes, her hands cupped over her mouth.

"You ok?" Faux-hawk asked.

Rebekah nodded. She needed air.

"Want to come in for some pizza?" Faux-hawk motioned to the door. "We're just about to get started with some ice breakers."

"Um, you know…I think, I think I'm just going to sit outside for a minute." Rebekah tried to laugh. It sounded like she was wheezing.

"I'll go with her," the woman to her left announced.

"Oh, Megs, you're just going to break her again," one student said.

"Yeah, Megsy, maybe we need to put you in a bubble first," said another.

"Oh shut up, you guys," the woman responded. She grinned at them. "The reason I was running was to bring in the nametags, which— let's not forget who left them in their apartment, right?" She held up a bag and shook it.

"Didn't your teachers ever tell you not to run with nametags? Or scissors?" One of the students, a tall, thin man, snatched the bag from Megan's hand. "I'll go set these out on the table." He turned to Rebekah. "Watch out for that one," he said gesturing at Megan. "She's trouble."

Faux-hawk turned to another student. "Can you go help him?"

"I was just going to do that. Later, ladies." The second student turned and followed the first one into the community room.

Faux-hawk stuck out her hand. "I'm Sam."

"Rebekah," Rebekah said, shaking Sam's hand.

"That one is Megan," Sam said, pointing at the woman who had run into her.

"I'm so, so sorry," Megan said. "I'm just a total klutz sometimes."

"That's ok," Rebekah said.

"You got this?" Sam asked Megan.

Megan nodded and put hand on Rebekah's shoulder. "Come on, let's go outside."

"Um, listen, I think I'm ok," Rebekah said to Megan.

"Yeah?" Megan's face lit up. "So you want to go inside?"

"Well, maybe in a minute. I think, um…." Rebekah paused while she searched for an excuse. "I just have a little bit of a headache, so I think I might run back to my dorm room really quick and just grab some ibuprofen and come back."

"Oh, well, someone might have some here. Want me to ask?"

"No, no, it'll just take me five minutes, and it will give me a chance to clear my head and stuff. I'll be right back."

Megan looked at Rebekah skeptically. She had a kind, open face, oval-shaped like an egg, framed by brown hair that hung down to her shoulders and bangs that hovered just above her eyebrows. Megan had broad shoulders and a square jawline, and she was tall, so tall that Rebekah had to tilt her head upward to look at her face.

"Ok," Megan said. "But you're going to come back, right?"

"I will," Rebekah confirmed, certain that she was lying.

"Ok." Megan looked over her shoulder at the event. Sam Ellis had just quieted her assembled students and was introducing herself and the schedule for the upcoming evening.

"Well, I'm going to go inside then," Megan said. "I'm so sorry. I'll see you soon?"

"Yep," Rebekah nodded.

"Ok, see ya." Megan waved and disappeared into community room. Rebekah watched her go, and then walked out of the Student Union, her night over before it had begun.

The next morning was like most Friday mornings on the USC campus: gently framed by manicured beauty, irrepressibly upbeat, and slathered in sunlight. A never-ending stream of young, backpack-wearing students—all cooked to the same faint-light tan—

walked past the Leavey Library reflecting pool. Anything that could possibly distract from these environs was kept out or quickly removed by police, campus security, or the students themselves. There was no poverty, no hunger, no death, no illness, no anguish on display here. Even winter, having once again baffled much of the country with its meanness, couldn't penetrate the Southern California campus. There was nothing to feel here but contentment. Within that wholly happy speck on the planet, Rebekah Cohayn sat in her dorm room, safe and alone, miserable over her fear and self-imposed isolation. Rebekah was surrounded by thousands of students who were cheerful and generous in their obliviousness, who seemed to judge Rebekah by the standards of their own happiness. Their smiles, their tans, their participation in intramural sports leagues and fraternities, their devotion to the college newspaper and to extracurricular activities—these were all indictments of Rebekah's exile. It wasn't that they wanted nothing to do with her, but that she wanted nothing to do with them; that she, living in a place with seemingly boundless opportunity, couldn't break out of a prison of her own assembling.

She sat at her desk, looking out the window at the students milling below, wondering if anyone below was thinking about her up here, just as she was thinking about them. But no one glanced toward the second window from the left on the fourth floor of her dorm. They kept their heads straight and their eyes forward, occasionally looking down at a book or aside to speak to a companion. But no one looked upward.

Rebekah thought about what might happen if she somehow pried off the protective screen covering the window and jumped. Would the students gaggle around her body on the concrete, horrified at the suddenness and morbidity of the morning? Would the police come and cordon off the scene, block the view, and quickly remove all evidence of her termination, leaving only the unbent white concrete to indicate what had become of her?

Rebekah had gone to bed early the night of the mixer, ashamed of having gone to the event at all, and even more scared of telling Carrie what she did. She woke up early on Friday, mortified at having snuck out under the false pretenses of an injury. You're a coward, she told herself. A liar.

And gay. Right? Or was she? This was perhaps the most tortured question that she faced all morning, one that would follow her around campus as she dragged herself to her classes during the next few weeks. Did she leave the event early because she was afraid she might not fit in? Or did she leave early because she was afraid of what she might have found out about herself—that, in fact, she might belong there?

But Rebekah smiled at her roommate when she woke up, and she told Carrie that the event had been fantastic. Rebekah navigated the faultless flowerbeds and red brick buildings on campus, blending in with the thousands of other students who all seemed to project unimpeachable confidence. She dutifully took notes during class, turned in assignments on time, airily chatted with classmates and acquaintances from her dorm, and called her parents regularly to talk about life on campus. Rebekah betrayed none of her turmoil, her anguish, her daily rounds of self-immolation. There was nothing for others to see but contentment.

On a Wednesday evening in mid-February, Rebekah received an email.

Hi Rebekah,
You probably don't remember me, but I ran into you…literally…at the LGBT mixer a few weeks ago.
I was just writing to see how you're doing…I haven't seen you around since…just wanted to make sure I didn't give you a permanent head injury. I'm so sorry!!
If you're up for it, Sam and I and a few others are going out for Ethiopian food this weekend. It's going to be fun….
Want to come?
Megan Nimble

Rebekah leaned back in her chair. What to make of this email? The days and weeks had tottered along since the mixer. She had spent them waking up at the same time every morning, eating in the freshman cafeteria—often by herself—and focusing her efforts on her homework. Weekends were dreary, lonely, and long. She often lived vicariously through her roommate's stories of Greek life, politely demurring when Carrie invited her to parties. She admired

Carrie's persistence in trying to up the ante on her social life, but she declined, just the same.

Rebekah had no desire to hang out with Megan Nimble or with any of the students she had met who were associated with the LGBT student group. Why would she? They represented a rocky, uphill path that could only lead to difficult conversations, to agonizing memories, to the kind of bold, decisive actions that Rebekah had decided she was simply not cut out for. Her year with Ruth was buried, her excruciating conversation with her mom firmly behind her, as if it belonged to another life.

And yet, there was something irresistible about Megan's email. It may have been that this was the first invitation that Rebekah had received to go out, excluding Carrie's nearly weekly pleas. Or perhaps it was something deeper, a desire on Rebekah's part to slip into a skin that held the promise of being more fitted, of feeling more right, than Rebekah had felt in a long time. She had been a coward at the mixer. More than anything, she regretted walking out. Rebekah hit reply.

Hey Megan,
So nice to hear from you! I'm fine…no lasting permanent head injuries. I'm as crazy as I've always been (haha!!) Sorry I bugged out from the mixer…I just wasn't feeling quite well, and once I got home I decided not to go out again. I hope it went well!
Going out for Ethiopian food sounds fun. I really appreciate the invitation. Where are we meeting?
Rebekah

On Saturday evening, Rebekah walked to Megan's apartment. She'd slipped out when Carrie left their room for a few minutes, fearing dozens of questions that she had no stomach to answer. Rebekah walked quickly, her hands in her pockets, keeping her eyes down and her jacket pulled up closely around her neck.

A few minutes after seven, Rebekah arrived at Megan's house, where she found Megan, Sam Ellis, and another woman standing out front.

"Hi, Rebekah," someone said as she approached. Rebekah looked up from the ground.

"It's nice to see that you're still walking, after being taken out by Nimble," Sam said. She was wearing mostly black again, this time topped with a tight black beanie.

"Oh, God," Megan said. She towered over all of them, like a single stalk of corn that had accidentally sprouted a few months too early. She looked at Rebekah. "I am so, so sorry. I can't believe I did that. I'm such a disaster sometimes."

"No worries," Rebekah said. She glanced at the woman standing next to Megan. "I'm fine. It totally wasn't a big deal."

Sam stepped forward. "Rebekah, this is my girlfriend, Yuki."

"Hi." Yuki held out her hand.

Rebekah shook her hand and returned the greeting. Yuki had a pretty face with long lashes and a small nose. She was short—only a little over five feet—and looked even shorter standing next to Megan.

"I'm really glad you could make it, Rebekah," Megan said. She was talking with her hands, waving them in front of her to accentuate just how glad she was that Rebekah was standing in front of her. "I was having these panic moments that, like, you know, you never were going to come back or join, and then Sam would blame me forever."

"That's true, I would," Sam said, nodding.

"See?" Megan said, gesturing towards Sam. "This is what I would have to deal with, probably for the rest of my life."

"Definitely, for the rest of your life," Sam said.

"So…thank you," Megan said, pressing her hands together.

Rebekah nodded. "You're welcome," she said. She felt her stomach turn. Maybe there was still enough time to go home.

Sam glanced at her watch. "Ok, let's get rolling. I bet the boys will be late, anyway, but we should get there to get a table."

Sam walked around to the driver's side of the forest-green Volvo and opened the door. Yuki pulled open the door of the passenger seat. Megan followed Sam and sat behind her, so Rebekah opened the backseat door on the passenger side and took the seat behind Yuki. She looked straight at the back of the headrest and took a deep breath.

"Hey," Megan said, as she clicked in her seat belt. "Check it out. We're wearing the same shoes."

Rebekah looked down. They were indeed wearing matching black Chuck Taylors, just as she had noticed on the evening of the LGBT mixer. "Oh, yeah," she said. "Well, I guess you've got a pretty good sense of style."

"Well, it's hard to screw up with Chucks."

Rebekah looked over and studied Megan. She was wearing jeans and a puffy black down jacket. Rebekah noticed that she was also wearing a curious pair of earmuffs. They were covered in a faux-fur with a leopard print design.

"I like your earmuffs," Rebekah said.

"Oh, these things?" Megan took them off. "Yeah, aren't they silly? I won them in a contest that the LGBT held a few years ago. It was a Halloween contest, and they gave out prizes to the best dressed. Hey, Sam, remember when I won these earmuffs?" She held them up so Sam could look at them in the rearview mirror.

"Oh, yeah, dude, I totally remember that," Sam said. "That was freshman year, right?"

"Yeah."

Sam looked at Rebekah in the rearview mirror. "You'll never guess what Megan dressed up as that year."

Rebekah looked from Sam to Megan. "What was it?"

Sam grinned at her. "I dressed up as a phone. An old, boxy rotary phone."

"But she told everyone she was a homophone," Sam said. "Get it? Homophone?"

Megan laughed a loud, horsey laugh. "The only problem was that I had to explain what a homophone was all night. Besides a homo dressed up as a phone."

"So...really, you went as a pun," Rebekah said.

"Yeah."

"Geek," Yuki said.

"I've been trying to think of how to dress up as a homonym, but I can't figure out the 'nym' part," Megan said.

"It's probably better that way, Nimble," Sam said. "We wouldn't want your head to get too big."

"Oh, whatever," Megan said.

"So what's your major, Rebekah?" Sam asked.

"English," Rebekah said. "What about you guys?"

"I'm a gender studies major," Sam said. "These other two smarties are engineers."

"I just want to have a job when I graduate," Yuki said. Sam looked over at her and glared. Yuki leaned in and kissed her on the cheek. "Let's not talk about jobs," Sam said. She pulled off the highway. "Yeah, let's not," Yuki responded.

"Because in four months, I'll need to have one, and I'm not sure I'll have any practicable skills."

Rebekah looked out the window. The challenges of building a career felt like a cannibalistic next-door-neighbor set to eat them alive once they left the safe confines of college.

Rebekah sighed, turned to Megan, and studied her in the dimming light. Megan reminded her of a St. Bernard, without the droopy jowls: unusually large, a little gangly, but with a wide-open, charming, honest face. All she needed was a little barrel to hang around her neck, and Rebekah felt like she might trust this woman to carry her out of the Alps. She was amused that they had both worn Chuck Taylors, twice now, to different events. Might that not be the mark of a kindred spirit?

In a few minutes, Sam had parked her green Volvo a few blocks away from Tana, a cozy little Ethiopian restaurant in Little Ethiopia, near the intersection of Fairfax and Olympic. Holding hands, Sam and Yuki walked down the sidewalk in front of Megan and Rebekah. Rebekah walked behind them, a little cowed by their public display of affection. Even when she and Ruth had been deeply in love, they never held hands on the sidewalk. Their relationship was conducted almost fully in the confines of Ruth's house, in the evenings, when her mother was out and no one else was around. Sam and Yuki seemed unnaturally bold—far bolder than Rebekah could ever have imagined being. Megan walked beside her.

Tana was painted in bright hues and decorated with pictures, woven baskets, and bright pillows. There were a few tables near the front of the restaurant, low to the ground, designed for guests to sit on the floor. The other tables, near the back, were low and long, made out of wood, and covered in patterned tablecloths.

About ten minutes after they were seated, two men arrived. Rebekah recognized them as the students from the LGBT group who had razzed Megan outside the mixer. They introduced themselves to Rebekah as Asher and Ottawa. Megan later told Rebekah that the two—Ottawa, small and thin, and Asher, tall and bulky—had met in high school, and had each been the first to come out to one another.

The six split three plates of injera, meats, and vegetables. The dinner lasted until the six had cleaned their platters and leaned back in their chairs, utterly exhausted from their gluttony. Rebekah hadn't enjoyed a dinner so much since her evening with Andy Rowan, Jace, and Carrie, and before that, since being with her friends from theater in high school.

Rebekah was also enjoying sitting next to Megan Nimble, this giant, easy-going friend she'd made only a few hours ago. Megan was like an unvarnished wooden table: stripped down, simple, uncomplicated. When Megan was sitting, her shoulder weren't slumped. She sat up straight in her chair, alternately leaning lazily against its back and leaning forward, her chin on her hand, an elbow on the table, intently paying attention to whoever was speaking. Sitting, she was only slightly taller than Rebekah. And when she turned to Rebekah, their eyes met.

In Ruth, Ricky, Carrie, and many of Rebekah's other friends, charisma had always been something shiny and compelling, coolness wrapped in armor and shiny tin that kept her at arm's length. But Megan's charisma was cloaked in folksiness. Her mannerisms might have seemed out of place at a formal dinner party, but she was right at home here at Tana, commanding the attention of the table with her wit and charm.

Two and a half hours after dinner began, Asher checked the voice mail on his cell phone. "Friends," he announced loudly, "allow me to make a proposal after this fine meal we've shared."

"Only if you shut up and talk like a normal person," Ottawa said.

"I propose," Asher continued, ignoring Ottawa, "that we join some of our fellow Trojans at tonight's festive and very gay celebration at Storm." He paused and sipped his Ethiopian coffee. "Would anyone care to join?"

Sam and Yuki looked at each other. Sam shrugged. "Yeah, I guess that sounds fun. We haven't been out in a while." She looked across the table at Megan and Rebekah. "How about you guys?"

Rebekah felt her face get hot. She didn't know what Storm was, but it sounded like a nightclub. Not only had she never been to a club, but she was under twenty-one and wouldn't be able to get in.

Rebekah cleared her throat. "I don't think I can go," she said.

"Why not?" Asher asked.

"I don't think I'm old enough."

Asher smiled widely at her. "Well, my dear, that's not a problem. Storm is an over-eighteen club. You are over eighteen, right?"

Rebekah laughed, relieved. "Only on Saturdays."

Megan raised her hand. "May I speak?"

Asher swept his arm across his body. "The floor is yours."

"I, for one, think Storm is a little silly. It's an over-eighteen club filled with a lot of pretty gay boys—and straight girls!—leaving very little for the lesbian half of this table, which, I want to point out, is the majority of the current company. They don't even play good music."

"You're right, my dear Megan, on some points—particularly the one about pretty gay boys—which makes Storm worthwhile to visit, even if we must put up with a few minor annoyances," Asher said. "Besides, we've got two cars. Why don't we have a car going back to campus and a car going to the club?"

"I guess I'm in the car going to the club." Ottawa looked sympathetically at Megan. "If you come, I'll spend my evening looking for lesbians for you."

Megan snorted and started laughing. "You're a fucking liar, buddy."

"So, do you want to go, Megan?" Sam asked. "I suppose Yuki and I could go either way."

Megan sighed. "Yeah, I'll go." She looked at Rebekah. "I'll go if Rebekah goes."

Rebekah blushed. The whole table was staring at her.

"Well, shit, you guys," Rebekah said.

"And so it shall be?" Ottawa asked.

Rebekah nodded. "And so it shall be."

Although Storm was located in a nondescript, converted warehouse, a sizeable portion of Los Angeles' gay population had managed to find it. The line to get in stretched around the building, filled mostly with men: fit, skinny, beautiful men in tight shirts and tight pants, who smelled like mint and wood chips. Most of them had closely cropped hair, some wearing short, one-inch mohawks that snaked down the middle of their heads like giant earthworms. They were all young, as young as Rebekah, and they were trying hard to look bored, as if they'd stood in many lines for gay nightclubs. There were also a handful of women in line. Some were clearly dykes, with short, spiked hair, loose-fitting pants, and boots; others had the long blond hair and makeup-application skills of Carrie's Betas.

Asher and Ottawa immediately went to the back of the line, craning their necks to see if they were about to run into anyone they knew. Sam and Yuki huddled together against the cold, holding hands, and talked quietly to each other.

If Rebekah had been there by herself, she might have felt cowed. But she felt confident standing next to the tall Megan Nimble, with her sloped shoulders and goofy grin, who was sharing stories of their past trips to West Hollywood. There was the time, Megan whispered, on Ottawa's twenty-first birthday, that they took him out, and three of his friends—unbeknownst to one another—all bought him double shots of tequila. Three hours later, the poor guy was bent over the sidewalk, throwing up into the gutter. Then there was the time—Megan looked around before continuing—before Yuki and Sam started dating, when Sam really liked Yuki, but Yuki was still in the death throes of a relationship with a crazy older woman. Megan's voice trailed off. "It's a long story," she laughed. "You probably don't want to hear it."

But Rebekah was hungry for stories: hungry to hear about gay life in Los Angeles, hungry to hear about these new friends she had made. And then there was the enchanting, persuasive quality of Megan's voice. "I do," Rebekah told Megan. "Please keep talking."

Half an hour later, Rebekah made it to the front of the line. The bouncer stretched a big orange wristband around Rebekah's wrist to indicate that she couldn't drink alcohol. The inside of the club was dark, lit only near the bar and by a few neon lights above the dance floor. Asher, Ottawa, Sam, and Yuki disappeared immediately, leaving Rebekah to follow Megan into the hot thrum of people. With the deep, loud, thump, thump, thump of the DJ's bass in the background, Megan led her to a spot on the far side of the dance floor, up against a wall.

The two watched the dance floor. Gay men, Rebekah decided, had a very particular and elegant way of dancing. It was often a solitary activity, requiring space and balance. There was a lot of spinning, shoulder dipping, whirling and leaping, hands and arms gyrating in front of them, their eyes closed, their lips eased into wide smiles. They danced for each other, as much as with each other. It was fascinating, intimidating, and beautiful to Rebekah. She watched for a few minutes, mesmerized, aware only of the dancers and Megan standing next to her.

After a few minutes she turned to Megan, wondering what her new friend expected of her. Rebekah wasn't a particularly good dancer, not like these boys, anyway. What if Megan wanted to dance with her? So she hung back, leaned against the wall, and attempted to project an image of contentment. She also looked around for Asher, Yuki, Sam, and Ottawa, but couldn't find them in the crowd.

Suddenly, Rebekah felt a tap on her shoulder. She saw Megan jerk a thumb towards the dance floor. "Want to dance?" Megan seemed to be asking.

Rebekah, paralyzed by fear and indecision, only managed to answer Megan's question with a half-hearted shrug and a panicked smile. But Megan read her shy friend immediately. She backed up a few feet onto the dance floor and began dancing awkwardly to the music, her gangly limbs moving in all directions at once, her eyes wide, her mouth split into that same charismatic, silly grin.

Rebekah grinned back. She looked around. Some of the boys were watching Megan. One turned around and began imitating her, sending his own arms into the air and waving them, as if he was drowning near a sinking ship. Soon, Megan had a gaggle of boys around her, all amused by this tall, bold lesbian who couldn't dance like them, but was audacious enough to step out.

Megan motioned again to Rebekah. And Rebekah, slowly and reluctantly, moved onto the dance floor and began moving, ever so slightly to the music. Megan clapped and cheered her on, exhorting her to wave her arms in the air, then swing them low, then swing them up into the air again. Rebekah found herself laughing, getting lost in the music, her eyes fixed on Megan's as they danced together for the first time.

The morning after Megan left their home, Rebekah's alarm sounded, just as it always did. She switched it off, took a shower, and arrived at work at seven thirty.

At four thirty, Rebekah took the MAX train home. She walked to the Judge's house, opened the side entrance to the basement, dropped her backpack in the living room, and took up her vigil on the couch. She stared out the window. Checked her phone. Listened to the Judge and Claire walk around upstairs.

Rebekah and Megan had been having this fight for ten years. They'd had other fights too—little ones, about who would do the dishes, or where they'd go to dinner—but they were always able to trace it back to this one, the big fight. The "gay" fight. It always ended in yelling, accusations, and discussions about how to communicate about how to communicate.

Rebekah thought back to their first date, the night they went out for Ethiopian food, and then to Storm. The two girls had danced together for hours, surrounded by gay boys who smelled of boy-sweat and musk, and were propelled by pop music with high-pitched female vocals and heavy bass lines. Rebekah lost herself in the music. She allowed Megan to put her hands on her shoulders, to twirl Rebekah forward and back, and to hunch over and pull Rebekah toward her so that Rebekah's head lay on her collarbone. They were in a neon womb, just the two of them, along with hundreds of others who were there only for contextual purposes. When Rebekah and Megan walked out of the club, Los Angeles had turned into an inky black desert lit up by garish streetlights and car headlights. The air was frigid, compared to the heat generated by the mass of sweating bodies on the dance floor. The city felt big, imposing, unfamiliar, a city built for other people and accidentally inhabited by Rebekah.

Megan tried to hold her hand. Rebekah pulled away. Megan wanted to walk with her, a few steps behind Sam and Yuki. Rebekah kept walking faster to keep up.

Megan didn't say anything that night about Rebekah's behavior. She didn't say anything for a few months, in fact, as the two girls fell in love. It was only after a year of dating, when they started to finish each other's sentences and transitioned from easy compromise to light-hearted bickering, that Megan began to question Rebekah's public display of secrecy.

They ate dinners out together, all over Los Angeles, Rebekah always surreptitiously scanning the restaurant to see if she knew anyone. "Who are you looking for, the Pope?" Megan asked once.

David, Rebekah would think, knowing that he never ate out at restaurants that weren't kosher. "Maybe the Pope likes sushi," Rebekah said.

Megan and Rebekah went to the beach and museums, plays, concerts. If Megan tried to hold her hand, Rebekah claimed her palms were sweaty. When Megan tried to put her arm around her, Rebekah let it rest for a few seconds, then shook it off and said she was feeling antsy.

Rebekah reluctantly attended USC LGBT events with Megan. They were difficult to avoid, since both Megan and Sam were so involved, but Rebekah demurred when she could, most often citing schoolwork as the reason. Rebekah could identify no single reason for avoiding these events; it was a fear, an agitation that consumed her whole body. Everyone would *know.* And if everyone knew, then *everyone*—David, Grandma Simchah, the car mechanic, future employers, the tellers at the bank, coffee baristas and real estate agents—would know she was gay.

It was only when they were alone together, in a dark room, in Megan's bed, that Rebekah allowed herself to give in. She allowed herself to touch Megan, feel her, go inside her, sink into Megan's skin and hips and bones. She had sex with Megan furtively, anxiously, as if she was trying to feel her way out of a pitch-black cave. She pressed her hips up against Megan's, hungrily ground her thigh between Megan's legs, ran her fingertips over her neck and breasts and vagina, until the two lay clutching each other, dark and silent and breathing.

For three nights after Megan left, Rebekah slept alone. Those three nights were filled with paralyzing despair and frustration for Rebekah; with illusory conversations, some focused on accusations and conviction, others on apology and reparation.

Sometimes Rebekah consoled herself with the idea that this fight must be temporary, from necessity, at least. Megan would need to pick up her stuff. They would need to figure out what to do with the apartment, how to split up the furniture, who was going to tell the Judge that their relationship, and the wedding, was over. If Megan came back and stayed, then the fight would be resolved.

She shocked herself with these thoughts, with how easily she was able to bifurcate her relationship into two possible outcomes. Could her instincts have been wrong all these years? Could the relationship have been ill-fated from the moment it began?

Fangs, Rebekah thought. That's how her own parents had met.

Judith was a freshman at the University of Oregon. Her roommate, a vivacious, prone-to-party red-head named Dawn, told her about a Halloween bash hosted by friends of her older brother. The party would be safe, Dawn insisted, no boneheads or creepy older men. There would be alcohol. Weed. Costumes were mandatory.

The way Judith told the story, she loathed Halloween. She thought it slightly better than Valentine's Day in its crass commercialism. But Dawn had begged and pleaded, telling Judith that if she had to go to the party alone she would probably end up passed out on a sidewalk somewhere. Judith, opposed to Halloween but even more strongly opposed to being dangerously drunk, agreed to accompany her friend as a chaperone.

Dawn had worn a red leotard, red tights, red boots, a long red tail made from a chain of pipe cleaners, and red horns—Lucifer on a budget. Judith put on gray sweatpants, a ratty gray sweatshirt, bright red lipstick, and pair of white plastic fangs she'd picked up from the local pharmacy. She told Dawn she was dressed up as a shark.

The two walked to the party. Judith arrived soaking wet, unprepared for the predictable, steady Eugene downpour. She stood in the doorway, soaked purse in hand, her curly hair simultaneously frizzed out and stuck to her face. There were so many people crowded into this house—zombies, angels, demons, cowboys, evil nurses, and at least five Richard Nixons. All carried large red cups. She felt water from her sweat pants seeping into her socks.

"Nice fangs."

Judith turned around. A short, skinny boy in a black cape, starched white shirt, and red bow tie had walked up next to her. He smiled, revealing a set of identical white fangs.

"You too," Judith said. "You're a vampire?"

"I am," the boy said. "And you're a…?"

"Shark."

The boy grinned. "That's what I was thinking, but I didn't realize sharks wore red lipstick."

Judith shrugged. "I guess you've never really met a shark, then."

The shark and the vampire stood by the door and talked until the living room got too crowded. Then they moved to the kitchen, and then the backyard, where they stood under the tin roof of an outdoor deck, where the gentle pattering of the rain shrouded their conversation in an unexpected intimacy. They talked and talked, the only two sober partygoers at the house, until an intoxicated Dawn grabbed Judith by the arm and told her that the party was terrible and they needed to leave. The vampire ran into a bedroom, found a pen and a piece of paper, and wrote down the shark's name and phone number. The next day, Judith Abrams received a phone call from Daniel Cohayn.

It was so fucking easy for them, Rebekah thought. She had heard that story so many times, she just assumed she would have a cute, clever story to tell people one day. But what was her story? That her fiancée—possibly ex-fiancée—had run into her at a college mixer? That they had nearly married, except she was too spineless? That as the second-born child in the Cohayn family, she was fated for a life of almosts?

During the day, Rebekah was able to distract herself with work, commuting, answering emails, and the other mundane aspects of living that transformed the fight into a chimera. The Arts in the Halls event was only three weeks away. *Daft* was scheduled to be published in two weeks, and for the first time in the history of the newsmagazine, there would be no art in the center spread. Rebekah had placed Tony's fundraising letter just off center, slightly left and toward the top of the page. The background of the center spread was a bright white. The type was black, in 10-point Arial. The spread was plain, stark. A naked plea for money. At the end of the letter was a gray text box that Rebekah had created, linked to a separate website that the magazine's web viewers could visit. The text in the box said: "Save the Arts." Hard-copy readers received self-addressed, stamped envelopes for mail-in donations. At Rebekah's insistence, Micah and Jane grudgingly agreed to include the website information in the hard-copy magazine. Rebekah told them that this would increase the number of "clicks" on the page, a number she could use to demonstrate fundraising success.

The evenings were difficult. She couldn't avoid the empty seat across from her at the dinner table, the cold second cushion on the couch, and the tucked-in sheets on the other side of the bed. But the worst was the quiet: the stillness of the apartment felt like illness, or death, as if her world were encased in a bubble of syrup that blocked out noise and movement. Even the traffic outside seemed to be less noisy than usual, as if it was tiptoeing around her grief.

So the nights pressed on, each quieter and more suffocating than the night before. Calling Megan would have been giving in. And wasn't that what Megan *didn't* want? Wasn't this fight about Megan's insistence that Rebekah be herself, damn the world if it didn't love her?

It was Megan's responsibility to call her, she thought, to affirm the new steeliness in her backbone. In her stronger moments, she felt completely reassured that this was exactly what she was supposed to be doing. The failure to communicate was Megan's, not her own. If anything tangible weighed on Rebekah, it was the knowledge that their wedding—and its associated commitments, down payments, and invitations—hung in the balance. Maybe the finances were a distraction from thinking about Megan, but there were certain moments when they seemed all encompassing. Would she be able to get back the down payment on the facility they had rented? What would they tell the caterer?

Even more insistent was her fear of the deep humiliation that she expected when she told her friends and family that the wedding was off. She dreaded the conversation with Carrie Cline, who would want to know all the heart-wrenching details.

Only five or ten years ago, everyone Rebekah knew was homophobic. No one understood gay culture, gay people, or gay marriage. Gayness was something to be rejected and fixed. Gayness could be overcome with discipline and therapy.

Now, those people had changed. It had been so easy for them, such a natural progression to learn and grow, to discover that the gay people they knew were not freaks and monsters, after all, but their sisters and brothers, mothers, uncles, grandparents, sons and daughters.

But Rebekah's homophobia—and she despised calling it that—was deeply personal. For years, she had lived uncomfortably with her self-loathing. She welcomed it, in fact, as a path to humility. If she *did* fully accept who she was, she reasoned, she would become intolerably narcissistic. She wasn't perfect. She was flawed. With a martyr-like sensibility, she told herself that her sexuality was a blemish that would be borne with dignity. Her friends would love her anyway. They would embrace her in a polite way, carefully avoiding the lump in her stomach that held the frothing worms of her anxiety. She was stuck in her own decade of discrimination, and couldn't seem to pull herself out.

And Megan would simply need to accept that.

Saturday morning—four days after their fight, and two weeks before their wedding day—Rebekah woke up early. She decided to make pancakes. *I don't need Megan to make pancakes*, Rebekah told herself.

And indeed, she didn't. The directions on the box were perfectly clear. The first pancake came out a little burnt, but the subsequent eleven came out perfect: golden, brown around the edges, cooked in the middle, but not burnt on the outside. Rebekah set the table for herself: butter, syrup, fork and knife, and a glass of orange juice. She sat down at the table, took a bite, and congratulated herself on her cooking skills. She chewed in silence, staring out across the table. The bite of pancake felt like a bowling ball sliding down her throat. It seemed to expand in her esophagus, settling into her stomach like a shot putt. Rebekah put down her fork and took a sip of orange juice.

Worthless, Rebekah thought. Rebekah's lower lip trembled. She shut her eyes and squeezed back tears.

This wasn't what she wanted breakfast to look like on Saturday mornings. She wondered what Megan was eating. She thought it was most likely cereal and milk, since that's what Megan ate almost every morning. Where was she, anyway?

The thought was too much to bear. Rebekah pushed back her plate, grabbed her cell phone, and called Megan. The call went straight to Megan's answering machine.

"Hi, it's me," Rebekah said into the phone. "I miss you. I'm just…I'm miserable. We need to talk. Can you call me? Please?" Rebekah fought back the urge to apologize. *Not yet.* "That's it. I just miss you." Rebekah swallowed hard. "Ok, that's all. Bye."

The remainder of the day crept by. Rebekah watched television, flipping between HGTV and TNT, where a *Law and Order* marathon was playing. She kept her cell phone by her feet on the floor. It didn't ring once.

At one time in her life, Rebekah had assumed that she would be alone forever, that every Saturday would be like the Saturday she was experiencing. Adjusting to Megan's absence was like adjusting to a death, she told herself. Over time it would get easier. She would find ways to fill the day, plan outings around friends, and elevate herself out of her rut of solitude. It would take days, months, even years, maybe, for this to start to feel normal. Sure, Megan's absence felt like a gaping hole now, but soon, she told herself, it would be as though Megan had never been there.

Her chest felt tight, thinking about that. So she pushed it out of her mind, checked her cell phone again, and flipped the television channel back to *Law and Order.*

By seven, Megan still hadn't called. Was it really possible that she might never call? That she simply might disappear, leaving Rebekah with the apartment and all of their furniture? Was that really a more appealing outcome to the woman with whom she had spent nearly a third of her life?

Rebekah put three leftover pancakes in the microwave. When she pulled them out, they were steaming and heavy. They tasted like wet laundry. She considered calling Megan again. But what would she say? Would she leave a sobbing, wailing message on her phone to convey how sorry she was? Would she be indignant, angry, and leave an ultimatum? Would she threaten harm to herself? Cause permanent damage to their relationship?

Rebekah tossed her phone on the couch, grabbed her keys off the table, picked up a jacket, and walked out the door.

Walking was good. Walking was healing. Walking was putting one foot in front of the other, heel, toe, even steps, eyes forward and down, hands brushing her pockets, breath flowing in waves, almost too easily. How was it that breathing felt so involuntary?

Rebekah walked. Northeast Portland was a great place to walk, especially on evenings like this, when it wasn't raining. She walked on Broadway, past full bars and restaurants, and then up, past half-million dollar homes and the cars parked bumper-to-bumper in front of them. There was no shortage of neatly packaged neighborhoods, busy streets, and people-watching opportunities. Children wearing capes and Viking helmets as a form of make-believe. Adults wearing capes and Viking helmets as a form of irony.

She wandered through Northeast Portland for the better part of an hour. It was dark now. She figured that she was about twenty minutes from home, if she walked quickly.

Suddenly, Rebekah heard loud music blasting from a living room in a house to her left. The music startled Rebekah; she tripped over a bump in the sidewalk and fell to the ground, landing on her knees. Her glasses flew off in the initial stumble and landed ahead of her on the sidewalk.

"Shit," Rebekah said. She examined her knees. They were bruised, but her pants were intact. She crawled forward, leaning on her palms, feeling around for her glasses. Her fingertips touched the edges of her frames. She picked them up, and slid them onto her face.

The lens on the left side was fine. The one on the right side had taken the brunt of the impact with the sidewalk and had jagged scratches down the center.

Rebekah sighed, and put her broken glasses back on the bridge of her nose. She stood up, and turned toward the house on her left.

The front windows of the house were wide open. Rebekah spied a peculiar sight in the living room: half a dozen men and women clutching each other, moving slowly in time to the music, most with their heads down, staring at their feet. Everyone was dressed up, the men in dress shirts and slacks, the women in blouses, skirts, and heels. Almost everyone looked over fifty, except for one younger man, walking between the couples, who appeared to be in his mid-thirties. He was tall and graceful, a gazelle among buffalo.

Rebekah stared. Was that the Judge in there? His face hidden under a top hat, nearly unrecognizable, absent his ratty blue robe and slippers? The music stopped. The men and women let go of each other, laughing and clapping. The young one slapped the one who looked like the Judge on the back. The Judge looked out the window, directly toward Rebekah.

He can't see me, Rebekah thought. *It's too dark out here, and too light in there.*

Rebekah saw him squint. She ducked onto a darker part of the sidewalk, under an overhanging tree. The Judge was still staring. He moved toward the door.

Rebekah briefly considered running. She could run across the street, up about ten feet and around the corner, and duck behind a car. But what if the Judge followed her? He was still her landlord. She was assured of seeing him again. Rebekah backed closer to the tree, until she felt the bark against her back. She hoped that if she melted enough into the darkness, the Judge wouldn't see her.

The Judge walked out of the house and into the yard. He looked to his left and right, took off his hat, and scratched in the center of the messy white mop on his scalp. It looked sweaty, matted to his face and neck. He lifted one foot to scratch the back of the calf on his other leg.

He looked at the tree and took a few steps forward. "Rebekah?" the Judge called.

Rebekah stepped forward, trying to appear casual. "Oh, hi Mark," she said.

"Heya, I thought it was you!" The Judge walked toward her with a big grin on his face. He wrapped her in a hug, pressing her face into his shirt. He smelled liked mothballs.

"What are you doing out here?" the Judge asked.

"Oh, I was just out for a walk, and I saw you guys, you know…"

"Dancing?"

"Was that what it was?"

"Yeah." The Judge nodded. "Have you ever seen anyone tango?"

"Only in movies, I guess."

"Oh, boy." The Judge laughed. "Come in. You can watch for a little while."

"Oh, no…I don't think so."

"Why not?" The Judge hooked his arm through hers. "Come on."

Rebekah glanced down the sidewalk. It was dark, and her vision was obscured by the cuts in her glasses. She was beginning to get a headache. The Judge looked so silly in his outfit, shrunken in his knickers and bobs.

Rebekah unhooked her arm and followed the Judge into the house. All the furniture in the living room—a harried, cat-scratched gray couch, a tan armchair, and a wooden coffee table—was pushed back against the wall. A television was lying on its side on the floor. Framed pictures and empty flower vases were piled in a corner. The cord from an overhead light fixture had been taped to the ceiling.

"Lads and ladies," the Judge announced, walking in. "This is my friend, Rebekah Cohayn."

"Greetings! Hello!" the assembled called.

"Rebekah," the Judge said, sweeping his hand across the room. "These are the dancers."

The dancers saluted and nodded. The young one bowed. When he stood up, he pushed aside a thatch of dark brown hair that had fallen across his forehead.

Rebekah nodded.

"Aye, now we've got a lassie to perform for," one of the older men said. This fellow sported a long, ragged white beard, red tennis shoes, and multi-colored suspenders over a white dress shirt. He spoke in a heavy English brogue, one that seemed to hail from a vague, unidentifiable location in the United Kingdom.

"You're from England now, are you Smithie?" the young man asked. He was lolling back against the wall, hands in his pockets, one ankle crossed over the other.

Smithie folded his arms in front of his chest. "Well, I don't know wot you bloody expect of a transplanted Midwesterner doing Latin jigs in your living room."

The woman standing next to him draped her arm around his waist. "This one's mine," she said with a wink.

The young one looked at Rebekah. "I'm Haines. It's nice to meet you." Haines stuck out his hand.

Rebekah shook it. "Rebekah."

"This is my house," Haines said. "I teach tango in my living room on Saturday nights." Haines swept his arm around the living room. "Does everyone want to go around and introduce themselves?"

"You know me," the Judge said. "Mark."

"Hi, Rebekah," Claire said. She had emerged from the kitchen as Haines was introducing himself, holding a glass of wine. She walked over and stood next to the Judge.

"I'm James Smithie," the transplanted Midwesterner said. He seemed to have lost his accent. "And I'm from Illinois."

"Madeline Smithie," the woman standing next to him said. "New Jersey, originally."

The tango students continued to go around the room, sharing their names. Most looked married, or had at least brought a partner with whom they seemed intimately familiar. There were no strangers in this group, besides Rebekah.

"Nice to meet you all," Rebekah said.

The Judge clapped a hand on Rebekah's shoulder. "Friends, listen up. Rebekah's got some good news to share," he said.

Rebekah looked at him in horror. His timing was impeccably atrocious.

The Judge was grinning back at her, incapable of reading her eyes. She looked around the room. Everyone was staring at her.

"Um...I'm getting married," Rebekah said.

The dancers murmured their congratulations.

"Who's the lucky fellow?" Smithie asked.

Rebekah swallowed and cleared her throat. The dancers leaned forward slightly. A floorboard creaked beneath their feet. Rebekah took a deep breath.

"Her name is Megan," the Judge said. "And she is a lovely, lovely fellow."

Rebekah saw a few dancers nod and smile.

"Well, two brides are better than one," Smithie said, with a loud clap of his hands.

"I'll drink to that," Haines said, raising a bottle of beer. "To Rebekah and Megan, future brides!"

"Rebekah and Megan!" the dancers repeated. They clanked their glasses and bottles together and immediately began laughing and talking.

The Judge leaned toward her. "Never let an opportunity to celebrate go to waste," he said. "Can I get you a drink?"

The color was still draining from Rebekah's face. Her palms were clammy, and she could feel sweat stains forming under her armpits.

She wiped her hands on her pants. "Yes, please," Rebekah said. The Judge walked out of the living room into the kitchen.

Haines walked up to her. "So, how do you know Mark?" he asked.

"Um…well, I'm his tenant. I live in his basement. I also sort of knew him from before. He was friends with my parents."

"Ah," Haines said. "You live in his basement, huh? How does that work out?"

Rebekah shrugged. "It's fine."

"I bet. He's a nice guy." Haines nodded. "So, have you ever tangoed before?"

Rebekah shook her head.

"Do you want to try?"

Rebekah looked around the room. There was something dimly depressing about being here with a bunch of older, straight couples, all longtime dancing partners.

"Well, I'm really fine just watching," Rebekah said.

Haines studied her. "Hey, Mark!" Haines yelled.

The Judge walked out of the kitchen with two beers in his hand. "We dancing?" the Judge asked.

"As soon as you're ready," Haines said. "You gonna drink both of those?"

"One for you," the Judge said, handing a bottle of Sam Adams to Rebekah. The top was already popped. "And one for me," the Judge said, placing his bottle on the coffee table.

Haines motioned his head toward Rebekah. "You think we can teach this one how to tango?"

"That's really ok," Rebekah said.

"Of course we can teach Rebekah how to tango!" the Judge said. "That's what she's here for."

Rebekah took a long pull of her beer. She felt tired and dizzy, impossibly intoxicated after her day-long intake of half a beer, three pancakes, and the can of minestrone soup she'd had for lunch. She felt heartsick and headsick. The sensation of nausea was overpowering.

"It's really not necessary," Rebekah repeated. "I'm fine watching." Haines furrow his brow.

"Really, I'm fine," Rebekah said.

The Judge and Haines looked at each other. Some sort of unspoken communication passed between them, and Haines walked away.

"Rebekah," the Judge said. "No one is going to force you to dance. But may I ask why?"

Rebekah shrugged again. "I'm just tired."

"Right," the Judge said. "Everything ok with Megan?"

Rebekah closed her eyes. She willed herself not to cry. When she opened them, the Judge was staring at her. She looked around the room. Everyone was engaged in conversation; no one was paying attention to the old man with white hair and a top hat hunched over the younger woman. Even Claire was engrossed in a discussion with Smithie and Madeline.

"Listen," the Judge said quietly. "My house—it doesn't always block out sound. You know what I mean?"

Rebekah stared at the ground. She couldn't look into his eyes.

"It's ok, it's ok," the Judge said. "It's not like we sit around and listen. But sometimes we hear things, you know? I've been wondering this last week how you're doing. It's been quiet down there. Megan isn't back yet, huh?"

Rebekah wanted to run out of the living room. She looked past the Judge, and took another long drink of beer.

"Ok. Well…listen," the Judge said. "Here are my thoughts, because I know you didn't ask for them. You're here tonight. You're alone. You've got people who want to help you, who want to teach you to dance. Why not dance?"

"I don't have a partner," Rebekah whispered. Her voice sounded choked and froggy.

"You do," the Judge said. "Megan will come back. And tonight, Haines will dance with you."

"I don't know how to tango," Rebekah said.

The Judge shrugged. "No one knows how to tango in the beginning."

"What if I don't want to learn how to tango?" Rebekah asked.

"You don't have to learn. But if you don't learn, you'll always be on the outside, watching." The Judge leaned in closer to her. "Look. If you choose to be here, among people like this…" The Judge pointed around the living room. "You're going to have to dance with them, just as they are.

"You can always leave. Go somewhere else, where there's a different kind of dance. You know how many different dances there are? As many as there are types of people in the world. Every culture, every place, every group of people likes to dance in their own way. And here? In this room?" The Judge laughed. "No matter what Haines says, people still do it their own way anyway."

Rebekah looked around the room. Her eyes landed on Smithie and Madeline. They were leaning in, their shoulders barely grazing. "I'm still not sure I want to do this."

"And you don't have to," the Judge said. "You can watch all night tonight, if you want. But Rebekah, which dance are you going to learn? You've got to learn one. You can't watch forever. Do you want my opinion?"

Rebekah shrugged. She grinned. "I'm guessing you're going to give it to me, anyway."

"Learn the tango," the Judge said. "You're here tonight. You're not anywhere else. You're here, in this living room, where people are doing the tango. Why not learn it? Why not try it? If you don't like it, try something else. But for God's sake, try something."

Rebekah took a deep breath. She put her beer to her lips and finished the rest of the bottle in a few gulps. "I think if I'm going to do this, I'll need another one of these," Rebekah said.

The Judge took the bottle from her. "I'll be the judge of that. Haines!" the Judge called across the room. "We're going to need you to dance."

Haines walked over. "Awesome."

"I really have no idea what I'm doing," Rebekah said. "I've never done this before."

"Well, tell you what," Haines said. He tossed his bangs. "The men's part is much easier. Why don't I teach you that part? I'll do the woman's."

Rebekah looked at him skeptically.

"I like the woman's part better anyway," Haines said. "It's more fun."

"You gonna dance in those things?" The Judge pointed at Haines' tennis shoes. "If you're going to do the woman's part properly, you really need a pair of heels."

"Excellent point, Mark," Haines said. "I actually think I have some in my closet." He grinned at Rebekah. "I always bring them to my tango classes, in case we're short a woman. Like I said, I like that part better."

Haines disappeared into a back room, and emerged with a pair of strappy black stiletto heels. He kicked off his tennis shoes and squeezed his feet into the heels, his long toes poking out the front end like five little hot dogs squeezed out of a bun.

"Hey, look!" Smithie shouted. "Looks like Haines is changing his footwear!"

The room fell silent for a moment, and then everyone began talking at once.

"Nice kicks, Haines!"

"Don't injure yourself, buddy!"

"What's the occasion?"

"Well done, Haines! Those look good on you, boy!"

Haines stood up in his heels, teetered precariously, and grabbed onto the Judge's shoulder for support. "I'm going to teach Rebekah to tango," he announced. "And the rest of you can either watch, or join in."

His audience cheered loudly.

"You need to put your arm on my waist," Haines said, placing Rebekah's hand just above his hip. "Hold my other hand here. And stand just a few inches on my right, your left—like that."

Rebekah allowed Haines to gently push her into position. She felt herself shaking, her palms sweaty. The other dancers stood on the edges of the living room, quietly watching.

"Ok, now. The basic step for tango is, slow, slow, quick, quick, slow. Like this." Haines pulled her toward him with the five steps, shifting her slightly to the right at the end. He was so close to her that she could smell the lingering detergent on his clothing. He danced smoothly and with ease, defying the notion that he wouldn't be able to dance in heels. He'd clearly done this before.

Haines stopped moving but didn't let go of her hand. "So that's it," he said, speaking both to Rebekah and his audience. "That's all there is to the basic tango. Slow, slow, quick, quick, slow. Slow, slow, quick, quick, slow. Let's do this intentionally, with feeling. The rest of you ready?"

The other couples moved into position around the dance floor. The Judge and Claire lined up right next to Rebekah.

"Ok, ready?" Haines pulled a small remote control out of his pocket. He pressed a button and music started filtering down from the ceiling.

"Slow, slow, quick, quick, slow," Haines shouted. "Slow, slow, quick, quick, slow. Slow, slow, quick, quick, slow. Dance to your left, boys! Men, move your ladies to your left!"

Rebekah was nearly completely focused on Haines. He moved so fluidly in his heels, so elegantly and confidently in Rebekah's arms. He steered her while allowing her to lead, commanded her movements while doing only enough to make her think she was in charge. She focused on her steps, on her arms, and permitted her partner to tweak her posture, to nudge her movements forward and back. He was completely devoid of embarrassment.

Rebekah felt awkward, like a child just learning to walk. She fixated on her feet, willing herself to see them through her scratched up glasses. The way she had at Storm, Rebekah allowed herself to be taken by the music. *Slow, slow, quick, quick, slow.* Out of the corner of her eye, she saw the Judge bending over Claire, laughing.

There was freedom here. Freedom in the rules, freedom in the archaic institution. This wasn't her dance; not exactly, anyway. But the dance at Storm hadn't belonged to her, either. She fell into a netherworld, an in-between space, where both rules and autonomy held vast importance.

For the moment, Rebekah was preoccupied with her feet.

Rebekah gripped her broken glasses in her pocket. The Judge and Claire walked to her left, closest to the street.

"I really think that Haines is the most graceful dancer in the group," Claire said.

The Judge dropped his jaw in feigned shock. "More graceful than me?"

"Well, of course not, darling, that goes without saying," Claire said. "Haines is the most graceful dancer in the group, not including you. You are simply a god among mortals."

The Judge looked at Rebekah and raised his eyebrows. "Did you hear that? A god among mortals."

"Mm," Rebekah said. The sidewalk was a blurry white estuary, framed with hulking masses of greenery. The roots of trees planted in yards had disturbed the concrete, clawing their way out between the slabs and winding down to the street. The sidewalk rose and fell, as though little earthquakes had struck every twenty feet.

"How did you like dancing, Rebekah?" Claire asked.

"I liked it," Rebekah said.

"Really?" Claire asked.

"Yes," Rebekah said. It was true. Dancing with Haines had been a surprising treat at the end of what had otherwise been an abysmal week. It was unlike any other sort of dancing she'd done before. Freedom within a set of clearly defined, pre-determined steps. A focused creativity. Guidelines without predetermination.

"If you had danced with me, you would have enjoyed it even more," the Judge said. Claire lightly punched him in the shoulder.

"What?" the Judge asked.

"You're only supposed to dance with me, you fox," Claire said.

The Judge leaned down toward Rebekah. "Watch out when your lady gets possessive," the Judge said, just loudly enough for Claire to hear. "Give 'em an inch, and they'll take a mile."

"Who's that in front of our house?" Claire asked.

Rebekah squinted. She could barely see the Judge's house, let alone anyone in front of it.

"Is that Megan?" the Judge asked.

"Looks like Megan," Claire said.

Rebekah bit the inside of her cheeks. She shoved her hands in her pocked and looked at the sidewalk.

"Is she just sitting on the front porch?" the Judge asked.

"Well, if it's not Megan, then someone else is sitting on our front porch," Claire said.

"Maybe they're looking for a judge to marry them," the Judge said. Claire looked at him sideways. "I think there are easier ways to find a judge than sitting on our front porch at ten at night."

"But they wouldn't find a judge as good as me," the Judge said.

"You're right," Claire said. "You're a big helping of judge with a side of special sauce."

The Judge looked at Rebekah and raised his eyebrows again. "Did you hear that? Special sauce."

A few seconds later, the Judge, Claire, and Rebekah arrived at the house. Megan Nimble was sitting on the front porch swing, wearing a long-sleeve flannel shirt and corduroy pants. A new gym bag lay at her feet.

I've never seen that shirt before, Rebekah thought. *She probably ran out of clothes.*

"Well, if it isn't one of my favorite tenants," the Judge said.

"Your second favorite tenant," Megan said, motioning toward Rebekah with her head. Rebekah smiled. The comment was a sweet opening olive branch.

"We were just out dancing together," the Judge said.

"Oh?" Megan asked. She looked at Rebekah skeptically.

"It was an accident," Rebekah said.

"An accident?" Megan repeated.

"Oh, there was no accident about this," the Judge said. "You should have seen Rebekah dance. She was a natural."

"I wish I had," Megan said.

"She danced with Haines," Claire said.

"Haines…like the underwear?" Megan asked.

"He was definitely wearing more than underwear," the Judge said. When this elicited another puzzled look from Megan, the Judge added, "and according to Claire, he was only the second most graceful dancer in the room."

"I see," Megan said.

"Why are you sitting out here on the porch?" Claire asked.

"I think I left my key at my friend's house," Megan said. "So I knocked on the front door, and no one was home. I was about to go back to my friend's when I saw you three walking up. So I thought I would just wait."

"Oh," Claire said. "So you were staying at your friend's house?"

Megan glanced at Rebekah. "It's a long story."

The Judge looked at them. "Well, I don't know about you guys, but it's my bedtime. Claire's too, if I have any say in the matter."

Claire rolled her eyes. "Oh, Mark."

Mark unlocked the front door. "Are you two going to be able to get in the house ok?"

Rebekah fished her key out of her pocket and waved it at the Judge. "We're set."

"Ok," the Judge said. "Stay warm." He and Claire walked into the house and shut the door behind them.

Megan and Rebekah stared at each other for a few seconds.

"What happened to your glasses?" Megan asked.

"They broke."

"How did they break?"

"I fell."

"Dancing?" Megan asked.

"It just happened."

"With the Judge?"

"Like I said, it was an accident."

"Can you and I accidentally go dancing sometime, then?" Megan asked. She smiled at Rebekah. Megan's shoulders were hunched forward in her familiar crouch. Her long legs dangled off the swing, and the tops of her shoes grazed the porch.

Rebekah sighed. "I'm sorry."

"What are you sorry for?" Megan asked.

"For..." Rebekah paused. "For being dumb. For not listening to you. For being a bad partner."

"Ugh," Megan said. She shook her head and looked at the porch swing. "See? You always do this."

"Do what?"

"You apologize, but you don't know what you're apologizing for."
Rebekah blinked. "Well, at least I'm apologizing."
Megan pushed back her shoulders. "I'm sorry for leaving."
"Three nights."
"Well…" Megan shrugged.
"You were gone for three nights, Megs. That's a long time. I didn't know if you were ever coming back."
"Well, I did come back."
"I guess so, "Rebekah said.
"To be honest, I'm not really sorry for leaving. I needed to. I was really angry."
"Right."
"What?" Megan asked.
"I don't know."
Megan threw up her hands. "Well, do you want the truth? Or do you want me to make some shit up to make you feel better? Because that's what you've been doing the last ten years."
Rebekah closed her eyes.
Megan picked up her bag. "I can leave again."
"Don't."
Megan shouldered her bag and put her hands on her hips. "Rebekah, why are you with me?"
Rebekah swallowed a lump in her throat. "Because I love you."
"Fine. You love me. But you can love a friend, and you can love someone you don't want to marry. Why do you want to be my wife?"
Rebekah rubbed her face in her hands. She peered through her fingers at Megan. Megan suddenly looked angry. Rebekah sighed and dropped her hands. "Megan, the problem isn't being with you. The problem is being with you in front of other people." Rebekah swallowed again. She felt struck by how truthfully her words had come out.
Megan rolled her eyes. "So if we're hanging out in our basement, or in a dark movie theater, or having sex…" Megan let the thought hang. "Then we're ok. But if we're both dressed up in front of our family and friends, sharing our love for each other, then you have a problem. Rebekah…"
"No, Megan, listen," Rebekah said. Her voice sounded strangely calm, wavering slightly from the lump in her throat. "I know I've got

issues. I know. I've got shit to work on. Pretty fucking obvious, right? And I know I haven't been working on it enough."

"Enough? You haven't been working on it at all."

"Right," Rebekah said. "You're right."

"We've been dealing with this shit for a long time," Megan said. "And you know what? I've never heard you say that you're sorry."

Rebekah turned her face away so that Megan couldn't see her eyes fill with tears.

"I've been thinking about what I was going to say to you for days," Megan said. "What I did wrong. How I would do things differently next time. I've been thinking about my apology to you. "But it's like…I get the sense that you never do that. You never wonder about how you would do things differently next time. You're never really sorry."

Rebekah turned to face Megan. "Never really sorry? Megan, I'm always sorry. I'm sorry every second of every day. I'm sorry for who I am. I'm sorry I'm alive. I'm sorry that I can't seem to get a handle on myself. I'm sorry for hurting you. I'm sorry you love me, and I'm sorry you want to marry me. I'm sorry for being such a big fucking mess. I've been a mess my whole life, and I don't anticipate being able to change now."

Rebekah's throat felt raw and scratchy, as if she'd swallowed a thimbleful of salt. Her eyes burned, and her lips felt dry.

"Bekah…God. Just stop doing this."

"I can't change who I am." Rebekah was crying now. "I am who I am. And I'm flawed. If you want to marry me, you're going to have to marry this fucking mess."

Megan walked up to Rebekah and put her hands on her shoulders. "Beks…that's the whole point. I never want you to apologize for being you. I just want you to be yourself. And love yourself."

Rebekah sucked in a mouthful of air. "But what if who I am means I can't love myself?"

"That sounds pretty bleak," Megan said.

Rebekah nodded.

"It's like we'd be stuck in a Sylvia what's-her-name poem."

"Sylvia Plath," Rebekah said.

"See?" Megan tapped her chest. "Engineer." She reached out and poked Rebekah's collarbone. "Artist."

Artist. The word was loaded for Rebekah. Rebekah had listened to Tony's fundraising speech many times. "Art saves lives," he would say, as if he was talking about delivering sacks of rice to war-ravaged countries. Compared to Tony and Roberto, Rebekah had never thought of herself as an artist. She didn't have a portfolio; she had never taken an art class in her life. She had always considered herself a support person at Stella, a pre-destined drone in a world full of free will.

Artist. Could you really differentiate between being an artist and doing art? Between living as someone who struggled to articulate her identity on a daily basis, and someone who could successfully demonstrate her articulation? Was it a way of life, as opposed to a type of production? Was a recreational dancer an artist? Or a retired judge who married people for fun?

What about David?

When David was a child, he walked around with a healthy sheen of hubris, his chin sticking out like a balcony ledge on a penthouse. David had grown up into a man who wanted answers, who craved rules, and guidance, and the accouterments of righteousness.

But there was a nebulous lack of tidiness in David's life, too. He had taken on the good with the bad, the politics and the people, the linearity and chaos in one fell swoop. David couldn't pick and choose, piecemeal, what parts of Judaism he liked. He had swallowed it whole, like a religious sword swallower. Was it really so clear-cut for him, then? Was there simplicity in his lack of choice, or the most difficult of choices in his chosen simplicity?

"Maybe," was all that Rebekah could manage in response to Megan. "Yes," Megan said. "You are. And I'm not asking you to change. I'm just asking you to trust me. Just be. Just love me, and let me love you, and we'll be ok."

Rebekah nodded. *We'll be ok.* The most important words of the night.

"We ok?" Megan asked.

"Megs…"

"What?"

"Why do you want to be with me?"

Megan shrugged. "I like a challenge."

"No, really." Rebekah took a step back. "Tell me the truth. I'm feeling a little insecure about this right now."

"Rebekah, you're really fucking frustrating sometimes. You drive me nuts. Like really nuts." Megan put her bag down. "But what am I going to do? I love you. You hear that? I love you. For the last three days, I tried to convince myself that I didn't. That I didn't need this. I tried to think about breaking up with you." Megan sighed. "Maybe I'm an idiot, but I still want to marry you."

"You are an idiot."

"And I guess I'll be a happier idiot after our wedding."

"Uh-huh."

"So during our wedding, you're going to kiss me, right? In front of all the guests?"

Rebekah smiled. "Maybe."

"Maybe?"

"Only if you ask really nicely," Rebekah said.

"I want it to be an extra-long kiss," Megan said.

"Don't push it."

Megan leaned in and kissed Rebekah lightly on the lips. "It'll be like that. Just a kiss."

Rebekah put one hand behind Megan's neck and the other on the small of her back. She tilted her chin upward and pressed her lips against Megan's, kissing her long and hard, feeling Megan lean against her. She could feel Megan's breasts against her chest, her hips on her hips, and the long, lean muscles in Megan's back. Rebekah softly swiveled her hips, gently nudging one of her thighs between Megan's legs.

This is it, Rebekah thought. *I am. I am what I am.*

She pulled back slightly away from Megan's face.

"I think I can manage that," Rebekah said.

"And you're going to dance with me after the wedding. Just me and you. In front of everyone."

Rebekah kissed Megan again. "Whatever it takes," Rebekah said. She turned Megan around and gently guided her toward their basement apartment.

SPRING

The Dapple House sat on the southwestern end of downtown
Portland, a short walk to Portland State University and the interstate
highway that curled around behind the city. From the outside, the
house looked dilapidated, with peeling yellow paint, cracked and
drooping window frames, and a roof that had that been replaced so
many times that four layers of shingles could be seen from the street
below. The house had one small front door—six feet tall, if
measuring generously—and a big brass knocker instead of a
doorbell. To the left of the Dapple House was a tall brown events
center; to its right, a tall brown church. As the little squished yellow
building in the middle, the Dapple House looked like a piece of
faded American cheese in a whole wheat bun, an unappetizing, and
unwanted, blight on the sidewalk.

But critics needed only to go inside to discover the Dapple House's
raison d'etre. In contrast to its deteriorating exterior, the inside of the
Dapple House had been completely redone. The middle floors had
been removed, transforming the original three stories into a single,
open space. New curved beams had been put in to hold the ceiling in
place, and the wooden floors had been beautifully refurbished. The
walls were painted a deep red, with white wainscoting and crown
molding. A kitchen fit for caterers had been set up in the back of the
house. New bathrooms, with automatic toilets and sinks and high-
speed hand-dryers, sat tucked away in the basement.

The Dapple House was where Stella had opted to hold its Arts in the
Halls signature campaign, three days before Rebekah's wedding
date. When she first learned the date of the campaign, Rebekah told
Tony that she might not be able to attend. There were last-minute
wedding preparations to attend to, and out-of-state family in town.
Three weeks ago, Rebekah had suddenly had a change of heart; she
told Tony that she was going to be there, and she was willing to help
in any way the organization needed.

Tony set Rebekah up as a greeter at the front door. Rebekah stood
behind a small folding table, collecting tickets and handing out
information about Stella. Rebekah wore a long-sleeve, black top,

black slacks, black pumps with small heels, and a gray knitted scarf, a last-minute addition before she left the house.

The forecast had called for heavy rain that day, but "heavy rain" didn't do the weather justice. Pellets of rain and ice had been whipping the city for the last five hours. Winds upward of forty-five miles per hour blew through downtown Portland and reached more than seventy-five miles per hour at the crest of the Cascades. Rain certainly was not unusual for Portland in late March, but this type of rain—this angry, aggressive, militant onslaught—felt like winter's death rattle. This was most likely the last freak storm of the year in the Pacific Northwest, and the Pacific Northwest brought its tempest. Standing at the door, Rebekah braved blasts of cold air and the occasional discharge of hail. She kept her scarf wrapped tightly around her neck, sliding her palms underneath it when she had a few moments alone.

"Hello, is this the Dapple House?" one woman asked Rebekah. She peeled off black gloves lined with fur and shrugged off a long black pea coat. She had white-blond hair down to her shoulders, wore large glasses, and looked to be comfortably in her seventies.

"You're in the right place," Rebekah said.

"Oh, good, because my husband and I just had a miserable time finding it. We must have driven past three times before we figured that this little old thing might be the right place. Certainly doesn't look it from the outside, does it? We thought it might be the events center next door, but the address was clearly incorrect. And of course, there's no address on the front of this house, so we just kept going round and round."

"Well, I'm glad to see you made it," Rebekah said. "Do you have a ticket?"

"I do. It's somewhere in my purse." The woman clicked open a large handbag. "It's just terrible out, isn't it? Not only could we not find the place, but you can barely see anything, driving around out there. I was afraid some of that hail was going to crack my windshield. My husband is somewhere out there trying to find a parking spot. I told him to just find a garage, but…" she looked up and smiled at Rebekah. "He's going to do whatever he wants to do."

The woman handed Rebekah two tickets. "Here's one for me and my husband. Can you keep an eye out for him? He's tall, white hair, white mustache."

"And what's his name?" Rebekah asked.

"Oh, of course. Tom Jacobs. And I'm Mary."

"So nice to meet you, Mary," Rebekah said, holding out her hand. "I'm Rebekah."

"Well, very nice to meet you, Rebekah. And are you a volunteer?"

"No, no, I work for Stella."

"Oh! Well, my goodness, you look so young, I would have guessed you were a student. What do you do?"

"I'm the editor of *Daft*, the newsmagazine."

Mary smiled broadly. "Oh, you are? Oh, I just so much look forward to receiving that in the mail. It's always so fresh, so well-written. I just love to see what the students are up to."

"Well, thank you. It's a great job."

"Yes. This last issue I thought…" Mary's voice trailed off. "Well, I'll just tell you. I thought you all were a little blunt about your organization's needs," she said, her voice dropping to a whisper. "I understand why you did it, and it sure was effective. I read that and thought, 'Well, if they're going to those extremes, maybe they really do need help.' But I do really like seeing student work. I hope you decide to go back to that."

Rebekah nodded. "Yes, of course."

"Oh, and…" Mary looked around the room. "I did click on the fundraising link at the bottom of the letter." She winked at Rebekah.

"Yes, yes, good. Thanks again for coming."

"My pleasure." Mary glanced out the door again. "He's still not here. I bet he's still circling, looking for parking. Men." She shook her head. "When you get married, make sure you pick one who likes parking garages. Ask him on the first date." And with that last piece of advice, Mary Jacobs disappeared into the Dapple House.

Directly after Mary Jacobs, Roberto strolled in.

"Hello," Rebekah said. She looked Roberto up and down. "You managed to avoid the rain somehow."

"It's called an umbrella, dear." Roberto leaned in and gave Rebekah a hug. "You look nice tonight."

"As do you," Rebekah said. Roberto was wearing a navy blue suit, a pressed, white collared shirt, and shiny tan dress shoes.

Roberto tapped his foot and looked at Rebekah. "You doing ok?"

"I am."

"You sure?"

"Yes," Rebekah said. She felt her face getting warm.

Roberto smiled mischievously. He strolled past her table. "I'll just be inside, then."

Rebekah watched him walk away. She took a deep breath.

The event space filled up during the next hour. Adults, mostly retired baby boomers, appeared with tickets in their hands and spouses on their arms. Students armed with canvases and sculptures nodded to Rebekah on their way in and asked where they could set up their exhibitions. Rebekah directed them to the student table, manned by Roberto and Gregory Rimes. Next, each young artist was assigned a spot on the perimeter of the space to display his or her work. Students had been instructed to arrive before the event started at seven, but many students were trickling in more than half an hour later.

At eight, Megan Nimble strolled in, tall, slightly stooped, and damp. She shook her coat off at the Dapple House door, pulled off her hat, and stamped her boots on the doormat in the foyer. When she looked up, she noticed Rebekah standing in the entry. Megan walked up to her table.

"Is this the Arts in the Halls event?" Megan asked.

"It is. And you are…?"

"Megan. Megan Nimble," Megan said, holding out her fingertips. Rebekah grabbed them and gently shook them up and down.

"Welcome to our event, Ms. Nimble. I hope you're prepared to make a major financial donation."

"I brought my credit cards, checkbook, and a huge wad of cash," Megan said.

"Then you can come in."

"Good thing, because I sure as hell wasn't going to stay out there," Megan said. She took a few steps into the house, looked around the ballroom, and then walked back to the table.

"I have one more question," Megan said, leaning into the table. She glanced behind her to make sure no one was approaching. "Are there any single women here?"

Rebekah pursed her lips and looked around the room. Jane Salish was standing in the center, a plastic champagne glass in her hand, surrounded by people at least twice her age. She looked fetching in a blue dress over black tights.

Rebekah nodded in Jane's direction. "See that one over there? In the blue dress?"

"The blond one who looks slightly intoxicated?"

"Yes. You should go ask her out on a date."

Megan threw back her head and laughed uproariously.

"Stop it," Rebekah deadpanned. "You're drawing attention."

"That must be Jane."

"It is."

Megan studied Jane. "She's pretty. I like her dress."

"You and the rest of the world."

"She's not really my type, though," Megan said. "Too important. I much prefer door greeters."

"Good thing I'm a door greeter," Rebekah said.

"Good thing. I'm going to head inside. See you soon?"

"Yeah."

"You ready?" Megan asked.

Rebekah nodded. She looked around the room and pushed her new glasses up on her nose. She'd gotten them the day after she broke her old pair. They had black frames with small, square lenses, a new look that suited Rebekah's oval face. She'd had her old glasses for so long that wearing this new pair was like looking out of a new set of eyes.

After Megan walked away, Rebekah surveyed the space. At nearly two thousand square feet, the Dapple House could comfortably hold two hundred people. Tony had chosen this smaller venue—instead of the larger event space next door—to give the campaign a community feel. He wanted to know the name of everyone in attendance, and their kids' names, too; he wanted to learn where they lived, where they grew up, and why they were here. He wanted someone from Stella to call people after the event to thank them for coming. Tony understood that charisma took work. His gift was supernaturally innate, but it required a daily slog of routine maintenance.

About twenty students had set up canvases around the edges of the room. Nearly all of them had dressed up in suits and ties, dresses and heels. A few, perhaps unable or unwilling to conform to Stella's instructions, had worn clothes plucked out of their daily wardrobes. For one girl standing in a corner, this meant ripped jeans over fishnet tights, and a black, body-hugging shirt with large fake jewels on the shoulders. The boy next to her wore a large black trench coat, black pants, and black boots. They had set up their displays next to each other, and now they were standing very close together, shoulder to shoulder, between their canvases. Their paintings looked remarkably similar: splotches of red and black paint, wide arcs and small drips, a chaotic mess of intermixed color and untouched white space.

Other canvases looked similarly abstract, though a few students had done landscapes or still lifes. One canvas looked like a re-creation of Leonardo Da Vinci's *The Last Supper*. Instead of depicting Jesus and the disciples, the student had painted thirteen young people, in swim trunks and bikinis, huddled around a long surfboard. The painted young people looked frantically, desperately happy. The sun was setting behind them, descending into an ocean with frothy, white-capped waves. The work was titled, *The Last Summer*.

Event attendees walked around the room, champagne flutes and appetizers in hand, discussing student work. Rebekah could hear bits and pieces of conversations.

"This is really interesting," one man said to the artist behind *The Last Summer*. The two were standing about ten feet from Rebekah. The student said something unintelligible.

"Where did you get the idea to do this?"

Rebekah watched the student shrug and look around the room. He looked as if he didn't have an answer for the man. After a few moments, the student opened his mouth and said a few words. The man laughed.

"Yes, I suppose that's true," the man said. "It happens to all of us at some point."

Snatches of similar conversations bounced off the high ceilings and filtered down to the Dapple House doorway. Donors wanted to know how long it had taken students to complete their works, what they meant, and if the artists planned to try to sell them. A few asked students about their plans after graduation. Did they want to go to college? Study art? Try to become full-time artists? Rebekah wondered if these adults, these people who had been so successful in their lives and careers, and were now handing out money for charitable causes, would encourage these kids to follow their dreams. Was art a penniless and foolish path to happiness and starvation? Or would these donors—doctors, CEOs, lawyers, politicians—tell these kids that art could pay off?

Dom Turken had been given his own corner of the space to accommodate the crowds of people who wanted to see his work. Dom was a diminutive teenager: thin and hollow-cheeked, with long, straight, scraggly black hair that hung half-way down his neck. He had light brown skin—Vietnamese? Rebekah wondered—and the same set of hunched-over shoulders that Megan Nimble wore so well. But Dom was small, much smaller than Megan, and when he arched his back, he nearly disappeared into the walls of the Dapple House.

Dom stood to the side of his canvases with his hands stuffed in his pockets. He nodded politely to his admirers, shook hands when necessary, and retreated into the shadows of his corner in quiet moments. He looked bored, or embarrassed, or maybe both, trying to fulfill the business requirements of his vocation.

Tony had prepped Dom for this night, telling him what to say, how to act, and how to talk about his experiences in the organization in a manner that reflected well on Stella. Dom was his star, proof that Stella could be everything that Tony envisioned. Tony walked around the room, shaking hands, introducing himself, and selling himself and his organization. He stayed in one place just long enough to make his conversation partners feel important and attended to, but never so long that they felt a conversation had been finished. Tony would always say, "You know, I'd love to hear more. Can I give you a call about this, later?"

And Tony's genius was that he would.

The other Stella employees mingled to various degrees, depending on their positions and level of comfort with such fraught small talk. Jane appeared to be Tony's equal in hobnobbery, lightly descending on groups of people and easily slipping into and out of their conversations. Micah, hobbled by an inclination to introversion and a general disdain for chitchat, had volunteered to manage the AV equipment, and was busy setting up a microphone and speakers at the front of the room.

Rebekah checked the clock on her cell phone every few minutes. One month ago, she hadn't been planning to be here at all. But here she was, her anxiety level increasing with each passing second. *Tonight's a big night.*

It was a big night. One of the biggest nights of Rebekah's life. And who in this room knew it?

Megan knew it. Rebekah could see it in her eyes. She watched her soon-to-be wife walk around the room, talk with students, lean in and whisper to them. Sometimes they would turn to Rebekah and laugh.

Some of the donors knew it. They were checking their watches, looking around the room. Mary Jacobs kept glancing back at Rebekah and smiling. Her husband—who had presumably found a parking spot on the street—kept one hand on his wife, rubbing the small of her back.

Roberto might know. He kept glancing at her from across the room, that wolfish grin spread across his face.

Tony didn't know what a big night it would be. Jane didn't know. Micah didn't know.

Rebekah alternated between watching her cell phone, scanning the room, and staring down at the table, trying to breathe. She'd been preparing for this night for the last three weeks, and she had practiced with Megan incessantly. In her head, she had gone over the steps, the order, and the outcome. She'd readied her outfit for the event and prepared her resume for job hunting.

Tonight might be my last night with Stella, Rebekah thought.

The last three weeks had been fueled by anger. Rebekah resented Jane Salish's unchecked power, her political prowess, her ability to gobble Rebekah's pawns and knights and castles, until she had Rebekah surrounded in a checkmate.

Rebekah also knew that Jane's ability simply to *be Jane* was what set her apart from Rebekah. She was willing to take chances—to risk failure—because she knew that she could fall back on the safety net called Jane Salish. There was an iron anchor in Jane's feet, a titanium rod in her backbone, and fiberglass vertebrae in her neck that held her head up and kept her shoulders straight. And even if Jane Salish was putting on a show—even if there was another Jane Salish, a shy, vulnerable, insecure Jane Salish—she never let that Jane out at work. The only Jane Salish that mattered was the one people saw.

Rebekah knew that she had never found the courage to *be Rebekah* the way Jane was Jane. First, there was David, whom Rebekah persistently emulated; next, there was the coming out debacle in high school. In three days, there would be a wedding: a coming-into, stepping-out, showing up-maneuver.

Rebekah took a deep breath. *I am what I am*, she thought.

Rebekah looked toward the door in time to see the Judge stumble through the entrance. His girlfriend, Claire, had her arm wrapped around his back. Haines trailed in behind them.

Rebekah nodded to them. "Welcome," she said.

"Sorry we're late," the Judge said. "Had a devil of a time finding parking. And the weather—there was traffic all over the city! Good thing I knew where this place was, otherwise I never would have found it."

The Judge was wearing a loose-fitting black silk button-up shirt tucked into khaki dress slacks. Claire wore a short red cocktail dress, black tights, and two-inch black heels.

"I made him get dressed tonight," Claire said. She looked at her boyfriend. "He looks good, doesn't he?"

"I'd just like to say that I got dressed all on my own, thank you very much," the Judge said. He looked at Haines. "And I believe you know Haines."

"I do," Rebekah said. "Thanks for coming."

Haines put both his hands flat on the table. "I am so excited," he said. "Are you kidding me? I wouldn't have missed this."

"Neither would we," the Judge said. "Claire and I have been practicing," he whispered.

"Where do I set up?" Haines asked.

Rebekah looked around the room. "Anywhere, really. The AV equipment is up front, but you'd probably have to hijack it from Micah."

"Well…I don't want to do any hijacking. Getting arrested would really ruin my night. We can probably make do without it. I brought all my stuff." Haines held up a black bag. "I set it up on the car on the way over. I figured we wouldn't have much time."

"No worries. Megan and I brought some backup equipment, just in case." Rebekah smiled at him. She hoped she looked relaxed.

"Well, I'm going to head inside," the Judge said. "Maybe we can look at this artwork for a few minutes before the festivities begin."

The Judge, Claire, and Haines moved toward the center of the ballroom.

She checked the clock on her phone. Eight ten.

Ten minutes later, Tony stepped to the front of the room. He tapped on the microphone; there was no sound. He signaled to Micah, who flipped on a switch. Tony touched the microphone again, and a few muffled thuds echoed through the room.

"Friends!" Tony shouted. Conversations in the room slowly died. Everyone turned to the front of the Dapple House.

Tony Hernandez was standing on a small stage. He stood straight and tall, his dual rows of white teeth matching the wainscoting on the walls.

Chiclets, Rebekah thought. She looked at the table and closed her eyes.

"Friends!" Tony said again. "Thank you so much for coming tonight. It's such a pleasure to see all of your wonderful faces—so many familiar faces, and, of course, so many new faces. I know the weather is terrible out, so I doubly appreciate what all of you went through to get here. Thanks for braving this storm to spend time with us, and talk about the arts.

"First, I want to make sure everyone knows where the exits are in the building, in case of an emergency. There's one right behind you, where you all came in—Rebekah, can you wave?"

Rebekah waved from her table near the door.

"Thank you. Right there. And there are two more exits, one to my left, and one to my right. You can see the green exit signs on the walls. Please do not leave out of those doors unless it's an emergency, because it'll trigger the fire alarm.

"Now that you're here, I hope everyone has gotten a chance to make their way around the room and look at all of the student artwork. It's really, truly incredible. What each of these students has achieved is amazing. So please, let's give these students a round of applause for coming tonight and sharing their beautiful work with us."

The room erupted in cheers. A few of the students took bows.

"Incredible, aren't they?" Tony said. "Here at Stella, we don't create artists. We find artists, like these students, and try to help nurture their talents. We give them space and time to practice their craft, and try to provide opportunities, so they can continue working as artists after they graduate from high school, or go into something completely different in college. The important thing is that they go to college. They pursue their dreams. They challenge themselves to be and do what they never thought was possible before. Some, like Dom…" Tony pointed to Dom. Dom shrank into his corner. "Some will go on to be art superstars, will be able to make a living doing this. Others may become biologists, doctors, writers, or landscape architects. But they'll know the importance of art. And they'll always support the artists who grew up in Stella."

The audience started clapping again. Rebekah noticed that even Megan seemed impressed by Tony's speech.

Tony took a few steps on the stage while he waited for the room to quiet down. He moved with such calm, such poise. Even when he was pacing, he looked as if he knew exactly where he was headed. Rebekah checked her watch. It was eight twenty-six now. She loosened the scarf around her neck and wiped her hands on her pants.

"Stella has come a long, long way in the last five years," Tony said. "It's blown me away, how much we've grown. Five years ago, it was just me. I didn't have an organization. I didn't know what I wanted to do with my life, or even if I wanted to stay in Portland. "And then I met a boy named Tom."

As Tony said "Tom," the door closest to Rebekah slammed shut. A strong wind, stronger than she'd heard all evening, blew against the walls of the Dapple House. It drowned out conversation and whipped against the walls. A few seconds after the wind started, the lights went out.

A gasp swept through the room, followed by laughter.

Tony looked around. He tapped the microphone a few times, and then laid it on the ground. He cupped his hands to his mouth. "Can you all hear me?" he shouted.

"Yes!" someone in the back of the room shouted back.

"Good!" Tony said. Another gust of air hit the Dapple House, drowning out Tony's voice. The walls shook.

"Damn," the student near Rebekah said. He grabbed *The Last Summer*, took it off the easel, and gently set it on the ground. "Don't want this thing blowing over."

"I don't think you have anything to worry about, unless the walls cave in," a woman said to him. "And if they do, I think we all have bigger problems."

Rebekah checked her phone. Eight twenty-seven. Where was Megan? Rebekah scanned the room. Megan had moved to the center of the floor. She stood with her hands on her hips, facing her soon-to-be wife. Rebekah couldn't see her face, but she imagined that Megan was staring at her, willing Rebekah to move.

Rebekah checked her phone again. Eight twenty-eight. Two more minutes. She took off her scarf, rolled it up into a ball, and set it down on the table; she unzipped her jacket, folded it, and carefully set it down on top of her scarf. She took a deep breath, closed her eyes, and stepped away from the table. Her breath trembled in her throat.

She had thought about potential consequences three weeks ago, when she first concocted this plan. Losing her job was perhaps the most likely outcome. How could Tony possibly keep her on? He'd have to justify her betrayal. If they didn't hit development goals with this campaign, it wouldn't be because of the event itself, or a failure on Jane's part. It would be, Tony would say, because of this.

There was her upcoming wedding to consider. What would she tell her parents and her extended family when they asked about her job? How would she pay off her credit card? Would the Judge evict them, even though he knew the circumstances?

She shook her head violently and tried to reorient.

Her colleagues at Stella could have figured this out three weeks ago. It was right there in front of them the whole time. And no one had said a word.

She had practiced for weeks with Megan and Haines. She'd received emails from other participants. This thing was on, whether she had last minute doubts or not. It would happen, with or without the storm, with or without the lights, with or without anyone.

If a flash mob dances and no one can see them, does it still matter? Rebekah found Megan in the center of the room and gently touched her shoulder. Megan slid one arm around Rebekah's back and took her other hand. Rebekah leaned in to Megan, feeling the heat of her body, allowing her fiancée to support her. Rebekah sensed movement around them. The air inside the Dapple House was thick with anticipation. People moved in the darkness; they whispered to each other, positioning themselves around the ballroom.

"Friends!" Tony shouted. "I think it will only be a few more minutes until—"

No one could hear the rest of Tony's sentence above the notes of the tango song "La Cumparasita," blasting from the boom box and loud speakers that Haines had surreptitiously set up in the back of the Dapple House. Rebekah straightened her spine and picked up her feet as she felt Megan gently lead her backwards.

Slow, slow, quick, quick, slow, Rebekah repeated to herself. *Slow, slow, quick, quick, slow.*

Megan deftly directed her movements, steering her backwards and sideways, navigating through the crowd of couples suddenly doing the tango. She felt Megan's legs moving slowly into hers, felt the stiffness in her back as she worked to maintain posture, and her rhythmic footsteps, timed to the beat of the music.

She kept her eyes on Megan's face, as Haines had reminded her over and over again during their practice sessions. Out of the corner of her eye, she watched as other pairs moved in the same way, gliding around the dance floor.

Slow, slow, quick, quick, slow. Slow, slow, quick, quick, slow.

About fifteen seconds after they started dancing, the lights came back on. An audible gasp went up in the Dapple House.

Rebekah whipped her head around. About half of the one hundred and fifty people at the event had paired off and were moving in rhythmic step—though in a multitude of different directions—to "La Cumparasita." She caught a glimpse of Tom Jacobs accidentally stepping on his wife's foot; he moved back suddenly, then quickly moved his hand around her back and confidently stepped forward. Mary took his misstep in stride, falling right back into rhythm with her husband.

The girl in the fishnet tights and boy in the trench coat moved slowly, close together. They looked stiff, practiced, formal, and impossibly serious. The bottom of the boy's trench coat swayed with his steps, and the girl kept her chin up and her eyes closed, her face only a few inches from her partner's.

Out of the corner of her eye, Rebekah saw Dom Turken moving toward the center of the Dapple House. *Slow, slow, quick, quick, slow.* Dom didn't have a dancing partner; he twirled and leapt, pushing an imaginary companion in front of him, moving his feet in time to the music. He was smiling, and it was the first time Rebekah had seen him smile all night. Dom danced with abandon, completely ignoring the rules of the tango.

Dom doesn't need rules, Rebekah thought. *That's what makes him so incredible.*

Rebekah turned her head again. Megan was smiling, her eyes alight with excitement.

"Have you seen the Judge?" Rebekah whispered.

"Nope. But I'm sure he's having a good time," Megan said. She grinned. "What do you think Tony is thinking right now?"

Slow, slow, quick, quick, slow.

Rebekah looked past Megan, to the stage. First Rebekah saw Jane, who had apparently jumped onto the stage at some point during the last few minutes. Her eyes were wide, her hands clenched at her sides. Jane looked from Tony to the floor, finding Rebekah and Megan for a second, then immediately looking away. She walked over to Tony, picked up the microphone, and brought it to her lips. "Ok!" Jane said. "So…can I have everyone's attention, please?"

"La Cumparasita" continued playing. The dancers ignored her. "Excuse me," Jane said into the microphone. "Who's playing that music?"

Megan spun Rebekah around so that she could get a look at Haines. Haines was sitting in a chair in the back, one leg crossed over the other, recording the proceedings on his phone.

Rebekah marveled at how critical Haines had been to making this happen. Though the flash mob had been Rebekah's idea, it was Haines's organization, ingenuity, and understanding of the logistics that had enabled them to pull this off. The key to the flash mob's success, Haines had told her, was making sure that all the participants knew exactly what they had to do and when they had to do it. What kind of mechanisms did Rebekah have at her disposal?

Daft. The magazine Rebekah had built and loved would serve as the catalyst for her most glorious moment of audacity. It was the only way she could make this happen, the only avenue she had to reach Stella's supporters.

After the final meeting with Tony, Micah, and Jane, Rebekah had removed the story about the Washington High students and replaced it with the fundraising letter. At the bottom of the letter, right in the middle of the spread, she'd added the fundraising link.

At least, it looked like a fundraising link. "Save the Arts," it read. Jane assumed that the link went to Stella's fundraising page. Fundraising had been up since March; Jane was still bringing in double the amount of money that she had raised during the same period in the previous year. Jane never found the time to double-check the link's veracity.

Neither, for that matter, did Tony or Micah.

The link took readers to a YouTube video titled, "Flash Mob Tango with Stella at the Arts in the Halls Campaign." The video had been hastily put together by Rebekah and Haines, and featured Haines and Megan teaching viewers the steps to the tango.

"Spontaneity, joy, and self-expression are the elusive sustenance of the artist," the video's opening text read. "Help us. Join us. Be free with us—in an impromptu tango flash mob on March 29, 2012, at 8:30 p.m. during the Arts in the Halls campaign at the Dapple House. Watch this video to learn the steps. If you have any questions, contact Rebekah Cohayn. See you there."

Rebekah had received about two dozen questions about the video, a few from people who wanted both to dance and to make financial contributions. She instructed people who wanted to donate money to contact Jane Salish, and she confirmed to skeptical donors that the flash mob would, indeed, be happening.

Megan spun her around again. The room was full of dancers. People who weren't dancing had taken out their phones and cameras. Many attendees who didn't seem to have known in advance about the flash mob had joined the dancers. Some were doing the tango, while others were just dancing. Rebekah saw Jane put the microphone to her lips. Tony was walking toward her.

"So please, everyone, if you could just—"

Tony grabbed the microphone from Jane, turned it off, and set it down on the stage. He took Jane's arm and, despite her vehement protests, led her away.

At the edge of the stage, Roberto was waiting for Tony. He held his arm out. Tony scanned the room, glanced back at Jane, who was pleading with him to go back to the microphone, and looked at Roberto. Roberto grinned. Tony smiled back. He slipped his arm through Roberto's and allowed himself to be led to the dance floor, where, the two men began to dance, to the sound of raucous clapping.

Fucking opportunist, Rebekah thought. She smiled and shook her head.

"Look at me," Megan said.

Rebekah turned her eyes back to Megan. Rebekah's chest felt so full of air and light that it was nearly impossible for her to breathe, to fit any more oxygen into her lungs. Her feet slipped across the floor. Rebekah felt herself falling and slipping, completely reliant on Megan's direction. She was crying, free and out of control, dancing for the first time in her life in a way that really mattered. She gripped Megan's hand hard, feeling the contours of her fiancée's fingers and the strength in her wrist. The dancers in the room had become a part of Rebekah, unshackling her from her charges, giving her permission to dance alongside them.

The lights were on. She could see the other dancers. They could see her. Together they danced through the remainder of "La Cumparasita," until the music stopped and everyone cheered, and Tony walked back to the center of the stage with the microphone in his hand.

April 1, 2012

Rebekah and Megan chose the Satz Building for their wedding because of its spare aesthetic. The Satz was a space. It looked unfinished, lacked varnish, and appealed in its sparse, industrial qualities. Massive wooden panels held the ceiling in place. Cement beams, gray and raw, stood sentry in the main gathering spaces. The Satz Building also featured hidden doors, ornate doorways, steel-cut staircases, and old boiler rooms. New bricks had been sanded and roughed-up. The fixtures in the updated bathroom were stark and metallic, flushing and pouring out of tired necessity.

The Satz woke up at six on Sunday mornings. A janitorial crew, dressed in gray scrubs and black, rubber-soled work shoes arrived to clean up from the previous evening's wedding. They swept up the party fallout from the tables and wielded industrial-strength vacuums to inhale the bits of cake, glitter, and photo booth pictures that never found permanent homes. The janitors removed bits of food stuck to the walls and re-arranged the chairs and tables to the specifications set by the Cohayn-Nimble wedding party. Eight chairs would be set at each table tonight instead of the previous party's ten.

The caterer, Northwest Eats, arrived four hours after the janitorial crew left. The company specialized in salmon, huckleberry pie, lavender dressing, and salads made with local tomatoes and arugula. During their tasting, Rebekah and Megan had settled on chicken in a tomato cream sauce, sliced thinly against the grain, spiced with basil and oregano; steamed halibut, lightly seasoned with rock salt and freshly ground pepper; a polenta and bean dish for the vegetarians; and salad and sliced rosemary bread.

At three, a runner from Alphabet Bakery rolled in with the wedding cake. It was simple: a large, round vanilla cake with vanilla frosting and a single, small rectangular tier in the middle.

At four thirty, the guests began to arrive. Rebekah's uncle Julian wore a tweed suit and pushed his wife in her steel wheelchair down the aisle. Megan's aunt Anne wore a floral skirt over blue jeans and Teva sandals, along with a loose-fitted, white fabric shirt; she was carrying a camera so large that it seemed to take up half her torso as it swung from a leather band around her neck. Rebekah's uncle Stedman was dressed in a black suit. His wife Leanne carried their daughter, Callie.

There was a diverse contingent from Ingenue, Megan's engineering company: mostly men, some with wives and children. The ones without families, two rows of young men, shoulder to shoulder, who appeared to be discernibly single.

Carrie Cline, tall, regal, and stunning, showed off her black skin in a canary yellow cocktail dress. In a conspicuous omission, she had no date by her side. But she was resolute, walking with a determined straightness and carrying her independence like a barbell.

Roberto arrived early, looking dapper in a blue suit and white tie, and took the open seat next to Carrie Cline. In another universe, the two might have made a picturesque couple. Tony Hernandez came a few minutes later, talking on his cell phone, and hung up only when the processional music began. Jane Salish, clicking her way forward in white stilettos, stood next to Tony's chair for the duration of the ceremony. All of the Stella employees looked stiff and slightly anxious. They were caught between congratulations and criticism, between art and a hard place. What to do after Rebekah's sweet treachery?

"Sure, I'm going to Rebekah's wedding," Tony had said to them after the Arts in the Halls event. He shrugged. "I'm going to eat and drink and celebrate. I'm going to tell Rebekah, 'congratulations.' What else am I supposed to do at her wedding?" Tony looked around at his employees. He cleared his throat and stuffed his hands in his pockets. "We'll deal with what happened at the fundraising campaign next week."

Guests attending a Jewish wedding for the first time may have wondered what to do with the circular pieces of fabric handed to them by a small child. Some eventually put them on their heads, copying the Abrams, Abels, and Cohayns; others kept them wrapped tightly in their programs, unsure of the religious significance of such a thing.

At the head of the processional, a white cloth hung on four birch poles set into wooden blocks. The program described this structure as a chuppah, or wedding canopy. A few minutes after the guests finished arriving, Rebekah and Megan would enter the chuppah. They would read vows, exchange rings, listen to the rabbi chant the *sheva brachot*, and raise their heels to jointly stomp on a glass that had been tightly wrapped in paper. They would break the glass to acknowledge that there was still darkness in times of happiness, to commemorate Jews who had perished in the Holocaust, to acknowledge all the work to be done in the world. The breaking of the glass would mark the end of an era.

There was also one aspect of the wedding that very few guests noticed: an empty seat in the front row for the absent David Cohayn.

"Where are our parents?" Megan asked, tapping her foot.

It was four ten on the afternoon of the wedding. Rebekah and Megan were standing outside of the small dressing room, thirty minutes before they were supposed to sign the ketubah.

"I bet they're just stuck in traffic," Rebekah said.

"I can't even get ahold of my mom on her cell phone. This is totally bizarre." Megan looked as though she was on the verge of tears.

"Megs, just calm down. They'll be here." Rebekah tried to touch her shoulder, but Megan shrugged her off. "And don't pace like that. You're going to ruin your suit."

"My suit. Right. I can't believe that crazy bitch at Brenda's talked me into this." Megan looked down at her outfit. Now tailored to fit her broad shoulders, narrow hips, and long torso, the suit made Megan look like a dressed-up centaur.

"What? Are you crazy? You look great."

Megan sighed. "Rebekah, this isn't me. I don't feel like me."

"Right. Because you're getting married. You can't wear jeans."

"I should have just worn what you're wearing."

Rebekah shook her head and smiled, despite her best efforts to maintain a straight face. She had been outfit-less until a week ago, when she got a call from Carrie Cline.

"Bekah!" Carrie had sung over the phone. "You still don't have your dress, do you? Am I right?"

Rebekah confirmed that her situation was nearly calamitous.

Girl, it is such a good thing we're best friends," Carrie said. "I've got you all figured out. I was looking through my closet for something to wear to your wedding, and I just found the most beautiful thing— you'd look perfect in it!"

Rebekah, remembering the disastrous evening during which she had shrink-wrapped herself into an outfit of Carrie's choosing, politely declined.

"Bekah, I'm going to overnight this to you, and you're going to try it, ok?" Carrie had said. "I promise-promise that you'll look good in this one. Trust me."

Rebekah didn't say anything.

"Oh, shit, girl…you're thinking of that silly double date in college, aren't you?" Carrie laughed. "Well, forget it. This is totally different. Let me make it up to you; just try this on. Ok? For me? For old time's sake?"

The next day, a slim box with a northern Virginia return address arrived on the Judge's porch. Rebekah took the box into her basement bathroom, locked the door, and sat down on the toilet. She took a deep breath and opened the box.

Rebekah pulled out a long, white linen skirt. It had large lace eyelets over a silk slip. She held it up for inspection, and then slowly pulled it over her legs. It moved and swished, rubbing up against her ankles and flying out toward the edges of the bathroom. It was large, roomy, and comfortable. Rebekah bent over the box, pulled out white linen shirt with long billowy sleeves, and slipped that over her head. It was more form fitting, hugging her breasts and lying neatly over her stomach. Rebekah turned from side to side in astonishment, marveling at how well the two pieces fit.

She ran out of the bathroom to show Megan.

"Wow babe…beautiful!" Megan said. She leapt up from the couch and dropped her jaw in exaggerated astonishment. "Spin for me, spin for me!"

Rebekah twirled, feeling the skirt billow beneath her waist.

"Do you like it?" Megan had asked.

"I love it," Rebekah said. "It's perfect. It makes me feel so free."

"Goddamn that Carrie Cline," Megan said. "Saving your ass."

Now, standing outside the dressing room, Rebekah giggled. She twirled again for Megan.

"Yes, darling, you're beautiful," Megan said.

"You look beautiful," Rebekah said.

"I think it's more like beauty and the butch," Megan said. "And you're not the butch."

"You think Disney would make that into a movie?"

Megan shrugged. She looked past Rebekah and frowned. Rebekah turned around.

An old woman was walking toward them. She was wearing a white headscarf and a long yellow dress. She walked slowly, leaning on her cane, frowning at the brides.

"It is so humid out," Grandma Simchah said. "I barely made it here, you know. If the cab driver hadn't walked me up to the building, I would probably still be lying on the sidewalk out there, waiting for God to take me. You had to choose a wedding date in the middle of monsoon season?"

Rebekah smiled. She leaned in and kissed her grandmother lightly on the cheek. "I'm so glad you could be here, Grandma. Are mom and dad coming?"

"I'm always here, aren't I? And they're downstairs." Grandma Simchah looked Megan Nimble up and down. "You must be the other bride."

"I am," Megan said.

Simchah studied Megan's suit. "For women, they make suits?"

Megan pushed out her broad shoulders. "You like it?"

"Let me tell you something," Simchah said. "You know what my mother would have said, if I had worn pants to my wedding?"

Megan looked at Rebekah, panicked. Rebekah shrugged. "What?" Megan asked.

Simchah flipped her wrist at Megan. "Never mind. My mother's dead."

"Um, Grandma…" Rebekah said. "You can go inside. Mom and Dad are in there."

"Are they? Ach." Simchah leaned on her cane and began shuffling towards the door. "Such a party, this is. I had nothing when I got married. Just a rabbi and my parents and that man I used to call my husband. Dead now, too. Now—look at all this. Such a new world." Grandma Simchah paused and frowned. "But you know, I've gotta tell you. I can't say that I miss the old one." Grandma Simchah cackled, and disappeared into the dressing room.

Rebekah shifted her arms. She was sweating so profusely that her underarms were sticking to her shirt.

"Oh, my parents are here. Fucking finally." Megan waved. "Over here!"

"Hello," John Nimble said as he walked up. He looked at his daughter. "You look very nice, sweetheart."

"Dad, you're late."

John checked his watch. "It starts at four thirty, right? It's only four fifteen."

"You were supposed to be here at four."

John raised his eyebrows. He was wearing a charcoal suit, tightly fitted around his chest and legs, with black wingtip shoes that he had spent an hour of the previous evening polishing. He smoothed down the front of his suit. "Well," he said. "Let's just get rolling then, huh?"

John Nimble walked into the dressing room. Amy Nimble embraced Megan and kissed her on the cheek. "I'm so proud of you," Amy said. "And I just love your suit."

"Really?" Megan straightened her shoulders and stuck out a leg to admire her pants.

"Yes, you look beautiful." Amy looked at Rebekah. "Is that the right word? To me, you're beautiful. And Rebekah, you're just stunning. That skirt is perfect for you." She smiled at both of them, her chin to her chest, tears in her eyes.

As Amy walked into the dressing room, the Judge and Claire approached. The Judge was wearing a suit. His hair was combed, parted on the side of his head. He was wearing running shoes, but this seemed a small concession given that he had emerged from his apartment robe-less. Claire wore a short yellow dress, yellow pumps, and a white jacket. Her arm was resting on the Judge's.

"So sorry we're late," the Judge said. "But my, don't you both look stunning!" He looked them up and down. "Megan, I'm just so taken aback by your suit. It's wonderful."

"You think?" Megan twirled. She delighted in the Judge's attention.

"It's true, you're both so gorgeous." Claire leaned in and kissed Rebekah on the cheek. "I'm so happy for both of you."

"And very honored that you asked us to be your ketubah witnesses," the Judge said. "Now I'm going to be on your ketubah forever, you know. You're never going to be able to forget me."

After Jacob had told Rebekah and Megan that they needed two Jews—to whom they were not related—to sign the ketubah as witnesses, the only people the girls could think of were the Judge and Claire. The day after Rebekah ran into the Judge at the tango lessons, she made an impromptu request. Both the landlord and his girlfriend accepted.

"I don't think we'd forget you, anyway, somehow," Megan said. The Judge laughed. He motioned for both of them to come closer to him. Megan and Rebekah leaned in.

"Listen, you two," he said, his voice a hoarse whisper. "I want to tell you something. This moment, these next few hours—they're going to go by really quickly. And at the end, the end of the day, you're just going to have each other. Your love for each other—it is what it is. It will hold you together. It's your glue. But everyday, choose to love each other. Choose to be with one another. Choose each other all over again. Because it goes by really fast."

The Judge squeezed each of their shoulders, and looked over his shoulder at Claire.

"I suppose you're going to tell me that you choose me every day?" Claire asked.

"I do," the Judge said.

"Well, let me tell you something," Claire replied, slipping her arm through his. "The reason we're still together is because I choose you." She kissed his cheek.

"I am a very fortunate boy," the Judge said. "This is the ketubah room here?"

"It is," Megan said.

"Ok." The Judge winked at them and walked into the dressing room with Claire.

Rebekah heard a quick clicking on the wooden floor behind her. She turned around. Judith was power walking down the hall, and Daniel was nearly running to keep up.

"I'm so sorry we're late, we ran into traffic," Judith said when she reached Rebekah. "What time is it? Are we going to need to push back the ceremony?"

"It's fine mom, everything is fine," Rebekah said. She smiled. "Everything is ready to go."

"Just in time then," Daniel said. He rubbed his wife's back. "Calm down, honey. We're here."

"I know we're here, but if we had left when I wanted to leave we would have been here on time," Judith snapped.

"I know. It's my fault." Daniel winked at his daughter.

Judith took a deep breath. She looked at her daughter again, finally noticing her wedding dress. "Wow, Beks, you just look so beautiful."

"Thanks mom."

"Really, your dress is gorgeous," Judith said. "And you too Megan. That suit is so becoming on you."

"Thanks Judith," Megan said.

"You both did so well, with everything," Judith said. "This venue, your outfits, the caterer…this is really going to be a phenomenal wedding. I'm so proud of both of you." Judith smiled through the worry creases on her forehead.

"Thanks mom," Rebekah said. "It really came together. Mostly because of Megan."

Megan nodded slowly. "I won't argue with that." She looked at Rebekah. They grinned at each other.

Judith looked at Daniel. Daniel looked at the floor.

"What?" Rebekah asked. She glanced from parent to parent. She could feel her store of confidence slipping out through her knees.

"I've got some news," Judith said.

"What? What news?" Rebekah asked. *Someone died. David died.*

"We got something in the mail a few days ago. From David. He asked that we give it to you at your wedding." Judith pulled a small white envelope out of her purse and handed it to Bekah. "If you don't want it, don't take it. I'll hold onto it until later."

Rebekah stared at the envelope. It was still sealed shut. She tried to stare through the stocky white envelope paper to read whatever damning message David had in store for her. He had almost a year to reach out to Rebekah. Why now? Why crash the biggest moment of her life?

Her first instinct was to hurl the envelope across the room. She wanted nothing to do with it.

"Really?" Megan asked. Rebekah looked up. Megan was shaking her head. "I'm sorry Judith, but that's not right after all he's done. Or not done."

"I know," Judith said. She put her hand out to take back the envelope. "I just thought I'd offer."

Rebekah held up the envelope to the light. She could see black ink—about a paragraph's worth of writing. Whatever David had to say, it was short.

"He could have said whatever he needed to say to her last week," Megan said. "Or even yesterday. He just…" Megan shook her head. "It's like he can't just let go."

Can't let go. Rebekah considered the words. She hadn't been able to let go of her own self-loathing for more than a decade. She hadn't been able to let go of her mother's judgment, her deeply scarring coming out experience, since high school. And she hadn't been able to let go of David since she was old enough to say his name. It was only in the last two weeks that she had started to shed layers of her old skin.

Did she even want to let go? Or did she simply want to forgive— herself, her family, Megan, David—and begin anew?

Not a rebirth, Rebekah thought. *A Yom Kippur.*

Rebekah sighed. "Megs, I'm going to read it."

"What?" Megan exclaimed. "Bekah, no. This is fucked up. Totally emotionally manipulative. If he wanted to be at your wedding then he should have grown up and figured out a way to get here." Megan looked at Judith. "No offense, Judith."

Judith shrugged. "You're right. It hurts me to say it, but you're right."

"Megs, it's ok," Rebekah said. "I want to do this."

Megan rolled her eyes. "Fine. Whatever."

Rebekah took the envelope from her mother and walked a little ways down the hall. She kept her back to her parents in case she started to cry. She opened the envelope slowly, gently tugging at the sealed edges until the folded-over part of the envelope lifted off in one piece. There was a small, folded up piece of paper inside, with a short handwritten note:

Dear Rebekah,
Mazel tov on your wedding. I'm sorry I can't be there. I'll spare you any sort of insufficient explanation…there's none that will do justice to the complicated lives we both lead.
Despite what you must think, I love you. I wish you the best in love and life. May you be blessed with happiness and righteousness.
B'shalom,
David

Rebekah folded the note, slipped it back in the envelope, and walked back to her family.

"So?" Judith asked anxiously. She searched Rebekah's face.

"David sends his love," Rebekah said. She leaned over and kissed Megan on the cheek.

"We're still getting married, right?" Megan asked. "You're not changing your mind?"

"No," Rebekah said. She slipped her arm through Megan's. She felt nimble and unraveled, and if she had been a tight spool of yarn that was finally unwinding. "Let's go."

Rebekah and Megan walked into the dressing room. Judith and Daniel followed behind them. Jacob stood in the center, hovering over a long wooden table, wearing a white collared shirt and black pants.

Jacob walked towards Rebekah and gave her a hug. "Mazel tov," he whispered into her ear.

"Thanks, Jake."

He gave Megan a hug and shook hands with Judith and Daniel. He slowly walked back toward the center of the room and waited until conversation ceased.

"Welcome," Jacob said. He looked around. "Welcome to the wedding. Welcome to the ketubah ceremony. Welcome to the union of two people we love and cherish: Rebekah Cohayn and Megan Nimble."

Rebekah stared at Jacob. His eyelids were relaxed, nearly droopy underneath his eyebrows. His smile was easy, confident, the same smile that Rebekah had admired since their early days in elementary school.

Rebekah stole a glance at her parents. Judith's forehead was an undulating mountain range, and her cheeks were puffed out in anxiety. She looked at Rebekah and smiled broadly, too broadly. She was stuffing, pretending, her happiness for Rebekah tempered by a hidden sorrow. Daniel's thumbs were hooked through his belt looks, and he looked remarkably placid.

"I would like everyone to close their eyes," Jacob said.

Rebekah closed her eyes. She tried to push everyone out of her head. Megan, standing next to her. Her parents, up against the wall. She felt a lump in her throat and tears on the edge of her eyelids.

"With your eyes closed, I'd like you to imagine a moment of love; not romantic love, but an enveloping love, a giving love. Close your eyes, and imagine a moment of love."

Rebekah took a deep breath. Her mind wandered to her childhood, when her parents tucked her into bed at night. They would read a book together, and then her mom would sing, and her dad would hum along with them. Sometimes David would climb into Rebekah's bed, so their parents could sing to them at the same time. Those were the best moments: David curled up next to her under the covers, giggling or breathing into her ear as their parents put them to sleep. She envisioned David smiling kindly, no trace of reproof in his strong jawline and high cheekbones. David racing down a dirt mound on his bicycle, leaning forward over the handlebars like a ski jumper. David staring blankly ahead with tired eyes and a furrowed brow, struggling under the weight of unbridled idealism and circumscribed worldliness.

David was an image, more than a man, to her; a god, more than a brother, an ephemeral standard by which Rebekah had been measuring herself for the duration of her life. Did the David in her mind really exist? Was her time with him augmented by her own fantasy of their relationship?

Surely David existed. Rebekah had smelled him, held his hand, taken hundreds of family photos with him. His physical presence had dominated much of her childhood. But his spirit—the constant threat of his judgment—ate up her psyche and still loomed over Rebekah like a moon shadow. David was less a daily part of her life than a daily reminder of her own perceived shortcomings. He wasn't here today: another absence coupled with censure.

Rebekah took another deep breath. *That's not the David I want with me today.* His reality, she knew, was far more complicated. He was a kind man, devoted to his family, single-mindedly pursuing a life that he hoped could live up to standards of piousness. David had always chased the impossible, held his sister to the impossible. In David's own quest for self-discovery, he'd found comfort in rules, in the thick black lines that come with living a devout life. Rebekah understood the need for walls and ceilings; given the choice, she might have done the same thing.

Jacob cleared his throat softly. "I want you to hold onto that memory—whatever you were thinking about. Parents and friends, I want you to think about giving that kind of love to Rebekah and Megan. Give it to them right now, in your minds. Rebekah and Megan, I want you to give it back to your families, and give it to each other."

Rebekah took another deep breath. She imagined Megan, the love of her life. Rebekah wrapped Megan in her warmest, tightest mental hug and tried to imagine years passing in that hug. They would become bent over, wrinkled, maybe even a little overweight and out of style—and she was still hugging her, still holding her, as their hair turned white, and they gripped walkers and shuffled together to sit on park benches and watch children play.

She imagined giving the love back to her parents—tucking them in bed, singing to them, trying to make them feel as warm and safe as she had felt when she was a child. She thought of the Judge, of spending time in his apartment, giving the old man good company.

"Open your eyes," Jacob said.

Rebekah opened her eyes and found herself staring at Megan. Her wife-to-be had her head bowed. She slowly lifted it up and looked at Rebekah. Her lower lip was trembling. When she caught Rebekah looking, she nodded slightly, un-slumped her shoulders, and smiled.

"I want you to hold onto how you feel," Jacob said. "I want you to hold onto that through the marriage ceremony, through the party. I want you to hold onto that tomorrow, through the next week; and on bad days, I want you to return to this moment, and grab a little bit of the love you're feeling right now."

Rebekah looked around the room. Her parents looked teary-eyed and overwhelmed. John Nimble stared straight ahead in a failing attempt to keep his composure. Amy was weeping openly, trying to wipe her eyes as quickly as the tears poured out of them. The Judge and Claire leaned against each other. Megan stood across from Rebekah, shoulders back, chin up, and lower lip trembling.

"One of the things we do in Jewish ceremonies is sign a Jewish marriage contract, called a ketubah," Jacob said. He picked up the rolled ketubah from the table and unfurled it.

"This is the first step in any Jewish marriage. When a couple signs a ketubah, it means they're bound together in the eyes of the Jewish community and the eyes of God. Rebekah, please come stand next to me," Jacob said. Rebekah approached the table.

"Rebekah, do you choose Megan as your wife and loving companion?"

Rebekah nodded slowly. "I do."

"Please sign on this line." Jacob handed her a pen, and Rebekah signed.

"Megan, come stand next to me on my other side."

Megan took a big step next to Jacob.

"Megan, do you choose Rebekah as your wife and loving companion?" Megan closed her eyes and took a deep breath. She balled her hands into fists.

Jacob looked at her. He raised his eyebrows. "Megan, do you…"

"Yes," Megan choked out. She was crying now. Rebekah heard Amy sharply draw in a breath.

Jacob nodded. "Good. Sign here."

Megan wiped at her eyes. "Oh crap, I'm ruining my makeup."

"I'll help you fix it," Claire whispered. She was leaning on the Judge, her own mascara running in streaks down her face.

Megan picked up the pen and signed her name under Rebekah's.

"Great," Jacob said. "Now, I would like to call up our witnesses." The Judge and Claire walked up.

"Do you," Jacob said, turning to the Judge, support the marriage of Rebekah and Megan?"

"Of course!" the Judge said. "They're perfect for each other." Claire elbowed him in the ribs.

"What?" the Judge asked. He looked around.

"Sign here, please," Jacob said. "Under 'witnesses.'"

"They are perfect," the Judge said to Jacob. He turned to Rebekah and Megan. "You are perfect." He signed the ketubah.

"And do you," Jacob said, turning to Claire, "support this marriage?"

"Yes," Claire said. She picked up the pen and signed her name under the Judge's.

Jacob nodded. "Now, Rebekah and Megan, I want you to pick up the ketubah by its ends."

Rebekah and Megan lifted the document off the table.

"This is your marriage contract. This is what binds you together. Now that this is signed, we just have one more step to complete: the marriage ceremony. But the ketubah is the legal piece. As you hold it, I want you to feel its power. There's a lot of beauty here."

Rebekah smiled at Megan from across the table. Megan, her face streaked with black mascara, smiled back.

"Ok, Jacob said. "That's it. Mazel tov. Now we need to do the marriage ceremony, and dance at your party, and it'll be official."

"Hear that?" Claire said, looking at the Judge. "You're dancing with me tonight."

John cleared his throat and approached Megan. "That was beautiful, sweetheart." His voice was hoarse. He planted a quick kiss on her head, then walked up to Rebekah and did the same. Chin up and back straight, he left the room.

Megan rolled her eyes. "My dad is emotionally challenged sometimes."

Judith and Daniel walked up to Rebekah. They embraced her in a hug together.

"We love you so much," Judith said. "So much. We're so happy for you. And we're so proud of you. I know this hasn't always been easy, and I know David not being here…"

Rebekah cut her off. "Mom, it doesn't matter. I'm happy that the people who are here are here."

Judith looked confused and overwhelmed. Rebekah knew she was a fixer and that she desperately wanted to fix things, to clip and tuck and hide the messy bits. There were many messy bits still left for Rebekah, like chubby love handles hanging out the doors of the Satz Building.

"I know. I know." Judith blinked back tears and smiled. Rebekah knew she was thinking about the empty chair. Each day without David would always be pockmarked, always a little black around the edges.

Rebekah smiled and looked down again.

"You look so beautiful," Judith said, kissing her cheek.

"Reasonably beautiful, you mean?" Rebekah asked, slipping her arm through her mother's.

Judith laughed.

"Very reasonably beautiful, honey," Daniel said. He took her other arm. The three Cohayns walked out of the dressing room toward the chuppah.

Acknowledgements

Thank you to my stable of excellent frienditors: Andy Garland-Forshee, Imelda Ortiz, Alanna Hein, Brad Tait, and Sarah Bowman. Your feedback, support, and love are irreplaceable. This book exists because of you.

Thanks to my editors, Kate Haas and Merridawn Duckler. Your feedback was challenging and insightful. You made me better.

Thanks to the many, many friends, family, and colleagues who have been my witting and unwitting sources of inspiration: the extended Levy, Angel, Perre, and Sprecher families, Naomi Angel, Mitch and Nate, Rabbi Adam and Rabbi Joey (better rabbis, I've never met!), the A-P family, the Bowmans, Callaghans, and that whole New York City-crowd, S.E. and Beth, Mr. and Mr. Tait, Jill, my Forest Service and BLM families, and my awesome Havurah Shabbat group. I love you all.

Mom: You taught me how to write. You were my conductor, my role model, my editor. I'm sure you've read through a lot of crap during the last thirty-one years. Thanks for always being supportive, honest, and gentle. Thank you for guiding me, as you always have, in my writing. I hope it's getting better.

Dad: Thank you for teaching me how to think: outside, around, beyond, and in between. I've never known anyone more creative than you.

James and Elizabeth: My inspiration, competition, and teammates. My bookends. Thanks for never making fun of me for getting rainbow sprinkles on my ice cream when I was younger. We all know how that turned out.

To my in-laws, the Sprechers, Perres, and Fissells: Where would I be without you? Where would our house be without you? Thanks for all the love and support for the last six years. And thank you for keeping Katy alive since 1980.

Pickle: You're the houseplant of the decade.

Mimi: Little girl, you've changed my life in an infinite number of ways. Thanks for bringing me so much joy, and love, and heart-full moments of bliss. And thanks for starting to sleep through the night, so I could finish this damn book.

Katy: My wife, lover, and best friend; my rock, my muse, my river boat captain. Thank you for the unwavering, never-ending support. Thank you for loving me completely. Thank you for encouraging me to write, even when it came at the expense of conversation and movie nights. Thank you for picking me up in my moments of despair, keeping me in clean laundry, and being the most consistent source of love and empathy. Thank you for bringing me on as an intern in Challis, Idaho. Sorry I still can't pull a horse trailer.

www.ingramcontent.com/pod-product-compliance
Lightning Source LLC
Chambersburg PA
CBHW071055250626
47159CB00002B/472